PRAISE FOR

"There are still books being written that you cannot put down . . .
Beach Lawyer . . . is just that kind of read."

—*American Bar Association Journal*

"A page-turner."

—*Bloomberg Law*

"A fast moving, interesting, exciting ride . . . This book is hard to put
down."

—*Portland Book Review*

"*Beach Lawyer* is a multilayered tale of backstabbing, greed, and
manipulation that continually surprises readers with where Duff's
mind takes them."

—*Chattanooga Times Free Press*

"A roller-coaster ride with twists and turns and unexpected
happenings . . . great read."

—*Fresh Fiction*

"Great legal suspense."

—*Great Thoughts*

"So tense . . . I found myself holding my breath . . . A great summer
read!"

—Nancie Claire, *Speaking of Mysteries*

THE
BOARDWALK
TRUST

ALSO BY AVERY DUFF

Beach Lawyer

THE
BOARDWALK
TRUST

AVERY DUFF

THOMAS & MERCER

Published by Thomas & Mercer, Seattle

www.apub.com

Amazon, the Amazon logo, and Thomas & Mercer are trademarks of Amazon.com, Inc., or its affiliates.

ISBN-13: 9781542046909
ISBN-10: 1542046904

Cover design by Jae Song

Printed in the United States of America

This book is dedicated to my friend West Oehmig.
The most delightful fellow that ever was.

PROLOGUE

San Bernardino County, California

As he slowed the SUV in the deep sand that grabbed it from out of nowhere, he fought the shuddering steering wheel; his armed passenger braced against the door.

Behind him, the pursuing Mercedes started slowing in the same sand. Doors opened, and two men he'd never met jumped out with pistols.

He found the four-wheel-drive button, left of the steering wheel, and hit the accelerator. The tires grabbed traction, the car moving away from the Mercedes, the two gunmen hesitating, unsure, as he put precious yards between them.

What was it—twenty-four hours ago?—he'd been chased across another expanse of sand, where the storm-darkened sky spewed electric and sluiced water down on him? Death by garrote, knife, or blunt-force trauma had been out there somewhere, the dread and danger of that other moment once again vivid, the taste of blood and death again coppering his tongue.

Now, in his rearview, the armed men scrambled back into their Mercedes.

Screw 'em, he was thinking. *We're outta here!*

But speeding across the sand, Robert Worth, attorney-at-law, saw other armed figures pouring from hillside scrub and knew from their slickers that they were the last people he wanted to see right then: *the FBI.*

❧

Northern California, Six Weeks Earlier

The girl slipped farther into her cocoon sleeping bag, not because of forest frost but because the men's voices grew louder out by the fire. Through the tent's flap, she saw them passing a bottle, same as they did every night, and until lately, she had joined them and the other women they sometimes brought in. The women laughed at her, she was pretty sure, made fun of her small breasts and slender legs, and spoke the same language as her new boyfriend.

She wondered: *Any of you bitches ever runway models in San Francisco's TECH Fashion Week?*

By now, it dawned on her they'd moved camp so many times, she didn't know the way out. But when she'd asked about it, she'd been told not to ask again. What had started as a lark, driving up from Los Gatos, had now turned scary-serious. Her friend Xavier had dropped by her parents' house, said he was writing a paper on the pot-growing scene up in Northern California's Emerald Triangle. He would drive them, then they'd get picked up by his contacts and taken to a modest grow, about one hundred plants. He'd work on his report, get loaded, and make decent money if he was a good enough trimmer. He'd warned her, though, the work was hard, focused, and boring.

But the experience? This wasn't Paris abroad where a "team of dedicated students will create fashion designs to eventually *change the world!*" This was very cool, edgy. Who else at school could say they'd been a dope trimmer her semester off? Rubbing elbows with real people, criminals, probably. An adventure designed to grab that real-world experience her father always talked up. The same real world her mother assured her was overrated as long as you had the right looks. And admittedly, she and her mother did.

On top of that, this was the first secret she could recall keeping from her family. Something they would forbid her to do. Sex in her bedroom at thirteen? Use a condom. Smoking dope at fourteen? Yes, but at home and no driving. Cocaine?

"We're certain, darling, you'll make the right choice."

Her parents sure had—their stash was the best she and her friends had ever tried.

Now, though, she found herself inside a tight sleeping bag, knees shaking, teeth chattering, remembering her trip from down in Los Gatos up to this forest.

Right after Xavier had picked her up, he had insisted they were just friends and insisted they have sex their first night on the road. After she'd convinced him she was gay, he'd backed off. Next, Xavier's growers had sold out. Once Xavier had met up with the new owners, a couple of hippies, he'd said they looked okay, so they'd started work in the trimming tents of this bigger operation.

That was the one thing Xavier got right—the work was hard and boring, but if she put on her tunes and took a few tokes, the days went by.

You did what? her friends would ask. The thought of it made her smile until the hippies had disappeared. Other men appeared who spoke little, their accents sounding, best she could tell, Russian. The men would move quietly through the work tent and occasionally stop behind her. One man in particular.

"Back your ass off," she'd told him, tough-sounding, she'd thought. He'd smiled at her. "You are very beautiful girl."

3

She'd noticed his deep-set eyes, accent, and thick features and decided he was dangerous-looking and *hot*. Especially now that it looked like Xavier had split. So had those hippie owners. One week later, she'd slept with the new man under the stars and towering spruce, and he'd told her about his country's raw beauty, how one day they would travel there. She wasn't in love. That, she knew. Still, she'd always have this memory tucked away no matter what direction her real life took.

Looking outside the tent now, she saw him toss a bottle away and come toward her. Slipping inside the tent, he sat beside her, knees drawn. He reached out and stroked her hair. She trembled because the sex had gone from intense to perverse. He'd started choking her, tying open the tent flap so the others could watch them. Exposing her body to the others, playing to them.

Two days ago, he had no longer been able to get hard, and that's where they'd stood when he came inside the tent tonight. He began by telling her she would leave for the road in the morning. A car would take her to the Eureka airport, and he'd already bought her ticket.

"I will never forget you as long as I live," he said.

In the dark, she saw his body shaking, his head between his legs, rocking back and forth. Reaching out, she touched his arm.

"I'll never forget you, Penko," she said, with tears of relief.

"You are cold," he said, and tucked her arms back inside the cocoon, zipping it up.

Then his powerful hand gripped her long hair, twisting until she cried out. Now she saw a small baseball bat in his other hand. She tried to roll away, but he'd zipped her in, and as he raised the bat against her thrashing and screams, the firelight caught his face. He'd been laughing, not crying, and he was still laughing when the bat crashed into her skull and ended her world.

CHAPTER 1

Two Weeks Ago

The case had started out easy enough. Robert Worth was pretty sure the little girl sitting with her father across Venice Boardwalk had been eyeing him, off and on, for the last half hour. Lounging beside him, at Robert's faux-bamboo conference table, just-retired LAPD cop Erik Jacobson thought the same thing.

At the moment, though, Robert had his hands full with a prospective client.

"You call yourself a beach lawyer?" the prospect was telling him. "Beach lawyer, my ass. I can see you not giving full props to what I'm sayin'."

Whatever that means, Robert was thinking.

But the prospect across the table from him had it right. He'd lost interest once the guy wormed the interview away from his initial beef—a neighbor's barking dog—to his recent divorce, despite Robert's laminated placard clearly stating: *No Divorces! ¡No Hay Divorcios!*

"Man's right," Erik said. "You're no beach lawyer."

That was Erik's two cents from a sturdy beach chair. Kicking back, reaching into the Igloo for another Gatorade, a half tube of SPF 50 slathered on his massive, ever-pale frame. The other half tube had found a haphazard home on his forty-year-old face. Protected by both a beach umbrella and a cowboy hat, he was enjoying his role as court jester.

"Maybe you could tell me," Robert asked his silver-haired hipster prospect, "why public picnic tables at Venice Pier belonged to you . . ." Checking his notes. "To you and Sweetie before she split?"

"'Cause it was me'n Sweetie's spot, dude, is why." Looking around at a nonexistent audience, bobbing his head in appreciation of their support.

"Your *spot*'s what I'm asking about."

"Me and Sweetie's, yeah. Where we always got our groove on, did our thing, got greasy," the prospect said.

Got greasy on one of those tables? Erik and his two sons picnicked on them, and Erik had a light gag reflex. Fortunately, he'd slipped on earbuds and missed the exchange. Another two minutes of Sweetie-talk followed, and the free fifteen-minute consult ended. Robert stood, photographed the prospect's signed release, and sent him on his way.

At this point, no one was waiting to see him. Six weeks ago, the situation had been different after *Yo! Venice* published an article during a Santa Ana winds–induced heat wave.

"Is This the Hottest Lawyer in LA?" the headline asked.

After that, he had been jammed with prospects and gawkers. So much so that when the spirit moved her, mail carrier Sharon hand-delivered postcards addressed only: *Beach Lawyer, Venice CA, 90291.* Two hotshot producers even planned to make a movie about him, but only if Robert signed over his life rights and wrote a screenplay about himself gratis.

With Sweetie's ex now gone, Robert caught the young girl squinting at him from across the boardwalk. Best guess, she was eight or nine, sitting with her father, about forty, who squatted beside her. Then Robert waved; she looked away.

Actually, the pair was familiar. He and Erik had run into them a half mile south of here behind Muscle Beach. That's where an upright steel beam with a hook had been sunk into concrete and where Erik liked hanging his heavy punching bag. Working it, Erik reminded him of George Foreman's big-bag workout—Robert almost felt sorry for the bag as it jumped away from body shots and skirted sideways from the follow-up hook to the head.

Erik had given the girl's father—Matteo but called *Teo*, he'd told them—a turn. Once he'd started, Robert and Erik had exchanged a look: *Damn*. Looked like Teo had spent time in the ring, and a stretch in prison wasn't out of the question. In and out, up and down the bag, his footwork and torso creating different angles of attack. Feinting, slipping counters, his punches messengered energy from the soles of his feet through his roped calves and torqued body till the punches hit home. *Bam. Bam. Bam.*

The girl—Delfina, he'd learned later—watched and read books in the nearby Joe Weider Stadium bleachers. No matter what, every thirty seconds or so, Teo stopped banging and looked her way, making sure she was safe. Robert liked that about him; as a father of two, Erik loved it.

So far, hanging his shingle on the boardwalk wasn't a decision Robert regretted. Several recent prospects promised to blossom into clients. Situations that called for a strong push outside of court for a client getting the short end of the legal stick. The courtroom, he still believed, was where both sides of a dispute went to lose.

Top of his list: an employee overtime situation. The prospect had full documentation of her hours worked and was due $150,000 once her damages were trebled under the state statute. A big plus: her employer was as solvent as he was unethical. A hard letter to her boss, hinting that other employees could well surface if he didn't settle quick, might net a winner.

Working an ultraflex schedule—whenever he wanted—and taking only the cases he liked suited him fine. His parking-place-size alfresco office slot was on the First Amendment side of the boardwalk—the ocean side—in one of 205 rent-free spaces. Landward, brick-and-mortar stores facing him paid rent and sold their wares.

Boardwalk regs and the First Amendment allowed him to communicate with the public on legal matters if he didn't charge a fee. Gia, now in first-year law at Loyola, once joked that, because boardwalk regs also okayed giving away items of nominal value, his advice already qualified.

Passersby could ask for a free consult, and after they'd signed his release, he'd give it his best shot. As long as he claimed a spot early enough, he never had a problem except on holiday weekends, when the boardwalk became a landlocked sluice of families in matching T-shirts and spandex; of skateboarders, fat-tire bike renters, and in-line skaters; of drunks, stoners, unwelcome nudity, dope smoking, fistfights, knifings, and just plain fun.

Where his slot sat, there was less in-your-face boardwalk activity. In fact, the entire area, once 100 percent seedy, had become seedy with a splash of hip. Argentine and Peruvian cuisine, poke bowls, gourmet coffees, and panini alongside boardwalk staples: Twinkies, Oreos, and Ding Dongs, all deep fried and a stoner's throw from the medical-marijuana green cross and the well-located candy store IT'SUGAR.

He and Gia were still together six easy months after their rental Ferrari ride back from Santa Cruz, a city where he'd been jailed as a murder suspect until he'd bent the truth enough to set himself free. Now, he was living at her place in Brentwood and paying rent. Still, he held on to his rear over-the-garage apartment on Ozone Court, a few beach blocks away. On his tax return, he called it his office. Gia called it their Love Shack, and they both thought that her nickname, alluding to its most frequent use, would be much easier to defend in a tax audit.

On their southbound drive, they'd agreed to wait at least a month before making love. To their credit, he thought, they'd waited an hour after reaching the LA County line. Meaning, they were in her bed moments after crossing her threshold.

He and Gia had a history—not of dating and dinner and weekend flights to Cabo or Napa Valley. Their history dealt less with what they wanted to do and more with the type of people they wanted to become. She'd blown her twenties following her destructive urges with a dangerous man, then a senior partner at Robert's law firm. Robert had been fired and decided to quit burning himself out to make partner. No doubt, his decision to chill out as the Beach Lawyer, and to be selective about cases, had been boosted by the $1.8 million settlement he'd banked for his first solo client by going after his old firm. An ongoing negotiation involving Gia's former lover, Jack Pierce, could bring as much as another $1 million his way.

Erik stood up, stretched, and asked, "Want me to transport a few steaks over to Gia's tonight?"

"Chicken and shrimp, grilled vegetables. We got dinner covered."

"You know, in some cultures, steak's considered a vegetable. And tonight, don't forget to bring up my new investigator gig with Priya."

"Got you covered, too, Erik, when the time's right."

Erik announced he was going to hit the public restroom before heading home.

"If I'm late," he liked saying to Robert, "they'll slaughter me."

Hard to imagine. Erik's Thailand-born wife, Priya, plus their two boys, all told weighed less than Erik.

Robert started to empty the melted ice from his Igloo, planning to walk across the boardwalk to see whether Delfina needed anything from him. By the time he looked up, three locals had rolled up to Teo. Each had a load on and distinctive hairstyle: a Mohawk, cornrows, and shaved bald. Heated words flew at Teo, but as the trio closed on him, Teo kept squatting.

Robert had learned way back to never get involved in a boardwalk beef. For all he knew, Teo had just stolen their car or worse. Then again,

Delfina was there, so Robert shucked his Reef flip-flops, slung away his VB Surf cap, and headed over just as Teo eased to his feet.

At first, Teo moved away from the pack, his daughter's hand in his, but they followed. Maybe he was letting concern for his daughter override street sense: backing down showed weakness.

Then Teo turned, swept his daughter behind him with one hand, and looked down. The locals must've mistaken that for fear, but Robert knew he was tucking his chin. Right then, the white guy with the cornrows and biggest mouth stepped inside Teo's invisible line, and Teo stretched that boy out with a chopping left hook. Blink, and you'd have missed it. By the time Robert got between Teo and the others, Teo had scooped up his daughter, and the other two locals were striking aggro poses and crotch-grabbing in a united front against who the hell knew what.

Erik showed up, badged the conscious pair with his retired cop ID. "Hey, pipe down, you clowns!"

They did until the real cops came. Then the locals started up again about Teo assaulting them for no reason.

Robert and Erik both said that, from where they'd stood—and they'd both been standing close—Whitey laid hands on Teo first, even though he hadn't.

Turned out, Teo told Robert later, it all started because he had stared at them walking by. They'd asked Teo the age-old question: "The fuck you looking at, bitch?" A standard boardwalk riposte would be, "The fuck *you* looking at?" followed by everybody getting bowed up and moving on.

Instead, Teo told them, *"Looking at myself."* That's what set them off.

Whitey was back in the game now, on his feet and talking smack to the cops about Teo. "He was looking right at me, disrespecting me."

Was it possible not to disrespect a grown man with Bubble Yum stuck to his cowboy jacket fringe?

Erik was looking at Whitey—looking down at him, actually. "Am I disrespecting you?" Whitey muttered something, and Erik said, "Trust me, son, I am disrespecting you. Lucky I don't coatrack you, right where you stand."

"*Coat*—say what?" Whitey asked.

Robert added, "Said *coatrack*, dude. Speak up. You want some or not?"

"Yeah, right, bro" was the best confused Whitey could muster, and once nobody filed charges, things broke up quick. Robert noticed that Teo had stayed calm through it all. Even after the cops came, he hadn't tried talking up his version, like most people would. Just listened, said he was defending his daughter and himself, and left it at that.

After Erik left for home, Teo and Delfina joined Robert across the boardwalk at his conference table. He handed each of them a bottle of water. Teo opened Delfina's for her, then poured his over his left-hook fist.

Robert asked Delfina, "Did you want to talk to me about something?"

She checked him out one last time: early thirties, with his slightly bent, flat-brim VB Surf cap over his short brown hair; Reefs on his feet again; board shorts; and lightweight hoodie.

"It's okay. I'm a real lawyer, I promise."

"Daddy doesn't want me to go."

"Go where?" Robert asked.

"To the court."

Teo gave Robert the go-ahead nod. Robert lifted her onto his table.

"First, I need you to sign a release. Your dad needs to sign, too, and I bet he will."

She said, "He won't do it."

Teo reached over and signed as his daughter's guardian: *Matteo Famosa*.

"There you go, baby."

11

"What does it mean?" she asked Robert about the release.

Before Robert could answer, Teo said, "Means he's trying to help, and if he does, we won't do anything bad to him for trying."

"That's exactly right," Robert told her, surprised at Teo's down-to-earth clarity.

"Now, baby, go ahead on and tell him what's on your mind."

She reached into her well-worn Hello Kitty backpack and pulled out an *Argonaut*, a local paper of record.

"There," she said, pointing to the classified ads.

Opposite the last page of real estate ads was a personal ad that read:

> Important Notice. Hearing in Matter of Vincent
> Famosa Family Trust.
> Final Accounting. Stanley Mosk Courthouse, Room
> 356.
> Don't Forget!

Famosa, their surname. The hearing date was Monday, three days from now.

"*Important*, it says," she told Robert.

Could be, Robert thought, but this wasn't an actual legal notice. Those appeared in the Legal Notices section, where you'd read about corporate name changes and individuals notifying the public they were doing business under a fictional name: *Bob Smith d/b/a Acme Plumbing*. This ad or notice, whatever it was, looked a little squirrely.

Delfina explained how she'd happened across the notice—she'd spotted her last name while browsing the *Argonaut* for open houses. Over time, she'd learned the names of the real estate brokers who served the best snacks and food.

"Carrots, celery, broccoli, ranch dressing," she said.

"She loves those little wrapped-up hot dogs," Teo said.

"Pigs in a blanket," she told Robert. "Yum."

"They're so good," Robert said. "I love 'em, too."

She asked, "Will you come to the court with me? It says *don't forget*, and I don't want Daddy to get in trouble."

"Let me think about it," he asked, knowing better than to answer right away.

Teo insisted on carrying the light conference table back to Robert's place on Ozone. On the way, they stopped by Teo's truck so he could disinfect his hand. A cutaway cube, separate from the old Ford's cab, provided living space—their home.

Watching the pair talk and plan, Robert had next to no doubt their bond was strong and healthy. Delfina, so vibrant, sweet and innocent, still a little girl, even though her home was the inside of this cube. And Teo? Robert found himself already hoping that Teo wasn't one of those guys trouble followed around, just for kicks.

♋

Teo opened the cube's padlocked, shuttered rear door, and light fell into the interior: ten by fifteen feet, eight feet high, its floors rough, wooden planks. About four feet inside the doorway, a rolled-canvas separator hung from the ceiling. Whenever Teo hauled either brush or bagged trash, he told Robert, he dropped the canvas and sealed off their living area.

"On a rare good day, I can clear a couple hundred after gas and landfill fees and keep us a step or two ahead of the game."

Teo had customized the living space himself: a pop-up skylight, a venting fan, built-in bunk beds stacked on one side with a dolphin— *delfina* in Spanish—wood-burned into the frame. Open wire shelving lined the other side. One self-contained section of shelves had plastic drawers with combination locks: private spaces marked *Delfina's Stuff* and *Daddy's Stuff.*

Delfina jumped onto her bunk and told Robert she thought the place was awesome and her dad awesome, too, for putting it together. He was relieved that Delfina's situation wasn't as dire as others who actually lived on the street. Not even close.

"You a carpenter?" Robert asked as Teo swabbed alcohol on his left hand.

"Not really, just handy."

"Looks professional. Why don't you two shower and change over at my place?"

Instead of at the public showers down the boardwalk.

"Mighty nice of you, Robert. That'd be great."

"What's *coatrack* mean, like that big man said?" Delfina asked Robert. Meaning Erik.

"Well, have you ever seen a real coatrack?"

She nodded. "Downtown at the Mission. To hang your coat by the door."

"So *coatrack* doesn't really mean anything. It's something my friend says to people when they're acting bad. Not acting polite. It might make them stop and think about how they're acting."

"Oh," she said, and gave him one of those kid smiles that sticks with you. *"Coatrack."*

After that, Teo grabbed clean clothes and towels for himself and Delfina, locked the cube from outside, and lifted Delfina onto his back.

Robert took the conference table this time as they headed over to Ozone.

"This trust," Robert asked. "You have a copy of it?"

"Not anymore. That trust, it caused me so much trouble . . ."

❧

In Robert's bathroom, Delfina was bathing in the old claw-foot bathtub. All of Gia's beach-stay emoluments were on hand to occupy her, giving

Robert time in the kitchen to learn more about Teo's situation. As Teo washed out Delfina's backpack in the sink, Robert assured him that nothing would happen without his say-so while Teo filled in some gaps about their current situation.

"Delfina's not in school, but I'm gonna enroll her soon as I have a real address. Right now, though, right this minute, I have one item top of my list: stay sober. Stay sober, and keep working. Stay sober, and put a real roof over our heads. Stay sober, and keep Delfina out of the system."

Got it, Robert was thinking. *Stay sober.*

Teo's phone interrupted them. He took the call to the living room.

When he came back, he said, "That was my new AA sponsor. Almost."

Turned out, Teo's former sponsor had slipped up—gotten drunk—and had suggested as his replacement a regular at a Venice Beach AA meeting.

"Supposed to meet him up the boardwalk, but all that mess got started," Teo said. "He told me being late was one of his big things, the wrong way to start off with him, so he gave me some other numbers. I'll start calling around tonight."

"Okay," Robert said, a little confused.

"Wasn't my fault I was late, right?"

"Crossed my mind," Robert agreed, because it had.

"You thinkin' like a sober person. A drunk—that's what I am—a drunk can't afford to think that way. Drunk starts thinking like that, pretty soon he's dwelling on how unfair life is, telling himself, 'Minding my own business, get set upon by those men, and I'm just trying to protect my daughter.' Then the resentment and anger kicks in—right anger or wrong anger, don't matter—and pretty soon the angry man goes looking for the man in the bottle, the man with all the answers. 'And Delfina?' I'd be telling myself. 'The world's unfair anyway, so who cares? She might as well learn about it now.'"

"Stay sober," Robert said. "Got it."

"For me, that simple, that hard."

Teo's move toward sobriety had started when he and Delfina had lived downtown at the Union Rescue Mission. There were AA meetings on site, where he'd found his first sponsor.

"I was still drinking some," he said, "but they let you stay so you won't be out on the street. I was thinking about quitting, but I sat, back of the room, didn't share. Still don't share, but I don't drink, and I listen good and take it all in."

Once he'd left the Mission with Delfina, his next sponsor—downtown was too far away then—was a self-described step-Nazi. Ninety AA meetings in ninety days, and all that time they worked the first three steps.

Teo said, "I admitted I was powerless over alcohol—that my life was unmanageable. Came to believe that a power greater than me, my higher power, could restore me to sanity. And I made a decision to turn my will and my life over to the care of God as I understood him."

"Where are you in the process?"

"Well, I'm powerless over booze, that's for damn sure. Believe a higher power can restore my sanity, and my life's unmanageable on alcohol. Taking a personal inventory, that comes next."

"You drinking? That's why you two left the Mission?"

Teo told him, "Nah. There's a woman was taking a beating over dope down on San Pedro, and I backed the guy down. But he lost face, so him and his boys came up on me after I put Delfina on the school bus. Let me know that—well, they asked personal questions about her. Just a matter of time before they hurt her or I killed somebody, so I put together some money, said goodbye to Reverend Andy down at the Mission, and took off outta there."

Robert was curious about the trust, and finally, they got around to it. As Teo told it, it was a family trust set up by his father. Far as Teo knew, the trust owned LA real estate. LA real estate, over time, had been a winning bet.

"You're a beneficiary?" Robert asked.

"Me and my brother, Carlos, both of us. And once I shuffle off, Delfina."

"Did the trust pay for your truck?"

"No, got the truck off a doper I used to know needed cash right then, so it didn't cost much. But the trust? I don't fool with it anymore. Haven't in a good while."

Teo offered more about how the trust started out.

"There was a rental house way, way back. Then Vincent sold it and bought something else . . . apartments . . . I never kept up with it. After Vincent died . . ."

"Your father?"

Teo nodded. "After that, my brother took over as trustee, in charge of the buildings and the money. By then, me and my drinkin' and dopin' and all the rest, I just . . . I caused some problems. And money? It caused me more problems than it solved, and once it stopped coming in, Bee—that's Delfina's mom—she split."

Robert could tell that his past pained Teo, but Teo had more to say.

"You know, Vincent, he always liked to tell me, 'Your brother, he's a bookworm, and you? You nothing but a thug.' Maybe Vincent got that one right."

Ugly words to hear from your father. Before Robert could ask about Teo's brother, he heard Delfina moving around in his bedroom.

"Want me to go to this hearing, or you want to drop it? Your call, Teo."

"Guess going won't hurt. She's had plenty to worry about in life. No point me adding to it."

"I'll have more questions about this trust, so how about you two stay here till the hearing? That way, you'll both be fresh."

And three days from now, I won't have to run around Venice trying to find your truck.

Robert expected token resistance, but Teo said. "Anytime I can get her closer to what's normal, that's a good day. I thank you, bottom of my heart, Robert."

By the time Delfina joined them in fresh clothes, Robert was typing her engagement letter. He limited her contract's scope to attending the hearing at Stanley Mosk Courthouse in three days and advising her on all legal matters that might arise from that hearing.

"So you'll be my lawyer?" she asked, jumping up and down.

How do I say no to that? Robert wondered.

"But your father needs to sign for you."

"Because I'm too young?" she asked.

"Too young and too cute," Robert said.

Once Robert printed out her contract, Teo signed as her guardian.

"Dealing with trusts isn't what I usually do," Robert told them, "so if there's a real problem, I'll find another lawyer to help me out or to take over."

Teo said, "Never heard of a lawyer saying there's things he didn't know."

"I know just enough about trusts to be dangerous."

"Then I think we can trust him, Delfina."

Then to Robert: "You mind running off one of those engagement letters for me?"

CHAPTER 2

In Gia's living room, fresh-cut roses from her front yard spilled from several clear vases. Robert found her scrubbing vegetables in the kitchen, slipped his arms around her waist from behind and nuzzled her neck.

"Better hurry," Gia said. "Robert'll be home any minute."

"Not Robert *Worth*? They say nobody alive can handle that dude."

"Watch me," she said.

In her backyard, a small going-away barbecue was under way for Erik's wife, Priya, and their two kids. They were off for a two-month visit to her family's village in Isan, the largest Thai province. A couple of Erik's cop buddies had showed up, too, along with the neighbors from either side of Gia's house.

Erik was trying to throw horseshoes with his sons in the backyard pit Robert had built.

"They getting the hang of it?" he asked Gia.

"What happens is, they run the horseshoes from one stake down to the other one."

Robert pulled sausages and marinating chicken out of the refrigerator.

"Then they . . . ?"

"Then they drop the horseshoes and run around the yard."

"Win-win," Robert said.

Six years ago, after a blistering American divorce, Erik had headed for Bangkok with one idea: "To have sex as many times as possible. With women," Erik had added.

After sleeping off his jet lag, he'd grabbed his depravity list of Bangkok bars and clubs and stopped at the hotel's front desk for advice. After all, it was a Buddhist country, accepting and all too familiar with depraved behavior by tourist *farang*, as the Thai people call foreigners. Alone, behind the desk: Priya, the first Thai woman to whom Erik had spoken. Petite, beautiful with delicate Isan-Thai features rightly considered a national treasure.

Erik had lost his mind on the spot. Instead of getting liquored up, he'd scheduled a temple tour and insisted she join him. The next ten days, he'd spent either with her or thinking about her, and before he'd left for home, she'd kissed him on the cheek, touched his nose.

"You han'some," she'd told him.

Two children later, they were living in Mar Vista.

Robert and Gia walked outside to the barbecue, its coals already glowing, thanks to Erik. Robert started to grill the sausages and chicken.

"Whoa, there he goes," Gia said, heading over to join the Jacobsons.

Erik's boys had pulled him to the ground, swarming him with Muay Thai elbows, and were now bouncing on him like he was their own private bounce house. It wasn't unusual for Priya to join them, but she was laughing with Gia at the moment, uncorking wine bottles and waving at him. Robert waved back and saw both of Gia's next-door neighbors—she called them *Brady Bunch* and *Full House*—still at the party, even after making a point of telling Gia they could stay only a few minutes.

He guessed that was because earlier, Gia had let slip to each couple: "I'm really going to miss living in this house. Hope you like grilled sausages?"

Miss this house? You could see the wheels turning. *The house will be for sale?*

Gia actually *was* thinking about selling her house into this red-hot market, but with no rear-alley access for parking—street parking only—it was a hard sell. What an unknown third-party buyer might do with the lot, as Robert liked to say, *you never know,* so that made the house most valuable to her neighbors as a teardown. With the *miss-this-house* trap baited, Gia would wait and see what might happen.

As he grilled, Robert watched Gia stroll around the get-together and wondered how a first-year law school student pulled off staying so calm. His own first year at Hastings College of Law in San Francisco? He'd have been grinding all weekend. He guessed that Gia's decade-long experience managing a law firm made much of law school seem impractical. Her reaction to the *Peerless* case in first-year contracts came to mind.

In *Peerless,* one party agreed to sell cotton shipped on the ship named *Peerless,* leaving Bombay, as it was then called, for London. Another party agreed to buy the cotton from the *Peerless,* also leaving Bombay for London. The problem? Two ships named *Peerless* each left from Bombay for London, one in October, the other in December. The buyer refused to accept the cotton because it was not on the December *Peerless.* The court agreed, voiding the contract because there was no mutual agreement as to what *Peerless* meant.

Gia had understood the case right away, but she'd jumped past the facts.

"Why are they even in court? Cotton is cotton, and they agreed on the price, didn't they?"

She'd guessed the buyer found a better price and used the *Peerless* coincidence to weasel out of the deal.

Probably right. But back in his own first year, Robert's study group spent more time arguing about how to pronounce *demurrer* than wondering about who was weaseling whom.

His advice to her on *Peerless*: "A mutual mistake of fact about an ambiguous, major contract term equals no contract. And the professors like it when you act interested."

Giving him a Marilyn Monroe pout, she said, "Like this?"

No doubt, her teachers were interested in her, even though she dressed down for school. For her, that was an effort. On the boardwalk, he'd watch her coming toward him, covered head to toe in a sarong, long-sleeved shirt, and wide-brimmed hat. Even then, single men had stared, and husbands endured wifely arm-jerks in her wake. Gia's looks were a problem, Robert decided. A problem he could endure.

The party broke up around 10:00 p.m., after Gia had chased out her new-best-friend neighbors. At this point, Robert and Erik's plan about Erik's employment status came into play.

Even though Erik had sold his novelty flatulence-device company (a.k.a. Natural Gas) for a significant chunk of change and had his pension from the force, Priya believed her husband was happier when he was productive.

Robert liked reminding Erik of that fact when they were banging the bag, throwing baseballs into their high school gloves, or running the Venice Beach soft sand, the Santa Monica Canyon stairs or the Los Liones Trail, just up the coast.

Even so, Erik was no layabout. Robert had seen that firsthand with the sale of Natural Gas. Erik knew at least one thing in life would always be true: all men think passing gas is funny; replicating each variety of that sound with a handheld device was a winner.

"Not a trend," Erik liked to say. "We're dealing with scientific fact."

Gia told Erik her own scientific corollary: "Even though women find no humor in passing wind, women do think it's funny that men can't get enough of it."

Scientific or not, Erik had been right. His company had been bought by the largest novelty company in the western United States.

Robert had negotiated the sale, but Erik had been very savvy up to that point.

At their first and only meeting, he'd showed the other side an order from the police union for five thousand units at $4.99 a unit. His manufacturer in Rosemead could make each packaged device for less than twenty cents. The retail price, the novelty people believed, was closer to $9.99. A profit margin to kill for, and off that single order, the novelty guys had thrown a real number at Erik, and he'd grabbed it—even agreed to a three-year noncompetition clause for any flatulence-related novelty products.

On Gia's front porch, Robert told Priya that Erik would now be working as his investigator.

She often spoke "Thai-sty"—Thai-American shorthand. "What mean, *inwestigatah?*" she asked.

Erik said, "Means I find out things for him, ask questions he's not smart enough to ask."

"Means he gets a paycheck when he's working for me," Robert told her.

"Oh, you have client now?" Priya asked Robert.

"Signed a new client today," he said, catching Gia's when-were-you-going-to-tell-me look.

Priya said, "So Erik files W-2 form? Files 1099?" Priya was a fast learner and, Erik liked saying, smarter than he was about everything important.

"A 1099," Robert said.

Priya gave Erik a long hug. "Working now for beach *lawyah*. Okay, *na*," she added, Thai-sty for *okay, okay*.

Erik slung a son under each arm and walked with Priya down the walkway to his flex-fuel Prius. Somehow the entire Jacobson family piled inside, screaming what sounded to Robert like: *The Beach! The Beach!* Whatever they were saying, Robert was gratified Erik had followed his advice: *Do not buy a hot new car for one year after your deal closes. One year, dude.*

Later, while cleaning up the after-party backyard mess, Robert caught Gia's image through the kitchen window, hitting the books for tomorrow's class.

They'd been going out less than a month when she revealed she'd been accepted to law school. Walking arm in arm down the boardwalk, from Ozone to Dudley Court, for an early dinner at Osteria Venice West. Robert was telling her about the *garganelle* with truffles, pretty sure he was pronouncing it correctly, when she said: "I visited Dorothy today. Up at her house."

"Dorothy." He left it at that.

"We talked about Jack. I thought about telling you beforehand—if I did, I probably would've listened to you, done the sensible thing, and let it lie."

She was right about what he would have advised. "How'd it go?"

"Well, I told her I was sorry about my affair with her husband. That I'd been angry and hurt and stupid—mostly stupid. I told her I wasn't raised to do the things I did, that I felt like both my parents had turned their backs on me, and I was ashamed."

Both her parents had died when she was sixteen. Speaking of their ghosts in that way wasn't something he'd ever heard from other Americans and had probably originated with her Chinese mother.

"How'd that go down with Dorothy?"

"She said she knew what it was like, doing stupid things on account of him. *Jack stupid,* she said, and then she made me lunch in the coolest kitchen I've ever seen. Oh—and I got into law school."

Turned out she'd taken the boards and applied before they'd ever started going out. That moment on the boardwalk—seeing her setting serious priorities—that was when he knew it was just a matter of time before he fell in love with Gia Marquez.

In bed after the barbecue, Gia snuggled into Robert, one arm across his chest. She was scented with roses and, for some reason, lavender.

"Tell me about your new client."

"Didn't already?" he asked.

"Don't think so."

"My bad. She's female," he said, messing with her. "Exotic. Quite stunning, really."

"Didn't you learn your lesson about stunning?" she asked, referring to his previous client and girlfriend for a month, Alison Maxwell. A stunning woman, sure, but to describe Alison as a serial liar would be generous.

Robert felt his earlobe between Gia's teeth; the bite wasn't at all sexual.

"How exotic?" she asked, without losing her grip.

"Quite. I let her stay over at Ozone," he said.

"You what?"

Her fingernails dug into his rib cage. That wasn't sexual, either.

"Ow—she's a nine-year-old," he said. "With her father."

Gia sat up in bed. "Nine years old? What's she going to do over there?"

"I have cable and . . ."

"Disney Channel?"

"Maybe. I don't know, but—"

That was followed by: *Did you change the sheets? Was the kitchen clean? Was there anything in the refrigerator? What was she doing when you left?*

A little to his surprise, Gia wanted to meet Teo and Delfina the next day.

"Long as you finish your homework, baby, you can meet her tomorrow," he said.

"Already done."

With that, his hand slipped between her legs.

CHAPTER 3

Fifty miles north of San Francisco, Kiril Dragonov opened his motel room's curtains, eased onto his small second-floor balcony, stood at the metal railing, and looked down on the parking lot. Two sedans—a white Ford and a blue Chevy—were visible from here. He dropped the bedding on the balcony and eased to the floor, his back to the wall.

Driving through San Francisco tonight, all the way down to LA— that would've been his preference. But when you were hauling contraband, blending with tomorrow morning's San Francisco rush-hour crush was the smartest way to go.

Across the motel parking lot, Penko hid in a dark landscaped area, standing guard over the money, too. Then again, he might be with the teenage night clerk who'd clocked out as Kiril had checked in. Penko's accent was catnip to women in America, and Penko knew how to use it. Men, though, always saw him for what he was: the most dangerous man in any room.

Kiril's thoughts returned to the Emerald Triangle, by now two hundred miles north. Their marijuana extraction from the national forest had gone well, no thanks to Penko. After beating the girl to death in the tent, he'd bashed out her teeth and snipped off her fingers with her own trimming shears.

Why not dig a hole in the woods? Kiril had wondered at the time. *Lure her there first? Quick and quiet without your theater of cruelty in camp.*

In spite of being top dog, Kiril knew not to question Penko's judgment in front of others if he valued his life.

Once their forest extraction was under way, though, Penko's aggression turned into an asset; he moved through those mountains like he owned them, an OverBoard waterproof bag over each shoulder, another strapped to his chest.

Behind their fast-moving group, far upstream on the Salmon River shore, Kiril's men had half-assed hidden two inflatable kayaks. By now, those decoys would have drawn the attention of Agent Pascoe and the other federal agents who'd infiltrated the area to root out interstate transport of contraband. Alongside the two kayaks they would find a single bag of second-rate product, enough to convince Agent Pascoe to wait there so that she could link grower to product at the time of arrest.

Once Kiril, Penko, and the others had reached their true entry point on the Salmon River, the men surged into the fifty-five-degree water, floating the swift current downstream. Cold, yes, but warm compared to glacier-fed Dreadful Lake where he'd swum as a child.

In the old country, smuggling had run in his family's blood, no matter who'd been on top. In World War II, the Nazis came first, then the Communists. After them, the Allies, then the Communists again, but through it all, smugglers, drug dealers, extortionists, and killers like his family remained in strong demand.

As the sun rose that morning, Kiril's men floated till they were far outside the federal perimeter and had reached a deserted RV park. There, prearranged buyers waited in a cargo van; Kiril traded their harvest for two large bags of cash, and the cargo van left immediately. The cash bags had gone into the false-bottomed trunks of the Ford and Chevy that currently sat below Kiril in the motel's parking lot.

After the exchange, two just-washed Lexus decoys—two women inside each—headed out of the RV park, well before the money cars.

For the drive down to LA, Kiril had bet on Highway 101—right through the Garberville corridor. It was an open secret that Garberville was the pot-growing mecca of Northern California. Hardware stores in town sold weed trimmers and turkey-basting bags by the hundreds, and the local football team, the joke went, had a sealable Baggie for a mascot. No surprise, then, that in and around Garberville's freeway exit, police presence was a constant.

Both Lexuses had LA tags, new paint jobs, and lightly tinted windows, and stood out in this depressed, mostly rural area, so it was no surprise when the second Lexus was pulled over. Immediately, a prearranged text went to a burner phone in Kiril's Ford, seven miles back. That was his go-ahead. Less than ten minutes later, his car and Penko's Chevy passed the pulled-over Lexus, Kiril eyeing the five police cars already gathered for the feast, lights strobing.

Perfect, Kiril thought as he'd rolled by.

When they searched the Lexus, the cops would find a folder of twenty prepaid money cards under the passenger seat. The cops' ERAD machines would scan the cards and siphon funds from each account. What the cops would quickly learn: each account held only $100, and each was, the women would explain, a gift for extended family in LA County.

Later, back at Garberville, the pair would be released on a bullshit misdemeanor, if that. Total risk of the operation had been $50,000, if both cars were confiscated. That plus attorney's fees, if an attorney was called for, and Kiril had just moved $2 million cash straight through the belly of the Garberville beast.

Below Kiril in the parking lot, that young motel clerk—skin and bones like the dead girl—appeared with Penko. She must've gotten sweet on Penko because she skipped across the lot. Now Penko stepped from the shadows, looked up at him, and grabbed his crotch, mouthing the word *penko*. It meant "stone" in their native tongue, but to Kiril, *penko* described the other man's head, not his cock.

Kiril rose from his seated perch on the balcony. It was after 2:00 a.m. Given the move toward legalization and shrinking profit margins, those two money bags from the Emerald Triangle would be the family's last-ever dope grown on public land. Already, more than $20 million cash had been hidden somewhere down south—cash the Draganovs would use for new business ventures, depending on what *Gospodar*, the master, decided. But no matter what direction the Draganovs' business went, to Kiril, America was still "Eye of the Tiger," blasted from Burmester speakers in a Porsche Turbo, pedal to the floor, burning doughnuts in a Tiffany's parking lot.

Eye of the Tiger, Kiril was thinking. *Then, once I've dropped off the money, I'll be hitting the beach and clubs in LA . . .*

CHAPTER 4

"Ever see a movie being made, Delfina?" Gia asked the little girl.

"No . . . not really."

"Want to? It's not far."

"If it's okay with Daddy."

When Gia and Robert had reached the Ozone apartment late that morning, Delfina sat at the top of his exterior stairs, eating cereal from a bowl. Teo had already hit an AA meeting on the beach and mashed out God knows how many crunches, bottom of Robert's stairs. By noon, Robert, Gia, and the two Famosas had started down the boardwalk toward Hinano Cafe, a mile south on Washington Boulevard, where Robert's buddy, Reyes, was acting in a scene being filmed for *Street Cred 6*.

On their way to Hinano's, Erik checked in with Robert. He'd dropped off his family at Bradley International Terminal at 6:00 a.m., and five hours later, Robert suspected, was already at loose ends. At Windward Plaza, Delfina pulled Gia over to the enclosed public showers and bathroom. The building's exterior design suggested concrete waves, its surface embedded with glazed ocean-themed tiles, hand-painted by local schoolkids.

Delfina showed Gia her favorite tile: a white dolphin skimming the blue ocean beneath a smiling yellow sun. "Look, that's me."

"Delfina, sí, comprendo," Gia said.

Robert and Teo watched Gia and Delfina, the pair now whispering and laughing. Then Delfina looked at them and waved. Even from ten feet away, Robert had no choice—he waved back.

Robert said, "She's a happy little girl."

Teo nodded. "Even with her mom and me messed up all the time, she was always loved, but never loved all the time like . . . *la palabra correcta?"*

Robert tried picturing Delfina's chaotic family life.

"Consistent?" Robert asked.

"Not consistent, yes. We were high on alcohol and drugs and filled with our own selves."

"Where's her mom?"

"Money ran out, and she ran off. Looked all over for her—Manchester Square, Arroyo Seco, Skid Row—but nobody'd seen her, so I'm guessin' she's back up in Bakersfield with her people, or, well . . . *gone-gone.* But that ain't right, me speakin' ill of her. Turns out, we're just bad for each other."

Outside Hinano's, a stone's throw from the Venice Pier, Erik joined them.

"Lonesome already, big boy?" Gia asked.

"Hell—" He noticed Delfina and toned down his language. "Heck no, Gia, I'm a free man, and I do as I want."

"Lonesome for who?" Delfina asked.

Erik knelt down and told her about his family flying out that morning. "I don't miss them at all. I'm glad they're gone." Then he screwed up his face like he was crying.

Delfina got a kick out of Erik.

"It'll be all right, sir," she said.

"Promise?"

"Promise," Delfina said.

The director was between shots, so Reyes came over to shoot the breeze, vibing rapper T. I. Harris in crisp jeans, a white T-shirt, thick gold chain, and a quilted-leather moto jacket. Reyes and Erik were natural enemies. Ex-LAPD and *the other side*. While Reyes was not gang affiliated, he knew his way around that world, and by recommending legit gangbangers as extras—a glamorous job, even though the movie was *Street Cred 6*—Reyes scored major points in that world.

Robert introduced him to Delfina as Raymundo Reyes.

"Are you the star?" she asked.

"Ain't gonna lie, *chica*, no," Reyes said, "but I play a real, real important role."

"Thug Number Seven," Erik offered.

Reyes had insisted Robert run lines with him, so Robert knew Erik was off by four thugs.

"Thing is," Reyes told Delfina, "guy I'm playin', he's working out things in his personal life, same as what the whole movie's about."

"His street cred?" Delfina asked.

"Exactly that," Reyes said.

"There a cop in this picture, Reyes?" Robert asked.

Gia gave Robert a rib shot. "Don't stir 'em up," she said.

Too late. Reyes and Erik were about to get into it.

Reyes said, "*Seguro*, Gia, and the cop, he takes money from bad people, making him even worse than they are. The cop, see, he's the only one took an oath to uphold and protect."

"Oh," Delfina said, thinking about it.

Erik looked to Robert for help, but Robert shrugged: "Sorry, dude, it's in the script."

"What happens to you in the movie?" Delfina asked Reyes.

"Wind up in jail—for a crime I didn't commit."

That he was making up, Robert knew. Thug Number Three died in a hail of gunfire alongside Thugs One, Two, Four, and Five.

"An innocent man?" Gia offered, ignoring her own advice.

"True to life, Gia," Reyes said.

"His big problem in jail," Erik said, making it up on the fly, "he winds up in the same cell as that cop, and the cop's real big. Uh-oh." Erik traced air *x*'s in front of Reyes' eyes. "Lights out."

"Oh, no," Delfina said.

Robert could see this encounter was taking on a life of its own. "Teo," he said, "a walk?" From the probate court website, he'd gained only limited visibility into Monday's hearing, but one thing was clear. Even though the *Argonaut* notice hadn't been issued by the court, the hearing was real and involved a final accounting of the trust's assets and distribution of those assets to beneficiaries. Meaning that, as beneficiaries, his clients ought to show up.

Once Robert worked out that Gia and Erik would keep an eye on Delfina, Teo agreed to that walk and to talking about the trust along the way.

❧

From Hinano's, Robert led Teo two blocks inland to the Venice Canals, past the locks, onto Grand Canal's sidewalk. He hoped Teo might warm to a deeper conversation where foot traffic was sparse to none.

Grand Canal paralleled the beach and formed the western boundary of the Venice Canals area, about twelve square acres. All the houses, both landlocked and on the three islands, faced the canals. Laced with arching white footbridges and split by Dell Avenue, the canals and islands offered a calm oasis amid their 1920s canal cottages and modern, three-story glass-and-steel houses.

"Heard these canals used to run all over Venice proper," Teo said.

Robert explained that the few canals still left had been the brain-child of developer Abbott Kinney, who'd re-created Venice, California, in the likeness of Venice, Italy. Not exactly an obvious idea, but for years, people had swarmed to his creation, despite Kinney's amusement parks and piers being blown away by storms or burned down by arsonists.

With upkeep and crime a growing problem in the '60s, the city filled in and concreted over most canals. Even so, the Venice streets were still dotted with cottages where imported Italian gondolas had once picked up passengers from front-door docks, paddling them slowly down to the boardwalk.

At this point, Teo had relaxed enough, Robert believed, for him to switch gears.

Robert said, "I've never been to a probate hearing, but it's a family trust, so I'd like to know as much about your family as you're comfortable sharing. Maybe even a little more."

For a while, Teo seemed lost in thought as they walked along Grand Canal.

"*Don Vincent*, I'd call him sometimes."

His father had reminded Teo of that blowhard in *The Godfather: Part II*, always in an impeccable white suit: Don Fanucci, a neighborhood big shot who preyed on his own people. The guy young Vito Corleone—played by Robert De Niro—shot dead in an apartment hallway on his rise to power.

"My father was Don Fanucci without the good suit. Took me years," Teo added, "before I figured out Vincent owned three Goodwill suits. Just those three, and had him three fedoras and three sets of shoes—all different colors, resoled Stacy Adams. All of it, he'd mix and match so it looked like he had a deep closet back home."

As Erik would've put it: Vincent was *all hat, no cattle*.

Vincent would take young Teo and his older brother, Carlos, to do cleanup work on Vincent's first run-down rental property.

"Pretty sure it was the first one, but with him, it's hard to know anything's true for sure. Except one thing: no physical labor for Don Famosa. We'd take the bus over to Highland Park, and he'd leave me and Carlos there, tell us what to do, then he'd split for something real important. *Real important*, but taking a bus to get there. Couple times, he came back with a woman—girlfriend, investor, beats me—saying she might buy it from him. He's the big dog, right, but it was *her* car they'd show up in."

That was all Teo said for a while. For the next mile, he didn't speak. Robert could see him sorting through his past, and by the second mile, Teo had warmed up again.

Vincent was a part-Creole, part-Cuban from New Orleans; his wife, Zara, a Jamaican, her family up from the islands. In their late teens, the pair had run away to LA without her parents' blessing. This was the early '60s. Not too long after, they'd married and wound up in Rampart, west side of downtown. A year later, they had a daughter, Felicity. Zara would take the infant with her on the bus over to Hancock Park, where she cleaned those big houses.

"She even saw Mae West and Nat King Cole. But after Zara and Vincent lost Felicity . . ."

"Lost her?"

"Drowned in the bathtub. Both Vincent and Zara were home. They never talked about it to me, but people in the building thought Zara passed out drunk when she was supposed to be watching Felicity. And Zara, she's outta Jamaica, so back of her mind, her momma musta put a voodoo curse on her for runnin' off with Vincent."

Teo's guilt-ridden mother was never the same. By the time Teo was born in '70, three years after Carlos, the household was in turmoil. His parents blamed each other for the baby's death, but Teo believed if it hadn't been Felicity, it would've been something else.

"Zara brought the alcoholic gene to the family, not Vincent. When me or Carlos found her passed out on the floor, Vincent would tell us she's in a voodoo trance. I bought it till I was a little older. By then, she's angry and mean-talking, then she'd turn on a dime and be sweet as can be for weeks on end. And I tell you, nobody in the world's as sweet and loving as an island woman."

Looked to Robert like Teo had more to say, so Robert gave him time to remember.

"I'm just now thinkin' about AA's fourth step—taking a relentless personal inventory. Starting to see why I gravitated to Delfina's mom in the first place. Bee, she was the whitest white woman I'd ever met, the opposite of my mother. But Bee, she was Zara in whiteface," Teo said. "Angry, sweet, an addict, so I'm thinking I just went with what I already knew."

The Famosas had lived in Rampart on Leeward Avenue in a stucco complex. Four separate buildings, two stories with four apartments apiece. Over the outside walk, an archway swept overhead with the complex's name in redbrick letters: *Stover Arms*.

"Swear to God, I think Vincent lived there because of the name. A run-down place trying to sound like more than it was."

Like Vincent, Robert thought, a firmer picture of that man emerging.

"By the time I's twelve, I could jump up and touch the arch, and every time I left the building or came in, I'd slap it till I wore out the stucco, and the bricks underneath was showin'. Later on, I'd stash my hash pipe or meth pipe up there, feelin' my way along to bein' a full-blown addict."

As they neared Santa Monica Pier, crosstown foot traffic swelled. Teo suggested they get off the main drag that was filling fast with tourists, gawkers, and the few residents who'd forgotten what weekend-tourist crowds felt like.

"Alleys feel more like downtown to me, more like home," Teo said, as they cut inland to the alleys between Second and Third.

As they paralleled the retail throng jammed onto Third Street Promenade, Teo shared more about Vincent.

"He'd tell made-up stories you couldn't believe. Like, he was at the Ambassador Hotel the night Bobby Kennedy was shot. Saw Sirhan Sirhan hanging around, wished he'd said something. Oh, and when he was older, he liked saying he'd come up with putting those beer girls inside the boxing ring. How he'd told some beer executives to have sexy girls in the ring. Always have 'em look at the camera and keep their beer-logo halter tops facing the camera, too. 'Always have 'em smile and never say nothin'. Fighter drops dead in the ring, just keep 'em smiling and those tits pointed at the camera.'"

"Wow," Robert said. The audacity of the lie.

Teo said, "I was out of the house by then, and the big man was trying too hard to be somebody important."

Robert admired the even-keeled way Teo was able to talk about him. As if he was *Vincent, the bullshitter*, not *Vincent, my abusive father*.

Teo explained that he'd hated his father his entire adult life till he'd started getting sober, working the steps.

"AA helped me shrink him and Zara down to size. Both of 'em, all they were was ill people who happened to be my parents."

"How much time you spend inside the ropes?"

It was a guess, but Robert had seen him working Erik's bag.

"Had a few fights coming up, Golden Gloves and so forth. Held my own. Wasn't half-bad startin' out, but I always knew why I was really in there. Think that poisoned it for me."

"Vincent?" Robert asked.

Teo nodded. "He's my corner man. You hear how it's bad, a father being in his son's corner—dads don't like seein' flesh and blood take too many punches, tend to throw in the towel early. Mine never once stopped a fight. 'Get your ass back in there' is all he ever had for me, and I'd go in till I got dropped, or the ref stopped it."

Jesus.

Teo had fought for a few purses downtown. Unsanctioned fights, smokers: club patrons eating steaks and smoking cigars while two up-and-comers beat each other's brains out for a few hundred bucks.

"Manager took half of next to nothing, and age twenty-four, I hung 'em up."

Just then, as they cut toward the ocean again, Gia texted Robert. He showed it to Teo: Take your time, fun w/Delf. Going to beach. Ask if that's OK w/Teo.

"Okay with you?" Robert asked.

"Sure," Teo said.

Robert texted her a thumbs-up, then he and Teo descended from Palisades Park onto Entrada Drive in Santa Monica Canyon, less than a half mile from the ocean.

Teo started talking again. As it happened, Zara and Vincent had arrived in LA a few years before the Watts riots, when racial tensions in the city erupted over a traffic stop gone bad. Vincent had heard all his life about the Cuban revolution, and Zara believed in evil spirits, so Vincent decided to get out of LA with Zara and Felicity.

"Later on, Vincent'd tell me and my brother he always knew what was coming, like he had special powers. Way he put it, he could *just tell*, but Watts riots was the only time he ever got it right. Every couple of years, Vincent could *just tell* something bad was gonna go down, so he'd pile us in whatever car he could borrow and get gone. By the time Rodney King got beat up in the '90s, I'd moved out, but Vincent made a point of telling me, 'Don't worry, the King thing's gonna blow over. Just wait and see.'"

"He could *just tell*, right?" Robert asked.

Teo shook his head. They reached the bottom of the stairs on Entrada.

Robert asked, "But the trust, the real estate. How'd a guy like Vincent manage to pull that off?"

"Want the long or short of it?"

Robert stared up at the 187 stairs looming overhead. "Take your time," he said, hoping that talking would slow Teo's pace. It didn't.

"The fight game," Teo said. "Vincent said money to buy that first rental house came from betting on fights."

Inside the boxing ring—that's where the family trust had been born.

"The Olympic Auditorium was still a big deal downtown. Main Street Gym, too, and Vincent did have an eye for fighters, picked a few solid winners by watching fighters train. Saw who was in shape, whose old lady just split on him, who was hitting the bottle, that kinda thing. But don't get me wrong: he's never driving home in a Cadillac, a'ight? He's small-time, bringin' home a sack of steaks or a used TV in a new box."

Robert figured those gifts helped fill Vincent's *big hat*. They topped the stairs the second time, Robert sucking a little wind. Teo spoke like they'd been lounging in deck chairs.

"Ever heard of the Ramos versus Ramos fight?" Teo asked.

Seemed to Robert that he had, but the specifics escaped him.

"That fight was in '70, before I was born. But later on, around the dinner table, Vincent said the Famosa Trust started the night of the Ramos fight."

The lightweight fight was billed as Night of the Ramoses because the boxers had the same last name: Sugar Ramos, a Cuban-Mexican, and Mando Ramos, a US-born Mexican. People had started calling Mando "Wonder Boy" when he'd turned champ as a teenager.

Teo knew all about that fight—a black-and-white postfight photograph had hung on his apartment's dining room wall.

"Vincent's at the fight, and somehow he's inside the ropes. That picture was always in my face. To Vincent's right at the dinner table so he could point at it or take it off the wall. His guy, Sugar, the Cuban, lost the fight in a ten-round classic. And in the picture, there's Vincent, big as life, with his arms around Sugar."

"Sure it was Vincent in the picture?"

"He was there, all right. Once we were older, Mom had passed, he liked bragging that a sweet young thing took a shine to him, and they'd made it after the fight. Nice picture. I'll show it to you sometime."

"How does Vincent put together a stake to buy real estate?"

"See, that's the thing. Vincent says Sugar—Cuban, like Vincent— told him before the fight he'd go the distance, gonna die before he lets Wonder Boy knock him out. All the Mexicans were lined up strong for Wonder Boy to knock out Sugar, so Vincent found somebody to take his action on Sugar going the distance, the full fifteen rounds. Bet every nickel he could find and took home three hundred bucks. All during the '70s, he kept parlaying that three hundred, according to him. Bet big on the first Ali-Frazier fight in the Garden—he *knew* Frazier was gonna drop Ali with that big left hook. Knew Ali was gonna make a comeback, too, so he bet their second fight right. Same with the Thrilla in Manila—sayin' they're gonna give it to Ali because he's got history on his side. And Holmes-Norton, Duran-Palomino, and on and on, he called 'em and kept winning till he put together right at ten thousand dollars."

Robert asked, "So in 1980, let's say, he buys that first rental house?"

"About that, yeah."

"And the trust was set up when?"

"Mid to late '80s, about, and Vincent's the only trustee till the end of 2005."

"What happened in '05?"

"Somebody beat him to death, age sixty-five. They found him in West Hollywood, back of a gay club, had a dildo shoved up his rectum."

"Was he gay?"

"Nah, hetero. That mouth of his, he was bound to piss people off. Police let it go unsolved—guy like Vincent, no witnesses, where do they even start?"

At that point, Teo begged off for his second AA meeting of the day. Robert said he'd pick up some takeout, and they could all meet for dinner over on Ozone.

"Sure you don't have a copy of the trust agreement?" Robert asked.

"Not for years," Teo said.

"The hearing's Monday, first thing—I want to talk tomorrow, too."

Teo said, "I have a morning job out in Malibu. How's two o'clock on Ozone sound?"

"Two sharp. You'll be back in time from that job, right?"

"Right as rain," Teo said.

◆◆

After Teo took off for his AA meeting, Robert stopped by Cha Cha Chicken, a long block up the hill from the beach and Shutters hotel. Given Teo's Jamaican heritage, Robert bought jerk chicken, jerk chicken enchiladas, sides of jerk sauce, plantains, and dirty rice and beans.

Once he met up with Teo, Gia, and Delfina back at Ozone, they grabbed a basket and a blanket for a picnic dinner on the beach.

As they walked across Speedway toward the boardwalk, Delfina told Robert and Teo, "We went in the ocean with boogie boards today. It was exciting."

"Were you scared?"

"No. Mr. Jacobson said I was very brave."

"She was so good all day," Gia told Teo.

"Makes me proud to hear that, Delfina."

She took his hand. "Thank you, Daddy."

"Hey, Beach Lawyer."

Robert saw a man angling to intersect him on the boardwalk, a red plastic party cup held aloft. Robert told the others to keep going, he'd meet them on the beach.

"Sir, I just need a minute of your time, sir." The loud-talking drunk wore a linen jacket, deck shoes, and a cloth belt with ducks, beak-to-tail feathers, circling his ample waist.

"What's up?" Robert said, aiming for abrupt—anything but welcoming.

"I need to know, sir, can they eject me from a movie without no refund whatsoever, just for using my phone?"

"Tell you what, Jack, you need to move on," Robert said.

"Sir, my name's not Jack, sir. It's Dave, and you're the beach lawyer, I'm told, sir."

"Take this piece of advice, Sir Dave."

Robert emptied Dave's cup, handed it back to him, and hit the sand running, catching up with the others shoreline.

As they spread the blanket and sat down, Delfina asked, "He talked too loud. Was he not polite?"

"Not at all polite, Delfina."

"Did you coatrack him, Robert?"

Robert winked at her. "Tell you what, sweetheart, we see him again, I'll let *you* coatrack him, okay?"

"Okay, that would be so fun. Daddy, can you make a chip for your phone out of this sand?"

"I don't know," Teo said.

She looked at Robert.

Robert said, "Gia's better at science than I am."

She looked at Gia.

Gia said, "Maybe if you heated it up so it was real, real hot, but I don't know."

Delfina said, "Fun Kid Facts online said the astronauts left a coin on the moon made out of sand. It had seventy-three little messages for aliens written on it and said we come from Earth and we come in peace for all mankind."

An inscribed silicon coin, Robert dimly recalled, left on the moon by the first astronauts.

"Exactly," he added.

After dinner, Robert and Gia drove over to her place in the Bronco. As he made a turn onto Wilshire, Gia said, "Erik claims you owe him a day's pay for today."

"For . . . ?"

"Any day he has to talk to Reyes costs you a full day's investigator pay, plus therapy. What was up with Teo tonight?" she asked.

He knew what she meant. Teo had been quiet during the meal, ate very little. Halfway through, he'd excused himself and eased down the bank and stood in the shallow tide. A few minutes later, Gia had caught Robert's eye, and Robert had walked down to check on him.

"What's up, man? You doin' okay?"

Teo kept staring out across the milky sea. A few straggling sailboats lazed across the horizon, headed back to the marina in light winds.

"Zara, the food. Her food. It's the smell of her. Cinnamon . . . cloves. Like I told you, she wasn't drunk all the time. I don't like the smell of her food and, same time, I do. I fear it and want it at the same time, but it's just food, right?"

Robert recalled the eucalyptus trees lining the Gilroy, California, driveway that led into the family farm where he had been raised. That crisp scent sometimes brought back the good things about his childhood: that hillside tree limb where Robert and his first cousin, Rosalind, used to sit and talk. But that scent triggered the bad times, too.

"Sure, just food," Robert told him.

"Teo's mom was Jamaican," he said to Gia now. "They had a troubled relationship, but he misses her anyway."

Gia nodded. "Boy, Delfina's such a good girl."

"Sure looks that way."

"All day long I wanted to buy her things. Clothes, books, anything. Bad idea, right?"

"Think so, yeah. This situation won't last forever."

"Really smart, too," Gia said.

"Fun Kid Facts? I was already in over my head."

"But sometimes she gets scared."

"About those men on the boardwalk coming back?"

"No. Afraid her father might go for a walk and never come back."

Teo and Delfina. Teo had surprised him with how soft he was below the surface; that ran counter to Robert's first impression. And Delfina? Anyone who didn't fall for her wasn't playing with a full deck. Robert liked them a lot, but what he'd said to Gia applied to him as well: better that he keep his distance.

CHAPTER 5

The next morning, Robert and Gia hung around her house, took a long walk up nearby Amalfi Drive. Between Amalfi and the ocean, Santa Monica and Rustic canyons wound their way back in to the hills, their giant eucalyptus and sycamores sheltering what had once been the Uplifters Ranch. Complete with polo grounds, its members included stars like Will Rogers and Bing Crosby, who cruised from LA proper to their secluded canyon clubhouse to *lift up* their glasses of booze and to pursue whatever else might come to mind.

Back at Gia's place, she cracked open her civil procedure book for Monday's class, and he started to organize his notes about Teo's family history in case he needed to know it for tomorrow's hearing.

"What's up in class?" he asked her.

"*Pennoyer v. Neff*, and the International Shoe case," she said. "Minimum state contacts sufficient to sue somebody in the state where you reside."

He remembered. First-year law cases about limits on where you could sue a person or entity and when you could bring them to your state. Doing so gave the person who'd sued an immediate advantage.

"Gripping, huh?" he asked.

"I'll say," she said.

Working for a law firm and seeing litigation firsthand, Gia already knew quite a bit about filing lawsuits. She'd even served papers on defendants herself. That had demystified what she was studying in her class full of eager beavers.

"You acting interested?" he asked.

She nodded thoughtfully and—no sexy pout this time—furrowed her brow in deep concentration. "How's that?"

"Intensely interested. You got a future in the law game, kid."

At 2:10 p.m., Robert drove up the Ozone alley for his meeting with Teo. Teo's truck wasn't behind Robert's apartment, so he parked there. At 2:30 p.m., Teo was still a no-show. No incoming phone call, either.

Robert walked up the stairs, went inside. Dishes were clean, the bed made, and the apartment empty. Trying to keep from getting pissed off, he cruised Venice, looking for the truck and wondering, *How long could his brush pickup job out in Malibu take?*

No luck spotting the cube truck roaming or parked around Venice, so Robert drove back to Gia's. Later, in the backyard, he fired up the grill and threw on some of the chicken from the barbecue.

"What were we thinking?" Gia asked.

"Teo didn't really want to talk about the trust. Thinks there's bad blood between him and his brother, the trustee. Too much to ask of him, I guess." He poked the chicken. "I tried, right?"

She gave him a squeeze. "I'm so smart."

"I know," he said, a little confused.

She kissed him on the mouth. "Smart for being with you."

"Oh, that," he said, and kissed her back.

It was after dark when Teo finally called.

"*Roberto*, man, I'm real sorry . . ."

Out in Malibu, Teo's and Delfina's cheap phones had failed to grab a signal. And instead of a morning job like he'd been told, the land-owner had asked Teo to haul the brush to another lot up the coast, close to County Line Beach.

"Took all day and two round trips, but I cleared four hundred dollars."

Robert was glad he hadn't lit up Teo about being MIA. "Okay, I'll come over there and . . ."

"Listen, man, I know I messed you up. Been thinking all day about what you need from me, so I'll tell you on the way to court. Won't take fifteen, twenty minutes in the car."

Robert agreed, signed off, and went into the darkened living room. He heard Gia in the shower and thought about Teo's call. This wasn't a corporate client with problems; this was a family with problems. But he'd taken it on and tried to make himself remember: all he could do was what Teo allowed him to do.

The mesquite fire he'd set earlier was on its way out. Jabbing the biggest log with the poker, he knelt on the hearth, stared into the fire, and counted his blessings.

❧

Robert picked up the Famosas on Ozone at 7:00 a.m. for the 8:30 a.m. hearing. At least they would be on time—barring a pileup on the eastbound I-10.

Delfina sat in back wearing earbuds, jacked into Robert's phone. With Robert driving, Teo filled in more family history, starting with his older brother, Carlos.

"Two years older'n me. Smaller, smarter, lived in his head quite a bit, and always did real good in school. I's a big kid, athletic, not dumb, exactly, but never accused of being too bright."

"Smart enough," Robert said, and meant it. He found Teo to be clear, logical, and clever.

Teo grinned at the compliment. "By the time I was seven, I could whip Carlos easy, and sometimes I did, but he was a pretty fast runner, lucky for him. Some nights, he'd find my report card from school first, bring it to the dinner table. Say what a dumbass I was not passing math or whatever else I's failing. And me? I might tell about Carlos' gym class. How he couldn't do push-ups or got picked last for some team."

Robert knew that brothers picking on each other wasn't unusual. In a few minutes, he changed his mind about these siblings.

"Mom, she was loaded most of the time by now or taking a nap. Sad, mostly, but the Don? Don Vincent was head of the table, always stirring the pot. Always taking sides with me or Carlos against the other. Depending on what *he* wanted, how *he* felt that day. Dinnertime," Teo said, "was most always a nightmare."

Teo turned around in his seat. "How you doin' on Waze patrol, baby?"

"Fine, Daddy." She gave him a thumbs-up and a smile and said, "Get off I-10 up here."

Robert took the 110 off I-10 East, headed for the north side of downtown Los Angeles. On their right, the Microsoft Theater and STAPLES Center, and he could just make out the top of City Hall.

Delfina, from the back seat: "Sixth Street exit, take it, take it!"

He took Sixth, went downhill to the first light.

Teo spoke again: "In the movie about me and Carlos, the brothers gonna tell each other, 'Don't listen to Dad; he's a bully.' And one night, after the brothers had enough, they'd stand up to him and tell him off. But wasn't no movie happenin' on my street. Whoever caught it that night lost; the other brother won."

"Until the next night," Robert said, despising Vincent even more.

"Yeah. It always hurt, but once I started boxing, things changed some. I was top dog then. Vincent made Carlos come along to the gym, called him *el Débil*, the Weakling. Vincent's in the ring with me, just me, and my brother's on the sidelines, doing homework or working those puzzles."

"Puzzles?"

"Crosswords, puzzle books, word games. 'His little faggot books and puzzles,' Vincent called 'em."

"And the trust. When did you learn about it?" Robert asked.

"Mid-'90s, Vincent told us he had apartment buildings in it, not that rental house anymore, and he was rich now."

"Left on Olive, Robert, left on Olive!" Delfina said behind him.

"Got it, good job," Robert said.

Passing Pershing Square, he reached back for Delfina's high five, got one back.

"So Vincent sold that first house and bought other property?" he asked Teo.

"Over the years, yeah. Apartments over in Monterey Park."

East of downtown. A predominantly Asian section, even back then.

"Once Vincent passed, that trust called for Carlos to be the new head honcho, but we're supposed to split the money down the middle after bills and whatnot were paid."

Whatnot? Taxes and property insurance, Robert was thinking.

"How long since you've seen Carlos?" he asked.

"Been years."

After that, Teo just stared ahead at the imposing courthouse carved into Bunker Hill.

Seemed to Robert, the closer they drew to court, the more he retreated.

"You okay?" Robert asked.

Teo gave him a nod. That was all, his eyes still fixed ahead. In a half hour or so, he and his estranged brother would come face-to-face, whether Teo liked it or not.

After parking in a public lot, Robert got out. Teo stayed buckled in. Robert let Delfina out on his side; by the time they circled over to Teo, Teo had gotten out but looked pale.

"Ready when you are," Teo said, taking Delfina's hand; his trembling voice betrayed his smile.

Robert walked alone to the slotted money box, taking his time. As he headed back, he saw Teo squatting by the car, holding his daughter, she holding him. Looked to him like a child comforting an adult.

Together, they crossed Hill Street and headed uphill to the courthouse entrance on Grand. Nearing the front door, Delfina looked up at the three marble-block statues over the bank of doors. Carved underneath the respective statues were the words: *Mosaic Law*, *Magna Carta*, and *Declaration of Independence*.

"What's Magna Carta?" she asked Teo.

"Dunno, sweetie," Teo said, his face drawn tight as they went inside.

After they made it through security, Robert held back to speak to a security guard. It was one thing to tell a client about his inexperience, another for them actually to see that he couldn't find the courtroom. Once the guard told him how to locate Room 356, he rejoined his clients, and they walked down a two-block-long marble corridor.

Lines spilled out of landlord-tenant court and the clerk's office; still farther along, Robert led them left onto the escalators. In short order, they stepped onto the third floor and found the courtroom from the *Argonaut* notice: Room 356. A plastic sign ID'd Judge Hardwick Blackwell as presiding judge.

They were twenty minutes early; Teo looked borderline nauseated.

"No need for you to come inside yet," Robert said.

"Man, sorry, I . . . I might need to catch a meeting real quick."

Robert didn't know much about AA, and at this point he didn't much care. He pulled Teo aside.

"You're here. There's no booze here—just you and your brother. I don't care if you two get square with each other or not, but you gotta stay, all right? Gotta deal, okay, then it'll be over. Stay here, all right?"

"I hear you, okay."

Robert pushed through the door into the courtroom. To his left sat a cop, who looked up. Robert nodded to him. To his right, a court clerk sat up on a dais. She was talking to a man in a suit who looked to Robert like a lawyer.

Robert approached the clerk. Her nameplate read: *Valerie Chou.*

"Excuse me, Ms. Chou?"

"It's pronounced *Joe*," she said.

Must happen a lot; she smiled at him.

"Sorry, Ms. Chou, am I in the right room for the Vincent Famosa Family Trust hearing?"

She didn't bother checking. "Yes, you are."

Robert shook her hand, then did the same with the lawyer, Bruce Keller. He was a court-hired probate lawyer and was assigned to all Judge Blackwell's cases.

Bruce asked, "And you represent . . . ?"

"Two of the beneficiaries. Matteo Famosa and his daughter, Delfina."

A loud bang echoed from outside. That cop's radio barked, and he took off for the door.

Shit, Robert just knew: *Teo!*

Robert made the hallway and saw three cops struggling with two unfamiliar men. All along the hall, doors opened, heads appeared. Teo was nowhere in sight. The cop from Blackwell's courtroom headed back Robert's way. As he passed, Robert heard him mutter: "Families and money, oil and water."

Corner of his eye, Robert caught Teo and Delfina down the hall. She was drinking from a water fountain, her father watching. Robert hurried to another cop at a nearby courtroom door.

"Sorry to bother you. Which side of the courtroom do the beneficiaries sit on?"

"On the left. Trustees, they sit on the right."

Robert thanked him and met up with Teo and Delfina down the hall.

"See Carlos anywhere?" Robert asked him.

"Not yet," Teo said.

"Okay, then . . ."

Robert held open the door; they went inside. Now Valerie Chou was talking to a woman in her fifties, brunette, in a dark designer suit. Given her dark looks, he'd guess she was Latina. Robert set his ultrathin case file on the left-side table as the woman walked over to him.

"I'm Evelyn Levine," she said. "Val tells me you're Robert Worth. That right?"

Val, not Valerie. Evelyn was a probate court regular.

He shook her hand. "That's right, here on behalf of Matteo and Delfina Famosa." She didn't bother looking at them. "And you?"

"Here for the trustee and the trust. Val said you didn't have the case number, so I assume you know little to nothing about probate practice."

Coming right at me, huh?

"I was retained Friday afternoon. I did what I could to bring myself up to speed."

"If you're relying on Matteo Famosa for information, I doubt you know much at all. Here's what I think we should do. Judge Blackwell will walk in here any moment, and when he does, I'll ask him for an extension. If that's all right with you?"

She was already way ahead of him; he didn't care for that.

"If you don't mind, I'll hear what the judge has to say before I agree to anything." He looked around, making sure Carlos hadn't just now slipped in. "If your client ever gets here."

"Oh," she said. "Then you don't know?"

"About . . . ?"

"Carlos Famosa is dead. I'm here as executor of his estate, and as such, I stepped into his shoes as trustee of the Vincent Famosa Family Trust."

Carlos Famosa dead? Definitely in over my head. That extension looks better than ever.

"Just now," Evelyn said, "I gave Bruce Keller a notarized original of Carlos Famosa's instructions appointing me his executor. Right about now, Bruce slipped it to Judge Blackwell, who is now reading it. My document, together with Carlos Famosa's final accounting as trustee, will create an unhealthy head of steam for Judge Blackwell."

Before Robert could react, Judge Blackwell came in fast through a front-corner door and headed to his perch, that *head of steam* Evelyn had mentioned visible. No time to tell Teo what he'd learned and no point pretending: he'd just gotten blindsided. In spite of Evelyn's hard edge, she'd been trying to toss him a line.

"That extension, Ms. Levine, sounds like a plan. Thank you."

"All right," Evelyn said. "Brace yourself."

After allowing Robert to identify himself and the Famosas, Judge Blackwell thanked him and launched into Evelyn.

"Ms. Levine, do you mean to tell me Mr. Carlos Famosa was able to avoid hearing this court's opinion of his final accounting as trustee by the simple expedient of dying?"

Evelyn: "Your Honor, I—"

"Where will this imbecile be buried?"

"Your Honor, if it please the court, I would like to ask—"

"No, Ms. Levine. Absolutely nothing pleases me today. I'd like to attend the man's funeral for one reason only—to tell him I've never seen a clearer case of negligent management of trust assets *and* to impose court sanctions against him as trustee."

Robert looked on as the judge railed against Carlos. Finally, there was a break in the action.

Evelyn said, "Two things, Your Honor. First, there's a child present, so please lower your voice. And second, Mr. Famosa was my friend of long standing, regardless of what the trust's final accounting may or may not contain. So on both counts, please cool down, Your Honor. That's all I have at this time."

Judge Blackwell made a half-hearted attempt to regain the upper hand, but Evelyn was right, and he knew it. Once he simmered down,

Judge Blackwell granted a joint motion for a two-week extension of the hearing and dismissed the court.

Teo looked to Robert like he had been poleaxed by news of Carlos' death.

"You got all that?" Robert asked.

"Yep."

No time to console him. Robert needed a copy of the case file from the court because Evelyn was right—he had no idea what was going on.

"Are we in trouble?" Delfina asked him. "Is Daddy in trouble?"

He knelt beside her.

"No, not at all. Everything's all right, Delfina." Then to Teo: "I need to talk to the other lawyer. Don't go anywhere."

"Got it," Teo said.

Robert noticed that the hearing had drawn a gallery in the back rows: ten men and women in suits, who had just now filtered out.

Joining Evelyn, Robert asked, "Is that kind of outburst normal?"

"Blackwell's going through a divorce, wife cleaned him out, took the kids. He'll e-mail me later to apologize." They exchanged business cards, and she said, "Tell you what, I have some ideas about how to move forward. Why don't we take five, ten minutes, look each other up online, and go from there?"

"Good idea," Robert said.

Taking a seat nearby, Robert Googled *Evelyn Levine*. Martindale-Hubbell had given her their top rating, same as his own. Currently a sole practitioner, she'd had several articles printed in *California Trusts and Estates Quarterly* and was a member of the Real Property, Trusts and Estate Law Section of the American Bar Association, the latter making him grateful he hadn't crossed swords with her just now.

Evelyn motioned him over to her table.

"Robert Logan Worth. Five years with Fanelli and Pierce. Corporate and securities transactions, banking, M&A. I knew Pierce by reputation only, but Philip Fanelli was always top-notch by all accounts."

"Definitely," Robert said.

"On your own now, Beach Lawyer?"

Thanks, Yo! Venice.

"Yes. And your qualifications are . . . you're good to go."

Not done with him yet, she asked, "You left Fanelli's firm on good terms?"

"Good enough," Robert said. "There's an NDA connected to my departure, but I'm partnered with Philip on another case, if that helps." NDA: a nondisclosure agreement.

"Helps if it's true. So if I called Fanelli right now . . . ?"

He showed her Philip's number in his contacts. "His cell. Give him a call."

"Maybe later. For now, let's you and me quit screwing around."

She pointed to the large legal file bungeed to her rolling briefcase.

"That's *my* Famosa file. It includes not all—but almost all—the correspondence between me, as trust counsel, and Carlos Famosa, the trustee. I'm thinking about turning it over to you. But first, mind if I tell you about attorney-client privilege for California trustees?"

"Go ahead."

"Some idealists argue that the privilege belongs to the beneficiaries, *your clients*, so they could look at my work product anytime. But people who actually *work* with trustees—*people like me*—we know that the trustee and the trust should have the privilege, and that's how California case law stacks up."

Off the top of her head, she cited book and page of a California Supreme Court ruling. Just for fun, she gave him a Texas case that agreed with California. Sounded like she was gearing up for a fight over his access to the Famosa trust's privileged documents: *her work.*

"I have to believe you'd like to see the trust's file, including my privileged correspondence with Carlos about trust business."

"Couldn't hurt," he said. That way, he avoided begging for it.

"For a moment, pretend we're big-boy lawyers. That we have deep-pocket clients. What would happen next?"

"We'd fight about it, no matter what the California cases say, and after a year or two, you'd win. If the cases you cited are on point."

"They are, but I'm sure you'll check them anyway. And after that?"

"After all that, the lawyers would pocket big fees, and the bankers, who usually serve as trustees, don't really care. For them, it's a cost of doing business."

"But this is different, right? Different because there is nothing at stake."

She let that news sink in: *nothing at stake.*

"Because . . . ?"

"This trust is worth nothing at all. Glad you're here, Robert. Nice to meet you and all that, but I could've saved you the trouble."

"Real estate that's worth nothing?" Robert asked.

"I'm exaggerating a tiny bit to make a point. Don't take my word for it. You have the case number, so check the court's file, along with what I'm going to give you." Evelyn took a deep breath. "The child with Teo Famosa?"

"Delfina, his daughter."

"Mind if I meet her?"

"Not at all."

Teo stood when Evelyn approached the table. She ignored him and knelt in front of Delfina.

"Hi, Delfina. My name is Evelyn. It's very nice to meet you."

"Nice to meet you, too," Delfina said. They shook hands. "Are we in trouble, Evelyn?"

"Not at all, dear."

She turned back to Robert and spoke, not quite a whisper:

"The Famosa family—welcome to Crazy Town."

CHAPTER 6

"Hey, Sharon, don't go cheating on me over at Eggslut," the Latina clerk said from the counter of a Grand Central Market burrito bar.

Sharon Sloan said, "I'm not eating today, just window-shopping," and pointed to her baby bump.

"Where's your boyfriend? Killer?"

Killer. That was Bruce Keller's nickname for himself.

"Getting a facial's what he said," Sharon joked.

Sharon had planned to eat lunch today with Bruce, her fellow probate attorney. Then her marching orders came in, and she'd canceled—but not before Bruce had dropped by her office to dish about Judge Blackwell's morning session.

"J. Black went *off*," Bruce told her. "It was classic, but he made the mistake of trying it on Levine."

Bruce Keller, a one-man probate court newswire.

"Evelyn Levine could've been a probate judge herself if she'd wanted it," Sharon said.

She halfway listened as Bruce kept going. "Only death saved the trustee from J. Black's wrath."

She locked her office door, and they headed toward the escalator.

"Oh, well," she said, for lack of anything better to say.

"And we had a newbie lawyer at the hearing. Robert Worth. What a cutie."

"New guy get out alive?"

"He skated unscathed," Bruce said. As she ascended the escalator, he added, "Okay, Basic, you're buying next time."

Bruce and his nicknames. Sharon Sloan's being "Basic" after Sharon Stone in *Basic Instinct*.

After that exchange, she'd left Superior Court and headed down Hill Street beneath the stainless-steel curves of Walt Disney Concert Hall. Four months pregnant, just beginning to show; she and her husband had told the other two kids last week, and they'd seemed okay with it.

As Sharon made it onto South Broadway, Latino street flavor kicked in hard: frilly bride's dresses, *mantillas*, mother-of-pearl *peinetas*, baby-blue *charro* outfits for kids with baby-blue sombreros.

She wondered what Bruce would think if he knew about the people she was meeting. Bruce wouldn't know what to think, she decided. It was beyond his reach and, depending on the day, beyond her own.

Passing through the buzzing indoor food courts—Japanese, Chinese, Latino, fusion, barbecue, high and low cuisine—she headed to the rear of Grand Central and took the basement stairs.

From the first landing, she saw the two men sitting at a metal picnic table. Easy to spot them in those black leather jackets, black jeans, chains, and white T-shirts. Her hand went to a 14-karat Christian Orthodox crucifix, nestled against her growing breasts, the sacred dancing with the profane.

She took a seat next to Kiril, the least obvious of the two. Penko's appraising stare from across the table reminded her why seeing this pair, twice already in one month, was her limit.

"We will keep it short," she said, her cadence and syntax deliberate, more in their manner of speaking. "Today, things changed. Maybe it means something, maybe it does not."

Penko reached into his leather jacket and showed her a bottle.
"We drink?" he asked, his accent thick with booze already.
"You will do well to remember your place," she told Penko.
She handed Kiril a slip of paper.
"Go online," she said. "Do it in your hotel lobby. That is the case number and my password. All new developments from court will be entered by now. You will find the information you need in that case file."
Kiril asked, "On Internet, I go to Superior Court site, then to Probate?"
"Yes," she said.
"What is expected of us?" Kiril asked.
"For now, monitor the address in the probate file, nothing more," she said. "If you have more questions, I will meet you here in two days. Same time, understood?"
Kiril nodded. "Very well."
"Sharon?" Penko asked her. "Does TMZ tour visit home of the Kirk?"
The Kirk. She knew who he meant. Kirk Douglas had played Spartacus in the movie. Legend was, the real Spartacus, a Thracian, was born in Sandanski, a Bulgarian village, and even though Kirk Douglas was Russian, they all overlooked that fact.
"Call them and ask," she said.
"*Spartacus, Bad and Beautiful, Champion.* Which movie you prefer?" Penko asked her.
Even Kiril got into it. "No. *The Vikings.* An excellent picture."
"*Spartacus,*" she said. "Hands down."
Penko again: "The Kirk say, 'I am Spartacus.' Fuck *Terminator.* The Kirk, he is all-time top movie badass."
This could go on forever, so Sharon stood to leave. Penko stood, too. He lifted her crucifix from her chest, stroked it with his thumb, his eyes on hers. She didn't back down. This one must be drunk and overvaluing

his aunt's role as *Gospodar*'s current mistress. He fancied himself something special, but men like him were a dime a dozen in Sofia.

"*Lust for Life*, a good movie, too," Penko said.

She said, "That movie is for *tapak* only." Idiots only.

He kept stroking the crucifix, grinning that cocky grin.

She looked at Kiril. "He shows no respect for me. You should have a long talk with him."

"Penko. Enough."

Penko dropped the crucifix, not the attitude.

"I need a small box," Penko said to her. He held up his pinkie. "About that big. Like jewelry box, small and very tight."

"Jewelry District's not far. Walk there and clear your foolish head."

"Walk with me. Maybe I buy you ring, we get married."

"You," she said, "are filth. After you lick clean the ass of my dog, you will praise me for letting you do so."

That fake smile of his got bigger. The reaction of a violent man without enough power to lay hands on her.

She motioned to Kiril and walked him away from the table.

"I am sorry about him," Kiril said. "He is useful but hard to control."

She nodded. "I have eyes."

"The big celebration out in San Bernardino. You will be there?"

"Yes," she said. "Of course." She gave him advice on new clothing to fit in around low-key Westside neighborhoods. Then, turning her back on him, she said, "By the time I come out of the bathroom, you will have taken that scum away from here."

❦

Kiril finished his *probate court* computer search in the Millennium Biltmore hotel lobby, then joined Penko, already waiting outside, pacing the wide sidewalk across from Pershing Square.

"Where is our fucking car?" he asked Kiril.

"Coming," Kiril said.

Penko spit on the ground.

"Grozna curva, ya chukash!" Unkind Bulgarian words about Sharon. Draining his liquor bottle, he slammed it into a trash can marked *LA Sparkles!*

"She is right about how we look, *dobre?*" Kiril said.

"What is wrong with twelve-hundred-dollar leather jacket? We have no tattoos. Now we are told to wear no good jackets—"

"It is not like home here, *dobre?* We have no pull, no family, or judges to help us."

Kiril understood the frustrations of Penko and the other men, up in the forest all that time. Hitting town now, they wanted to look sharp, cut loose.

Kiril said, "We will shop the Westside. I promise you, we will look cool, but no black tracksuits, all right? No black jeans, no black nothing."

Penko was getting ready to spew again when a private Mercedes Mauck 2 Sprinter tour bus pulled up to the curb. The door opened, and Kiril stepped inside.

"Our very own ride," he told Penko. "I rent. You like?"

Penko lit up. *"Fantastichen,"* he said, joining Kiril.

Inside the Mercedes: six captain's chairs, a bench table in back, a kicking sound system, and disco lights. The other three men from the Emerald Triangle were already getting their swerve on with the five women on board—call girls Kiril had summoned from the family's online escort business. Dark and beautiful, a morale booster for the men.

Penko wrapped Kiril in a big bear hug, then moved in on the women. The driver hit the head mike:

"Welcome aboard, gentlemen . . . and ladies . . . to Tip-Top Tours of Hollywood. Today, our first stop will be the home of film legend *Mister* Kirk Douglas."

Kiril threaded through the cheering men, taking a table seat in back with his special woman, Ilina. Not demure, but quieter than the others. Avoiding that slutwear the other women liked.

He poured two glasses of champagne and handed one to her.

"Wonderful to see you again, Ilina."

"And you, Kiril. Will this visit to LA be longer than your last?"

He toasted her. "Yes, and you have been greatly on my mind."

"Oh?"

As the Mercedes pulled away from the Millennium Biltmore, Kiril laughed along with the others, but his thoughts returned to the address he'd just seen on the hotel-lobby computer.

A Westside Los Angeles house on Amherst Avenue that belonged to Carlos Famosa.

CHAPTER 7

On Tuesday, Robert still had a hard time believing what had happened to the Famosa family trust. Evelyn's enormous legal file was spread out over Gia's living room table, where he'd been plowing through twenty-plus years of records, correspondence, and documents.

He'd started with the most recent item—the final accounting Carlos Famosa had filed with the court before he died.

At the end of the current quarter, the trust had no real estate at all and a cash balance of $18,000 and change. Compared to two years ago when its assets and cash totaled $3,840,607.

No wonder Judge Blackwell lost his temper. What in God's name happened? he wondered.

It was simple enough to find out. Starting two years ago, Carlos began selling off all the trust's real estate. Once the trust went all cash, he invested in two start-up ventures— SoccMom and Vegas Rail. Both went under. As in total loss, belly-up, zeroed out.

Even after those disasters, the trust still had over $220,000 in uninvested cash. But according to bank statements, Carlos had blown through all but $18,000—including the $1,400 left in his personal checking account. And now Carlos was dead.

Walking with Evelyn through the courthouse's underground parking, he'd learned Carlos' gardener had found the body. When he'd shown up at Carlos' house, late afternoon, the study's curtain had been open, and Carlos had been sprawled on the floor by his desk.

Evelyn had told Robert, "We live in the same neighborhood, use the same gardener, and he ran straight over to my house."

"Carlos was alone?"

"All alone," she'd said. "Because he died *unattended*, as they say, an autopsy was called for. Report came back, massive heart attack. Suicide wouldn't have surprised me."

"Because . . . ?"

"The trust. Life's little tragedies. His life had fallen apart."

In court, she'd shown little regard for Teo. When he'd pressed her about it, she'd said, "Teo Famosa and Bee, his sometimes wife. You have the file. See for yourself what your client pulled."

She'd eased into a 2012 Volvo sedan.

"Sad to say," Evelyn had said, "your client has a right to look through his brother's personal effects—as his sole heir, they belong to him now. If you want to check Carlos' computer, any other records at his home, I'll call later today, and we can set up a time."

"Sure," he'd agreed.

That was yesterday. So far today, Evelyn hadn't reached out to him.

Checking the trust's legal file again, Robert didn't see anything contradicting what Teo had told him. The trust had been set up in 1985, and from what he could tell, whoever had done the legal work had turned in a professional job. The trust's '85 real estate inventory had been over in Monterey Park, too. Four apartment buildings, twenty units total—the first Highland Park rental house had been sold years earlier. Photos of the apartment buildings appeared in the file, along with their addresses. All well maintained, from the pictures. Between 1985 and 2005, Vincent, then the trustee, hadn't sold anything and had managed them himself.

Then in October 2005: a West Hollywood police report. Vincent Famosa had been beaten to death and sodomized with "an external object." Under the trust, Carlos had been named Vincent's successor trustee.

Robert could see how that choice might've hurt Teo, maybe even pissed him off. Then again, with his addiction problems, Teo wasn't the guy to run a trust, especially with a CPA brother. After Carlos' death, no successor trustee had been named.

According to year-end reports in the file, Carlos didn't mess up for a long time. The opposite, in fact. Prior to the trust's decline into its current state, it had churned out about $300,000 gross income a year, before taxes and *whatnot*. After that, the brothers had split what was left, even steven. Carlos, though, was directed to serve as trustee without compensation, and Robert imagined over time those unpaid duties could cause resentment on Carlos' end.

Robert's cell vibrated on the table. Philip Fanelli was calling.

"Philip," he answered. "I wondered when you were going to surface."

Philip said, "I'm just back in town from Santa Cruz. When can we meet to discuss our case?"

After arranging to meet the next day, Robert put Philip and his former law firm out of his mind to refocus on the Famosas.

Searching the file again, Robert found a budding problem for trustee Carlos. In 2009, Carlos' letters to Evelyn mentioned Teo and Bee, who'd started showing up at Carlos' house. Reason being, they wanted more income, and if they didn't get it, they planned to find a lawyer and sue.

Those visits led Carlos to ask Evelyn about the trust's so-called In Terrorem clause. The two Latin words meant "in fear"; Section 17 of the trust, with Carlos' underlining, read:

> *In Terrorem. If any beneficiary shall <u>at any time commence proceedings in any court</u> to have this trust set*

aside or declared invalid or <u>to contest any part or all of</u>
<u>its provisions, they shall forfeit any and all interest in</u>
<u>my trust</u> without further action necessary by the trustee.

In Carlos' letter to Evelyn:

That part of the trust I underlined. Can I threaten to
take away Teo's interest in the trust if he and his insane
wife keep threatening me with lawsuits? Looks to me like
it applies to situations just like this.

Evelyn's legal memo and responding letter were clear. The In Terrorem clause—meant to strike terror in beneficiaries before they contested a trust—only applied when the trust was first presented to the court. Meaning right after Vincent's death. That's when Teo might've complained about how Vincent had treated him under the trust. Grounds for complaint would've been Vincent's incapacity, his incompetence or his being under someone else's undue influence.

Evelyn's memo to Carlos:

Undue influence, Carlos. Like Anna Nicole Smith and
her ninety-year-old husband's will. Remember? The in
terrorem ship has sailed. At this late date, that clause
no longer applies to the trust. My best advice to you, try
reasoning with your brother . . .

Robert could see why Carlos had been confused about the underlined language, but a quick trip to the California cases confirmed that Evelyn was right.

He wondered why he even bothered second-guessing Evelyn Levine.

Back in the file: The trust's troubles escalated—again because of Teo. Three different civil suits had been filed against both Teo and the trust. The amounts ranged from $250,000 to $350,000. All in, nearly three quarters of a million dollars. Each involved assault and battery, and each had been filed by a different lawyer.

The trust and Teo—the trust had handled Teo's side of it—filed a brief answer to each of the complaints, denying every allegation without giving any facts in its favor. The trust's, and Teo's answer, did raise self-defense as justification for the assaults, but again, no specifics.

Looked to Robert like the trust was trying to buy thirty days to figure out what to do. Understandable, given the medical reports and pictures of the guys Teo had beaten up. Busted-up faces, bruised and broken ribs. Men named Peterson, Novak, and Daniels, ages thirty-two to forty-seven, who alleged Teo beat them without provocation downtown, in Culver City, and near Koreatown.

Robert recalled the trust had a spendthrift clause, so called because it was designed to keep outsiders from suing and collecting from a spendthrift beneficiary. That is, a beneficiary likely to squander money, with alcohol or drug problems, or a garden-variety black sheep.

In other words, a guy just like Teo who was bound to blow his family money once he had it in hand.

The spendthrift clause was long, its language complicated, but the gist of it was: the outside world could forget about suing a beneficiary covered by such a clause. Even if the beneficiary had assaulted you, even if you had a court-awarded money judgment against him.

Even so, the trust settled all three cases for real money. Copies of canceled checks showed that the three beaten pugilists received around $350,000 total over three years. Roughly thirty cents on the dollar. Releases signed by Teo, the trust, and each plaintiff showed up in the file.

With a spendthrift clause protecting Teo, Robert wondered why the trust had paid out that much.

That is—until he read Evelyn's memorandum to Carlos. A serious piece of work, it ran five pages, single spaced. He checked the cases backing up her arguments—he couldn't help it. The memorandum was one of the best pieces of legal writing he'd ever seen. She'd billed $15,000 for the legal work on the Peters case, the first of the three assaults. He was about to reread her memorandum, just to see how she'd done it, when he saw Delfina across the room, her hand raised, like she was in school.

"What's up, Delfina?"

"I have a question about Magna Carta?"

"You don't need to raise your hand to talk."

"Daddy said you were busy and not to bother you unless it was important."

"Right . . . okay, then . . ."

Daddy told her not to bother him? Teo had been pacing around the house while Robert was trying to work. Robert finally suggested he drive to the beach and take a long, long run.

"You're not bothering me," he told Delfina. "Why don't you come over here and . . ."

"I'm okay here. I'm still not sure what Magna Carta means."

He walked over and sat down beside Delfina, her phone in her lap in case her father called. From the window, he realized, she could keep an eye on the street below—see her father the moment he returned.

He Googled *Magna Carta* on his laptop, digested what was on his screen.

"It means 'big map,' like a big map for people to follow."

She wanted to know more; he showed her England on the map.

"Well, over in England, a long time ago, there was a king named John. His earls and barons, those are important people who . . . who worked for him. They didn't like King John. But the king was a big deal back then, much bigger than we can imagine today."

"Bigger than the president?"

"More like God, so King John didn't care what they thought about him. Nobody ever told the king what to do, but those guys kept giving him a hard time, starting fights with him. So finally, King John got worried and told them he'd try to treat them better. Not like they were horses and cows, more like they were people. But they didn't trust King John, so they made him write down his promises. And that piece of paper, where King John wrote those promises, that's what they call the Magna Carta."

"Why was Magna Carta Man standing on the courthouse?"

He thought about it. This was tougher than he'd thought.

"Pretend like you and I are in England now, and all of a sudden somebody came in this house, right through the door, and said, 'Give me that chair, Delfina.' The one you're sitting on. What would you say?"

She frowned. "It's Gia's."

"But they tell you, 'No, it's not Gia's. Everything belongs to King John.' And they take your chair, and you can't do anything about it. That's what it was like back then."

"Are you teasing?" she asked.

"No. And so the Magna Carta, it said no king could take your stuff unless there was a trial where everybody gets to tell their side of the story. King John didn't like it, but they told him, 'Hey, King John, too bad.'"

"Yeah, King John, tough luck," she said.

They high-fived.

"The courthouse where we went, that's where trials happen. Trials about people taking chairs and other stuff that doesn't belong to them. So they put Magna Carta Man over the door. That way, people won't forget: that getting to have trials in America is really a big deal."

He hoped that was her last question. Any more and he'd be over his head. Teo saved him, though, pulling up in the truck and parking on the street. In a flash, Delfina was up from the chair and out the door.

At the window, he watched her run down the front walkway. Watched Teo get out and catch her in his arms as she jumped into them. Again, that visible bond. On his way down to join them, he found it hard to reconcile that image with those assault-and-battery lawsuits, the ones that Teo hadn't mentioned to him before the hearing.

Once Robert joined them, Teo asked, "Was she any trouble?"

"She was real bad. She made me drive her to Las Vegas, and I gambled and lost all my money. We just drove back home."

Delfina picked up on the joke. "We ate ice cream all day long, Daddy."

"I can't leave you two alone, can I?" Then Teo told Robert, "I dug up that Night of the Ramos picture I told you about. In the truck. You want to see it?"

Vincent Famosa in the ring with Sugar Ramos after the fight.

"Later, okay? First, let's talk about the trust."

❧

In Gia's backyard, Robert and Teo took turns throwing a Frisbee with Delfina, running her around the fenced-in yard, hoping to burn off some of her pent-up energy.

Robert asked Teo if he remembered asking Carlos for more money, threatening to sue the trust if Carlos didn't come across.

Teo said, "Yeah, but Carlos told me I'd lose everything if I sued him, and he read it to me, right out of the trust. Said his lawyer told him that's how it was, and he *hoped* I sued him so I'd lose my piece. Then he could have it all."

Now Robert knew: in spite of Evelyn's memo about the In Terrorem clause being irrelevant, Carlos had lied to his brother about it. Hard for Robert to judge Carlos too harshly. After all, Teo was a raging addict with an addict wife, and they'd showed up at his home, out of control, wanting lifestyle money.

"So you backed down after Carlos threatened you?" Robert asked him.

"Me and Bee find a lawyer, show up for court? Didn't think so at the time, but we didn't need more money. More money woulda kept us high longer. What I needed was to hit bottom and sober up. If anything, Carlos did me a favor."

What Teo said made AA sense to Robert.

"Why didn't you tell me about the three men you beat up?"

"Guess I should've, but the trust handled all of it. Swear to God, Robert, I's blacked out. Don't remember nothin' about beatin' those boys up."

"Anton Peterson, Stanley Novak, and Martin Daniels. Know any of them?"

"Know 'em? No. Seen 'em around where I was drinking. Barflies, people like that."

"No memory of the assaults?"

"*Nada.* I signed a release, and it was done. But Carlos? He was real pissed off I got the trust sued over my bullshit."

"You blame him?"

"Did back then, hell, yeah. 'Hey, Carlos, you'da given me more money, fights wouldn't've happened.' That right there, that's my shame talking, my alcoholic thinking, but it was never on him—it was all on me."

They kept running Delfina around the yard with the Frisbee. Looked to Robert like she was just getting warmed up.

"She ever get tired?" Robert asked.

"She can *go*, baby. Takes after me that way." Watching her, proud, Teo still seemed concerned. "My mom, alcoholic. Me and Bee, alcohol and drugs. Chances are good my little girl's got the bad gene, and she's seen enough bad things already to self-medicate down the line."

Hard to imagine looking at this healthy young girl, but what Teo said sounded right.

Teo asked, "What I did back then to those men. Is it important now?"

"Hard to say, Teo. Lots of times, you don't know what matters till it matters."

"Here's the thing about that trust, *mi abogado*. You heard me talking about how Vincent acted, right?"

"Sure. The big man."

Teo nodded. "After Zara died, he'd have me and Carlos over Sunday dinners. Get wound up, say stuff like, 'How many trustees you two boys see at this table? Only one trustee here I can see.' Sometimes he'd tell us, 'You think anything's gonna be left for you two? A goddamn weakling and a goddamn thug? Think again.'"

"You're saying, what? Vincent didn't plan on you two getting anything?"

"Tellin' you what he liked sayin'. That he's the big man, and he's gonna live forever."

That night, as the fog rolled over the Palisades and into Brentwood, Erik made up an excuse to drop by with salmon, lemons, and capers. Robert grilled it in the backyard as the temperature turned SoCal cold—in the low fifties—so he blazed up the fire pit. He, Erik, and Gia ate dinner sitting around in the misted ocean air suffused by firelight.

Over wine, Gia told them about a professor hitting on her after civil procedure class.

"Stopped me by the door, asked if I had any questions about jurisdiction. I told him no, and he said, 'Minimum contacts, you sure?'"

"I told him, 'Thanks anyway.' So he asked what I thought about *maximum contacts*. Then he winked at me."

Robert said, "I ever see him, I'll give him all the contact he wants."

"Not fair. He's about Priya's size," Gia said.

"Priya'd slaughter your professor," Erik said, missing his wife and kids terribly.

"What's on tap tomorrow?" Robert asked Gia.

"Criminal law," she said.

A look passed between them. Her past dangerous urges had led her to cash malpractice-insurance checks under forged signatures at their old firm. No Girl Scout, she'd also been involved with the female banker Robert had been accused of murdering up in Santa Cruz. Given that, he decided to forgo any cute comment about criminal law as she headed inside to study.

Then Erik suggested that tomorrow they run the soft-sand shelf on Venice Beach, one of their regular get-in-serious-shape events. There was no getting out of it with his masculinity intact, so the next day, the run was on.

Once they hit the soft sand, the exertion kept their conversation to a minimum, and Robert's thoughts drifted to Teo's three assault-and-battery lawsuits. He pictured Teo on the boardwalk, where he'd tried walking away from a fight until Whitey got too close. Even though Delfina was scared, and even though he could've punished all three men, Teo hadn't. But he was sober, not blind drunk like he'd been when he'd delivered those other beatdowns.

Robert still hadn't mentioned to Teo the trust's remaining $18,000. The trust might have outstanding bills in excess of that, so why get his hopes up?

And so far, Teo hadn't mentioned his brother's death, either. On the ride home from the courthouse, Teo had asked to ride in the back seat. The morning sun had shone in on him through the back window, and in his rearview, Robert could see Teo facing the sunlight and smiling. Then, too—hadn't he seen Teo sleeve a tear from his cheek? Happy about Carlos? Sad? Hard to say, grabbing looks at Teo in the mirror.

It doesn't really matter, he decided. *Teo's feelings about his brother's death have no bearing on what I've been hired to do.*

The run with Erik only fueled his questions, so he was relieved when Evelyn called later that day to set up a meeting.

"At my house on Harvard, if you don't mind. And even if you do."

He knew her street. Several blocks from Carlos' house on Amherst Avenue. As Evelyn was signing off, she gave him the teaser.

"Maybe it's time to tell you about *the girl* . . ."

CHAPTER 8

Tucked away in a Harvard Street neighborhood, several miles east of the beach, Evelyn's seventy-year-old house had been redone top to bottom under what she'd told Robert was a twenty-year lease. Open floor plan, high ceilings, exposed beams. Original hardwood floors and oversize wooden furniture custom-made in Mexico, he guessed, from the inlay and carvings. Black-and-white photographs hung on the living room wall, an array of them behind where he now sat, each with the same look: white borders and black frames.

When she'd first let him in, he'd noticed she was moving slower than at the courthouse, and she chose to sit in an easy chair with an ottoman. They'd settled in across from each other.

Then she asked, "Do you mind indulging me? The two of us just talking for a while?"

A little tit for tat. She had a way about her that he liked, so for a while they *just talked.*

"May I ask about one of those photographs behind me?"

"Sure, I took most of them. Guess which ones?"

"Let me think," he said, smiling.

In the one that interested him, a brunette in a black cocktail dress glanced at the camera from a nightclub two-top. Expressive eyebrows, wavy hair, an all-knowing Angelina Jolie–esque smile. Beside her, a heavy-lidded man in a long-sleeve paisley shirt and fringed leather vest. He knew exactly where the camera was and looked right at it. About as stoned as you can get and still be conscious. A male graced with movie-star good looks, and that's what he was.

"You and Chet Jordan?" he asked.

"China Club, way back when."

"I loved his movies," Robert said. "His comedies were great. Then he'd be serious in the next one. One of those actors who could pull that off."

"Not many of them can do it. Robert De Niro, Matt Dillon, Kevin Costner . . . I'm sure there are others. What Chet most enjoyed was losing a limb or being disfigured. It made him appear deeper than he actually was. Chet, you might've guessed, was a firm client where I worked in the '80s."

Evelyn's hand was entwined with Chet's on that white tablecloth.

"A client?" Robert asked.

"Oops. Okay, we dated for a while."

She told him about table-hopping lunches at Le Dome, stars and agents at most every table. Dinners at Chasen's, more stars, drinks at Skybar, more rock and rollers. Private jets to Las Vegas, New York, and Zihuatanejo, Mexico.

"Zihua was perfect before the tour ships started showing up. Looking back on it," she said, "that might've been the tail end of Old Hollywood."

"Chet Jordan. Supposed to be the next Marlon Brando, right?"

"*The next Brando?* No such thing. I was such a huge fan of Brando's—I even joked about it in my high school yearbook—but no one will ever be the next Brando. Truly one of a kind, but 'the next Brando' is what Chet's people put out there. Same old story, Robert. Chet was a great actor and a great big mess."

Robert recalled Chet Jordan had died in a car crash. Drunk, they said. Tour buses even stopped by the site on those morbid movie star death tours.

"We broke up not long after that club picture, and he died a few years later. Fame's supposed to fill that empty spot inside, but when they find out it doesn't work, look out below."

He told her about farm life up in Gilroy, life around the Bay Area, his days at UC Berkeley as an undergrad; after that, Hastings for law school, then coming south to work at Fanelli & Pierce. After a five-year stint, he'd left the firm last year. Single, he lived with a great woman named Gia over in Brentwood.

She asked, "Do any serious wills or trusts work while you were with Fanelli?"

"Several very specific research questions for clients with trusts, but nothing practical."

Then her: "After I decided against becoming a professional photographer, I worked in a real estate office downtown. Saw that I wasn't going to get anywhere without a profession, so I saved up for Southwestern. Trusts and estates. I was drawn to that area of practice because no one I knew growing up had either a trust or an estate. Rich people—they'll always have money, and they're always going to die."

And they're always going to have problems. Robert thinking this about his own family.

When it came time to find a job, Evelyn told him, all the top midtown firms were just then starting to look for women attorneys.

"Not a darker-skinned woman who way back then rolled her *r*'s. So around then, that's when I married Syd Levine and took his last name. After that, doors opened up, and I wound up at Holtzmann and Shapiro. I was with them almost a decade, but I grew tired of grinding it out as a junior partner. I managed to leave on good terms, along with several of their big clients."

"Grinding it out," he said. "I feel you."

"My husband, Syd, I loved. A beautiful man, and by that, I mean a gay man. Early '90s, we divorced, and I kept nothing but his name. He moved to West Hollywood and died of pneumonia a few years later. Get it?"

"AIDS," Robert said.

When Evelyn called to set up this meeting, she'd mentioned *a girl*. She'd get around to it when she was ready—not before—so he didn't bring it up.

She asked him to bring her a photograph from the wall. It was her father, with Evelyn's mother. Both posed beside a limousine parked in front of a white-frame house.

"Dad drove limos for the studios, Paramount, MGM, and Columbia—before it was Sony—and always brought home romantic tales of driving big movie stars around town."

"Like who?"

"Burt Reynolds, Cybill Shepherd—and did I mention Marlon Brando?"

"Might've," he said.

"Isn't it funny?" she asked. "Where else would it matter if you were Brad's proctologist or gave J. Lo bikini waxes, or you were so-and-so's limo driver?"

"Crazy, yeah," he said, smiling along with her.

He asked about another photograph. Her father, standing alone on the porch of that same house.

"That one's later on, much later. He always wanted me to take him by our old house. He'd been so proud of it, a homeowner in a neighborhood of renters. But by then, I'm not even sure he knew what he wanted, but I did it anyway."

Robert gauged the pained, confused look in her aging father's eyes. Dementia, he guessed, but didn't mention it. He thought of his own father, Garrett Worth, diagnosed with late-onset schizophrenia after cashing out, then losing his inheritance from the family farm. The turmoil had split his family apart.

From out of nowhere, Evelyn asked: "My memo on Teo and the trust's spendthrift provision. What did you think about it?"

Toning down his admiration, he said, "I thought you covered everything. And given the way the California statute reads, I thought you were right."

California's spendthrift statute made an exception if Teo's assaults had led to a felony conviction. If that happened, it would be open season on Teo's portion of trust assets. In her memo to Carlos, Evelyn reminded him that Teo had been a professional boxer. If one of Teo's victims pressured the district attorney, the charge could be aggravated assault, a serious felony. If Teo were convicted, the spendthrift clause protecting Teo and the trust from lawsuits would fly out the window.

Evelyn said, "The Peters case, my favorite. I located Mr. Peters' lawyer's office—not his PO Box, his office. It was in a two-story strip mall near Crenshaw and Wilshire."

The opposite of a high-rent district, Robert knew.

"I set up a lunch meeting, let him choose the restaurant, even promised to pick up the check."

"He picked Fatburger, right?" He settled into the story.

"Pacific Dining Car, downtown," she said. "Making me drive to him, but I was a no-show. When he rolled into work three hours later, loaded, I was at his dump of an office door—pretty sure he slept in there, too. In one hand, I held a certified check for—how much was the check, Robert?"

"One hundred two thousand dollars and no cents."

She nodded. "In my other hand, I held releases of the trust and of Teo Famosa. I told the guy: 'Suing the trust, even *you* know that's a nonstarter. That gets thrown out of court first. And Teo Famosa? You're going to settle his claim before I leave your office with this check. If you don't, you'll never see it again because the trust will pay criminal lawyers twice that much in fees to make sure Teo Famosa is never convicted of a felony.'"

Then the shyster would get paid nothing.

"And?" Robert asked.

"He dashed off with the releases. I waited at the nail salon next door, and a half hour later, he brought back his client's notarized signature. After that, I advised Carlos to start setting up reserves against Teo's future misdeeds. As you now know, Teo did not disappoint."

He nodded. Two more assaults. No guesswork now why she didn't speak to Teo in court. For years, his behavior had been a problem for her friend Carlos.

"Now," she said. "About *the girl.*"

"Oh, that," he said.

"Think you know by now that two years ago, the trust started selling real estate and went all cash. You saw my letter to Carlos?"

In it, Evelyn had told Carlos she approved of selling the apartment buildings.

"Yes, I did."

"Out here, earthquakes make real estate a decades-long game of Russian roulette, and maintenance on those buildings had increased every year. Carlos told me he was tired of plugging the dike with temporary repairs, and I didn't blame him. Some big-ticket repair would come along, sooner than later."

Robert thought about it. By the time Carlos had sold out, LA real estate had made an epic run from its lows in 1998. Carlos' decision to sell was easy to justify as a trustee's prudent investment—and the sale put him in a position to diversify the trust's assets.

"At first, it was *girls* Carlos was involved with. Nothing wrong with that—God knows he needed companionship. But, I'd say, eight months ago, he met *the girl* and started spending more—a great deal more. Traveling, new clothes, a rented 1150 Mercedes—he even took me for a quick ride. Oh, and the cigars, vintage wine, connoisseur marijuana—sorry, *primo weed*—and God knows what else he spent on her. She really got her claws into him."

Claws. Robert had a feeling *the girl* was why the cash in the trust and Carlos' personal account did that nosedive from $220,000 to $18,000.

"Who was she?"

She shrugged. "He called me on one of those fake phones. You know the ones?"

"A burner."

Disposable, bought with cash, sold by the hundreds in Venice Boardwalk storefronts. He recalled Carlos' phone bills—nothing more than the data package for Internet and TV.

"He brought her over here, right out front, on their way back from somewhere—Vegas, that's right—making a big deal out of dropping by. He rolled down the window, wearing designer shades. I looked in. The girl, she was blonde—that week anyway—and if he said her name, I didn't catch it. The he flipped me a five-hundred-dollar chip from the Bellagio, told me I should get out more."

She made light of it, but it was easy to see that his treatment had hurt her.

"Anyway, after he met her—that's right about when he started talking up those two garbage investments. That's why I sent him letters threatening to resign, hoping he'd see I was serious and come to his senses."

"When did I resign?" she asked from out of nowhere.

A test question?

"March of this year."

"The exact day?"

He shrugged.

"Guess," she said.

"Guessing March twelfth."

"Bravo."

She fished a flash drive from her pocket and tossed it across the room to him. For some reason, that throwing motion seemed to pain her.

"Our personal and our formal correspondence. Should give you more flavor for the situation." She sat back in her chair. "Over the years, Carlos and I had become friends. That nail salon meeting, for example? I never charged the trust for the actual meetings, but Carlos and I would get together, have a glass of wine and a few laughs. Oh, like telling him how that shyster brought the release back to the salon, and I'm holding up my hands. '*Sorry, dear, my nails are still drying,*' making the guy wait till they dried before getting his check."

"Wish I could've seen that."

"Priceless."

"The girl? What ever happened with her?"

"Don't know, but she dropped him cold. After that, he was a beaten man. He wrote me several e-mails, wondering if he'd offended me. I didn't respond, so he began to drop by my house, all hours. Crying, upset, stoned . . . some of it's on that flash drive," she added.

She stood up slowly, but when he moved to help, she waved him off.

"You spend years thinking someone's a friend. A good friend, even though he behaved badly toward me . . . Now that he's gone . . . I know I could've behaved better on my end. Extended myself more when he reached out, but I didn't."

She motioned him into the kitchen. As they passed her gallery of photographs, she pointed out one of Carlos and her, standing on her front steps.

"That was the day he moved into his new place. Couple years after I moved in here," she said.

It was the first image of adult Carlos he'd seen. Teo was on the money about his brother: slight, five nine or five ten, receding hairline, and glasses too big for his face.

Evelyn leaned down to pick up a bag from her kitchen trash can. Looked like it took some effort.

"I got that," he said.

"Thanks." She pointed at a nearby kitchen drawer. "Grab my clicker, would you?"

He slid it open. Inside the drawer: two garage-door remotes. One had her address felt-tipped onto the plastic; the other was clean.

"It's the marked one," she said.

They walked out the kitchen door. In her garage, he dumped her trash into the black can and opened the door with her remote. She let him pull her can into her rear alley for pickup.

"It's only a few blocks over to Carlos' house. Mind if we walk?"

"Not at all. Teo's expecting my call. I'll have him meet us over there. Gia wants to take care of his daughter today while we're busy."

"A man with a plan," she said.

He clicked the door closed, handed back her remote.

They headed up her alley, which angled back to Harvard Street. Several houses up from her garage, she stopped behind a neighboring house; an old chain-link fence encircled the lot, flush with the garage on each side. Stepping back, he could just make out its rusting downspouts and overgrown yard.

"Can't count how many times I called the city about this deserted house. Even circulated a petition, but the owners do just enough to keep the city off their backs."

One in every neighborhood, he was thinking. Gia's house might qualify as the nuisance in hers.

Before he could add his two cents on this eyesore, she pulled up her sleeve. A thick, black band covered her forearm. A needle ran into her arm.

"After our morning in court, a chemo port was installed. So no matter what, Robert, time is no longer my friend."

"I'm sorry," he said.

"So am I. When you see me wearing a wig, pretend like you don't notice."

CHAPTER 9

Three ficus-lined blocks from Evelyn's house, a black Lexus SUV was parked near the address Kiril had seen in the probate court file. From the driver's seat, Kiril watched Penko twist the miniature human hand on his gold necklace and cracked the window against the sour smell seeping from party boy's pores.

First night on the tour bus, they'd made the rounds in Hollywood; the next night, they'd found the Santa Monica apartment building where the feds finally had grabbed Southie gangster Whitey Bulger.

Black Mass, a movie about Bulger's rise and fall, was one of the men's favorites. His, too. Others were *New Jack City* and *Ray Donovan*. But *The Godfather* always ranked number one in their hearts: Francis Ford Coppola's passion play of family, revenge, and severed horse heads.

Outside Bulger's building last night, they'd paid their respects— toasting, pissing on the sidewalk, and wondering which windows gave into Bulger's apartment.

"His apartment wall, he hide all his money inside," Penko said. "Almost a million stinkin' dollars."

So they all drank to Whitey's hidden million and anything else that came to mind.

Even so, Kiril had held himself back because he'd been with Ilina again. Because he wanted to keep an eye on Penko, too, never knowing when the man could cross the line from civilized to barbaric. As the tour guide had dropped them off at the Biltmore, he'd asked them all if they knew about Elizabeth Short's death. The so-called Black Dahlia murder.

"The lobby of your hotel was the last place Elizabeth Short was ever seen."

Kiril had last seen Penko squatted next to the driver, fascinated with the Short woman. She'd been burned with cigarettes, butchered, surgically cut in half, a smile carved into her face, and her body dumped in a vacant lot.

Glancing at Penko then, he'd wondered how long he would be saddled with this man. This nephew of Pinky, the coarse, overperfumed woman who'd taken over as mistress of *Gospodar*? *Not much longer,* he prayed.

Early this morning, this SUV had been delivered to the Biltmore hotel's garage, with further instructions about what was expected of them today. The SUV belonged to a couple who'd bragged about an upcoming two-week cruise at a body shop the Draganov family owned and operated in San Bernardino. Their car would be back in the shop and repaired a week before they came back into the country.

Now, next to Kiril, Penko's eyes drifted to his laptop where an early episode of *Ray Donovan* played.

"Love the Ray," Penko said. "He is serious badass."

From the back seat, Alexandra sat up from her nap. One of the party girls from the tour bus.

Alexandra said, "Love the Ray, too. Very handsome, very strong. *Very virile.*"

"I have not one care about what you love," Penko told her without turning around.

"Last night you say you love me very much."

Kiril saw Penko's neck swell with blood, his eyes narrowing. Kiril spun on Alexandra.

"Mouth of a whore. Shut it before that man shuts it forever."

She started to go at Penko again but caught Kiril's warning, even hungover as she was.

"I am sorry, Penko," Alexandra said. "You make love to me so good last night, but today you don't even speak to me." She massaged his neck. "I am woman, darling, after all."

"Whore woman," Penko added.

"Yes, your anytime whore woman."

Penko eased. Kiril winked at Alexandra—*smart girl*—and settled into his seat again. Wondering: *Who wears a right-hand replica on a neck chain? Even if it might represent the missing right hand of Bulgaria's Saint Ivan?*

Kiril had to admit, their country was brutal like Penko; even their version of Christianity was laced with savagery.

The murals at the Rila Monastery, south of Sofia, depicted sinners thrown into a fiery lake, winged demons devouring them, and snakes slithering around naked virgins. Saint Ivan's left hand was considered a holy relic in their country and rested alone in a silver casket inside the monastery. The right hand had been stolen on its tour of Russia; Kiril tried picturing a single right hand on a countrywide tour and could not.

And the heart of Tsar Boris? That relic had its own chapel in the monastery.

Let the Russians steal Boris' heart, too! he was thinking. *Let the Russians keep the hand and the heart.*

The right hand of Saint Ivan figured in his own family's history. Once they'd filtered into America, the Draganovs had wound up in Chicago, same as most Bulgarian immigrants. Chicago worked out for years; smuggling cigarettes to and from Canada made for a good life.

Their problems in Chicago began on Bulgarian Liberation Day, during celebrations for freedom from the five-hundred-year brutal Turkish Ottoman yoke.

How the Draganov family recalled that day and their own Ivan: as a drunk Turk had exited the bar, he'd made his last-ever boast to Ivan Draganov and his cousin, Emil; he'd wiped his ass with Saint Ivan's right hand and jacked off with Saint Ivan's left. All fun and games until the Turk's dead body washed up at Wolf Point, his heart removed and both hands hacked off. But because of the dead Turk's wire into local politics, Ivan and Emil had to flee Chicago fast, eventually settling in and around San Bernardino.

San Berdoo, Kiril was thinking.

Like Ivan, Penko and he were part of the northern clan, called that because its members had gravitated north to the Bay Area. The southern clan had stayed behind for the weather, using their graft and strong-arm skill sets and pursuing foolish dreams of stardom.

"Pussies," Penko would say of the southerners.

Even though the two halves of the family worked together, Kiril agreed with Penko's opinion of the southerners. In fact, the tale of the dead Turk had been refined by the northern clan: Ivan Draganov, it was said, did all the cutting on the Turk, while Emil, a southern weakling, puked on his shoes in the alley.

Now in the SUV on Amherst, Kiril watched a Ford cube truck park up the street. No one got out. Didn't matter. No direct action was to be taken without definite instruction from *Gospodar.*

Ten minutes passed. Then a man, early thirties, and an older woman walked toward the house. Another man, looked Latino, and a young girl now got out of that Ford truck, and they all stood around talking. Another car pulled up and double-parked, engine running. A dark-haired woman got out. A knockout, that one. The young girl ran over to the dark-haired woman and took her hand.

"Very nice," Penko said, looking at the woman and the girl.

Kiril wasn't sure which female Penko meant as the pair got in the double-parked car and drove away.

After that, that early-thirties dude and the older woman went inside Carlos Famosa's house. That last man, the one who'd driven the little girl here, sank down on the front steps of the house.

"That him?" Penko asked.

"*Da*. Matteo. He is the one . . ."

CHAPTER 10

"As Carlos' executor, I simply think of myself as if I am he," Evelyn told Robert.

They were inside Carlos' house, in the study. Robert sat in Carlos' desk chair, and Evelyn had turned on the desktop computer's screen.

"I notified Carlos' landlord, paid his rent through the end of the month, notified gas and electric, too. The gardener—his family came in, cleaned the house top to bottom. I'd planned to have Saint Joseph's empty out the place, but it's all yours now."

Robert understood: Teo was sole heir to Carlos' estate. Dealing with the house's contents was in his court now, not Evelyn's.

Robert said, "Whatever Teo doesn't want, I'll put together a garage sale, Craigslist, whatever works best."

Across the simple room, Carlos' movie posters and print reproductions had been removed from the walls and were leaning against them. Daylight streamed through a mullioned double door that opened onto a narrow side yard.

"That yard," Evelyn said, pointing. "That's where the gardener was working when he spotted Carlos sprawled on the floor in here."

In the rest of the house, Carlos had made his own interior-decorating mark, and it wasn't a good one. Oversize leather furniture filled a small living room. Sub-Zero appliances dominated a kitchen far too small to handle them. A twelve-by-fourteen media room held a seventy-inch flat-screen TV, leather chairs, and an oval, onyx coffee table. Like a crib designed by a nineteen-year-old male with new money.

On Carlos' computer in the study, Evelyn showed Robert his client records, formatted by business software: *Client, Hours Worked, Description of Work*, and *Notes*.

"His computer was on when I came in. I left it that way in case he had a password. Checked his mail, too, hoping there might be a client who owed him money. So far, nothing's come by mail, and I don't expect the situation to change. See for yourself," she said.

Robert scrolled back in the client program a couple of months, worked his way forward. All the entries were blank until a couple of weeks ago. At that point, he saw a trio of what looked like new or prospective CPA clients.

Robert skimmed over the first one:

- *Client: Monumental Park West Only*
- *Hours Worked: TBD*
- *Description of Work: Startup company/advise*
- *Notes: Profits. Evergreen, Yuck*

The second one:

- *Client: Rx Samuelson*
- *Hours Worked: TBD*
- *Description of Work: Startup/advise*
- *Notes: Truht/Faiht. Granted, a real chiseler.*

Then the last client:

- *Client: O'Meira*
- *Hours Worked: TBD*

- *Description of Work: Startup/advise*
- *Notes: Angle Mann. Sticky Mickey, a real prick. Meet Karen. Your Decision! Don't Forget! Dance Wif' me 'Inri (not cockney)*

Robert thinking: *Word games, like Teo said, or stoned. Or stoner word games.*

Evelyn watched the screen, too: "Angle Mann? Looks like gibberish to me."

"Wow," he added.

"He liked smoking dope. Can you tell? Maybe we should've started in his bedroom."

They walked through the living room, down a short hall to a door.

"If Carlos hadn't had this trust, I think he would've developed his CPA practice, done quite well."

"Trust income took his initiative?" he asked.

"Something like that."

She unlocked the bedroom door. "You first."

In the bedroom, burglar bars protected the windows. The black-satin, zebra-stripe motif and smoke-mirrored walls didn't surprise him. What did: the pulled-back throw rug that exposed a floor safe.

"Rug was pulled back when I came over. Feel free to look inside."

He knelt, pulled open the safe's door, and shined his iPhone flashlight inside: two and a half feet deep and three feet wide, much larger than its door suggested. He made out a few items stacked on one side.

"When the medical examiners came for his body, they didn't bother with a walk-through."

Once he'd put the safe's contents on the bed, he no longer wondered why. First, a half pound of shrink-wrapped hashish. Then one each of a boxed woman's Patek Philippe watch and a Rolex; three bottles of vintage Louis XIII Rémy Martin cognac; three boxes of Davidoff Oro Blanco cigars.

"Can't tell you what the drugs are worth—bet Teo can. Cigar store tells me the Davidoffs went for four thousand a box; cognac's thirty-five

91

hundred a bottle. With the watches, the whole thing, ex-drugs, cost right at thirty-five thousand. What it would all bring now, I have no idea."

He looked at the stash. This was how Carlos had pissed away his money while his brother and niece had lived at the Mission or rolled around town, living in a truck.

As they walked out the door, Gia texted him. She and Delfina were going for lunch; Teo had okayed it.

Out in the living room, he and Evelyn sat on that oversize leather couch.

Evelyn said, "All my questions earlier, my lawyer shoptalk, quizzing you, I know it was odd."

"A little," he said. "I enjoyed it." And he had.

"I think we can agree on the legal situation. Carlos negligently mismanaged this trust by any imaginable standard. Investing in two start-ups and only those two things? Even if the trust agreement had said what Carlos did was okay—had actually *allowed it*—the law won't allow it. Carlos is personally responsible for the loss, and it's clear that anything Carlos owned, or that the trust might own, belongs to your clients—either as Carlos' next of kin or as the only beneficiaries of the trust."

To Robert's clients, that meant $18,000 in the trust's bank account and whatever that swag in the safe might bring.

"Sounds right," Robert said.

"But," Evelyn said, "I have unbilled fees as Carlos' executor. Roughly fifty hours dealing with the house, preparing for court, and going to the hearing. Fifty hours multiplied by my friends-and-family rate of four hundred fifty an hour"—she smiled saying that—"puts what I'm already owed at well over that eighteen thousand in the bank."

He nodded. Looked like there was more bad news.

"Then there's the question of my unbilled fees to the trust. I found at least a hundred thousand I never billed. Not a problem documenting it, and I can go to probate court and lay claim to everything here, including what's in the floor safe. Then we could fight about it, but you'd lose."

Here we go, he was thinking. *Her fees. In excess of everything Carlos and the trust owned.*

She must've seen his look.

"Robert, hear me out. I said *could.* A few days ago, I would've gone to the mat for every nickel I'm due rather than see Matteo Famosa get a goddamn dime. Once I met his daughter in court . . . well, she's a different story, isn't she?"

He hoped so, and waited.

"I want three things, Robert. That woman's Patek Philippe in the bedroom. I looked it up. It retails for twelve thousand five, and you won't get eight for it. Second, there's a photograph of Carlos and me in his study. It can't be of value to anyone else. And last, I want to petition the court for you to take over from me as sole trustee of the trust."

He was nodding, grateful, until she hit that *sole trustee* part. When he leaned back in the leather couch, it made an unpleasant noise. Wasn't this supposed to end at a hearing for a worried girl on the boardwalk? Hadn't he signed her and her father to a limited task? How would that client conversation go now?

Listen, Delfina, Teo, let's go over the specific language in your engagement letter. As you can see, the scope of my services was limited . . .

What about hiring a skilled trust lawyer to take over for him? Just paying that firm's retainer would eat up everything Teo and Delfina now had coming to them. He walked over to the front window that gave onto Amherst.

Outside, Teo still sat on the front steps, slumped into his thoughts.

"All right. Let's do that," he said. "And thank you, Evelyn."

After that, Evelyn copied all of Carlos' files onto a flash drive for him and handed him a key to the house. With her Patek Philippe and the photograph of Carlos and her in hand, she said, "That hashish, Mr. Trustee, that's on you to deal with."

Looking outside, he watched as Evelyn walked past Teo. She didn't speak a word to him.

CHAPTER 11

Robert joined Teo on Carlos' front steps. For a while, they sat without speaking.

"What's going on?" Robert finally asked.

"Can't go in yet."

"He's gone, man. All his things, they belong to you now. We gotta start dealing with it."

"Since hearing he was gone . . . dead." He stopped. "I mean, before I knew about it, I was mad at him and resentful and, mostly, ashamed of myself. And then he was dead, and I started having different . . . I started thinking different about him. Having better thoughts. More like memories of the two of us. I don't know. It's hard puttin' into words."

Teo fell silent again. Robert gave him his space.

"Been thinking that the two of us were brothers, after all."

"Sure," Robert said, standing. "C'mon, let's go. You need to go inside, take care of business."

Teo kept his seat, looking up at Robert.

"What I mean is, I know Carlos had no love for me after how we were raised, after what I did to him, to the trust, and I don't blame him.

But that don't matter to me now, *Roberto*. No matter what, I feel love in my heart for Carlos."

Robert felt his throat tighten. Teo stood, and they headed inside.

෨෨

Looking around inside Carlos' house, Teo didn't have much to say. He wandered the rooms, and Robert followed in case he had questions. Then they reached the study.

"Where he died," Robert said.

"Mind if I have a while alone?" Teo asked.

Robert nodded, closed the door behind him.

In the kitchen, Robert flipped on the garbage disposal, thought about grinding up Carlos' hash. Then he had another thought: *How about asking Reyes for a little off-the-record advice?*

When he switched off the disposal, he thought he caught a noise. Waited. Nothing. Then a wail came from the study.

By the time he reached it, the front door of the house was open, and Teo had made it outside, already unlocking the cube's sliding door. Robert ran down the steps. When he peered into the truck's dim interior, he found Teo kneeling in front of his open personal drawers.

"What's going on? You okay?"

Teo pocketed something from the drawer, relocked it, and headed Robert's way, looking shaken and agitated, not unhappy. In fact, Robert couldn't put his finger on Teo's mental state.

"Roberto," Teo said, "I need a AA meeting. It's important to me, and I know I've imposed on you and Gia so very, very much already. But . . . please. Do you mind? Is it possible? Is it okay?"

"Sure, let's go."

Teo shook his head. "I'll walk, need to walk right now, sort things out. Delfina . . . she's my higher power, you know. I'd be dead without her. You know that, don't you?"

95

"Teo." The word came out sharp, but Robert didn't know how else to get through to him: "Don't screw up, man. Not now. Things are gonna get better now for you and Delfina, all right? Do you understand that?"

He handed Robert the keys to his truck.

"Better? Things are better already. I ain't running away, Roberto. I'm running *toward*."

He headed up the street, first walking, then jogging.

As Robert headed back inside Carlos' house, he didn't pay attention to the SUV starting up down the street. Or notice who was sitting inside as it cruised past.

CHAPTER 12

Ahead of Kiril's Lexus SUV, Teo jogged down Amherst, took a right onto Wilshire Boulevard. Kiril wheeled a right, and when he saw Teo jogging along the sidewalk ahead of him, he pulled into a bus stop, idling.

"You like how the car drive?" Penko asked, keeping an eye on Teo.

"*Da*, good car," Kiril said.

"Maybe I buy one like it but flex fuel. That way, I, too, am friend of the planet."

The idea of Penko being a friend of anything made Kiril smile.

"Call San Berdoo," Kiril said. "Make sure about replacement grille after we finish job."

Penko grabbed a burner, put the call on speaker. On the other end, a man said, "Body shop."

"You know the part we wait for?" Penko asked.

"*Da*, grille is in stock," the man said.

"Double-check," Kiril said.

"I am looking at it. Front grille is still inside box."

"Open the box. Double-check model number," Kiril said.

The speaker voice said: "You already give me model number. Model number on box is same as the model number you give me. Nothing more to do."

Kiril watched Teo cross Wilshire three long blocks ahead; Kiril pulled out into traffic.

Kiril told the speaker voice: "What if person making that grille at car plant was smoking dope or snorting drugs and made mistake? What if shipping box has wrong model number by mistake, or a single screw is missing from a plastic bag inside the box? Then you are permitting my friend—the one sitting beside me in the car—to fit that part all the way up your ass."

Now Penko leaned closer to the speaker.

"Do not listen to Kiril. Do not bother checking box. Nobody ever makes mistake in great country of America."

The voice changed tone. "Looking in box now. Will call you back, for sure."

Once Kiril caught up to Teo, he was jogging south on Twenty-Sixth Street: wide sidewalks, a busy road, no parking lane. Kiril checked his rearview. Alexandra was lying down in the back seat.

"Get out," he said to her. "Follow him. Call me when you know where he's going."

"Still running?" she asked, sitting up, rubbing her eyes.

"Yes, follow and sweat out your poison."

She slipped on a pair of tennis shoes and opened the door.

Kiril watched her begin to jog along Twenty-Sixth. Long strides, her head erect like the track star she had once been.

"Hey," Penko said, reading his Subway app, "Subway on Colorado, not too far. Twelve-inch meatball sub with cheese? And toasted, right?"

"*Not* toasted—how many times do I tell you?"

He looked over. Penko was laughing at him.

"*Lunyo glava,*" Kiril said. *Shithead.*

As they pulled into the Subway parking lot, Penko said, "Ilina, she is good girl. You like her very much, no?"

"Just a girl," Kiril said.

Penko opened his car. "Give me her number," he said. "I want to try her out."

"Sure," Kiril said, and watched him walk into Subway, wondering, *How do I get the go-ahead to kill this co co alkoholik and not die myself?*

CHAPTER 13

An hour after leaving Carlos' house, Robert arrived early for his scheduled meeting with Philip Fanelli and managed to grab time to learn more about the trust, courtesy of Evelyn's flash drive and his own records.

At a corner banquette at Bistro Fresco, laptop open, he read a personal e-mail chain between Evelyn and Carlos.

Like she'd said, her warnings had started about eight months before he died. About the same time, Evelyn had told him, Carlos had met *the girl*:

> Carlos,
>
> What's gotten into you? My God, these investments are not suitable for you—and no, I didn't review them closely at all. I just know. Look at them. They're too risky for the trust—for that matter, they're too risky for you, personally. I don't want to hear about it anymore and don't want any association with it, so do yourself a favor and drop it.

A few more similar-in-tone e-mails followed from Evelyn, threatening to resign, until Carlos received this one in their attorney-client thread:

> Subject: Vincent Famosa Family Trust ("Trust")
>
> Effective as of the end of business today, I resign my position as counsel to the Trustee of the Trust, and as counsel for the Trust itself. I wish you continued success in this, and all of your other endeavors. If you have any questions, please do not hesitate to call. Today, I am returning the trust's files to your home office by courier.
>
> Regards,
> Evelyn Levine, PC

Her letter of resignation was professional, to the point and without recrimination. Nothing she wrote to him in his capacity as trustee could ever bounce back and hurt Carlos personally, a man she'd believed to be making an epic investment mistake with SoccMom and Vegas Rail.

Six weeks later, this from Carlos:

> Morning, Evelyn,
>
> Wanted you to know, I received my first monthly payment on the SoccMom note today. Right on time. Always said, you worry too much!
>
> Best, Carlos

Evelyn's reply:

Carlos,

In case I wasn't perfectly clear with you, I resigned as counsel to both you, as trustee, and the Vincent Famosa Family Trust. Whenever you have time, catching up on a personal basis would be welcome.

Best, Evelyn

Interspersed with these e-mails and others that followed were personal volleys—*shots*, really—from Carlos:

Evelyn,

Sunrise outside Sonora, there's nothing quite like it. We both believe there's something spiritual about this place.

You and I always talked about going to our favorite places in the world. You should travel more. I insist!

Best, Carlos

Several days passed:

Carlos,

I managed to travel a bit in my younger days. Days gone by, I'm afraid. Glad to hear you're expanding your horizons.

Best, Evelyn

For Evelyn, *travel a bit* meant Chet Jordan on Learjets, yet she didn't rub Carlos' nose in it.

Then this short one:

Evelyn,

In San Francisco this week. Between Fiat Lux and Bulgari, it's hard to decide between the two for top-of-the-line trinkets. Good problem to have, right?!

From Evelyn:

Carlos,

Happy travels!

From Carlos:

The Four Seasons, Santa Barbara. Elegant, quiet, yet sensational. We love it, would move up here in a heartbeat!

More of Carlos' travelogue and big-spender e-mails appeared after Evelyn resigned. He might as well have told her: *I'm happy. I'm getting laid. On a spending spree. I'm in love. You have none of those things. Your former friend, Carlos.*

Reading how this man had cut her off, maybe his only friend, after two decades of service, much of it unbilled, Robert marveled at Evelyn's restraint. Carlos Famosa, the little man who was going to hit it big, now stepping out on his own. He remembered something Evelyn had told him: *I never knew his father, Vincent, but I believe that man cast a long shadow over his son's life.* Putting that together with Teo's tales about Don Vincent's three suits, Robert had to agree.

Then he read trustee Carlos' first written letter to SoccMom Corporation:

> *Mr. Saxon,*
> *Your next monthly payment, which was due on the 1st, is now late. Be advised, by the terms of your promissory note, the late payment penalty is due as well, on top of your regular payment. Please remit your check for the new total by return mail.*
> *Sincerely,*
> *Carlos Famosa*

Over the next several weeks, more snail-mail letters from Carlos followed, similar in tone and content. Then this e-mail from SoccMom showed up in Carlos' in-box:

> Mr. Famosa,
>
> I understand your dealings with the company to date have been unproductive. I fully comprehend your frustration and fully intend to make good on all of our promises, both written and verbal.
>
> Sincerely,
> Jake Saxon

Fully intend, huh? Robert was thinking.

After that, it sounded like Saxon started answering Carlos' e-mails by text, if at all:

Mr. Saxon,

I don't consider a tossed-off text an adequate response to my correspondence: "Your payment is in the works, I assure you"??? That doesn't cut it, and your assurances mean nothing to me. We will meet this week—in person—or have no doubt at all, I will refer this matter to legal counsel, and the trust will pursue it with all the means at its disposal!!!

Triple question marks and triple bangs. Good, Carlos, that'll get Jake Saxon off your ass.

Robert already knew from the e-mail dates and the trust's bank balance: Carlos had no resources to go after these guys anyway.

According to the next e-mails, Jake Saxon was a no-show for their first meeting at the Lobster in Santa Monica. Then more excuses from Jake Saxon until he stopped responding at all.

After that, Carlos' tone with Evelyn changed dramatically:

Evelyn,

Think it would be a good idea for us to grab a cup of coffee sometime. It's definitely been way too long since I saw you.

Your friend, Carlos

And then:

Evelyn,

Haven't heard from you since my last e-mail. Are you okay? Should I be worried about you?

Carlos, your friend

Evelyn,

Beginning to think I offended you somehow? If so, I'd like to talk about it when you have time. Either way, let me hear from you, please?

Carlos

He'd started showing up at Evelyn's house, too, and Robert understood Carlos' about-face. Carlos was wigging out about his two investments, and about the same time, *the girl* had disappeared on him.

He pictured Carlos, alone in his rented house. The girl, *adiós*. Carlos smoking one of those $500 Davidoffs, slugging top-shelf brandy, smoking dope, and wondering why he'd decided to screw up his life. Wondering who else to blame. Maybe blaming spendthrift Teo because of those three lawsuits. But knowing—if he had any sense left—that all of it rested on his own frail shoulders. A man fully invested, both body and soul. Carlos had put it all on red, and Robert knew where the roulette wheel stopped: Carlos Famosa, DOA in his study.

He'd already reviewed Carlos' autopsy and a short police report. Carlos' death was deemed to be from natural causes. Time of death about 1:00 p.m., from a massive coronary, traces of THC in his bloodstream—not alarming levels, according to the report. Evelyn's account squared with the police report: Carlos' body had been found by the gardener about 5:00 p.m.

Philip Fanelli's voice roused him: "A familiar sight, Robert Worth buried in his work."

Robert looked up. Philip and his fiancée, Dorothy Brightwell, stood there, her arm hooked inside his. If possible, they were even more besotted with each other than he and Gia.

He slid from the booth and gave her a hug. "Philip, Dorothy, have a seat."

❧

The two lovers were still glued together as they all ordered lunch and caught up with one another and with the case involving Jack Pierce.

Jack had been Philip's partner, Dorothy's ex-husband, and—Robert still found it hard to believe—Gia's boyfriend of many years. Jack had wound up in a vegetative state after stabbing Robert on the cliffs near Santa Cruz.

Once Robert had been released from jail and returned to LA, he'd called Philip for an urgent meeting, in spite of their falling out. He'd reminded Philip that Dorothy had thirty days to back out of her recent divorce from Jack and to assert her prenuptial agreement against him. If she did, given Jack's provable infidelity, *he was due nothing* under the prenup. Meaning that the $5 million she'd paid in the divorce settlement would go back into her pocket.

At first, Philip wanted to let sleeping dogs lie.

"Dorothy's money has disappeared, Robert. What's the point?"

"It's in the Bank of Hong Kong. I have Jack's flash drive and the password to his account. Feel like sharing?"

Sharing the money, he'd meant.

Philip liked sharing. So did Dorothy. They would unwind her divorce in Santa Monica court; on her own, she would use Jack's flash drive and password and reclaim her divorce settlement from Jack's Asian account.

She had just the charity for the proceeds—less, of course, Robert's 15 percent finder's fee for making it possible. After all, he'd almost died getting his hands on the flash drive.

Only one wrinkle: Alison Maxwell's portion of Jack's Hong Kong account balance. Alison had been Robert's client, then his girlfriend. A big chunk of the Hong Kong account, over and above Dorothy's divorce settlement, was money Robert had won her based on Alison's fraudulent claim against Jack and Philip's firm.

The real question became: If Dorothy claimed Alison's portion, too, would Alison ever be able to collect it from Dorothy? After some back-and-forth about Alison's credibility problems and easy-to-prove reputation as a scammer, they reached a collective decision: *Screw Alison. If she ever found out about it, let her try to come after her money.*

At Bistro Fresco, Philip brought Robert up to speed on neutralizing any objections from Jack's legal guardian in Santa Cruz. That is, to keep the guardian from challenging Dorothy's unwinding of her own divorce. So Dorothy had offered to set up a separate $1 million account for Jack's benefit. To be administered, of course, by Jack's guardian.

Philip said, "The man works harder surfing than on his law practice. The idea of controlling a million-dollar account, doling it out for Jack's extras, sounded fine to him. He can pull down fifty thousand a year in fees for doing what he does best."

"Nothing?" Robert asked.

"Give the man some credit, Robert. Next to nothing."

Their food came—steamed fish, vegetables, pot stickers—so they hung out and ate. Robert had always liked Dorothy, and they both liked messing with Philip, who gave as good as he got.

Philip asked, "Thriving in your new practice, Beach Lawyer?"

"Can't beat the rent," Robert said. "I put in almost twenty hours last week. Gonna take a month off, recharge my batteries."

Dorothy chimed in. "How many years would you have needed to work at my darling's firm to earn what you'll earn from our one case?"

"That would've depended on my year-end bonus."

Philip's turn: "Given your customary billable hours and work quality, sadly, your bonus would've been a token amount. A single dollar seems more than fair."

"In that case, Dorothy, I'd need three salaried years working at Boss Man's hideous sweatshop just to break even."

"*Sweatshop?*" Philip asked. "If only."

Dorothy always enjoyed Robert's back-and-forth with Philip. Robert knew if it were up to her, he and Philip would be practicing together, but that scenario wasn't in the cards.

Philip wanted to hear specifics about the Beach Lawyer's unorthodox practice.

"I took on a pair of trust beneficiaries earlier this week."

"A large corpus?" Meaning assets in the trust.

"It was set up to buy LA real estate in the '80s, and we both know about LA real estate."

"Again, the corpus? Significant?"

Never a good idea to run one past Philip Fanelli.

"Hard times. Mismanagement. Not much at all. My clients are virtually homeless, and I'm trying to help out if I can. Looks like I'll take over as trustee. So yeah, I'm killing it."

"Who is on the other side?"

"There's not really an 'other side.' But a lawyer, Evelyn Levine, handled the trust's legal. Smart, reputable, I think. She's been published in *California Trusts and Estates Quarterly.*"

Philip remembered her.

"Quite a woman-about-town back then. Word was, she pulled it off—hard work and hard play. Quite stunning, if I recall," he added.

Dorothy winked at Robert and asked Philip, "Did you happen to date this Levine tramp?"

Philip said, "How could I? I was hard at work, dreaming of the day you would marry me."

"You didn't even know me back then."

"I dreamed you before I met you," Philip said.

Dorothy told Robert, "He's good at this, right?"

Robert nodded, thinking: *Philip is good at lovers' repartee. Who knew?*

Philip said, "I noticed Evelyn Levine at Le Dome once or twice, back when my firm tried going after entertainment clients. Tried and failed, thank God. She was with that movie star, Chet, you know . . ."

"Chet Jordan?" Dorothy asked.

"Drunken degenerate," Philip said.

She mouthed *gorgeous man* to Robert.

Philip said, "She was at Holtzmann and Shapiro. Top-notch couple of guys, solid firm, but we never dealt with them directly, that I recall."

"*Bradley* Holtzmann?" Dorothy asked.

"Think that's right," Robert said.

"I dated him decades ago," she said.

"Was it serious?" Philip asked, joking but not.

"How could it be, dear? I didn't know *serious* until I met you." Then to Robert: "I ran into Bradley at Bel-Air Country Club last month. Arthritis pain has all but crippled him. Poor dear, he's in very bad shape."

"Want me to give *poor dear Bradley* a call, ask him about that *Levine tramp*?" Philip asked Robert.

"Why not?" Robert said. "Couldn't hurt."

Later, the three of them waited as the valet brought the Brightwell Maybach around.

As Dorothy started to step inside, she kissed Robert's cheek and whispered, "Tell Gia I said hi. She's a lovely person, Robert."

Once Philip had closed her door, he said, "If you decide to take on that trusteeship, you'll need a rider to your malpractice insurance."

A moment of regret for their past surged through Robert—their bond wasn't what it once was.

"Hadn't thought of that, Philip. Thanks a lot."

"You're welcome, Robert. As always, so very good to see you . . ."

CHAPTER 14

Driving his Bronco down to the beach, Robert called probate court to set up a get-acquainted meeting with Bruce Keller.

"I'll set aside as long as you need," Bruce told him, "and don't forget to let me know if your plans change."

"Okay, you got it."

They set a meeting for later that week.

Don't forget, Bruce had said. The same phrase that ended Carlos' *Argonaut* notice. If he remembered right, *Don't Forget* appeared in Carlos Famosa's work notes, too. *Gibberish.* That's how Evelyn had described Carlos' notes, and with good reason. Not a single bill had gone out in months. No client meetings, either, unless he counted those nonsensical work notes.

As Robert parked in the alley behind his place, Reyes waved from down the way. Robert got out, tossed a garbage bag into his blue can, and joined him.

"What's up, BL?" Reyes asked. His shoe soles featured multicolored flashing lights.

BL? Beach Lawyer. Jesus.

They took a stroll down the boardwalk to Figtree's Café. Reyes ordered a grilled ahi tuna sandwich to go, and they waited for the order out front on the boardwalk.

"Where's Ed McMahon got off to?"

"Meaning . . . ?"

"Your sidekick, *Oso Polar*." Calling him *Polar Bear*.

"Working on his tan," Robert said.

A dreaded-up bikini girl on skates began circling Robert, blowing soap bubbles at him through a plastic circle on a stick. "You that Beach Lawyer dude, right?"

"Not right now, I'm not," he said.

"Want to buy me a drink?"

"Talk to my lawyer," Robert said, nodding at Reyes.

"You want to buy me one, *el Guapo*?" She asked Reyes this time, calling him the handsome one.

"Can't you see I'm talking to my client, Roller Girl? So go ahead and piss off."

She stopped circling, went *en pointe*, and with a toss of her buttocks and dreads, she pissed off down the boardwalk.

Robert began easing into the idea of Reyes selling Carlos' hashish.

"How's your license and registration these days?" he asked.

"So-so," Reyes said.

"Again, meaning . . . ?"

"Means I'm always better off rolling in *el carro de mi novia*." His girlfriend's car.

"That's what you're driving today?"

"*Sí.*"

"That little girl you met the other day. How'd you like to help out somebody like her?"

"Dolphin Girl?" Reyes asked.

"No. Somebody *like her*."

"Oh, not *her*. *Like* her. *Sí*, anytime."

"Tell me this, Reyes, all these drug hospitals around. What happens if they got a good deal on some dope? Let's say, a half pound of hashish?"

"Quarter kilo? Westside, they won't touch it. But out my way, there's plenty of 'em will."

"So if a guy was to drive by my place tonight, reach in my blue can, and find something like that?"

"Sayin' maybe somebody dumped it there?"

Robert shrugged. "Dunno, they could've."

"Maybe somebody come running by, had to ditch it real quick."

"It's Troubletown, right?" Robert asked.

"Fleeing felon in Troubletown, happens every day. But one thing, *jefe*. Guy should've known blue cans are for paper and plastic. Green cans're for grass."

Robert tried not to smile and said, "Guy like that wouldn't wear Peter Pan shoes like yours, right? Shoes everybody remembers."

"Even bangin' as these are, I doubt it."

"What kind of cut do guys take for moving things *like that*?"

"Guy's gonna say he's taking twenty, thirty percent, winds up takin' half. But doin' it for a little girl *like* Delfina? Guy'd hafta be *un monstruo* to take anything . . ."

CHAPTER 15

The church grounds filled half a city block in Ocean Park, a half mile from the beach, but Teo's walk from Carlos' house brought him to a ground-floor room inside the church's annex. That's where he sat now, at an AA meeting in a mini-mart-size room. A table held fifteen, twenty people, all of them strangers, adults of different ages, and once the meeting started, everyone introduced themselves, first names only, and declared they were alcoholics.

That's what he did when his turn came: "My name is Teo, and I'm an alcoholic."

"Hello, Teo," everyone said back.

It was hard to know why their simple words held so much comfort, but they settled him down and gave him confidence.

Today's meeting leader had already picked one of the twelve steps to discuss. A young man who hugged himself, he looked like he worked in movies with his tinted lenses and tipped hair. Not that it mattered. Nothing mattered here except you were here and hadn't had a drink since the last meeting. On both counts, Teo qualified.

Waiting to share for his first time anywhere, Teo recalled a kid at his first AA meeting. Once the teenager heard the rules, he'd whispered: "Dude? Not drink. Do they mean *not drink at all?*"

"Think so."

"Too much red tape," the kid said, and split.

Teo tried to pay attention to this meeting leader's share: his anger, his everyday problems that looked easy to solve by drinking alcohol, the value of going to meetings without needing a reason—just go. Cool that he didn't talk like he was someone important but like anyone who'd messed up his life. Like every person in the room, and that comforted Teo, too.

The time came for others to share, no more than two minutes per person.

Nearly last in line, Teo sat with his eyes closed, head bowed, waiting. He knew he wasn't respecting what others were sharing, but raw emotion had bubbled up inside him ever since he'd learned about Carlos' death.

Before knowing that, he'd wondered what he'd say to Carlos in the courtroom. *Exactly* what? What would Carlos look like now? Would Carlos turn his back, shame him in front of his daughter?

Did Carlos know that his own brother had broken into his home and stolen from him to buy his Ford truck? No matter that he did it for Delfina. No matter it was to get her away from those badass people downtown. No matter that he wasn't drinking when he did it. Back then, anything would've been better than asking Carlos for help, even going to jail for B and E. But now Carlos was dead.

Like he'd tried telling Robert: the shame he'd felt about facing Carlos was gone and made way for good things like forgiveness. Like gratitude. Good, positive things.

And Roberto, his lawyer. *Boy, did I luck out meeting him.*

Not like lawyers he'd met in the system. Tough like them, sure, but Robert didn't look past you like they did. Grew up on a farm, maybe that was why. How many lawyers would sit down with him outside Carlos' house, tell him to come inside, and do it for his own good?

He knew Robert wasn't a saint, that Delfina had roped him into helping them. That was okay. Okay, too, that soon enough he and Delfina would part ways with Robert and Gia—the way of the world.

But if it weren't for Robert, he wouldn't have gone inside Carlos' office. After Robert left him alone at the desk where his brother had died, no doubt about it—he'd been afraid. Shaking and ashamed in the room where his brother took his last breath. Looking around at Carlos' computer, his brother's glass desk with no drawers, a few puzzle books in the bookshelves, those big doors out to a garden, and those posters and prints leaning against the far wall.

The puzzle books—like the ones Teo'd grab from Carlos and throw in the garbage or tear up in front of him. He wondered if Carlos had held on to any of them, with his name and address printed neat in the front like always.

Seeing all of it had driven him from Carlos' chair to his knees. He'd cried out. To ask his brother to forgive him. As his face touched the floor, he felt like his stomach had pulled up inside his lungs, his throat too tight to speak. How long he was on the floor, he didn't know. But when he lifted his face, he saw everything he needed to see in this world. Right across from him—against that wall. After that, everything had been clear, and his mind had flooded with long-muted memories of Carlos.

Then he heard his name in the AA meeting. Saw it was his turn to share.

"I know this is off topic for today's step, but my brother died not too far back, and I need to talk about it. We didn't get along. I was bigger'n he was, and I bullied him. He was real smart, and he picked on me in his own way, every chance he got. But . . ."

Closing his eyes, he kept talking, picturing himself with Carlos, back seat of that car, his parents in front, and describing what he pictured to the meeting. How what he pictured made him feel about his brother. He kept talking till he had nothing left to say.

When he opened his eyes, he saw they'd let him run way over his allotted two minutes. Around the table, a few people were crying; others looked at him, clearly touched.

As the meeting ended, several people told him his share had been powerful and thanked him for it. He thanked them for the meeting. For being here, and he hoped what he'd said might help someone else.

Across the room, he noticed an older guy with short white hair, thinning on top. The man nodded to him, and Teo nodded back. Something like knowledge passed between them.

Out in the parking lot, Teo caught up with the white-haired man.

"Said your name was Benny, right?"

"That's right, Teo." Remembering his name.

"How long you been sober?" Teo asked.

"Twenty-eight years and change," Benny said.

"Any way you'd think about being my sponsor?"

"I'm big on walking," Benny said. "Want to walk around the block?"

"Need to call my daughter first. That okay with you?"

CHAPTER 16

When Alexandra called Kiril, he drove to Ocean Park and found her at a bus stop, not far from Santa Monica College. Once she was in the Lexus' back seat, the car moving again, she asked if they'd bought her a Subway, too.

"Want this?" Kiril offered her the last half of his.

"Like mine toasted," she said, waving it away.

Then she told him Teo had gone into a church not far from here.

"Going to pray?" Penko said. "Good idea for him today."

"Not to pray," she told him.

She'd followed him inside. He went into a room for some kind of meeting.

"About a half hour ago," she said.

Kiril drove where she told him to go and parked where they could see the annex door Teo had used. Then more waiting.

Kiril asked Alexandra, "What are you reading?"

"A college course catalog." She mentioned a course about geology. "Introductory course. They study different rocks, all the formations, take field trips. We live near San Andreas Fault, and one day, *whoof*, it's gonna be very bad."

"Have special college deal for *prostitutka*?" Penko asked her.

"*Neh.* But a course for *lainarl* only, starting next semester." Calling him a shithead.

"Get out," Kiril told her, his voice sharp.

She slid out. He did, too, and motioned her to him.

"My life is difficult already," he said. "You understand?"

"Life always difficult."

"Next time you want to mess with him, go ahead. And next time, I will not stop him."

Tears filled her eyes; she looked down. "Maybe next time I start to run and keep running."

Kiril saw that man, Teo, coming out of the church annex. Not alone. With a white-haired man. The pair crossed a parking lot. The man and Teo stopped, and Teo made a call on his cell phone.

Kiril told Alexandra, "If you wish to drown, do not torture yourself with shallow water."

A Bulgarian proverb that fit her situation. And his own. He reached over, wiped her eyes.

"The girl, Ilina. Have her call me, *dobre?*"

She nodded, reversed her blue jacket to red, and zipped it up. He reached inside the car for a Dodgers cap and snugged it onto her head.

"Ilina, you like her?" she asked.

He stared at her until she said, "*Dobre*, I tell her to call you."

They watched Teo heading down a quiet residential street with the older man. Alexandra, head down, started after them. Then she turned back around. Raised her hand so that her limp little finger pointed at the ground.

"Him," she said, meaning Penko.

Penko can't get it up, she was telling him. In its own way, that made perfect sense.

A half block away, a Town Car stopped. Its lights flashed. Kiril walked over.

The darkened rear window rolled partway down, revealing a thin-faced man with hair dyed jet-black, oiled, and swept straight back like a '50s car fin: *Gospodar*, the clan leader from San Bernardino. Beside him, Kiril could make out bulbous breasts in a cinched-up leather bustier—Pinky. *Gospodar's* woman, Penko's aunt. No mistaking her sharp perfume that clung to him even outside the car.

"*Gospodar*, what brings you out this way?"

"Your phone locator had you two blocks away."

Kiril checked his settings, handed his phone to *Gospodar*. He knew better than to lean down and look inside. But if he had to guess, two other people sat in front, still another in back.

Kiril shrugged. "Locator is always on. I don't know what happened."

"Technology." *Gospodar* handed back his phone. "Where is the best surf and turf near ocean?"

"For steak, I hear BOA, over by pier. Seafood, try Ivy at Shore, or Enterprise Fish, just for the fish and the price. For surf and turf together, I cannot say."

"*Dobre*," *Gospodar* said. "It is time now for the other thing. Make it happen."

"*Da, Gospodar.*"

The car drove away. Kiril walked back to the Lexus, grabbed a large stiff envelope from the trunk space, and got behind the wheel.

Opening the envelope, Penko asked, "*Leyla* Pinky, she riding with *Gospodar*?" Aunt Pinky.

Tits and all. "*Da,*" Kiril said, looking at the license plates and clear plastic zip ties.

They each took a tag and a few zip ties and got out. Halfway done putting these new plates over the owner's, Kiril saw Teo and the older man round a corner, coming back. Thirty seconds after that, Alexandra showed up, strolling behind them. Kiril cinched the last zip tie in place and stood.

Hope she's ready for business, he was thinking.

CHAPTER 17

Sunset at Venice Beach had bathed Robert's Ozone apartment in muted pink and melted orange, and as darkness fell, he glanced out the alley window for Reyes' blue trash can pickup. The alley was deserted, and he returned to the two offering circulars, trying to figure out the trust's last investments.

His phone rang; it was Gia.

"Hola, Roberto," she said, calling him that sometimes when she felt the Latina side of her puzzle. When she was feeling Chinese, she'd ask, *"Ni haw ma."* How you doing?

"Hola, chica," he said, just because he liked the way it sounded.

Gia told him the two *chicas* had visited Gia's law school, late afternoon, and made it home about a half hour ago.

"Teo called Delfina," Gia said. "He wanted to pick up Chinese on his way home."

"Where is he?"

"Didn't say. He's walking, I think."

"Why not have it delivered?" he asked.

"Think about it."

"Oh. She's listening?" he asked.

"I don't care what they say. You're pretty sharp."

Then he realized: If the food was delivered, he and Gia would pay, not Teo. This way, Teo paid for dinner, end of discussion.

"Showing us his appreciation," he said to her.

"Yep. Pot stickers, chicken with snow peas. Sound right for you?"

"And half of whatever you ordered."

"Lose that thought right now, big boy."

Getting a rise out of her. The most generous person he knew; still, she didn't like sharing her food.

"I'm from two cultures of scarcity," she once told him. "You're from a farm in the land of plenty."

"You're American," he said.

"I run deep, *amigo*."

Joking with him, but she did run deep. One of many reasons he loved her. Before he ever told her how he felt, she'd taught him how to say *I love you* in Chinese: *Wo ai ni.* She made him repeat it till he got it down. Both of them already knew how to say it in Spanish: *Te amo.*

"*Wo ai ni.* Just in case you ever need to use it," she'd told him.

About a week later, he'd used it. First in English, then in Spanish, then in Chinese. Gia didn't seem to mind his batting order, as long as he got the words right. She'd told him she loved him, too, in English, and had loved him for a long time. He didn't try to nail down her time frame; she'd tell him *when* later, if she wanted. They weren't in any hurry, and he knew what she meant by saying *a long time*—he'd been having those feelings since their boardwalk conversation about her visit to Dorothy's house.

Now she said on the phone, "I'm alone now. Our girl's getting antsy about her dad."

"He just called, right?"

"Not seeing him, not knowing where he is, it bothers her."

He remembered Delfina, earlier in the week, waiting for Teo at Gia's front window.

"He'll be there soon. I'm on my way."

As Robert headed out the door, he saw Reyes parking by the trash cans in his girlfriend's car. Saw him pull that bundled hashish from the blue can and heard two honks before he drove away.

Don't honk! Robert was thinking. *C'mon, man!*

CHAPTER 18

Teo headed up a Santa Monica alley, still a couple of miles away from Gia's house. To his left were parking lots for businesses fronting Wilshire; to his right a cinder-block wall. Teo felt like he was flying. Not light-headed. *Light.* Finally, he had a new AA sponsor, this Benny guy. Sober almost three decades, Benny had the same kind of pain Teo knew about. Similar bottle issues. Anger, resentment, an overbearing father, and enough screwups along the way to pave a freeway with excuses to drink.

"Every excuse under the sun," Benny had said.

Teo's drill with Benny: seven meetings a week, more if possible, keep a journal, and call Benny whenever he felt the urge to drink. *All the right stuff,* Benny called it.

A plastic bag filled with Chinese swung from his left hand, ginger and garlic scents swirling around him. On top of finding Benny, after Teo had left Carlos' house, Robert had told him good news was on the way. Could be that father and daughter might be able to head indoors soon, sleeping in the truck a fond memory. A permanent address, Delfina enrolled in school, making friends. The truck, though, he'd keep it, use it for hauling and—

He slowed down his mind, thinking: *Get too happy and pretty soon your disease starts sayin', "Time to celebrate. Hey, you earned it, didn't you?"*

Thinking, too: *Don't get ahead of yourself, Teo. Be grateful. Don't paint some rainbow picture for what's ahead. Nothing's gonna be easy about it. Delfina might have problems, the life she's led. So keep it real, take it as it comes, one day at a time. Stay sober. Be grateful, not excited. Got it?*

"Got it," he said out loud.

Another hundred steps up the alley, it didn't matter how hard he tried keeping an even keel. A wave of emotion hit him: remorse, joy, regret, and elation, and it brought him to tears. Crying, he laid his face against a green metal trash bin, this huge, raw day of his life seeping from his soul again—first in Carlos' office, then at AA, now here.

He decided: *Better I break down here than at Gia's, where Delfina might see me.*

Then he heard someone yelling. He looked up from the dumpster and saw an angry man waving a silver baseball bat at him.

Get out of here! he was saying, with some kind of accent. *Go on! Get moving!*

Teo held up both hands, "All right, man, no problem, all right."

He stepped back into the alley, took twenty steps, and never heard it coming. But he felt the vehicle's force wave behind him, bearing down, and as his powerful calves coiled, he sprang into the air.

CHAPTER 19

For the past two hours, Robert and Gia had been trying to distract Delfina. Anything to get her away from Gia's front window, to help her stop obsessing about Teo.

"Where is he?" Delfina asked again.

"He was in Santa Monica," Gia said.

"Where in Santa Monica?"

"I'm not sure."

"What Chinese restaurant?"

Gia said, "I don't know. He'll be here. He was okay when you talked to him, wasn't he?"

"Sometimes you can't tell," Delfina said. Then a flurry of other questions, but all asking the same one: *Where is Daddy?*

Robert and Gia weren't sure. Robert had slipped into the bedroom and called Teo three times already, but his phone had gone straight to voice mail. Back in the living room, Gia was reading to Delfina near the front window. Headlights would pass. Delfina would look outside, even knowing Teo was on foot. Gia would coax her into a book again.

Then Robert got a call.

"Is this attorney Robert Worth?"

"Yes." His heart sank.

"This is Officer Tedrow, Santa Monica police. Do you know a Teo Famosa?"

"He's a client, yes."

God, no. What's he done this time . . .

Nothing. There had been a hit and run. Police had found one of Robert's business cards in Teo's wallet and called him to see if he knew how to locate family members.

Driving over to Saint John's, the nearest hospital to the crash, Robert kept telling himself to calm down. As far as Delfina knew, he was headed to the drugstore to pick up a prescription for Gia. Then Evelyn came to mind: she was still trustee, and the trust's sole beneficiary had been hospitalized.

He voice-texted her: Evelyn, it's Robert. Teo is in Saint John's. Very serious. A hit and run, police are saying, and I wanted you to know.

He left his car with the valet and entered the ER entrance. The ICU was on the eighth floor.

It was another half hour before he met Dr. Vivian Wan, a brain surgeon, head of the neurological team working on Teo. About fifty, still in scrubs, her purple side combs gave off a curious blend of hipness and intelligence.

Robert identified himself as both a friend and a lawyer for her patient, someone who'd been notified by the Santa Monica police.

"Mr. Famosa was struck by an automobile and is in intensive care. His right arm is broken, and his left hip, crushed. His brain, though, there was swelling, and after an MRI, we decided it essential to induce coma via propofol."

"Propofol, that's what . . . ?"

"What Michael Jackson was using when he died, but properly supervised, we hope to give him time for the swelling to subside."

The idea of inducing a coma, she told him, was to keep the swelling brain from damaging itself by pressing against the skull.

"Any way to gauge the odds?"

"Impossible to say at this point. We'll know more in a few days."

Robert asked, "Would it be possible for his daughter to see him?"

Right then, operating staff rolled Teo down the hall into his glass-walled room. Robert looked through the window as they slid him off the gurney onto a bed. His head was wrapped in bandages, only his eyes and nose visible.

"How old is his daughter?" Dr. Wan asked.

"Nine."

"Oh. Under twelve, we really don't allow visitation. It's not a good idea, for them or for our staff."

Not a good idea. But he didn't hear a firm no, so he called Gia. Rather than let Delfina's vague worries escalate, they decided to bring her to Saint John's. If there were ever visitation exceptions for children, he believed Delfina would somehow make the cut.

A half hour later, Robert met them outside. He knew Gia was upset, but he stayed focused on Delfina as they walked down the ground-floor hallway and stepped into the elevator. Going up, he knelt in front of her.

"What I want you to do, Delfina, is look the doctor in the eye and tell her why you want to see your daddy, all right? She's very nice. Her name is Dr. Vivian Wan. I met her before, and she knows you're coming, so there's no reason at all for you to be nervous."

"Okay," Delfina said.

He stood. "And once we're there, if you decide you don't want to . . ."

Gia caught his eye, held up nine fingers and mouthed, *Too much information.*

Right, she's nine. Too much info.

The elevator door opened. Delfina surprised him when she took his hand and walked with him over to the doctor's station, where Dr. Wan was entering case notes into her computer.

Delfina said hello and looked Dr. Wan in the eye.

"And your name is . . . ?" Dr. Wan asked.

"Delfina Famosa. I'll be good, Dr. Vivian," she said. "I promise."

That was pretty much it. Dr. Wan explained that her father would be asleep for a few days, maybe much longer, and that he couldn't speak to her.

"But it's okay if you want to say something to him, maybe give him a little hug or a kiss. I bet he'd like that," Dr. Wan said.

Dr. Wan was accustomed to this kind of thing; Robert and Gia were not. Robert led Delfina into the room, and she approached her father.

Taking his hand, Delfina said, "Hi, Daddy. Are you okay?" Nothing registered. "I'll see you tomorrow. I'll bring you a present. I'm with Gia and Robert, and I'll be good. I promise."

After she kissed him on the cheek, she spotted Teo's backpack in the closet and put it on.

They left the room. Robert pointed to the backpack and asked Dr. Wan, "Okay if she takes it?"

"Of course," she said. "Was there a plastic bag in the closet?"

Robert checked the room. Back at the desk, he told Dr. Wan, "No."

"Then his belongings will be inside the bag, too."

On the way out of the hospital, Robert knew he and Gia had guessed right: Delfina had calmed down after seeing Teo.

"He'll get better here," Delfina said in the elevator. That was all she said.

Outside, the valet pulled up with the Bronco. Gia opened the back door for Delfina, who climbed inside with Teo's backpack. Delfina rolled down her window and gazed back up at the hospital as Robert paid the valet.

A Volvo sedan pulled up beside them. Evelyn eased out of the driver's seat.

"Didn't expect to see you here," Robert said.

"Didn't expect to be here," Evelyn said. "Hello, Gia."

"Evelyn," Gia said.

"Daddy's sleeping, Evelyn," Delfina said, yawning.

"That's good," Evelyn said. "That's the best thing for him right now, sweetheart."

She took Robert and Gia aside. "Sleeping?" Evelyn asked.

He told her about Dr. Wan and the induced coma.

"Did you notify children's services?" Evelyn asked.

Robert and Gia weren't her parents or legal guardians. Robert knew that legally, notification was the next step.

"No, not yet."

"She belongs with her father, don't you think?" Gia said.

Robert nodded. "Definitely. If the city steps in, with Teo's living situation . . ."

Gia said, "He'll have a real hard time getting her back."

"If ever," Evelyn added.

"What I plan to do, then," Gia said, "I'll skip school till they figure out his status."

"Skip . . . ?"

"For a week or so. I can keep up from home."

Evelyn said, "If need be, I can help, too. Gia, mind if I borrow your sweetheart for a minute?"

"Plenty to go around," Gia said, and headed for the Bronco.

Evelyn looked stricken as she spoke to him.

"Listen, I've been awfully hard on Teo. Somehow, in my mind anyway, I blamed him for starting the trust's troubles. And he did. Guess it's because the trust worked so well before that. I shouldn't have taken it personally, but I always do—and I'll feel better if I have a few words with him."

"Doubt anything's registering with him."

"He'll hear me, or he won't. Too little, too late. One of life's hard lessons."

"Need a hand getting up there?"

"Not yet, but give this chemo another week or two."

With Delfina buckled into the back seat, Robert drove down Santa Monica Boulevard. Gia turned around in her seat. "Should we stay at the beach or at my house? Which would you like better?"

"Either one," Delfina said.

She was tapping out. What a long, miserable day for this child. He took Gia's hand.

"You sure about ditching school?"

"She's on her own, both her parents are . . . *away*. When my parents didn't come back from Mexico . . . even at sixteen . . . it was so hard. So lonely. And she likes us," Gia added.

"Both of us?"

She poked him. "'What do you think Robert's doing? Do you think Robert's eating lunch now? Do you think Robert could be an astronaut?'"

He parked in front of her house, left the engine running.

"Was Teo in an accident, or what?" Gia whispered.

"I don't know. Mind if I drop by Erik's?"

CHAPTER 20

In the body-shop office in San Bernardino, Kiril watched the Lexus SUV rising on the rack, repairs to its damaged grille under way. Stacked around him: cases of booze, beer, and vodka for the christening. Earlier that week over on Foothill Boulevard, Kiril had helped dig the backyard pit where coals would soon be set for slow-cooking sides of beef and lamb, salted and stuffed with garlic. Enough to feed more than twice the expected fifty people.

Out in the body shop's garage, Penko was clowning around, drinking, firing the pneumatic hose at the shop dog. Alexandra and Aunt Pinky were out there, too, dancing, listening to music through shared earbuds.

Sitting with *Gospodar* and four other men playing cards, Kiril went back over the aftermath of the hit and run, how he'd stood at the Santa Monica Pier's wooden rail, keeping an eye on their SUV in the beach parking area. Farther down the pier, Penko and Alexandra had ridden the roller coaster, and the girl had already swallowed pills to take the edge off. For once, it was hard to blame her. Driving sixty miles an hour, she'd killed that man in the alley less than an hour earlier.

A female driver. Always the plan because of traffic cameras all over Santa Monica. Just as bad: cameras in the rears of many shops and restaurants. Smarter, it was decided, that Alexandra drive.

Once Alexandra had cleared the alley, Kiril and Penko rose from their seats. One block later, keeping to side streets, away from cameras, Kiril took over behind the wheel. Now they became two males and a female, a male driving, in a common Westside car. Not foolproof. Not bad, either. Little things made all the difference.

The damaged grille couldn't be helped, but the left headlight still worked. Once they'd sprayed down the grille in the beach parking lot with shaken-up quarts of soda water, they'd changed tags back to the owner's legal originals and headed up to the pier to wait.

On the pier, Kiril could hear the pair behind him. Penko buying tickets for the carousel, Alexandra wasted but upright. The pair's venom for each other had run its course, until the next wrong glance or word passed between them or until her drugs wore off.

An hour later, it had been a breeze driving to San Bernardino; they'd picked up the I-10 at the pier and headed east.

Now, out in the garage, Penko had found a *martenitsa*—red-and-white yarns twined together—and tied it to the dog's collar. Another one he tied to his own wrist and placed a shop rag on his head. Penko was dancing with the dog now, pretending to be Baba Marta, the mythical grandmother who ushered springtime into Bulgaria. Penko opened the office door, Pinky and Alexandra behind him.

Penko said, "Baba Marta has come early this year and is looking for young girls."

As Pinky's foul perfume blossomed in his nostrils, *Gospodar* and the others laughed, and Kiril joined in.

Similar in spirit to the American groundhog, Baba Marta was unpredictable like spring, depending on whether she saw young girls, and so on the first day of March, young girls went outdoors to meet her with gifts to keep *baba* happy.

Sure, Kiril laughed along at Penko screwing around, but Kiril liked March because spring was coming. When Penko spoke of *young girls*, Kiril wasn't sure what he was driving at.

Very nice.

That's what Penko had said earlier today, looking at that young girl from the cube truck that had parked on Amherst.

Very nice? Kiril asked himself, about a girl no more than ten years old.

With any luck, he and Penko were done working together. If so, he needed to find a way to get permission to kill him, even with his Aunt Pinky being *Gospodar's* woman.

"Look," he heard a card player say. The mood hardened. The same card player pointed at the TV and said again: "Look."

On the area-wide news, a reporter was in the middle of saying that a hit-and-run victim in Santa Monica had been hospitalized. The victim's name was being withheld, pending notification of his family.

Kiril felt certain that was bad news for him, even before *Gospodar* turned to him and said, "Alive? Alive is not what I asked for, Kiril."

CHAPTER 21

Just before midnight, Robert rolled over to Mar Vista, a neighborhood of large lots, a few hills, and Erik Jacobson's home. Lights shone from Erik's backyard, so he followed the driveway back to the locked garage door and got out. On a brick patio close by the house, fat dripped from a grilling, twenty-two-ounce T-bone. The late-night steak made sense—Erik had eaten mostly Thai food since marrying Priya. *Nonsteak food*, Erik called it.

Farther away from the house, beneath a mammoth avocado tree, Erik skill-sawed a two-by-six-foot support for a tree house. At loose ends, Robert knew, with his family overseas. In madras shorts, a hunting vest, and goggles, he vibed a supersize Bill Murray. He motioned Robert over, turned off his saw.

"Avocado, meet *abogado*," Erik said. "Been waiting a long time to say that." Then he caught Robert's expression. "What's up, man?" he asked, raising his sawdust-crusted goggles.

Robert laid out Teo's situation.

"Jesus, no," Erik said. "And Delfina?"

"With us for now. They're not giving out details yet on where it happened."

Erik pulled out his cell phone.

"Matteo Famosa, right?"

Robert nodded. Erik made a call to the Santa Monica Police Department and reached his contact. Santa Monica gave Erik a street number for the hit and run. He wrote it down, handed it to Robert. Not far, an address off Wilshire.

"Runner was eastbound," Erik said. "I can pick up a full report in the morning. What's the deal on your end?"

"Every year, how many hit and runs they get in Santa Monica?"

"Venice and Santa Monica combined, three or four. How come?"

"I need an investigator. You busy?"

❧

When they drove over to the alley off Wilshire, it was easy to see where the Lexus had struck Teo. Chinese food cartons still littered the pavement near the end of the alley farthest from them.

"Damn," Robert said.

"Cops must've just now finished up," Erik said.

The Bronco rolled up on the cartons behind a place called Sonny's Gyros. Robert started to get out.

Erik said, "Wait, back up first."

A hundred yards back, Robert stopped, idling, and looked ahead. Forty yards back from the cartons, a row of dumpsters jutted four feet into the alley. Ten yards past that, a concrete utility pole intruded into the alley, and sixty yards past Teo's cartons, the alley ended.

"See?" Erik said.

Robert thought he did. Unless Teo had been walking down the middle of the alley—and from the cartons' location, he hadn't been—someone had angled left past the bins and power pole to clip him.

Erik said, "See any skid marks?"

"Nope."

"Like somebody went out of their way to run him down."

Erik said, "Fifty miles an hour, roughly eighty feet per second. Twenty-five, thirty yards a second . . ."

"Three, four seconds to stop after they hit him," Robert said. "Three seconds to stop and make a hard turn."

"Hauling ass and had to stop fast."

Anyone following Teo was running out of alley. Another thirty seconds on foot would've put Teo up on the busy Wilshire Boulevard sidewalks, heading to Gia's house. Whoever hit him decided to take their best shot behind Sonny's Gyros.

Intentional. Robert had no idea why this might have happened.

"You free tomorrow?"

"What time?" Erik asked.

"All day, maybe longer . . ."

᠔

Gia's house was dark when Robert eased through the front door. Trying to stay quiet, he made it into bed. On his pillow, dim lamplight shone on a child's drawing. He picked it up and saw a castle with two turrets, a big gate splitting the middle. A man and woman stood above the gate, each holding the hand of the little girl between them. All three had big red smiles. In the sky overhead, a gray figure flew around, a yellow cape fluttering from his back.

At the bottom, he read Delfina's printed words: *Magna Carta Man.*

Checking out the flying figure's chest, he could make out the letters *MCM* and guessed the gray color was armor. Gray like the granite courthouse statue, too. No one was going to see this drawing and sign Delfina up for art school—her talents lay elsewhere—but Delfina's good and brave heart was on full display.

Gia was looking at him now, half-asleep.

"Sweet, huh?"

"Too sweet," he said.

Across the hall, he crept into Delfina's room. Reaching for Teo's daypack, he saw her stir. She saw him, too.

"Thanks for my picture," he said. "I like it so much, but you need to go to sleep, okay?"

"Why do they want to hurt my daddy?" she asked.

What a question for a kid to ask, he thought.

He sat down beside her. "I don't know." He noticed an object in her right hand. "What you got there?"

"My rock," she said. "Daddy bought it for me." She showed it to him. In the dark, it looked like a river rock. Oval, smooth, dark gray. "He's so sweet. Why'd they hurt him?"

With no idea what else to say, he said, "I'll find out, okay?"

"Thank you, Robert," she said. "Good night."

"Your drawing? It's my favorite drawing I ever had."

Out in the living room, he went through Teo's backpack. He found Teo's phone and wallet, his jeans, and jacket, too. All their pockets were empty.

Teo's phone battery icon pulsed, the phone dying, but he couldn't find a charger in the backpack, so he hurried through Teo's sparse number of calls over the last few days. Three days ago, based on the time, a call had come in from that AA sponsor who'd turned Teo down.

Next, an incoming call from a 310 number—that brush-clearing job in Malibu, Robert guessed. After that, several other calls to and from the same number, setting up that job and hauling the brush out to County Line.

After that, Teo had called him—Teo explaining why he'd been late for their meeting.

Then ten other calls to and from Delfina's number.

Among all those calls back and forth with Delfina, he noted paired calls—not to Delfina—between the time after Teo had left Carlos' house and the time he was struck by the car.

He looked up the unexplained number online—registered to Benjamin Smartt—wondered whether to call so late, and decided: *Why not?*

A generic machine-voice told him to leave a message. He identified himself, referenced Teo Famosa, and asked this outlier to call him back ASAP.

As the phone began dying for real, Robert was fading, too. Leaning back in the La-Z-Boy, he thought over his day. Recalling how Teo had bolted out of the study and gone straight into the truck cube. Whatever he'd found inside his personal drawer, he'd put it in his backpack and left for AA about a minute later.

And whatever *it* was hadn't been his phone or wallet—those he had on him. But whatever *it* was, was gone.

Something worth killing him for? That didn't seem possible. Not impossible, but very unlikely.

In bed later, Gia rolled into him, half-asleep.

"Refrigerator . . . framed?" she mumbled.

She must be dreaming, he decided, turning off the light. Lying there, he thought about Delfina's drawing. The man and woman had to be Teo and Bee. The child, Delfina, stood between them, holding their hands. That was him up in the sky, looking out for them. Magna Carta Man, protecting her.

It came to him now what Gia had mumbled just now. Should he put Delfina's drawing on the refrigerator or frame it?

No contest. Frame it. He'd never have another client like Delfina Famosa.

CHAPTER 22

The Greek father and son at Sonny's Gyros looked to Robert like they'd argue over whether water was wet. The next morning, he and Erik had shown up before Sonny's opened. Now they waited at the counter while the pair argued about whether a tray of refrigerated food should be thrown out or saved.

The boy had turned his back on his father by this time, so Sonny peeled back the Saran wrap from a stainless-steel serving dish—cucumbers and onions—and held it out to Robert and Erik.

"Smell it. Still good, right?" Not the best question for customers.

Erik gave it a shot anyway. "Good enough for me. Not good enough for my wife."

"I'm onion intolerant," Robert said.

From experience, Robert knew the problem wasn't food. The son didn't want to be here, and the father dreamed of the whole family working the counter, just like in the old country.

Sonny's Gyros showed up in the police report Erik had picked up this morning. In it, Sonny had given a statement to police about the hit and run. Once he'd handed each of them buy-ten-gyros-get-one-free cards, he tried to help out.

First off, his parking lot camera didn't archive video. It simply spotted trouble in back in real time and let whoever was behind the counter deal with it.

"Lots of trouble, bars, especially," Sonny said. "Customers come out drunk, urinate, use my dumpster for trash. I say something, they tell me go eff off, so I show them *thees*."

His silver baseball bat came out from behind the counter; it was plastic, spray-painted silver.

"See, last night, I'm closing up, and I see him back there." Meaning Teo. "Walking slow, then he stop, and I say to myself, 'Uh-oh, here we go.'"

Now, Sonny headed outside with the bat. Sonny's boy, texting, looked like he wanted to be anywhere else in the world.

Robert held back and asked him, "Business any good?"

Beyond caring, the kid said, "It sucks. He's gonna lose all his money. Mom's gonna kill him."

Outside, Robert walked up on Sonny asking Erik what he thought about renaming the place Sunny's or Mr. Sunny's.

"A new sign," Sonny said. "I would put a bright sun on it, then have a new grand opening."

The desperation of a failing business.

Erik said, "Don't ask me, Mr. Sonny. Ask the Beach Lawyer."

Sonny turned to Robert. "You are the Beach Lawyer? I see the article. My daughter thinks you are very handsome."

Robert shrugged off the compliment. "How's this, Sonny? Tell me everything you remember about last night, and I'll give you some free legal advice."

Hearing that, Sonny got with it: "Last night, that man in the alley, the man they run over, he stopped. Carrying a bag in his hand, I can see that from inside, so I think he will use my dumpster. Every single month, each and every year, my dumpster fees cost my restaurant at least—"

Robert stopped him. "The man in back, Sonny."

"So the man, he stopped, and he leaned against my dumpster." Sonny bent his arm and put his forearm on his forehead. "Put his face on his arm like this, and when I get closer, I shout at him, wave my bat, and he looks up, and—I see he is smiling. Crying and smiling, and then he waves to me and walks away. Then the woman drives by, and I hear it."

"The woman driving the Lexus?"

Sonny nodded. "Black Lexus hit him, and I run out to the alley. The woman, she hit that poor man and never stopped." Picturing it again, Sonny said, "But before that? The man, he was happy. I am sure of it."

Sonny's son called him back inside, so Robert and Erik searched the area. Looking for whatever Teo had put in his backpack the day before. After rolling Sonny's two dumpsters out of the way, they still came up empty-handed.

They walked back inside. Sonny and his boy were going at it again, so Robert and Erik each ordered two falafels, loaded, to go.

"No onions," Robert said, servicing his earlier lie. "Ready for that free legal advice?"

Sonny said, "From Beach Lawyer, sure."

At a nearby table, Robert talked to Sonny about his family for a few minutes. Learned Sonny wanted to shut down the business but felt trapped. Five years ago, Sonny's corporation had signed a ten-year lease with the landlord. Sonny had started the business with his brother as an investor, took a small salary. His son and daughter worked for minimum wage. The son enrolled at Santa Monica College; his wife and married daughter worked for the city, helped out on weekends and took their pay mostly in free Greek food.

"Did you personally guarantee the lease?" Robert asked.

"No, but my brother signed. Put his name on the line. When we started out, he had very good assets."

"I see." Sonny was a good guy, worried about protecting his brother. "Where's your brother now?"

"Moved back home. We all miss him very much."

"Where's home?"

"Athens."

"Athens, *Greece*?"

"Of course."

"Where are his assets now?"

"His house in Pomona, he sell it. Stocks and bonds, all go to Europe. Please, I do not want landlord to find out about any of this."

"When's the last time you talked to your landlord?"

"Two, three years ago. We are still current with rent," Sonny said with pride.

"Think about trying this," Robert said. "Give him a call. Tell him you want out of your lease, and tell him you'll leave the equipment here. If he doesn't like it, tell him to sue your corporation. If he threatens to sue your brother, tell him to go ahead, but he won't."

"Why not?"

"Your brother has nothing in America the landlord can collect, and—no offense, Sonny—I gotta believe your company's in the same boat as your brother."

"Sadly, that is true," Sonny said.

"Over the past five years, rents in Santa Monica have done nothing but go up. He'll jump at the chance to get you out and get more money out of this place. Matter of fact, he should pay *you* to turn the lease over to him."

Sonny beamed, hearing that news. "Pay me how much?"

A few more minutes batting numbers around, and they settled on $20,000. Robert said, "But wait twenty-four hours, all right? Promise me you won't do anything till you talk it over with your wife and family."

Sonny stood and extended his hand: "Beach Lawyer. You have my word . . ."

As they stepped outside, Erik went into Don Corleone mode, the Don talking to the undertaker about his dead son: "Someday, Mr. Sonny, and that day may never come, Beach Lawyer will call upon you to do a service for me. But until that day, accept this justice as a gift from the Beach Lawyer."

"Gonna be a *Godfather* day?"

"My man, every day's a *Godfather* day . . ."

⁂

Driving toward the beach afterward, Erik passed Sonny's falafels off to three guys hanging out in the Seventh Street park. Then they hit Shoop's delicatessen.

"A Swedish chow paradise. You're gonna love it," Erik said as Robert parked the Bronco.

The menu was mostly variations of salmon: salmon wraps, salmon smoked, salmon in Caesar and spinach salads.

"Can't go wrong with gravlax," Erik said. Salmon raw but cured.

They ordered a couple of salmon wraps to go and grabbed a table looking out onto Main Street. Then Gia phoned. She and Delfina had stopped by the hospital early—no change in Teo's condition, but none had been expected. Gia had used Delfina's padlock key, checked inside Teo's truck but didn't find a charger for Teo's off-brand phone.

Gia said, "The ICU nurses know Delfina now, and she's being real good."

"You going by Aunt Gia?" Like Evelyn had suggested last night.

"Tell Evelyn that was a great idea. Delfina likes it, and we're both mutts, so nobody thinks twice about us being there together . . . not yet."

Delfina came on next and asked, "Hi, Robert, how are you today?"

"Good, Delfina. Sorry I missed you this morning. I had to get up early and go to work with my friend, Erik . . . Right, he's a very big man . . . Yes. I'll tell him."

Erik had been giving him a look as he talked. After he clicked off, Robert said, "What? Go ahead."

Erik asked, "What happens if Teo doesn't come out of it?"

"What if he does?" Robert asked.

"You ready?" Erik asked.

"I'm not sure, not at all. Gia and I haven't gotten that far, even talking about it, and—"

Erik stopped him, nodded at the counter. "Wraps are ready. Let's book?"

Oh, he thought. *Not ready to adopt—ready to leave.*

As Robert drove north to Calabasas, home of Vegas Rail, he went over his to-do list with Erik. First thing was, find Teo's last AA meeting. Erik had already downloaded the AA app onto Robert's iPhone; the problem was manageable. Backtracking to yesterday afternoon, they'd used Carlos' house as Teo's starting point and Sonny's Gyros as the end point. Only two meetings made sense: one in Ocean Park, another on Pico near the 405. Neither met again until the next day.

"Catch both meetings tomorrow?" Robert asked Erik.

"Yep. So tell me about these two knucklehead investments we're checking out."

Meaning Carlos' investments as trustee. Evelyn doubted Robert would learn anything, but he felt that looking into them was obligatory due diligence. He had read both offering circulars—forty-page legal documents describing the investments, their risks, and rewards—and had a decent grasp of them.

The first, a real estate deal called Vegas Rail, had an office halfway to Santa Barbara in Westlake Village, where they headed now. The second office in Playa Vista was for a technology investment: SoccMom.

Robert told Erik, "Both companies gave the investor notes and a first lien on each company's assets till the notes were paid off. SoccMom started paying heavy interest right away, but the real estate deal was more a long-term play on escalating real estate values."

"A first lien," Erik said. "Same as the bank has on my house."

"Close enough," Robert said. "And the company actually filed the right papers with the secretary of state and the county, so the trust's first lien looks good.

"On the real estate deal," he continued, "the investment would score on land optioned up in the high desert, around Victorville, one of the station sites for high-speed rail connecting LA to Las Vegas. Pretty straightforward."

"Eventually connecting to Vegas, *maybe*," Erik said.

"Right, and if high-speed rail doesn't happen in three years, they'll sell the land and return the investors' money. Starting in one year, they'll use rental income from the properties to pay fifteen percent interest to the investors. Worst case—according to Vegas Rail—Carlos clears thirty percent in interest over three years. The circular has notarized deeds of the properties they were buying, contracts with owners, and phone numbers to talk things over with management."

"You call?"

"Yeah. Disconnected."

Erik said, "Up thirty percent, long as land value holds up in Victorville."

Robert nodded. "Up front in the circular, they give you all the rosy financial projections—how big the numbers can get if high-speed rail comes through Victorville. But when you read the Risks section near the end, it discloses that high-speed rail might not happen at all, plus California requires the train's manufacturer to be American—and so far, there's not an American manufacturer in existence."

Erik said, "I get it. Invest in this deal, you're an idiot or a baller."

"Yeah, risky," Robert said.

Just then, a lawyer named Frederick Baker returned Robert's call. A partner in a big Century City firm, Frederick's name had appeared on the offering circular for the SoccMom deal.

After Robert explained why he'd called yesterday, Frederick got right down to business.

"Yes, this firm drafted the offering circular, but drafting's all we did. We made no attempt to verify any information—all of it was furnished by our client—and if any money was eventually raised pursuant to this offering circular, we had no contact with investors, before, during, or after the offering circular was prepared."

"Did you know your firm's name appeared on the circular?"

"No, I did not. If that happened, and I'm not saying it did, it happened without the firm's permission. So look, Robert, I called Philip Fanelli off your Martindale listing, and he said you're a straight shooter, not some shakedown artist. So again, this firm *did not participate* in the deal, and that's all you're getting out of me. Any more and it'll be pursuant to a subpoena, and this firm will fight you every step of the way."

"I hear you," Robert said, then clicked off.

Robert took the Westlake Boulevard exit; he'd heard Frederick loud and clear. By *did not participate*, Frederick meant their firm didn't lie to or mislead investors about the deal. Could be Frederick had been lying just now—Robert doubted it. There wasn't a single scrap of paper in the trust's files between Carlos and this firm. That meant Robert needed Carlos to fill in the blanks, but the talking-to-Carlos door had slammed shut forever.

A quarter mile off the freeway, Robert parked the Bronco in a visitor's slot at a two-story, modern office complex.

As they got out of the car, he prepped Erik: "Same as with Vegas Rail, we're in real estate . . ."

Robert had called ahead and set up an appointment with the office complex's leasing agent, Lauren Cairo. On another call to the building's receptionist, he'd learned Vegas Rail's office was on the second floor; that was all he could get out of her. Once he and Erik made the lobby—*Receptionist on Break*, a placard said—Lauren introduced herself.

Robert headed to the sign-in book, hoping to catch a few Vegas Rail names.

Lauren stopped him. "No need for sign-in. You're with me."

She led them past the shared reception area. It was the usual setup: individual offices, a shared conference room and kitchen on the ground floor. According to the complex's web page, these temporary offices were *superb* if you wanted a month-to-month lease with no need for giving a personal guarantee.

"What is it you're looking for?" Lauren asked him.

"A two-office suite," Robert said. "Something with a view. Upstairs if at all possible."

"We do have one on the second floor, end of the hall, decent view. Do you have a business card?" she asked.

"Not yet. We're still trying to decide on our logo."

"We're in real estate," Erik added. "I like the name Fault Line. My partner doesn't. What do you think?"

"Are you serious?" Lauren asked.

"Hell, no, Lauren. It's rare I'm serious."

Robert had no idea why Erik said the things he said, or where this was going, if anywhere, as they took an elevator to the second floor and headed down the hall. Robert stopped halfway to the end, at what had been Vegas Rail's door. Two painters had put down a drop cloth inside, and Robert walked into the suite.

"Love this," Robert said, walking over to the window. It offered a canyon view and looked down onto the complex's delivery area. A few guys on break kicked back on the loading dock.

"This office isn't available for another month," Lauren said.

Erik said, "I was told we'd have a view of Wayne Gretsky's estate. Needless to say, I'm disappointed as all get-out."

"Mr. Gretsky's estate is nowhere nearby," Lauren said.

"Looked at Gretsky's pad online. Has a fountain *and* a pool—that cool or what?"

Robert stepped in. "Looks like the tenants are done with this office. Why not let me call them? See if I can buy them out of that last month."

"Can't reach them. I've tried," she said.

"Mind if I try?" he asked.

"Let me show you this other space up the hall," she said.

Erik said, "How about I grab a bottle of water downstairs?"

"Sure, bottles on the refrigerator door are communal."

"Want anything? Beer? Cocktail?" Erik asked her.

Before she could answer, Robert said, "My head of sales. He has a hard time turning it off."

After Erik left, she turned to Robert and said, "Who are you two? No fooling."

He looked her over. Just a woman trying to do her job. "I need information about Vegas Rail. They ran off with some people's money, and I'm trying to get it back."

"Should've just said so."

"Would that've helped?"

"No, but it would've saved me the trip over here. I'm not allowed to talk about tenants, all right? So grab that Norski Tony Robbins of yours and hit the road."

Outside, Lauren squealed away, and Robert waited for Erik by the car. When he came out and started to get in the Bronco, Robert said, "*Fault Line?*"

"Playing the clown, I got the run of the place. Kitchen's always a gossip gold mine," he said. "All those bored assistants hanging out, and I hit the mother lode—that receptionist. She remembered the Vegas Rail guys from upstairs. They had accents, like they were from Russia, Poland, one of those countries. She said they talked like Frankenstein."

"She mean, *like Dracula?*" Robert asked.

"Yeah, like all those guys over there sound. To her, it didn't look like anybody did anything. Two guys, they'd show up once, twice, a week and wore cool suits like they thought suits were a big deal. I got the sense at least one of the assistants boned Boris."

"Boris, that's . . . ?"

"Name one of the guys gave himself."

"And you think she boned him because . . . ?"

"Asked if I had his number. The sign-in book. The receptionist let me go through it, but the two guys never printed their names like they're supposed to. Scribbled their signatures, so you can't read 'em anyway."

As they got back in the car, Erik said, "You're benefiting from my storied years on the force and my God-given talent as an investigator."

He had to admit, Erik's style was impressive.

"Angling for a raise?"

Erik shrugged. "God-given."

"Keep dazzling me, dude."

Instead of getting onto the 101, Robert drove around back to that loading dock and parked.

"Stay here, you look like a retired cop. And a Norski."

Robert got out of the car, walked over to three guys sitting on the loading dock, drinking Monster Energy drinks and eating snacks.

"Hey, guys, sorry to bother you during break."

They nodded, their mouths filled with assorted junk food.

Robert said, "Remember those two *pendajos* worked on the second floor? You're repainting their offices now."

One of them said. *"Los rusos."* The Russians.

"Know anything about 'em?"

Another one of them said, "Left the place a mess whenever they showed up. Food and liquor and trash, condoms in the wastebasket."

"Cocky dudes, noses in the air," the first one said. "Never spoke to me in the hall."

"Me, either, not once. Party boys."

Robert said, "They're not good guys, and they took some stuff that belongs to *mi conchita*. Know anything about 'em? Names, maybe, where they live? Anything you can think of?"

Nobody did, till the one tugging on a tough piece of jerky jumped up, said, "Hold on," and ran inside. When he came back, he tossed Robert a half-empty bottle of liqueur.

"Left this behind. They drank it all the time. It's not from America."

"Not bad-tasting," the third one said.

All three guys agreed, and when Robert left a $100 bill with them, they all agreed with that, too.

Back in the car, Robert handed the bottle to Erik. "Rakia," Robert said, from the label.

Erik dipped his finger, tasted it.

"Not bad."

"That's the consensus."

While Robert drove back to LA on the 101, Erik Googled *rakia* and found out multiple variations of it were popular all through Eastern Europe.

"It's plum brandy, popular in Balkan countries and, I quote, 'often served chilled.' Alcohol content, forty percent and up—damn," Erik said. Then he rattled off ten Eastern European countries where it was popular.

Sampling the bottle again: "Tasty."

A wreck on the 101 put them onto the scenic route over the Santa Monica Mountains, headed toward the Pacific Ocean. After the twin tunnels where Kanan Road became Kanan Dume Road, they cruised down a five-mile decline, the Pacific Ocean spreading out below them, a dark-blue curve kissing a light-blue horizon.

Erik told him about a secluded beach across PCH, not far from where Kanan Dume Road teed at Pacific Coast Highway.

"Great surf, but you need a gate key to get in."

"A private beach in LA?" Robert asked.

"The public can climb down nasty cliffs over at Point Dume or walk in from Paradise Cove at low tide. So yeah, as private as you're gonna get in LA."

At PCH, they hung a left and headed for Playa Vista. As they passed Malibu Colony and Pepperdine University, Robert briefed Erik about SoccMom.

"It was a technology play on youth soccer in the United States. Its platform would aggregate all youth-soccer teams in the United States by sucking up player and team information entered in its database. The company would also sell a small patch to monitor a kid's vitals on the field, and that data would go into the parents' phone or device."

"The patches wear out, right?"

"Last for one season—one patch per game. Cash keeps coming in, and the numbers get real big, real fast."

"They'd sell ads on the website?"

"That's what the database is for—so the company can talk to sporting-goods companies about SoccMom's targeted demographic."

Erik nodded. "Why their site's great for selling jerseys, shoes, balls."

Robert nodded. "Investor money was supposed to go for R and D, paying tech guys to build out the platform, create that database, and make it all work wireless. Supposedly, they'd done something similar before in India—only they did it with veterinarians and animals."

"After dealing with monkeys, kids should be a snap."

Robert wondered whether monkeys were indigenous to India but stayed on point.

"Up front in the circular, you get all those rosy projections about what happens once the product is up and running. Letters from moms and dads about how they really need something like this, and that the league needs it, too. But then you get to the Risks section—the technology doesn't exist, and once it does, maybe it won't work."

"Feeling smarter already for not investing. Carlos coulda used a beatdown from Mr. Wonderful on the *Tank*."

The mean guy on *Shark Tank*. Robert had caught the show a few times.

"Any people-people behind SoccMom?"

"No warm bodies in the public record. They used a filing service for their organization papers in California, and no signed tax returns are due for another month or two—as if that mattered to these guys."

Robert told him about the string of e-mails Carlos had sent Evelyn. Carlos gloating about how payments had been coming in, telling her she worried too much.

"How'd the company plan to start paying him interest so quick?" Erik asked.

"They claimed they had royalties coming in from that veterinary technology. They'd use that money till the soccer technology was up and running."

"Why not just rip Carlos off and split?"

"I keep wondering the same thing; they already had his money." Then: "Beats me."

Fifteen minutes later, the Bronco rolled over a wide concrete culvert under Lincoln Boulevard. A trickle of water flowed west across the Ballona Wetlands toward the Pacific Ocean, a marsh mile away.

"The mighty LA River," Erik said, eyeing the culvert.

Robert wondered if any other river had a tributary called *Arroyo Seco*, meaning "dry ditch."

Ahead on Culver Boulevard, a twenty-block mixed-use development massed on their right. Four-story apartment buildings, residential and business condos, all serviced by Whole Foods, CVS, Starbucks, and, he believed, another Starbucks. Built since 2005, after protracted environmental challenges, Playa Vista was part of Silicon Beach, given that Google, Yahoo, YouTube, and scores of start-ups had a presence here.

Robert parked on Runway Road near SoccMom's office address, not far from the cliffs where Loyola Marymount University and Summa Corp. coexisted, side by side.

Erik asked, "This time, we go in as some kind of tech outfit?"

"Does it matter what I tell you?"

"Some," Erik said. "What's our company called?"

"Here's what it's not called: *Virus. Hacker. Downtime. Crashed. Obsolete.*"

"Seriously, they're taken? Don't sweat it, I got a good one."

"Please don't . . ."

"Hey, man, I know you're worried about Teo and Delfina, and I care about 'em, too, but relax, go with the flow. I've seen you do it lotsa times, so . . . you know . . ."

Chill the F out, Robert was thinking. "All right," he said.

It didn't matter. The leasing agent waiting outside was already chill. *Ana Short,* her card said, and she loved their company's name: Priya Software, after Erik explained it meant *beloved* in Sanskrit.

"I've never heard of Priya Software," Ana said.

Robert stepped in. "It's not trademarked yet," he whispered. "So keep it on the down-low, Ana."

"Oh, I definitely will," she whispered back to him, serious as hell in her pinstriped blazer and tailored slacks.

Tenants gained entry to Building D's offices in the lobby via a password on a digital keypad. For visitors, there was a guard and a guest register at the front door, but neither a receptionist nor a communal kitchen were part of the plan.

Ana didn't mind telling them that all leasing applications were handled online and remained confidential.

"SoccMom has already cleared out of Suite 1108; it's been leased out to a new tenant. Never met them, I'm so sorry."

After thanking her, Robert and Erik followed her directions over to the maintenance department.

Erik asked Robert, "Has my wife been gone too long, or was she real cute?"

"*Too long?* Priya hasn't been gone one week."

"Figure of speech, dude. *'So keep it on the down-low, Ana?'* That has all sorts of sexual connotations."

"Cute, okay. Let's leave it at that."

A few fully developed blocks away, they entered the open bay of the maintenance building. After $200 changed hands with the *jefe*, the story on Suite 1108 emerged. These tenants—again, two guys in slick suits—weren't winning popularity contests here, either: never spoke to workers, trashed the office, never tipped, and partied hard. Then *jefe* came up with a case of rakia they'd left behind, a different brand from the first bottle, and Robert gave him another $100.

They headed back to Runway Road.

Erik said, "I said these deals Carlos bit on were knuckleheaded, but compared to what I'd see at LAPD? With the formal offering circulars backing them up, these two look like blue chips."

"What kind of LAPD deals?"

"Like, 'My dentist buys a ton of gold for fillings and knows gold is going through the roof.'"

"Buy gold off that?" Robert asked.

"No, sell gold—the dentist is always wrong. Not everyone has a good lawyer looking out for them."

Erik was thanking him—again—for keeping him on the straight and narrow with Natural Gas. Not letting him borrow money from friends in return for stock; keeping 100 percent ownership, less Robert's

10 percent equity for free legal services. All that sound advice plus: *do not buy a hot new car for at least one year after selling the company.*

"No hot car for a year. For any reason," Erik had promised.

Back in the Bronco, they compared the two rakia bottles. Both brands had been distributed from Sofia, Bulgaria. Robert Googled *rakia* this time; again, it was described as "a popular plum-wine drink enjoyed throughout many Balkan countries."

Balkan countries included Albania, Bosnia and Herzegovina, Bulgaria, Croatia, Kosovo, Macedonia, Montenegro, Romania, Serbia, Slovenia, Greece, and parts of Turkey. Robert laid out for Erik what he'd learned.

"A quarter-million square miles with a population of sixty million— twice that if you include Turkey, where it's the national drink. Bulgaria— capital, Sofia—has only six million people. That's six million Bulgarian rakia drinkers out of one hundred twenty million Balkan people."

Then he added: "Twenty to one, we have two party-boy a-holes in suits who drink Bulgarian rakia from Sofia, *because they're Bulgarian.*"

Then Erik asked Robert, "Let's go with the same two suits at both places . . ."

"Same two *Bulgarian* suits," Robert said.

"Marijuana," Erik said from out of the blue, typing on his phone.

"What're you Googling?"

"Might've remembered something," Erik said, and called out the search words as he typed. *"Marijuana . . . Arrest . . . Bulgarians . . . Northern California."*

CHAPTER 23

Driving over to Gia's with Erik, Robert called Evelyn so he could pick her brain. He told her about his day with a retired cop, his investigator, and that Erik was in the car. She didn't mind being on speaker as Robert finished bringing her up to speed on the investments.

"Bulgarians? Rakia?" Evelyn asked after hearing him out. "Seems a bit far-fetched."

"Tell me about it. Any idea where Carlos might've run into them?" he asked.

"At this point, you know more than I do," she said. "What do you think?"

"Erik remembered hearing about a marijuana bust, up north. A few years back, some Bulgarians got popped for distribution, and Carlos loved good weed, right?" he asked.

"Not good. His had to be the very best," Evelyn said.

"Think there's a connection?" Robert asked her.

"Could be, but it's so simple to buy now, right?"

"But for a weed snob like Carlos?" Erik said.

They dead-ended on weed at that point.

Robert told Evelyn, "There was nothing in the file about how Carlos found the investments. The deals seemed to drop into his lap from out of the blue."

"I asked him about it; he wouldn't tell me. Don't laugh, but when he was holding all that cash from selling the properties, I suggested Laundromats—recession proof as long as you find the right deal going in."

"What'd he say?"

"He thought it was beneath him. How would it look to his dates, emptying dollar-bill changers for a trip to Vegas?"

Robert saw her point. *Playboy Laundromat operator* had a bad ring to it.

"Glad you called," Evelyn said. "I was checking the mailbox at Carlos' house . . ."

"Any client money come in?"

"Afraid not; I slipped what did under his door for you." Then Evelyn said, "I can't come inside Gia's, but I wanted to give Delfina a few books. Are you headed there?"

"Just pulling up," he said. "That's nice of you."

"Feeling guilty doesn't make me nice," she said.

"Yes, it does," he said, hanging up before she could disagree.

❧

Later, Robert and Erik sat outside on the back patio, rehashing the case. Robert checked his notes. Gia sat with them and listened in while she studied; Delfina was inside, watching *Frozen* again.

Robert started out, saying, "Let's try this, okay? These two company offices were staffed by two Bulgarians. For about three months, one deal paid the trust like they'd agreed, and both of them gave the trust first dibs on their assets. But now, both companies have vacated their offices."

"How about suing them?" Erik asked.

"If you could find them, sure. But after suing them—correct me if I'm wrong, Gia—I'd wait thirty days for their answer to the complaint. They won't file one, so I'd wait another thirty to move for a default judgment. Once I get that, the trust could seize whatever they have."

Gia said, "If you filed a statement of damages with the complaint, you'd save thirty days after taking a default judgment. But if they made an appearance, *just their lawyers*, they can delay you for months, maybe years, for almost no reason."

Erik asked, "They teach all that in first-year law?"

Robert knew how she came by that know-how—her relationship with Jack Pierce. Before Gia could answer, he told Erik, "She's taking advanced courses because she's so damn smart."

Leaning over, she whispered, "Where'd you come from, handsome man?"

"What'd she say, dude?" Erik asked.

"My turn to do the dishes," Robert said.

"Hey, I know *do the dishes*. That didn't look to me like *do the dishes*."

"She's half-Chinese," Robert explained.

Moving on, Erik asked, "You ever watch *American Greed*?"

"A few times."

Robert knew the TV show about real-life sociopaths ripping off decent folks, especially decent folks who trusted them.

Erik said, "No episode ever ended with the bad guy saying, 'Oh, well, you found me. Here's all your money, my bad.' I mean, maybe he's got a busted Jet Ski and a mortgaged-up mansion, but no money."

Gia looked up from her computer.

"Who's this bad girl Carlos met?" she asked.

"No one knows," Robert said. "A bottle blonde, maybe. Evelyn got a look at her inside Carlos' leased Mercedes, then Carlos flipped Evelyn a casino chip and took off."

Gia said, "Try this. Shy guy falls for a beautiful woman, spends all his money on her. Then the money stops coming in, and she bails."

"Something like that," Robert said. "After that, Carlos runs down the street to cry on Evelyn's shoulder about losing the love of his life. Or, how about this? Maybe Carlos doesn't know the Bulgarians at first. Let's say the mystery girl introduces him to the Bulgarians, then they separate him from his money."

Gia: "Let's make the girl a mysterious *Bulgarian.* Those cheekbones, gorgeous women."

Robert started over: "Okay, so try this. Let's say a gorgeous Bulgarian girl ropes in Carlos. Or the Bulgarians use her to rope in Carlos. One way or another, he gets in front of these Bulgarians, who set up two sophisticated-looking investments—on paper anyway. Big-man Carlos, maybe a little stoned—in love, for sure—swallows the hook. The girl, she sticks around, milks the Carlos cash cow till he runs dry, then she splits. You're Carlos, and you lost all your money, and you screwed over your brother and his kid. What does that make you? *El Débil,* the weakling your father always said you were. So you're drinking brandy, smoking dope, worried sick because it's all your fault. No wonder the guy had a heart attack."

"Bleak," Erik said.

Like a Dickens novel, but Robert liked the feel of that scenario.

Gia stood, asked Erik. "You staying for dinner?"

"I could probably work it in," Erik said. "I'm thinking . . . steak?"

⁂

Erik took off to Brentwood Fine Meats to buy fine meats, as he put it, while Gia found a little study time sandwiched between interruptions. Robert walked Delfina down to Teo's parked truck for clean clothes. The books Evelyn had left for Delfina sat in the mailbox: *Wonder* and one of the *Princess* books. The watch that Evelyn had taken instead of her fee was in the mailbox, too.

Evelyn had a soft spot. Who knew? That watch meant another $8,000 or so went into Teo and Delfina's kitty.

Robert showed Delfina her new books.

"From the lady you met at the hospital. Do you like them?"

She hugged the books to herself. "Oh, yes, I read them when we lived at the Mission, but I never had my own copy."

"Let's call Evelyn tomorrow and thank her, okay?"

Jumping up and down, she said, "Yes, yes! Okay!"

Once he unlocked the truck and lifted Delfina inside, she looked through her things. Fully aware that he wasn't close to answering her question—*Why do they want to hurt my daddy?*—he checked Teo's padlocked drawer for whatever it might yield.

"When will Daddy wake up?" she asked from behind him.

She sat on her bed, looking at him. He knelt in front of her, at a momentary loss for words.

"I don't know exactly. Doctor Wan said in two more days they'd think about waking him up. Maybe it will be longer, though."

"How much longer?"

"Well, if I said I knew, I wouldn't be telling the truth, and I don't want to do that."

"Okay," she said. "I hope it's not much longer, Robert."

He took her hand and said, "I hope so, too, Delfina. Do you know your daddy's lock combination?"

"Mine's one-two-three. Guess what his is?"

"Mmm . . . three-two-one?"

She clapped her hands.

"Think he'd mind if I looked in his drawer?"

"No. He told me he trusted you a lot. A whole lot," she added.

"Well," he said. That was all he could come up with.

Inside the drawer, he found $300 cash. An album of family pictures, too: all of them some combination of Teo, Delfina, and her mom, a short blonde woman with fire in her eyes. To him, the album was a journal of descent. From a rental home with a yard to an apartment to a smaller one. Booze, more booze, and drugs in evidence, loaded friends, heavy eyelids, a larger tat count, and gang signs.

Other loose photographs floated in the drawer. Sifting them, he found an eleven-by-fourteen-inch black-and-white photograph, worn around the edges but a quality high-contrast shot of a boxing ring; the aftermath of a match.

Night of the Ramos, he decided. *The shot Teo never got around to showing me.*

Downtown at the Olympic, it would've been 1960. The night Vincent Famosa won the $300 that started him down the road to his first piece of real estate. For years, he had brandished this photograph at the dinner table to remind his sons who was king of the roost.

Robert recalled Teo's version of Vincent's tirades: *How many trustees you two boys see at this table? Only one trustee here I can see!*

In the photo, TV lights still blazed on the fight's aftermath. Assorted people milled about the ring. The loser, slumped; the winner, arms raised; two guys who'd just risked their lives for a *W.*

That had to be Vincent strutting his stuff among them—dapper, café au lait, his fedora perched on his head just so, his jacket buttoned against his trim frame. Vincent stood next to the beat-up fighter with his head down. He had to be the Cubano-Mexican—*Vincent's Ramos*—who'd just lost on the judges' scorecards. That was the fighter who'd given Vincent the prefight tip—that he'd die before going down against the Mexican Ramos.

Cool photo, he was thinking. *Newspaper quality.*

Looking on the back, he expected to see a stamp from the *Los Angeles Times* or the *Herald Examiner,* but it was blank.

Also in the drawer—several small photos of Vincent and Zara, with serrated edges like the Polaroids in his own family album. A little washed out over time, with rounded boulders in the background.

Vincent sat on a fallen tree—maybe a sawed-down log—scowling at the camera. Back straight, arms crossed, his sharp-looking Stacy Adams shoes shined. Like that log's his throne and he's the one sitting in judgment of the world. Zara stood over to his left in shorts and hiking boots, a bandanna around her neck, hands resting on her canted hips. Looking at Vincent—glaring at him, maybe? Could be he was reading too much between the lines, but it looked like *les bon temps* weren't rolling just then for this Crescent City couple.

"Robert," Delfina asked, "is it okay if we go see Daddy before dinner?"

"That's a good idea," he said.

As she ran inside for her Hello Kitty pack, he locked the cube. A car approached the house. Robert didn't recognize it. Then it stopped. The driver's side front window rolled down. A hand held out a paper bag. The engine revved. Robert peered inside at the driver—Reyes.

"Five grand plus, for the you-know-what," Reyes said. The hashish. "Best to *Conchita*. Brentwood, *estoy nervioso*. I'm outta here." Then Reyes took off, and just like that, Robert had dropped another $5,000 in his clients' kitty.

❧

Robert waited outside Teo's hospital room while Delfina shared private thoughts with her father. According to the nurses, nothing had changed with Teo's situation. Watching through the window, he saw Delfina talking to Teo like he could hear every word, and he tried not to let his heart break in front of her.

Ten minutes later, she joined him and took his hand.

"I told him I'd go to the chapel to say a prayer for Mommy. Is that okay?"

"I think the chapel is on the—"

"Gia takes me there. She prays, too."

Still holding his hand, she took him to the fourth-floor chapel. Near the front, they found a pew and slid into it.

In front of them, a stained-glass Jesus Christ hung from the cross, his feet nailed to its vertical beam, his hands nailed to the crossbeam. Above his head, the letters *INRI*. An acronym, if he remembered right, for *Jesus the Nazarene, King of the Jews.* A simple, backlit glass tableau, but the point was made: Jesus Christ suffered on the cross and died for our sins.

Delfina asked, "Aren't you going to pray?"

"I was getting ready to," he said, leaning onto the pew in front of them.

Lying to a child in church—you're off to a bad start.

Praying now, he put in a few good words for his father, hoping that schizophrenic Garrett Worth would find some kind of peace. He asked that his mother—living with his uncle—wouldn't upset the family applecart any more than she had already, and that his first cousin, Rosalind, once his best friend, would reach out to him one day.

And Delfina, he prayed. *What a wonderful little girl she is, with her limited wants. Just to be with her father. To know he's safe from harm, safe from the streets. Is there any reason that's too much for her from this world? I hope not—I pray not, so please, God, forget all the other stuff I prayed about. Just that one thing for her. Let her be with her father, and let his brain be normal after he wakes up. That would be great. Actually, that would be a miracle. Amen.*

Opening his eyes, he sat back in the pew. Delfina held that dark river rock while she prayed. The same rock he'd seen her with at Gia's. In this light, he noticed the rock had been altered.

"Amen," she said, and saw what he was looking at. "My rock, do you want to hold it?"

"Sure," he said.

He'd been right. Something, a stamping machine or a laser, had punched or carved all the way through the middle of it. Far from being a work of art or an artifact, it looked mass produced. Holding it up to the light, he squinted through the cored-out part. Still, the image eluded him.

"That's upside down," she said. She turned it around in his hand.

"I'm not very smart," he said, smiling at her.

Holding it up again, he saw what could be the outline of a bushy tree. Impossible to tell what variety, given the lack of workmanship.

Delfina took back her rock. "It's from when Daddy drove us to the desert. We were looking for Jesus. Want me to tell you about it?" she asked.

"Please," he said.

Warming up to the story, she said, "Okay. Daddy had a car, and he took me with him. Not our truck, we didn't have it yet, but he borrowed a car from somebody. One of his bad friends, I think, and so we drove in the dark, and I tried to sleep. Finally, I did, and when I woke up, I saw all the spaceships, and I got sick to my stomach."

Spaceships?

"Daddy said it was because I ate something bad from a food truck on San Pedro."

"But your daddy drove you to the desert?"

She nodded. "And on the way, he bought me a milkshake, and then we drove around most of the day looking for him."

Robert almost hated to ask: "Looking for Jesus?"

"Yes, I told you. And we drove around, but we never found him. So Daddy went to the ranger place to ask and went inside and left me in the car. And when he came back, he was upset Jesus wasn't there. So I went to sleep again."

"How long ago was this?"

"A long time ago. Two years, I think. It was really hot."

What kind of bullshit trip did Teo take his seven-year-old on? Was he drunk, stoned, crazy? Driving a car? Dragging his daughter to some desert to look for Jesus.

"He ate a big hamburger at McDonald's. I wanted animal crackers, but they didn't sell them anymore, so I had a milkshake again. Then Daddy drove around and found a drugstore that sold them and bought me animal crackers, and I didn't throw up again after I ate them."

"I like animal crackers, too," he said.

"And pigs in a blanket," she reminded him.

"Them the most," he said.

"And once it was dark up there, we were lost for a long time, but finally he found this motel he wanted to find, and we drove through the gates, and Daddy went inside."

"The office?" he asked.

"Yes, and there was a pretty swimming pool—I saw it from the car—but I think it cost too much money to stay there, so we left."

Then he remembered why she was telling the story. *The rock.*

"Did you find your rock somewhere in the desert?"

"*Waaaiiit,*" she said. "And *theeennn* . . . we went to a place where they had lots and lots of rocks. In baskets, and there were all kinds of them. They had gold, too, but not really gold, Daddy said, but Daddy was looking for the special rock. It wasn't there. So he picked out this one and gave it to me. Just for me."

"A rock your daddy gave you," he said. "I understand why you like it so much."

They started up the aisle, but she wasn't finished.

"Daddy told me to hold my rock and close my eyes. So I did. And then for me to think about how I want things to be. Think about how good things are going to be." She looked up at him then. "So that's what I do sometimes with my rock."

Just when he'd pegged Teo as a deranged prick, the man found animal crackers for Delfina and told her something magical like that.

"Daddy didn't smell bad," she said. "The smell from when he drinks. That was after we drove back to where we lived then."

"Back to Los Angeles," he said.

"Yes, back to LA," she said. "The end." Of the story, she meant.

So for Teo, it was back to LA and back into the bottle. *Inconsistent parents.* That's how Teo described his and Bee's parenting style.

Hard to argue with that, Robert thought, as they walked out of the chapel together.

After the door swung shut, Penko raised his head in the next-to-last row, where he'd pretended to pray.

CHAPTER 24

At dinner, Robert juiced Gia's outside heat lamp. Erik set a sizzling platter of steaks on the wooden table, right in front of Delfina. Gia poured the adults glasses of wine; then they held hands and blessed the food.

After Erik served the steaks, Delfina asked, "Mr. Jacobson, what's the most steak you ever ate in your whole life?"

"At one time?" Erik said.

"Yes."

"At one time, let's see, I was three years old, but I was real big for three."

"How big?"

"*Real* big, and I ate one hundred pounds of steak for dinner, and I still wanted more."

Delfina started laughing.

"May I have yours?" Erik asked, pretending to reach for hers.

"Yes," she said, and held out her plate for him.

"No, no, that's yours, sweetheart," Erik said. "You know, I'm used to my little boys, and they're not *neeeearly* as sweet as you."

Sometimes Robert found it difficult to reconcile this gentle man, now cutting Delfina's steak for her, with the hard-ass cop he'd gotten to know. Then again, by his own admission, Erik had mellowed out quite a bit since leaving the force.

Erik and Gia began talking about one of her criminal law cases. The facts: A homeowner set up a shotgun inside a vacant home, its trigger tied to a trip wire to deal with regular intruders. The legal question: Was using what could be deadly force against a trespass to property an excessive use of force and, therefore, an intentional civil tort of battery?

Robert kept up his end, best he could, but unanswered questions kept banging around his mind, tugging at him

Why did someone decide to run down Teo behind Sonny's Gyros?

Someone getting back at Carlos? A jealous husband or boyfriend of *the girl?* Carlos loved Vegas—what about gambling debts? None of that made sense. Carlos was dead—why kill his dead-broke brother? What about the guys downtown who'd threatened Delfina after Teo broke up that drug deal? Too remote—a year or two ago. What about the barflies who'd sued over Teo's assaults? Again, years ago, and they'd been paid off by the trust. Any chance it was an accident? No skid marks, and the angle of impact ruled out accident. According to Erik, the Santa Monica cops agreed.

"Even if it was intentional," Erik had said, "so what? Teo's rolling around LA, living in a truck. A former Mission resident, his wife's MIA. There's no irate next-door neighbor, no insurance-policy beneficiary. Where do the cops even start? That boardwalk beef with those ass clowns? They've been questioned about it and released."

What about that "Argonaut" notice Delfina happened to see? That tugged at Robert, too.

Why did Carlos pay for any notice at all? He wasn't flush with cash anymore. A first-class letter to Teo's last-known address—Union Rescue Mission, Skid Row, California. Legally, that would've been sufficient notice from the trust to Teo.

And given his monumental screwup, why file a final return with the court anyway? Even though the trust called for him to do it, the court hadn't been monitoring the trust. Why not do nothing? Maybe it all blows over. Your brother's not on your back about money anymore. Sell your swag, bank that money, and start work again as a CPA—even Evelyn Levine said you knew your stuff. The more he thought about it, the more his frustration grew.

At least his efforts for Teo—he hoped—and for Delfina, weren't all for nothing. Reyes' $5,000 cash would wind up in Carlos' floor safe. *Must've missed it first time I looked, Evelyn, wink, wink.* Carlos' swag would bring in even more now that Evelyn had waived taking any legal fees and had returned the watch. Pretty big of her, given her own circumstances.

How then to use the trust's cash—call it $35,000—once he had it in hand? Some lawyers would pay it to themselves and burn through it looking for the trust's assets. Totally legitimate and ethical, but Robert felt sure the assets were vapor and preferred to save any recovery for his clients.

Reporting to probate court under each scenario, he guessed, would go something like this:

Report #1: "Your Honor, I looked for the millions of dollars in assets. Unfortunately, my client ran out of money to pay my fees and investigators, and I had to call off the search."

Report #2: "Your Honor, I didn't believe I'd find the missing millions, so I didn't look anymore. Guess what—I saved the trust thirty-five thousand dollars!"

He decided to run it by Evelyn, but his inclination was to go with door number two.

Across the table, Erik was teaching Delfina and Gia the Thai words for *steak* and *wine* and *coffee*: *sateek* and *wiiine* and *guffee*, kidding around about how easy it was to learn Thai.

Just another SoCal barbeque on its surface. Watching Delfina, he felt fulfillment as well as dread, as he returned to the only question that mattered to her: *Why do they want to hurt my daddy?*

His answer came back, still the same: *I don't know.*

❧

That night, while Gia read *Wonder* to Delfina, Robert rolled a recliner into the backyard and lay down. Wanting to put the case behind him, gazing into the shrouded moon, he tried to turn off his mind.

You've done all you can, right? What's left? Becoming trustee for a trust with almost no assets? Sure, okay, you can do that, too.

Later, Gia slipped outside, easing into his chair and resting against him. They lay there a few minutes. So quiet back here with her heart beating against his body.

"Found a charger at Best Buy," she said. "Teo's phone's charging in the kitchen."

"Thanks. You still okay, laying out of school?"

"I'm keeping up, kind of. Did you pray tonight?" she asked. At the hospital, she meant.

"Uh-huh."

"For what?"

"Same as you, I'm pretty sure," he said. "When she holds my hand, it really gets to me."

"Sometimes I go in the bathroom and cry about her."

"I'm sorry, baby. You didn't ask for any of it."

"Told you already, don't say nutty things."

She touched his face, letting him know she meant it.

Then he told her, "I found her mother's passport in the truck. *Beatrice Brewer*, born in Bakersfield. On one of our walks, Teo said the odds are good Bee's no longer among the living."

"Anything we can do?"

"Should we?" he asked.

"What about the Mission downtown? They know Teo. If she went home, they'd have contacts up in Bakersfield, wouldn't they?"

"They'd have to, I think."

"I'll call, then. Kids," she said. "You ever think about it?"

"No. Well. Not until recently."

"Like, this week recently?"

"Yes, baby, this very week."

"Me, too, sweetheart," she said.

One thing about Gia: she never played guessing games about where she stood.

Robert said, "Erik talked to Priya. If Teo doesn't come out of it, if Delfina goes into the system, they'll put in for adoption. Unless we . . . you know . . . ?"

"I know," she said.

They dozed off, lying together that way, until she woke him and they stumbled half-asleep across the mist-covered grass. Passing through the kitchen, he noticed an *Argonaut* spread on the breakfast table. It lay open to that classified personals ad Carlos had placed.

"Don't forget," he mumbled.

He tossed it in the trash and headed into the bedroom, falling facedown into bed. Gia wasn't far behind. Sleep came but not for long. Something stirred in his mind. Rolling over, he recalled Delfina outside the hospital earlier tonight, stopping at a stack of *Argonauts* by the door, taking one. *The new one,* she'd called it.

That can't be right, his sleeping mind was telling him.

Getting up, groggy, he looked in on Delfina, then weaved down the hall to the kitchen. Retrieving the *Argonaut* from the trash, he checked the cover. It wasn't the *Argonaut* Delfina had showed him on the boardwalk. It had come from the hospital stack and had been published today.

He found the page he'd noticed before and read:

Important Notice. Hearing in Matter of Vincent
Famosa Trust.
Final Accounting. Stanley Mosk Courthouse, Room
356.
Don't Forget!

The date was for the following Monday. One week after the hearing he'd already attended. Then he noticed Teo's phone charging on the counter—muted but pulsing, a call coming through. As he picked it up, it looked like this was the fifth call from the same number.

"Hello?" asked Robert, waking up fast.

Someone on the other end ID'd himself as Benny Smartt—and he sounded upset.

"Teo? I been calling and calling and calling you. What the g.d. hell's going on?"

Turned out, Benny hadn't recognized Robert's number when Robert called him and hadn't listened to Robert's message. This was Benny trying to find his missing AA sponsee.

"He won't be coming to the next AA meeting," Robert said. He told him Teo was in Saint John's and asked if they could meet up tomorrow.

CHAPTER 25

Robert sat at a round concrete table next to Marck's Brentwood Newsstand. Fronting San Vicente Boulevard, forty yards long, the stand had current and back issues of the newspapers Robert needed to check out. By the time Erik unlimbered from his Prius and joined him, Robert had called several newspapers and had a clearer picture of what had happened with the *Argonaut*—but still no idea why.

Erik checked out Robert's buys: *Los Angeles Times*, weekend edition; the *Santa Monica Mirror*; the *Pasadena Star-News*; the *Argonaut*; *LA Weekly*; *Culver City Observer*; *Culver City News*; *Los Angeles Daily News*, weekend.

Erik said, "So last week, after his death, Carlos Famosa's ad ran in every one of these papers?"

"Prepaid, yeah, I couldn't believe it. And next week, according to the *Argonaut*, they're running it again."

"How effin' much that cost?"

"Has to total five grand a week."

"Ten grand so far? C'mon, that's deranged."

"I'm not so sure anymore."

"Is there another probate court hearing?" Erik asked.

"Nope. So hearing or no hearing, Carlos wanted his brother to meet him at Room 356—and please don't ask why."

For the next hour at the IHOP off Bundy Drive, Erik scarfed pancakes and bacon, and Robert contacted three of the newspaper's classified departments, explaining that Carlos Famosa was deceased and asking them to stop billing either Carlos or the trust. He spoke as the trust's representative, which he was—other than legally—but each office said Carlos had paid cash in advance for a discounted rate, and payment for next week—the last ad—was nonrefundable.

After that setback, Robert kept kicking it around with Erik, who had signed on for another day of investigative services and another side of sausage links.

"*Three* consecutive weeks of ads?" Erik asked.

"Pretty clear to me," Robert said, "Carlos' notices weren't just a random guilt trip before he died. Carlos was reaching out—he wanted to see Teo, face-to-face."

"If there's no hearing, why meet at the courthouse? Why not at IHOP, have a rasher of bacon, stack of cakes, get off on the right foot?"

"I know. I was in Carlos' shoes, probate court's the last place I'd go. Judge Blackwell was steamed. Carlos ran a real risk of getting sanctioned by the court to pay back Teo's share of what Carlos lost—almost two million dollars."

"*Sanctioned?* Like the NFL? Deflategate?"

The question sounded wiseass at first. Then Robert thought about it.

"Sanctioned exactly like Deflategate. Even so, Carlos still wanted to see Teo."

As a waiter cleared their plates, Robert whiffed down more coffee.

"Is it possible I'm totally wrong about what was going on with Carlos?"

Erik: "Hate to say it. Thought we'd nailed it down pretty good last night, but now?"

Robert spotted a man coming in. Looking around like a Match. com first date. Based on Benny's description of himself—*I'll be wearing a shamrock-green watch cap, reads "Benny Boy"*—that man was Benny. After motioning him over, Benny motioned back that he was hitting the head.

Robert told Erik, "Would you find Ana Short? Do whatever you can to look at that Playa Vista office's guest register."

"SoccMom? There's not one. It's digital, remember."

"Not the tenants, the guest register."

By the time Robert told him exactly what he was looking for, Benny was headed over.

Robert knew that getting an AA member to talk about what went on in a meeting would be difficult.

"Erik, let it slip with Benny that you're a cop."

"Got it. Subtle." Erik stood, shook Benny's hand, and held up his badge. "Hi, Benny. Erik Jacobson, LAPD, retired, lead investigator on the Matteo Famosa case. Nice to meet you, man, but I gotta go bird-dog a few leads."

Subtle?

As Erik headed out, Benny sat across from him. Robert handed him his business card, thanked him for coming.

"Robert Worth, Attorney-at-Law," Benny said, reading the card. "I called the hospital after you gave me Teo's last name. They backed you up. Teo's a patient, but just so we're clear, I liken AA sharing to a priest in a confessional. Not quite as sacred but almost, so me sharing anything Teo said with you's a doubtful proposition."

"You're Teo's sponsor?"

"Like I said on the phone."

"I doubt you know that Teo was a hit-and-run victim two nights ago in Santa Monica. Deliberate, I believe."

Robert explained the lack of skid marks and the protruding trash bins.

Benny said, "Guy like Teo, that's hard to figure."

"I was with him at his brother's house several hours before it happened. He went into his truck, took something from his personal drawer, put it in his backpack. Said he needed to go to an AA meeting right then. He was so ramped up after being inside his brother's house, where his brother died, that—"

"Overwrought?" Benny asked.

"Good a word as any. I thought he might start drinking again, but he said he wasn't *looking back*, he was *looking forward*."

"Doesn't matter what he said. When it comes to drunks like me and Teo, it only matters what we do."

"That's what I hear. Look, I'm trying to find out why anybody'd want to hurt him. His nine-year-old daughter wants to know, and I'm not asking if he confessed to a crime—I know he didn't do that. I just want to know . . . Look . . . he was very concerned about his relationship with his brother when I saw him. I'm pretty sure you were the last person to talk to him before he was run down. And I need to do everything I can to help him and to help his daughter."

"You just his lawyer?"

Robert thought about the question.

"Started out that way, but since I met him, I started measuring my own life, counting my blessings. I'm healthy, no financial worries, a great woman, great this, great that. Teo's had it really tough—lotsa people had it tougher, I know—but life's been tough on that guy, and he's been tough on himself, so I want to help him, Benny. Can you help me out, or what?"

"You a drinking man, Mr. Worth?"

"Not like you mean."

"Any addictions?

"Does caffeine count?"

"Afraid not. You'd be good at the lectern, leading a meeting."

Robert nodded but didn't speak and saw that Benny was getting ready to open up to him.

"In AA meetings, we hear about families where, for tons of reasons, there's not enough love to go around. A deficit, you could call it. Fighting, friction, background noise, and at AA, we hear variations of Teo's life quite a bit. But I never heard anybody pin down a moment quite as specific as he did. Never quite as focused as Teo's moment was."

Another nod. Robert let him talk.

"I know you're telling the truth about his emotional state—*looking forward, not back*—because of what he shared in the meeting. And I know you're right about his brother weighing heavy on Teo's heart. Starting out, he told the meeting he wasn't a good brother. He was a bully. Even though he was younger, he was bigger and picked on the older one."

"Carlos."

Benny, nodding: "Carlos, the weakling. Teo told a story, shared how it wasn't always that way between the two of 'em. What I mean is, it was almost always bad, but there was this one time with Carlos when it wasn't. His parents . . . ?"

"Vincent and Zara."

"Those two, yeah, usually fighting about something, but this one time their illness musta worked itself out. And the two of 'em, the brothers, were in the back seat of a car. Vincent and Zara sittin' up front, holding hands. Teo could see their hands between the seats. And so, Teo tells me, him and Carlos, each of 'em, had a rock. They'd bought 'em somewhere, cost maybe a nickel, dime apiece is all, and they started knocking 'em together. *Click, clack, click, clack*, stupid crap boys get a kick out of doin'. After a bit, his brother and him, they start swapping those rocks, still clacking away. Like it was a game or something—guess it was a game—and then they'd clack once, and swap rocks fast, and do it again, until one of 'em dropped a rock, and they stopped. But they kept on playing. Thing is, when they started out, Teo knew which rock was his, but after a while, he lost track of it. He didn't recall how long the game went on, coulda been fifteen minutes, coulda been an hour, just playing with his brother in the back seat. Laughing and smiling at each other, physically close, too. And when the game was over, he kept whatever rock was in his hand. Didn't matter which one he started out with, playing their silly, made-up game. For once, they were *real brothers*. Loving each other like real brothers. Funny what people hold on to, ain't it?"

"Sure is."

Robert often recalled sitting on a huge tree limb with Rosalind, two kids inside a spreading oak at the farm. That was before his family had been poisoned by his father leaving the farm—cashing out his inheritance, striking out for Texas, and failing miserably. That enormous live oak, canted into the farm's steep hillside, had been his and Rosalind's secret spot. *Their spot.* Where best-friend first cousins would drink cold Yoo-hoos from an Igloo cooler, wait for their rock-hard Abba-Zaba candy bars to thaw out, and share their childhood secrets.

Benny said, "Forever and ever, even after that car ride, Teo didn't think Carlos loved him at all. Turns out, Teo just now came to believe that Carlos loved him, too. That made Teo feel, guess you could say, made Teo feel fulfilled."

Robert was puzzled by that: on Carlos' front steps, Teo said him loving Carlos was enough. A couple of hours later, Teo's telling Benny, in essence: *Carlos loved me, too.*

Benny said, "Thought I could be of service to Teo in AA, but what do I know?"

"Sober all these years, you can't tell who's gonna make it?"

Benny laughed. "Two years into sobriety, thought I could size up a drunk, tell if the program was gonna take or not. After a while, I knew I couldn't tell, no matter how powerful their testimony was. Take Teo.

He inspired everyone who heard him, but he coulda had a bottle to his lips before he left that building."

Benny stood to leave. As Robert followed suit, Benny looked at him hard, as if what he'd just told Robert was actually a question. Robert figured out what it was.

"According to Teo's blood work, he was sober when the car hit him. And a store owner saw him right before it happened. Said he looked very happy."

Benny brightened as they headed for the door. "Shouldn't matter to me, but it does. Being sober when fate rises up, it makes a difference in how a man's perceived."

From IHOP, they walked up to San Vicente, where joggers ran the wide median beneath just-trimmed coral trees that reminded Robert of green French poodles.

Benny said, "Know why I decided to open up to you?"

"Not really."

"Teo showed me what he put in his backpack. And I believe you truly want to help him, so I thought you needed to know as much as I do."

Robert stopped walking. So did Benny.

"It was his rock," Benny said. "He had it in his backpack. About the size of an extralarge egg, but flatter."

"Was it a river rock?"

"Mighta been. Light gray, smooth. Thing is, you could see still white marks on the side of it where Carlos and him clacked 'em together. And it had something etched on it, too."

"Etched? Do you mean that the rock was kind of hollowed out?" Like Delfina's.

"No. Etched, for sure. Scratched into the surface. It was a Joshua tree etched there."

They talked a little longer. Benny said he was going back to IHOP for some bacon and syrup—some things were better than booze, Benny told him—and Robert said he'd get in touch when he had any news on Teo.

Even though he looked calm while they'd talked, Robert's mind spiraled on what he'd just learned. Two things were clear now: Teo had placed a rock in his backpack. And Teo's rock had been stolen—but only if Robert wanted to be hypertechnical about it.

CHAPTER 26

Robert was driving to Carlos' house to meet Reyes about selling the furnishings when Gia called from the Apple Pan on Pico. Evelyn was here, Gia told him, and they were about to order midmorning apple pie. Then Delfina came on the phone.

"Gia's skipping law school again."

Gia took back her phone.

"We were thanking Evelyn for the books . . . and for the other thing she brought over to my house." That wristwatch. "She's not feeling so hot from chemo, but she has something she wants to run by you."

Robert delayed Reyes and detoured to the Apple Pan counter. It had been rough enough at IHOP, not matching Erik pancake for pancake and bacon strip for bacon strip. Now, the Apple Pan? Old-school LA, counter seating only, home of everything the Westside svelte found unholy: hot, homemade apple pie with two scoops of melting vanilla ice cream. In a word: *Satan!*

When he reached the U-shaped counter, he took a red vinyl stool beside Gia. Delfina halfway faced him at the corner in a gold-braided, kitty-ears headband. Evelyn, Gia said, had gone to the restroom.

He put his arm around Gia. "Let's see, cutting class and eating pie—is there anything more depraved than that?"

Her hand snaked inside his shirt, slid up his back, and clawed its way down.

"Want two scoops of *that*?" she whispered.

"Not here, that's takeout," he whispered back. Then in a normal voice: "Have you seen any kitties in here?"

"No, why do you ask?" Gia asked.

"Because I'm allergic to kitties, and my nose itches. Pretty sure there's a kitty in here."

He looked at Delfina, who shrugged. "Maybe you have a cold?"

Looking under the counter, he said, "No, it's pure kitty. I can tell."

He caught Evelyn motioning from the bathroom alcove and walked over. She looked pale, thinner than last time he saw her.

"How's it coming, counselor?" she asked.

"Making progress," he said.

"And your Bulgarian connection?" she asked. He caught the hint of a smile.

"I know it's far-fetched, but that's what happened. And whether the girl led him to them or vice versa, I don't think it matters."

They both reached matching conclusions about the trust's money: Bulgarians or no Bulgarians, gone was gone.

Her take about what to do next: "Thirty-five-thousand dollars is a rounding error to most people on the Westside, but to your clients, it's a new life. Having a home, her being in school. You should tell Judge Blackwell that saving what's left is in their best interests. Do it on oral motion, and I bet anything it'll go your way."

Then she said. "I know I shouldn't buy her things . . ."

"Kitty ears?"

"I never was a kitty-ears little girl, but she seems to like them. And one more thing—bored yet?"

"Not a bit," he said.

"Thought I could handle sitting on a bar stool today, but . . . walk me out, would you?"

She said quick goodbyes to Gia and Delfina, pleaded a forgotten deadline, and headed to her car with Robert.

Evelyn said, "Doctors tell you, 'You might become a little fatigued from chemo.' Believe me, there's no such thing as *a little fatigued*."

"How much longer?"

"Another month. Beats the alternative—oh, listen. We—and by *we*, I mean *you*. We need to clear out Carlos' house or his estate will owe another month's rent. That money would end up coming out of your clients' pocket."

"Already working on it," Robert said.

They stopped at her Volvo sedan.

"Let me give you one of my rare compliments, Robert. When we met at the courthouse, I had a mixed reaction to you. At first, I thought you were going to try bullshitting me about your probate expertise."

"Hard to remember that far back, Evelyn." She was right on point.

"Instead, you consumed the trust files I gave you and did so quickly. You were right—I was testing you—you even remembered the exact date I resigned as counsel."

She looked at him until he said, "March twelfth."

"Good memory, too. I know you had to do your own due diligence, to get comfortable about Carlos' investments, about the money, but what you've done is much more than I could've bitten off lately. Maybe ever."

"Coming from you? Thank you."

She waved off the compliment. "So look," she said. "I want to set up a trust for Delfina. Not for her father, whether he pulls through or not. For her. Nothing grand—for education and for emergencies until she turns twenty-five. A trust vehicle that I could fund with, say, twenty thousand dollars a year, as long as I'm able. What I've had on my mind—would you be agreeable to serving as trustee with me? And as successor trustee when the time comes?"

"I'd like to do that, Evelyn. Thanks again."

"When are you going to disappoint me, Robert?"

"Give me time," he said.

She smiled and started to get into her car. Then she looked back at the Apple Pan: one-story green-and-white wood-plank construction, like a beach cottage.

"Chet and I used to come here at closing time. They'd see him at the door, stay open as long as he wanted." Smiling at the memory, she imitated the girls behind the counter: "'I can't let you drink that old coffee, Mr. Jordan. Let me brew you some fresh. Which do you like better, Mr. Jordan, the Boston cream or the key lime? I made 'em both myself!'"

"What was your pleasure, Evelyn?"

"Hot apple pie, straight-up. Embarrassing to admit how much fun it was, just along for the ride. Chet wearing his shades at midnight, so loaded he could barely talk, but those girls didn't care—a star! That beautiful, sad man, dying the way he did."

She came out of her reverie. Before he could speak, she said, "Think I'll drive home now and throw up."

✒

Back inside the Apple Pan, Robert took a stool between Gia and Delfina. Without hesitation, he ordered a slice of apple pie straight-up in Evelyn's honor. Delfina tugged on his sleeve.

"Can I order a slice of pie for Daddy? I can take it over to him tonight. Maybe he'll wake up and be hungry."

"Great idea," Gia said.

"Listen, kitty," Robert asked, "do you remember my name?"

"Robert Worth," she said.

"No, my other name."

She took a bite of pie, chewed it with her mouth closed. Then: "Magna Carta Man?"

"Right, and Magna Carta Man's job is to find out about your daddy, right?

"Yes."

"So if you know anything that might help, you'd tell me, wouldn't you?"

She nodded.

Gia nudged him. Her mouth was full of pie, but her eyes asked, *WTF?*

It's okay, he mouthed back.

He searched the ceiling for the right words for a nine-year-old.

"I remember your rock from the chapel, and the more I know about it, the more I can help you and your daddy. So if you know anything else about another rock that might help me out—"

Two sharp sounds on the counter. Two rocks lay there. Her own stamped rock and a larger one. Teo's rock. Like Benny said: Teo's rock was XL-egg sized. Twice the size of Delfina's and lighter gray.

Delfina looked sad. "I'm sorry I didn't tell you. Can I keep it?" she asked.

He realized that all this time, she'd been worried he might take away her father's rock.

"Of course you can keep it."

After talking to Benny, he'd remembered: Delfina had worn Teo's backpack from his hospital room. That night, he figured, she'd looked inside before he did and held on to this keepsake of her father.

"Mind if I look at it?"

She handed it over. Right away, he saw white clack marks on its sides. An image had been etched into its surface by a human craftsman. Faded a bit by time, he could still see the outline.

Like Delfina's, it was a tree. And like Benny had said: *it was a Joshua tree.*

CHAPTER 27

Once Robert dropped Reyes' $5,000 cash into Carlos' floor safe, he went back out to the kitchen. Reyes sat on the counter, drinking a beer, going over a furnishings list from his own walk-through of the place.

"These Sub-Zs," Reyes said. "They not original. Want me to find some refurbs to go in here?"

Robert knew that either the original stove and fridge were furnished by the landlord or bought by Carlos. Either way, they'd be fifteen years old, next to worthless to the landlord.

"Sell the good stuff. Don't bother replacing them."

Reyes said, "So there's that office desk, office chairs, leather living room sofa and two matching leather chairs, coffee table, a banging four-poster zebra bed, two other leather chairs, that sick sixty-five-inch Sony widescreen, four kitchen-counter stools, and this right here—the Sub-Zero stove and coolerator."

"That's about it."

"Gonna need an advertising budget you want to capture top dollar."

"How much?"

"Thousand oughta do it."

"What? What's this stuff worth?"

"Well, I put some half-assed yard sale posters on phone poles around this hood, stuff brings fifty-five hundred. I do my ad spend, and it's worth three, four times that."

"What's your cut?"

"Well, you're getting full benefit of my Chico State marketing degree."

Robert didn't ask. He waited for the explanation.

"Online degree, *jefe*. I'll take that flat screen. Not worth much with Best Buy and Amazon cannibalizing the market, but I got a home for it, out back in my game room."

Marketing? Chico State? Game room?

"And those books in the office?" Reyes said. "Gotta box 'em and junk 'em."

"What about all those framed pictures?" Robert asked.

"Worth whatever the frames'll bring. Except that one."

"Which one?"

"The good one."

"I didn't see it. Show me," Robert said.

As they headed to the study, a heavy knock rocked the front door. Erik's face filled the single windowpane. His scowl told Robert that he'd already seen Reyes' whip outside. Robert let him in. Reyes was, Robert believed, the only person who got under Erik's skin simply by breathing.

Reyes said, *"Hola, Yaycobson. ¿Cómo estás, mi tocino?"* My bacon.

"The fuck's he doing here?"

"Well, I asked him to—"

"Head of marketing, *Yaycobson. Es un trabajo muy importante.* Having business cards printed up as we speak."

"You know how to pronounce my name, don't you, Ray-Ray?"

"Don't see no *Ray-Ray* up in here. I see *Reyes*, meaning *king*, last I looked."

"King of bullshit, last time I looked, and popular worldwide as a girl's name. Gotta talk to you," he said. *You* meaning *Robert*.

"We're not done yet with—"

"Done with what, Double *R*? The yard sale?"

"No, my *Risky Business* event, *Yake*. My happenin'."

"Risky what?" That was Robert.

"Play your cards right, I'll get both ya'll an invite. No, wait. *Yake*, he's retired, hits Souplantation 'bout four, four-thirty. Two bowls of tapioca and he nods off at sundown."

Then to Robert: "Leave marketing to me and I'll get you top dollar for *Conchita*, ¿*sí*? That right there's no bullshit."

"No bullshit? Another first," Erik said. He took a seat on the couch, put up his feet on the coffee table. "What's this couch and chairs going for, Robert?"

Reyes said, "You can enter with the general public, *Yake*, and learn my price points."

"*General public?*" Robert asked. "What're you planning to do?"

"Home's a rental, *Roberto*. Look, I'll give you fifty-five hundred cash right now, or you can do it up right."

Erik said, "Yard sale with snacks? Never been done, Ray-Ray."

"Keep it up, both of you. Ain't nothing bad gonna happen up in here, unless you count *bad* as me makin' *Conchita* a pantload of *dinero*."

Erik said, "That's a pantload, right there."

Reyes said, "Tell you what, *Roberto*, this *casita* looks like this or better after the sale, or I forfeit my pay."

"You got a witness on that one, Robert, but I need a word with you. Legal business, Ray-Ray, highly confidential."

"Who cracked open your last case, *Roberto*? Who found Lark Man? That's right, you lookin' at him."

It was true. Reyes was the one who had scoured all the beach-area convenience and liquor stores that sold cigarettes, looking for a man who smoked Larks. Without Reyes, Robert never would've found Lark Man, Stanley Tifton, the man who had tried to kill him. And without learning Lark Man's identity, Robert might well have been facing tax-evasion charges.

He looked at Erik. *"Es verdad, Yake."*

Erik knew it, too, and it pained him. "When you're ready to talk about *this case*, lemme know," he said, and slammed a pillow behind his head.

"Gotta flex anyway." Reyes pounded Robert's fist. "Cast and crew, we takin' over Santa Monica Pier tonight."

"For *Street Cred Two Hundred*?" Erik from the couch.

"Wrap party, baby. Free rides on the Ferris wheel, roller coaster, free corn dogs, and Skittles."

Erik stood up. "For that low-budget, *maybe* straight-to-DVD POS? Bet you a thousand bucks that production's not taking over Santa Monica Pier."

"Don't wanna take your money, *Yake*. Wrap party's on, baby."

"A grand, Double Ray. Man up."

"How's it gonna work? You come down to the pier tonight, you not on the list, can't even get on. Oh, wait—you workin' security?"

"I'm not going near that pier tonight. You gotta prove to me it *did* happen and *you* were there because you *belonged* there."

"I gotta do all that extra, we notchin' it up to two thousand."

"Hear that, Beach Lawyer?" Erik said.

"Got it," Robert said.

Listening to these two go at it was like a paid vacation for him. By the time Reyes walked out, the bet was up to three grand.

Erik watched Reyes drive away. "What a bullshitter." When Robert didn't answer, Erik turned around.

"I heard you," Robert said. "Major bullshitter." He recalled that fresh $5,000 sitting in the floor safe—somehow Reyes always came through. "What'd you find out at Playa Vista?"

"Ana Short—*on the down-low*, right?—she got the guard to let me check the guest registry. I went back three months; Carlos Famosa never showed over there, even as a visitor."

"How long did it take you to drive over to Playa Vista?"

"From IHOP, twenty minutes, a little less."

"Let's say you might lose a ton of money with the SoccMom guys over in Playa Vista. What does Carlos do? He sends them twenty e-mails, sets up lunches, snail-mail threats, more e-mails—what doesn't he do?"

Erik was already nodding. "Drive twenty minutes to Playa Vista, park his ass in the lobby till they show up. But this guy's a flyweight, right? Not the same mentality as you and me."

Robert said, "Money. *Gone.* Girlfriend. *Going or gone.* Brother's money. *Gone.* Your father's legacy. *Gone.* Twenty-minute drive from your front door?"

"Catch the light at Culver, more like eighteen."

They sat in the living room, trying to make something more of it, and couldn't. Once Erik left, Robert was closing up the house when he remembered the framed picture Reyes had just mentioned. *The good one.*

Robert checked Carlos' office again. On the floor, leaning against the wall facing Carlos' desk: the lineup of framed posters and prints. On the end of the row, framed better by far than the rest: a two-inch-deep, black-enamel frame with tinted glass.

Picking it up, he held it out in front of him.

Carlos' match to Teo's rock.

The rock, with its own clack marks and etched Joshua tree, rested on a wooden ledge inside the frame against an off-white background. Not an exact match in the physical world—Carlos' rock being more irregular, slightly darker than Teo's—but the clack marks connected the pair. Now Robert knew—that moment in the back seat of their parents' car mattered. Both to Teo *and to Carlos.*

Teo's feelings conveyed to Robert outside this house, sitting on the steps, fearful about coming inside: *I loved my brother. It's all right if he didn't feel the same way about me.*

But sitting inside this office ten, fifteen minutes later, Teo had come to believe: *I loved my brother,* and *he loved me, too.* The same conclusion Teo had shared with Benny.

Teo must've breathed it in, knowing how much Carlos had valued their back-seat time together. A rare respite to their troubled childhood. That explained Teo's attitude leaving here for his last AA meeting: *I'm not running away. I'm running toward.*

Turning over the frame, Robert noticed a sticker for Omni-Tint, a glass-tinting process. Alongside that, the brand of scratch-resistant glass the framer had used on this job. At the bottom of the frame: an adhesive tag with information about Freize Framers, its address on Lincoln Boulevard, not far from here.

On the bottom right-hand corner, he then noticed a printed sticker: *Date of Completion* _____. Handwritten into the blank was a date— and one month after that date, Carlos Famosa lay dead on the floor, ten feet away from where Robert now stood.

CHAPTER 28

While Robert waited for the guy behind Freize Framers' counter to finish with a customer, he looked around the place. Lots of framed movie posters. Several of *Frozen*—the owner's pun?—*Star Wars*, *Iron Man*; a framed Penguins jersey; and a large framed print with Jimi Hendrix for the Clippers slam-dunking over Jim Morrison for the Lakers.

A voice beside him: "Running back Jim Brown as a Cleveland Cav, dunking on Dallas Mavs Willie Nelson. Like the sound of that?"

The guy from behind the counter stood beside him. Midforties, five ten, he weighed three hundred pounds, give or take a few, and moved quietly for such a large man.

"Sounds cool," Robert said, and meant it.

"Drew Freize. How can I help you this fine day?"

"Robert Worth. Let me show you something, Drew."

Over at the counter, Robert showed him Carlos' framed rock.

"I saw Freize Framers on the back. Date of the job was written there, too."

"And you are?"

"His representative."

When Robert tried showing him the tags—no more Fun Jim. Both hands went into the air: not my problem.

"On high-end jobs, using that nonglare glass, we date the work to set the warranty running. And I told Mr. Famosa, our glue might not hold the rock against that backing. Sooner rather than later, the rock's gonna come loose."

"It hasn't. That's not why I'm here, Drew."

"I know this frame was quite expensive, but that was up to him. Over the years, I stopped second-guessing customers on matters of taste."

"Again, I'm not here to complain. I think it looks perfect." He meant that, too.

"Oh. Are you here for the pickup?"

What pickup? Robert wondered.

"Carlos' pickup, yes, that was my next question," Robert said.

Drew went in back. Robert could see him sorting through finished frames, pulling one out, and returning to the counter.

"Thought Mr. Famosa had forgotten about it." Drew placed it on the counter. "What do you think?"

Another expensive frame with a white envelope taped to the glass. Mounted inside this frame: three stamped rocks, darker gray than the brothers' two rocks—but to him, they looked identical to Delfina's rock.

As Robert turned over the frame, Drew's voice buzzed in the background, repeating his philosophy on high-cost frames for cheap mementos.

Back of this frame, too, the name *Freize Framers* and this job's date, handwritten on an adhesive tab's blank line. The date of completion this time: five days after Carlos' death.

Robert tried tamping down his pulse. Trying to act casual, he pulled the envelope from the frame. Handwritten on the outside: *Hold for pickup 2 wks. Then deliver to Amherst Ave.*

Inside the envelope: Carlos' receipt.

Drew said, "We don't normally deliver, but it's not far over to his home. I planned to deliver it in a day or so."

"Looks great. Did Carlos mention where he'd found the rocks?"

"Didn't say. Why don't you ask him?"

Robert didn't answer. He read the receipt. Its date was the morning Carlos died. A few hours before his time of death, according to the medical examiner.

"Is Mr. Famosa all right?" Drew asked.

"Why do you ask?" Robert asked.

"That was the first time he asked me to deliver. I thought it was odd, but I—"

Drew stopped himself, that same man who didn't want trouble.

"Well, Mr. Worth, will that be all?"

Robert tried sounding semi-official: "No, Mr. Freize. Carlos Famosa died not long after he left your store, and I'm his legal representative. He died approximately three hours after leaving here, making this his last known stop."

"God, how'd he die?"

"Massive heart attack. Anything I can learn about his state of mind that day would help."

Drew Freize shut down. "Sorry, I can't help. Anything else?"

Robert took in Drew Freize's girth—no wedding ring, no framed family pictures on the walls or counter—and made a blunt assumption about this man's social life among the beautiful people. Guessed at the inevitable childhood nicknames: *Tastee Freez, Deep Freeze, the Freezer.*

"Mr. Freize, Carlos' mother and father died years ago, and he had no close friends. His only family member, his brother, is in an induced coma over at Saint John's. And I've been running around town for the past week, trying to find out as much as I can about Carlos. So if you—"

Must've struck a nerve. Drew said, "When he was here, he looked scattered, unorganized, not like himself at all. His receipt. He left it on the counter and walked out the door before I could stop him. I hurried over there—"

Robert looked at the open door, fifteen feet away. They walked over to it. Drew pointed at a metered parking spot about twenty-five feet up the street.

"He parked right there. I started to call out, but two men were already talking to him, right beside his car. Then the men got in with him; the three of them drove away. There might've been another car that followed them, hard to say."

"Did they force him into the car?"

"Not exactly . . ."

Drew looked like he was thinking it over. Robert gave him time to do it.

Drew said, "It was more like he was resigned to it."

"Like he gave up?" Robert asked.

"Kinda like he'd had enough. I feel like that some days, don't you?"

"Some days I do, Jim. Not today, though. You stepped up and helped me out. You didn't have to, but you did."

Drew looked down, might've blushed. Robert eyed that parking spot again. So close to the door.

"Why didn't you just walk over, hand him his receipt?"

Drew said, "I had another customer, and I needed to see if she . . ."

He stopped, looked down again.

"What's wrong?" Robert asked.

"I didn't say anything because of how those men looked. One of them in particular. Honest to God, I was afraid to go over there."

CHAPTER 29

Robert drove over to Ozone and took his laptop inside. Once he jacked Evelyn's flash drive into the USB port, he went back over the offering circulars for Vegas Rail and SoccMom. Scanning them, he looked for anything more he might glean about the two men outside Drew Freize's shop. Bulgarian men, Robert believed, maybe another car following them.

But the circulars revealed nothing new. The ideas behind them, bogus or not, had only one purpose—to separate Carlos from the trust's money.

He took another look at Carlos' e-mails to Mr. Saxon of SoccMom. SoccMom was supposed to pay an immediate monthly income stream, so Carlos' complaints to Saxon started on the heels of SoccMom's first missed payment, with Carlos doing his best imitation of a trustee about to sue for nonpayment.

After Carlos' "threatening" e-mails hadn't worked, he'd arranged lunch with Mr. Saxon at the Lobster, about six weeks before he died.

Mr. Saxon,

What the hell happened? I made the reservation for
12:30—at your request—and waited at the Lobster

bar for a full hour. You failed to return my texts while I waited, and I am left wondering about your total lack of professionalism. I expect an immediate explanation. S/Carlos Famosa

This e-mail from Mr. Saxon followed several hours later:

Mr. Famosa,

My phone failed to hold a charge today, and there was a big pileup on the 405 going from Playa Vista to the restaurant. Also, there was a death in my family. My bad. Reschedule?

Robert knew, same as Carlos, that taking the 405 from Playa Vista to the Lobster was like driving from LA to New York via Mexico City. Whatever Saxon's real name, he might as well have written: *Blow me. I already took your money. What're you gonna do about it? Smiley face.*

A few more half-baked e-mails from Carlos to Saxon followed, but he was screwed and knew it. Something churned inside Robert. An underlying thread he couldn't discern, much less untangle. Carlos—who never made the twenty-minute drive from his house to Playa Vista—set up a lunch meeting with Saxon at the Lobster. Stood up there, Carlos *still* didn't drive over to Playa.

Rather than go down that rabbit hole again, Robert looked at Carlos' last work notes from his accounting software: *Profit . . . Rx Samuelson . . . O'Meira . . . a real prick . . . Meet Karen . . .*

Gibberish, Evelyn had called the notes. *Nonsensical* was how Robert viewed it.

"Forget it," he said out loud.

Closing his laptop, headed out the door, he was already calling Erik. "Let's hit the hill," Robert told him.

"When?"

"Right now. I'm tired of being wrong."

"About what?" Erik asked.

"Everything," Robert said.

✥

Twenty minutes later driving north on Pacific Coast Highway, Robert finished bringing Erik up to speed: Delfina's stamped rock; Teo's larger, lighter rock and Carlos' own matching, marked-up rock in his study; the three framed rocks; the two men outside the framer's, maybe another car following; Saxon's no-show lunch at the Lobster.

At Sunset Point, a few paddleboarders downwinded toward Will Rogers beach, and several never-say-die surfers tried to make something out of mushy conditions. At Gladstone's restaurant, Robert hung a right off PCH onto Sunset Boulevard, then a left onto Los Liones. A quarter mile later, he parked at the hike's trailhead.

"No talking," Robert said, "until we reach the landing zone."

"Agreed."

For the first half mile up and into the Santa Monica Mountains, the incline was shaded, gradual, and as usual, they jogged. Once they made it onto the wide-open East Topanga Fire Road Trail, they slowed to a fast uphill walk, adding random sprints. The beauty of the fire-trail workout: it was relentlessly steep for a mile and a half. Some days, they'd take side trails—even steeper—that reconnected to the main trail. Today, they kept to the main drag, with its sheer hundred-foot drop-offs to their left. With Robert pushing the pace, his own rasping breath was the only sound he heard.

His primary focus—*don't think about anything except what's in front of you.* Another step, another breath. Taking in the bitter smell of creosote and staying alert rounding bends, hoping to catch sight of a coyote or the white tail flash of startled deer. Always keeping in mind the trailhead sign: *Beware of Mountain Lions.*

199

Erik liked pointing out, "Mountain lions're just as scared of you as you are of them. Unless they're consuming you."

To their right lay Pacific Highlands, an upscale development. Its meandering streets spider-webbed the adjacent hillside, and the relentless building had stopped only when someone finally screamed, "Enough!"

To Robert's left, a more serene view. Two miles down, Pacific Coast Highway and the becalmed Pacific Ocean; on a hilltop, the Getty Villa, a museum finished in the '70s and filled with J. Paul Getty's antiquities. *Old stuff,* Erik called it.

After the first mile and a half, the incline flattened, and they ran another mile and a half out to Parker Mesa Overlook. With no breather, they ran back to the bottom of what they'd named *Hill of Doom.* On all fours, they scrambled a steep hundred yards up the barren, rocky incline to its top, where they crashed in their landing zone.

A minute later, still sucking a little wind, Robert said, "Carlos Famosa."

"Check," Erik said.

"One month before Carlos died, he framed a rock that matched Teo's rock. Carlos paid a ton for the frame and hung it on the wall in his study. The brothers, they'd each owned their rocks nearly forty years."

"Check, check, and check. Forty years, damn."

"Right before he died, Carlos bought three new rocks, but these three were like Delfina's stamped rock."

"Check. No, wait. Check, check."

"Two years ago, Teo bought Delfina's rock somewhere in the desert. So I'm assuming Carlos bought his new stamped rocks in the desert, too."

"Almost certainly—so I'm giving you several *checks.*"

Robert thinking now: Carlos drove to the desert, bought three stamped rocks, brought them to LA, and had them framed. Those rocks were to be looked at, pondered, and understood by his brother. But Carlos *already* owned a framed rock in his study. If that rock signaled

Teo about their childhood moment, why did Carlos repeat that thought with three new framed rocks?

"What is it I'm missing?" Robert asked Erik.

Erik didn't answer. Robert looked over and found him stretched out on the ground, his eyes closed, asleep.

❦

"Asleep?" Gia asked. "You sure?"

"Snoring," Robert said, behind the wheel of the Bronco. "Hiking down, he said he thinks better that way."

Gia was looking out her window, laughing at Erik's dry comment. Delfina sat in back, absorbed in a book Teo had bought for her about historic Venice.

"I'm a crazy person, right?" Robert asked.

"*Shin jing bing*, for sure." Meaning *crazy* in Chinese. Same as *feng*. He'd heard both from her lately.

Since Teo's induced coma, Robert and Gia had made every effort to avoid doing things with Delfina as a trio. That way, they wouldn't feel like a family and confuse Delfina, or undercut Teo, if and when he came to. Today was a rare exception—the girls had asked him to run the Santa Monica steps with them.

"Like you did with Daddy," Delfina said.

How do you say no to that?

In the book Delfina was reading, remarkable twentieth-century photos showed Venice becoming the Coney Island of the Pacific, and its later decline. When Robert thought about what had once been here, he was amazed and saddened. The craftsman homes, board-and-batten cottages, the Italianate buildings, Ocean Park Pier, and Abbot Kinney Pier had given the place character beyond modern duplication.

Delfina handed Gia the book over the seat.

"I know this building. You showed it to me, the one near that circle."

"Windward Circle," Gia said.

Robert glanced at the photograph: a multiarched brick facade on Windward Avenue, the current home of the Poké Shack.

"That's right," Gia said to her. "What are those brick things called in front of the building?"

"Arches," Delfina said.

"How many kinds of arches are there?" Gia asked,

"Three kinds. There's circle ones, pointy ones, and the other kind. It starts with *p*, too. I can't remember the name."

"Robert?" Gia asked. "A type of arch beginning with the letter *p*."

"*Pointy,*" he said.

"No, that's one of mine," Delfina said.

Gia said, "The smart girl in back already said *pointy*. You need to say another one."

"That starts with a *p*," Delfina said.

"Um, pink arches," Robert said.

"Nope," Gia said.

"Purple! Purple arches!" Robert said.

"No!" Delfina said.

Gia said, "Maybe he's not as smart as I said. The correct answer . . . *parabolic arches*."

"Like on some kinds of bridges, too," Delfina added.

"*Parabolic* was my next answer," Robert said, "but you two were talking too much."

He parked the Bronco out on San Vicente; they walked toward the workout stairs.

"Want to warm up?" Robert asked.

He wanted to stretch his hamstrings, still tight from the Los Liones hike, but the girls kept walking, so he followed them down the eastern set of stairs to Entrada.

"Maybe you *are* overthinking the whole thing with Carlos," Gia told him on the way down. "Look, you're the lawyer every client wants. It's just that being that guy is hard on you. Anybody else would've waited for Teo to come to and asked him."

If he comes to, Robert was thinking. Dr. Wan had been clear that staying positive was the way to go, but positivity didn't guarantee a good result.

Down on Entrada, the western set of stairs loomed over them. Robert offered to go last and whispered to Gia, "So men can't look at your ass, baby."

"Were you this full of shit back at the firm?" Before they'd actually dated.

"No, I'm a work in progress."

"*Wo ai ni* anyway." Chinese for *I love you.*

Gia and Delfina started up the steep stairs in front of him. Delfina was an animal, but the stairs slowed her down a bit as he brought up the rear.

Watching them and climbing, he lapsed into a meditation on Gia: holding Delfina's hand, moving nice and easy. He'd never seen Gia hurry—move fast, yes, but never hurry. Always smooth, even on a rare trip to the gym. Working the StairMaster, she'd hit it with her long, slow pace, listen to music, and after an hour, she'd climb off like she'd just strolled down the CVS toothbrush aisle.

On the stairs, she looked down at him.

"Are you objectifying me?" she asked.

"Ogling you," he said.

"Carry on, then," she said.

He and Gia never talked about how she handled men, but he knew what he'd seen when men hit on her. Meeting him at a bar, her eyes would catch him at the door and follow him all the way to her side. By then, bar players with any sense had already caught on and split. If not, she'd put her arm around her man and ask the clueless player: "I'm sorry, you told me three times. What was your name again?"

Attention. She didn't crave it. In a look-at-me town, she had no look-at-me in her, unless he counted her karaoke version of Sir Mix-A-Lot's hit "Baby Got Back."

On the stairs, Robert still lagged behind, fighting how beat he was from hiking with Erik.

He returned to the other nagging questions he and Erik had discussed at the trailhead:

"Why'd the Bulgarians grab Carlos?"

Erik said, "Didn't sound like they forced him into his car, did it?"

"But why meet Carlos at all? They'd already ripped him off."

"Because Carlos could ID them?" Erik offered.

"But Carlos didn't ID them to the cops or make any effort to do that."

"No effort that you know of."

Halfway up the third set of stairs, Robert considered faking a hamstring pull or a heart attack, when the idea came to him and hot-wired a hidden thread woven though the Famosa family.

He hit the stairs two at a time, caught Gia and Delfina near the top.

"Pick me up at the Lobster."

He took off running. A mile away, he crossed Ocean Avenue by Santa Monica Pier, dodged cars driving onto it, and hit the restaurant's glass doors. Still sucking wind, he found the Lobster's maître d'.

"Listen, I'm working on a project, need to know if a guest was here on a particular date earlier this month."

"You mean, *made a reservation*."

Robert gave him the date, a couple of months back. "Made a reservation on that date, made it and canceled it, made it and was a no-show—whatever you have."

"You'll have to wait for the manager, and she won't be here for two hours."

"Okay, I'll wait," he said.

"I just started working here, but seriously doubt she'd share that with you."

"I need to know. It's important, so I'll wait."

"Suit yourself. Drink?"

"Modelo Negra, thanks."

He grabbed a counter stool in front of a plateglass window, checking out the tourist flow to and from the pier, the coastline, and the mountain trail he'd just hiked with Erik. Then the maître d' set his Modelo on the counter.

"Just spoke to Ernesto at the bar, and he said to tell you your party definitely wasn't here then."

He looked over at Ernesto, who gave him a thumbs-up.

"I didn't tell you his name. How could Ernesto know that?"

"Ernesto said the restaurant was closed that week. Actually, for ten days because of a roof leak."

After he gave the maître d' a hundred dollars to split with Ernesto, he walked outside and bent over. Hands on his knees, he reached deep for breath—this time from excitement.

Carlos, you dog, he was thinking. *You made bad investments, sure, but it didn't matter, did it?*

Almost immediately, like he'd always seen in movies, Gia pulled up in the Bronco. Once he slid into the passenger side, he reached back and gave Delfina a high five.

"Ready to go see your daddy?" he asked.

She high-fived him again. "Yes, thank you."

Leaning over, he whispered to Gia, "Watching your beautiful shape on the stairs set my mind free."

She whispered back, "Does this mean we can be lovers again?"

He realized it had been several days since they'd fooled around.

"Definitely," he said. "And you were right—I was overthinking it. Carlos—*he was in on it.*"

"In on what?" Gia asked.

"All of it."

CHAPTER 30

From his car parked on Entrada, with Penko again beside him, Kiril had watched the three of them start up the stairs. The woman and girl walked ahead; the man brought up the rear. Crowds of people filled this canyon, all of them exercising. Physical activity in this country was now a social event—new equipment, the right shoes, shorts, shirts, hats, and drinks.

Hydration, he was thinking. *A made-up word for drinking water and selling water to people with too much everything.*

He recalled his own childhood. Every morning his grandfather had told him to take the herd to the mountain and come back at nightfall—with a full herd. Age seven, alone and cold, running to mountain pastures with the sheep. A *real* difficult life, but on the Westside of LA, difficult had to be invented.

Penko had his eye on the stairs, too, their targets now halfway up.

"Woman walk ahead of him," Penko said. *"Pedal."*

Once Kiril explained to *Gospodar* the situation with Matteo Famosa—why they couldn't go back for another pass to check their result in that long alley—*Gospodar* had calmed down. Even so, here Kiril was again with the oaf beside him, keeping an eye on the lawyer and the two females.

"How fast did you make it up those stairs?" Kiril asked. "Your best time?"

"Never do before. Looks like easy run."

Kiril checked the weather on his iPhone, waiting for Penko to be himself. Seconds later, swinging open his door, Penko jumped out.

"I signal to you. Keep my time."

"Go," Kiril said, tapping his phone. "Best of five."

Penko ran down Entrada and stopped at the stairs. Pulling up his sweatshirt hood, counting down on fingers to Kiril: *Three. Two. One.* Then Penko took off.

Without bothering to set his timer, Kiril was already calling Ilina's burner phone. When she didn't answer, he hung up, irritated that he'd missed her. But how fair was that? Ilina had no control over client appointments. That moment when a man viewed the website and decided that Ilina's alter ego, Candi—sultry and intelligent—was the Internet girl of his dreams.

Last time they'd met, they'd laughed about the website's legal language that said in every way possible: no promise of sexual relations was expressed or implied. Even more to the point:

This Site Offers No Prostitution!

All the girls joked about it, she'd told Kiril. "So sorry, Officer, I am new to your country. I did not know fucking for money was prostitution. In my country, this is called commerce."

Alexandra had passed along his message to Ilina, and a few nights ago, Ilina had slipped out of the house where she lived with Alexandra and the other girls, even though she was supposed to be working that night. They'd met at the top of Elysian Fields near Echo Park's water tower.

Halfway down the steep hillside, he'd kissed her. She'd kissed him back. He'd turned her around, and she'd held on to a tree while he raised her skirt and took her from behind, the position not meant to degrade but to let him spot any oncoming danger instead of losing himself in her alabaster face. Afterward, they'd walked arm in arm among the dying eucalyptus trees, preyed on, she said, by an Australian aphid that sucked all the sap from the leaves.

"Nashville," she said. "You know people there?"

He'd looked into this place, Nashville, since last time they'd hooked up. It was there she planned to learn line dancing and visit the Grand Ole Opry.

"No, but you love their music, and it is home of country music. All singers have swimming pools, look like guitars with strings painted on bottom of pool."

"All of them?"

"Every one of them."

They were having fun now.

"After we move there, I will build a pool to look like your pussy, dig the hole myself. And after that, we buy a big house on the Black Sea, invite your family for a long visit."

"Short visit," she said. Dropping into her Candi routine, she said, "You must be a very strong, very wealthy man."

"Strong, yes. Wealthy? Not yet."

He'd known she was testing him. Asking him without asking, if he could live with the person she'd been: *Candi*. Kiril liked that about her. Not coming right out with it, telling him again and again how much she hated her life as an escort.

She'd squeezed his arm with hers, and he grew hard again. Smart girl, this Ilina. But most of these girls from home started out smart. Like the others, Ilina had always lusted for America. At home, her life would've beat her down in ten years. Rough, cruel men like Penko were the norm, beatings and rape common. But after she'd landed in LA, everything looked like she'd seen on TV.

"Even the *Baywatch* lifeguard towers," she'd told him. "It's LA, baby!"

But now that she wanted out, like most of the girls, she was afraid. She'd heard all the stories about *Poor Radka*, the girl who tried running away.

"When they found her," she'd told Kiril, "they did not act angry. They take Radka back to the apartment, tell her to pack her clothes, wear a nice dress for travel, get her passport because her flight leaves that night. 'Hurry, hurry,' they say, and drive her to the bank, wait while she cashes out her accounts—forty thousand, I heard. After that, she sat in the back seat with a man and asked questions, but no one spoke to her anymore. When they reach the Tom Bradley, they do not stop. Then the man in back take away all her money, go through her pockets, too, and they drive her to Skid Row. 'Take off your shoes,' they tell her. 'Why?' she asks. The man in back hit her and rip shoes off himself. 'You have no friends anymore. Get out,' they tell her. They keep everything, even her phone. 'Careful of the sidewalks—they pass along a flesh-eating virus.' And they leave her in the dark and don't ever come back."

It would be worse for Kiril. If they found him trying to run, they would kill him. Despite the risks, both of them wanted to break free of this clan and live a new life.

"In my mind," she'd told him, "whatever you do to make it happen is already forgiven."

Parked in the SUV on Entrada, Kiril watched Penko bolting down the stairs, three at a time. At the bottom, he looked over at Kiril, who stuck his head out the window.

"You can do better," he shouted.

Penko took off again. The only downside to getting rid of Penko: his stench afterward.

Kiril recalled what the girl, Alexandra, had said about Penko—that limp finger she'd shown him—and wondered if Penko's cock problem drew him to younger women. Slender, no curves, like the girl in the Emerald Triangle. And now, perhaps, impotence was drawing him to little girls, like the one on the stairs.

That gave him another good reason to run away with Ilina: leaving behind this sick man.

"Money," he'd told Ilina at Elysian Fields. "As much as we will ever need. That will come in time."

"How can you be sure?" she'd asked.

"Because I am certain of it," Kiril said, even though he wasn't certain of it at all.

CHAPTER 31

By the time Robert and Delfina reached Gia's house after visiting Teo, Delfina was asleep in his arms. He carried her up the front walk, and Gia put her to bed. Robert had been gathering his thoughts about Carlos for the past few hours, made a few notes, and assembled his panel of experts in the living room: Erik and Gia. They sat around a mesquite fire as Robert unraveled his latest theory about Carlos and the trust.

He started with a bang. "First off, let's be clear about one thing. Carlos was not a bad investor. Carlos was corrupt."

He let that sink in, then forged ahead.

"All the e-mails Carlos sent SoccMom complaining about nonpayment, the lunches Jake Saxon of SoccMom didn't show up for? All of it was bogus. The day Carlos told Saxon he was waiting for him at the Lobster's bar, the Lobster was closed that day. Carlos' entire paper trail about the missed meetings? All of it was subterfuge."

"Subterfuge for what?" Erik asked.

"Bear with me, okay?"

"I've eaten red meat. I can definitely hang."

"Carlos knew the Bulgarians," Robert said, "and let's keep calling them *Boris*. Doesn't matter how Carlos knew Boris—maybe he bought dope from them, I don't know—but he knew them."

"And *the girl*," Gia said.

"The girl, right. Evelyn told me that Carlos started dating a lot of different women. And I'm telling you that five-nine, one-hundred-fifty-pound, fifty-five-year-old Carlos Famosa doesn't all of a sudden start dating lots of women. I'm saying, *Boris made it happen*. Maybe Carlos starts hanging out with them, feels like one of the cool guys for a change, and Boris makes the introductions. One way or another, for the first time in his life, Carlos had beautiful women digging him. And along the way, he met another girl."

"*The girl*," Gia said.

"Let's call her *Svetlana*," Erik said.

"Done. And Svetlana, she's a cut above the others, more refined."

"Extremely hot, though, right?" Erik asked.

Before Robert could answer, Gia handed her laptop to Erik and Robert.

"See if this helps," she said.

The link's title: *Photographs of Bulgarian Women*. Five across and five down. An array of stunning women with radiant skin, mostly brunette.

"Forget the bottom row," Gia said.

Some troll had inserted shots there of Bulgarian farm wives who resembled NFL nose tackles.

"Supermodels, I get it," Erik said, both men still checking out the top four rows.

"*Oye, Roberto*," Gia said. "Over here."

He handed back her laptop.

"And Svetlana?" Gia asked.

"Svetlana. Like I was saying, maybe she's more refined, real girlfriend material, but that doesn't mean she doesn't like spending money, traveling, getting gifts. Could be she tells him her parents are about to lose their farm, her mother has cancer, maybe she'll have to go home. However it happened, it doesn't take Carlos long to realize he's punching above his weight. He needs more money, and his half share of the trust's income doesn't cut it anymore."

Gia nodded. "Makes sense."

"Erik?" he asked. "You good?"

"Solid. Keep going, man."

"And here's our boy, Carlos," Robert said. "All that cash in the trust, and half of it belongs to his brother, but Teo's not just any brother—he's Carlos' *drunk* brother. More than once, his spendthrift brother and his wife had showed up wanting more money for booze and drugs, threatening to sue, and the trust took three big hits over Teo's brawling. Still, after all the mess Teo's caused, the brothers are treated the same under the trust. For the past decade, Carlos hasn't pulled a salary for dealing with all the busted water heaters, leaking roofs, and pissed-off tenants. It was that resentment, *that and Svetlana*, that's why timid Carlos—*el Débil*—decided to do something bold with the trust's money."

"The investments," Erik said.

"Right. But first, let's look at Boris. He's been growing dope up north, like you said, Erik. What Boris winds up with is a ton of cash and a need to clean it. Clean money that can be explained with a tax return, so Boris sets up two shell companies. Both look legit, and they get a legit check from a legit investor."

"The trust," Gia said.

"Check," Erik said.

"After that, Boris pays out Carlos' invested money to people Boris owns. Tech consultants, limo companies, employees—consultants, that's how I'd do it. I mean, who's going to question a consultant who pays his income taxes and fails to come up with a SoccMom app that works? Happens all day, every day."

"The IRS doesn't care?" Gia asked.

Robert said, "Say it's one hundred million dollars, and your last name's *Escobar*? Sure, that's a red flag, but I bet every year in the United States, there are a half-million transactions of three to five million dollars. Long as the IRS get paid its income taxes, it's game over for them. Now, Boris? His money's clean—he gets a tax return—and he can do anything he wants with it now. Buy a house, stock market, gift it to his boss."

"Whatever he's *told* to do with it," Erik said.

"Yep."

"And Carlos?" Gia asked.

"On the surface, Carlos gets IOUs from Vegas Rail and SoccMom. They can be converted to stock, but it'll never get that far. Day one, it's worth nothing—*and Carlos knows it*. So what's really going on?"

He let it hang there till Erik said, "Oh."

"Cash," Gia said. "Carlos takes Boris' dirty cash under the table."

Robert said, "*¡Exactamente!* Boris pays Carlos with dirty cash. *Not the trust*—Carlos. Let's round the trust's three point eight million up to four million—Carlos is taking a risk and doing Boris a solid. So let's say four million in unwashed cash goes into Carlos' pocket. Well, not his pocket—his floor safe."

"So he's single, dating Svetlana, has four million in cash," Erik said. "What's not to like?"

"What floor safe?" Gia asked.

"A triple-XL safe in his bedroom," Robert said. "Evelyn thought it was grandiose for his VSOP brandy, cigars, and watches. Same here, but I was wrong."

Gia said, "Sure, the safe was practical."

"For his stacks of money. And think about it. You're Carlos. Which would you rather have? Close to four million of trust cash that half belongs to your brother? Or four million tucked in your floor safe, all of it yours?"

Robert went over Carlos' lifestyle. All his recurring bills, even his rent, were on autopay. His monthly nut came to $4,000 or $5,000. Once the plan was really up and running, he could've slipped that much dirty cash into his checking account each month, easy, and never have drawn attention to himself.

Robert kept going: "Evelyn said Vegas was high on Carlos' list, and cash is king over there. On a given day, he gives Svetlana, say, ten, twenty thousand cash. She pays for a suite at the Bellagio or the Four Seasons, first-class everything else. Watches, jewelry, sure, and she pays for rental cars on her card, takes his cash reimbursement. He could fly around the world that way, paying her cash, using her credit card—all that and still keep a low profile."

Erik said, "I can see my man Carlos in his bedroom with super-model Svetlana, the bed covered in thousands, rolling around in it like the *Wolf of West LA*."

Gia threw a pen at Erik. "That Carlos you're talking about or you?"

"A good investigator paints a mental picture," Erik told her. Then to Robert, "Keep talking. I'm right there with you."

"Carlos' biggest problem just became: How do I spend all my cash money on the girl I love?"

Erik said, "I don't want to throw cold water on your theory—"

"Not a theory, *mi Oso*. It's what happened."

"What about probate court sanctions? You said the judge could sanction Carlos about two million for losing Teo's money?"

"So what? To the legit world, Carlos owns next to nothing. His house, rented. Car, rented. Stocks and bonds, *nada*."

"Nothing for the court to seize," Gia said.

"Even if that judge sanctioned him, Carlos is golden," Erik said.

"How I see it, too," Robert said.

"Until Svetlana split on him," Gia said.

Robert nodded. "Once Svetlana split—more like got her marching orders—Carlos lost his mind, went running back to Evelyn. Sent her real e-mails, trying to apologize, but Evelyn? She didn't make time for him and still feels lousy about how she left it."

Robert continued: "And there sits Carlos, alone with the money, no girl, sold his soul. And he starts thinking about how he treated Teo."

"That's it? Leaving all those clues, just to tell Teo *that*?"

"More than *just that*. Carlos took the money out of the floor safe—took the money to the desert and hid it."

Robert let that critical piece sink in: *Carlos hid the money in the desert.* Then he waited. Wanted to hear one of them say what he wanted to hear.

Gia said it first. "Carlos was afraid. Boris was coming back for his money. And Carlos knew it."

"Son of a bitch!" Erik said. "That's why Boris picked him up outside that frame shop. Boris was gonna to take back his money, and why the hell not? What's Carlos gonna do about it?"

Gia jumped up. "But Boris was too late."

"Carlos already hid it," Erik said, on his feet, too, low-fiving Gia.

"*Excellente, mi chica!* Gia was right—I *was* overthinking Carlos' last trip to the desert. All these clues weren't for me; they were for Teo. The *Argonaut* notice—come to the courthouse, Teo. I need to talk to you, to see you."

"And why didn't he pick the IHOP for a tall stack of flapjacks and a rasher of bacon?"

"Scared? Thinks he's being watched?" Erik asked.

"Hell, yes, and the courthouse? There's a metal detector to get in and cops everywhere. A great place to talk, especially if you're freaking out and afraid you're being followed."

"Whether Carlos saw Teo at the first hearing or saw him there one or two weeks after the hearing, he didn't care. He could tell Teo what he did, maybe set things straight between them. And if he never saw Teo at the courthouse, and somehow Teo wound up in Carlos' study—even if Carlos was dead and Teo made it there as next of kin—Teo might've seen the three framed rocks Drew Freize was supposed to deliver. *I went to the desert, and I went recently. That's* what Carlos wanted to get across to Teo if Carlos wasn't around to tell him."

"Where? Which desert?" Gia asked.

"The Mojave," Robert said.

On Gia's laptop, he Googled *Mojave Desert*, clicked *Wiki*, and handed it back to her. "Ms. Marquez, if you'll do the honors."

Gia started reading. "The Mojave Desert is an arid rain shadow desert and the driest desert in North America. It is located in the southwestern United States, primarily within southeastern California and southern Nevada, and it occupies a total of 47,877 square miles."

Erik: "Say, how many square miles?"

"I know. I need to narrow that down a bit."

"You think?"

"No more outbursts, please. Ms. Marquez, if you'll continue."

"'Very small areas of the Mojave also extend into Utah and Arizona. Its boundaries are generally noted by the presence of Joshua trees, which are native—'" Gia looked up. "Erik, listen to this. 'Its boundaries are generally noted by the presence of Joshua trees, which are native only to the Mojave Desert.'"

"Native *only* to the Mojave Desert," Robert repeated.

"When did you do all this research?" Gia asked.

"This afternoon. After we came home and, you know, talked about all that stuff."

"Oh, right," she said. "That stuff."

Meaning *made love*.

"Now look," Robert said. "I gotta believe Carlos and Teo each went to the same place in the desert. Teo first, two years back, and Carlos, recently. Delfina said the destination was about three hours from LA, and Teo went into a ranger station. So if you take all we know—three-hour drive, a state or federal park, a desert where Joshua trees grow—oh, and there's spaceships. What does that tell you?"

Robert stopped. Waited for one of them to confirm what he believed.

"Spaceships? I don't follow," Gia said.

Erik said, "Those wind farms . . . the wind turbines out by Palm Springs. I tell my boys they're *robots*—they kinda believe it." Erik kept going. "Three hours from LA, the desert, wind turbines."

"Oh, near the designer outlets. Morongo Outlets—it's Asian American Xanadu," Gia said.

"Priya would live in Morongo if she could," Erik added.

"What's the park near there?" Gia asked.

Robert said, "Joshua Tree National Park. According to Wiki, it's only one thousand five hundred square miles. See? Already knocked down the search area from forty-seven thousand."

Before Erik left that night, Robert had nailed this much down for sure: years and years ago, the Famosa family had visited Joshua Tree National Park. More recently, Teo and Carlos had each driven there, too. For some reason, that desert was important to the Famosa brothers. And somewhere inside that park, Carlos had hidden millions of dollars of Robert's clients' money.

CHAPTER 32

On the street at the base of Gia's front walk, Kiril drove past Erik's
Prius. End of the street, he braked for Penko. Acting the late-night,
sweatshirted jogger, Penko jumped into the front seat. The reek of garlic
and nicotine reached Kiril, a toxic reminder of the *shkembe korba* Penko
had eaten for lunch.

"What did you see?" Kiril asked.

"Nothing to see from back alley, so I climb over fence. Check it
out close-up."

"You did not go inside that house," Kiril said.

"Was told not to go inside, so I do not. From outside, I see them
talk, they laugh. Nobody look worried about nothing. The young girl
looked like she was sleeping."

Kiril looked at him. "How do you know that?"

"I see through her bedroom window," Penko said.

The young girl again, Kiril thought.

Penko knew how to infiltrate in silence, a skill he'd learned in the
army. Other habits he'd picked up in the service, Kiril was beginning
to see those, too. He recalled the blue jewelry box he'd seen on Penko's
bedside table—Penko had asked Sharon Sloan where to buy such
a box—but Kiril had assumed the question was only Penko's crude

come-on. When Penko had been taking a rare shower, Kiril opened the box. Inside it: a shrink-wrapped index finger, no doubt from that dead girl's hand—the one Penko had killed up north in the Emerald Triangle.

Kiril rolled down the window against Penko's smell, knowing that sooner or later, this deranged man sitting beside him would somehow bring him down, too.

"What about the cop?" Kiril asked. He had seen a blue-and-white bumper sticker—*LAPD Retired*—on Erik's Prius.

"He don't act like a cop. Act more like friend. Cop drives woman's car, not car for man."

Kiril thought about joking—*if Spartacus was alive today, he'd drive a Prius*—and decided against it. Winding up Penko never went anywhere good.

Instead, Kiril asked, "If Spartacus was alive, what car does he drive?"

Penko said, "Black Enzo Ferrari, six hundred sixty horsepower, top speed two twenty. Serious mindfuck, that car."

He answered so fast, Kiril knew he'd already thought about the absurd question. Rather than mention the $1 million LaFerrari, with its *790-horsepower* hybrid engine, he gave in to the conversation.

"Enzo Ferrari, black, yes," Kiril said. "Great car driven by Spartacus, a great man."

❧

That night in bed, Gia wore a long T-shirt with a HoneyBaked Ham logo. Robert joined her, and once the lights were out, they caught up on the nuts and bolts of their lives. Midday tomorrow, he was headed downtown for a get-acquainted meeting with the probate lawyer, Bruce Keller. Taking the Metro, for once, so he could meet up with Erik and ride back together.

"Erik's downtown, too?" she asked.

"He wants to look into those guys who sued the trust, see if they had a criminal background."

"You two big boys rolling home in his Prius?" she asked.

"Yeah, why?"

"Just asking," she said. "Your negotiating strategy on the house is working. *Brady Bunch* asked us over for drinks, and *Full House* wants to know if we like charades."

"We're not going, are we?"

"I don't care. Want to?"

"Charades? Tempting."

He understood why their reactions jibed. A week or so back, Gia's dueling neighbors had seemed important. Now, selling Gia's house had receded into the background because a nine-year-old girl slept across the hall. How long would this situation go on? A few days? Longer? Much, much longer?

Dr. Wan hadn't shed any light on Teo's timetable. This morning, she'd told Gia she wanted to wait a few more days before bringing Teo up. Her prognosis after that? She couldn't and wouldn't say.

"This isn't like taking out a gall bladder," she'd told Gia. "Not an exact science."

Reaching over, Robert touched her, stroked her belly, and waited. Hearing her exhale, he lay back to watch her get out of her T-shirt, something he never tired of doing. Sometimes she slipped her arms inside the shirt and slid it over her head. Other times, she'd reach around her body and pull it over her head. Either way worked for him, because afterward, she'd be sitting up in bed, looking at him in the dark. Her thick, black hair tousled, waiting for him to make a move. No matter how he made it—reaching for her arm, her neck, around her waist—she always made it look like his move was exactly what she'd been waiting for.

Later, she quartered the bed for her missing T-shirt: "Where the hell'd it go?"

"Beats me," he said, holding it in the air.

"Damn it," she whispered. Leaping on him, she grabbed it. "I can't believe Delfina slept through that," she said.

"We were quiet, no?" he asked.

"I meant out in the living room. You, me, and *Señor Oso*."

"Didn't think we were that loud," he said.

"We weren't, but I closed her door, and later it was partway open."

"She probably cracked it open, likes hearing us talk, more light in her room . . ."

CHAPTER 33

Yuccas.

That word rolled around in Robert's mind, picking at him, until it woke him at 5:00 a.m. Slipping out of bed, he eased into the kitchen and put on a pot of Urth's Honduran coffee, light roasted for an extra caffeine boost. Once he'd turned on Gia's iMac in the living room, he jacked Evelyn's flash drive into the port and pulled up Carlos' work notes.

Something else Gia had read aloud about the Mojave Desert last night stuck with him: *Joshua trees belong to the yucca genus of plants.*

That's what woke him up: his certainty that Joshua trees—*yuccas*—would lead him closer to the trust's money. Back in the kitchen, he poured a cup of coffee, grabbed a banana, and headed back to her computer.

In LA, yuccas were plentiful: green plants with radiating, pointed fronds. Two or three feet tall, when they stuck you—he knew from hiking—it hurt like hell. Occasionally, the plants bloomed white flowers that came and went in a few months.

But Joshua trees? For starters, they were trees, not plants; evergreens, not cacti. Then there were their trunks. Not friendly-looking at all, their trunks looked hairy, like tarantula legs.

Looking at online photos, even a layman like him could see why they were classified *yuccas*—the branches had LA yucca plants growing from their tips, and in mature trees, that meant twenty feet aboveground or higher.

"Yuccas," he said out loud.

The trees' limb formation gave Joshua trees their name. Mormon pioneers first came upon them in the Utah desert and decided the limbs resembled upheld human arms. That brought to their minds the prophet Joshua, Moses' brother, waving to the children of Israel, beckoning them into the Promised Land.

At that point, Robert turned to Carlos' accounting software.

Gibberish. Carlos' word games.

That, he no longer believed. The notes were dated over the last two weeks of Carlos' life and appeared to show him meeting new clients. Evelyn hoped that he'd been getting back to work, trying to generate cash as a CPA.

Robert knew better. The dates of so-called meetings were real-time dates, built into the software, and couldn't be fudged. And Robert now knew: by that point in Carlos' life, Svetlana had left him. Carlos feared Boris. His life had become a two-pronged effort: to make amends with Teo in person, or failing that, to guide Teo to the trust's assets.

Stoned and drunk? Probably, and he'd been under extreme stress, but as Robert began reading the work notes again, he knew he was on the right track.

Valerie, What follows looks so great!

- *Client: Monument Park West Only*
- *Hours Worked: TBD*
- *Description of Work: Startup company/advise*
- *Notes: Profits. Evergreen, Yuck*

Yuck, he was thinking, underlining that word. *Yucca.*

Closing his eyes, he put himself in Carlos' shoes and went over it again: *I feel you, Carlos. Boris is coming. You feared him. You wanted Teo to meet you at the courthouse, even if you met after the hearing date. It was safe at the courthouse, right? You could talk, and if you didn't make it, even if Boris got to you first, maybe Teo gets to your study. He's your only heir, your brother. He would've known what your clues meant, right? But Teo can't help me now. There's a good chance he'll never be able to help, so let's find the money, all right? Help me find the money, Carlos—*

"I heard you." Delfina was standing behind him.

He must've been mumbling. Turning to her: "Morning. Did the grown-ups make too much noise out here last night?"

"No. What are you doing?"

Communing with your dead uncle?

"Not much," he said, standing up. "Want pancakes for breakfast?"

And later, as he poured batter on the stove-top griddle, he knew that it was just a matter of time before he headed out to the Mojave Desert.

❧

The Metro Rail from Culver City let Robert off at Pershing Square; he walked the remaining five blocks east to Stanley Mosk Courthouse. Pausing at the courthouse door, he gazed up at Magna Carta Man. That first trip downtown had been slated as a quick in and out, but a phrase he liked using with clients came to mind: *You never know.*

He pushed through the courthouse doors and took the escalator to the third floor. Ten minutes early for his meeting with Bruce Keller, he came to a hallway of probate lawyer offices. Not a bad job. Nine-to-five job, great benefits, a little courthouse power on top of that.

Each office door had memorabilia of some sort affixed to it: a sport's team pennant, a Star of David, family vacation photos, that *Hang in There, Baby!* cat hanging from a tree limb. Taking a seat across from Bruce Keller's plastic nameplate, Robert noticed Bruce wasn't memorabilia averse: a rainbow motif notepad, a Key West postcard, Madonna ticket stubs from the MGM Grand.

Sitting there, his thoughts returned to the Famosas. What was it Evelyn had said about the Famosas? *Welcome to Crazy Town. Better get used to it. Guess what, Evelyn? I'm getting used to it.*

"Robert Worth," he heard.

Robert stepped inside Bruce's office; Bruce sat behind the only desk. On his wall and desk: photos of Bruce cuddling another man at various spots: the beach, a bistro . . . and was that another bistro?

As they shook hands, Bruce said, "Gonna let you in on two little secrets, Robert. I'm beginning to suspect I'm openly gay. And my handle down here is *Killer.*"

"Keller . . . Killer, not bad," Robert said, liking the guy already. "We met in court."

"Got it. The Vincent Famosa Family Trust."

Then Robert explained that his clients were indigent, Evelyn was in poor health, and he planned to take over as trustee. Pleading general ignorance of the nuts and bolts of how probate court worked, Robert asked what he needed to know before signing on.

"Not too much."

Bruce explained that by looking into similar files in the clerk's office—Bruce would help with that—Robert would get the hang of things. Also, it was Bruce's job to make sure everything was in order before it was presented to his boss, Judge Blackwell.

"So don't worry too much about having things exactly right. They will be by the time you come to court. In that trust, there's no way to pick a successor trustee, is there?"

"Nothing like that, no."

"Any other heirs besides your two clients? Any creditors?"

"None known. My minor client's mother's been MIA, going on two years. Before his accident, Teo Famosa told me she could well be deceased. Meth," he added.

"A drug most unkind," Bruce said. "Pretend you're under oath. Are the assets truly in a shambles?"

"I'm doing what I can to raise cash. I'd be lucky to get my hands on thirty thousand."

Not mentioning the hoped-for desert money—the truth for now, as far as it went.

Bruce said, "Down here, we don't turn a blind eye to reality. Let's face it, you already represent every known trust beneficiary, and Evelyn won't have any objection?"

"I'm actually here at her suggestion."

"So if the court appointed an outside attorney to act as guardian for the minor, that will eat up twenty percent of that thirty thousand. Pretty sure that money can be better spent elsewhere."

"Anywhere else," Robert said.

Bruce seemed to like that lawyer jab. "Then a simple motion to the court to change trustees would suffice, but for your own protection, publish notice in a paper of record with the hearing date, saying you'll be the new trustee. Makes it harder down the line if some troublemaker comes out of the woodwork, raising hell about your appointment."

Robert asked, "And that notice process takes how long?"

"Six weeks, start to finish."

Six weeks. That's why Carlos didn't bother sending out a formal notice through the court. He didn't know if he had six weeks. And his primary purpose was seeing Teo—not the hearing itself.

Bruce said, "You'd show up with the minor and her father, health permitting; Evelyn would appear for Carlos Famosa's estate, or file a motion waiving any objection to your taking over. After that, the judge would consider—and grant, I'll make sure of it—a court order making you sole trustee. I suggest you submit a revised final accounting, too. That way, unless that random creditor or heir shows up . . ."

"Very unlikely on both counts," Robert said.

"If not, you'd wind the whole thing up then and there, and make application for your fee."

Bruce explained the usual lawyer's fee was one percent of the trust's assets: $300.

"Good chance I'll waive my fee," Robert said.

"I hear you, but that will indeed be a first," Bruce said.

After that, Bruce filled him in on what he thought of the Metro Rail, STAPLES Center, the downtown Arts District and condominium prices, freeway traffic during Dodgers season, and the LA Rams. Meanwhile, someone was blowing up Robert's pocketed iPhone with vibrating texts.

"That about does it," Robert said. Standing to leave, he asked Bruce, who was standing, too, "Tell me—all the people who showed up at the hearing, back of the gallery, who were they?"

"Oh, them," Bruce said, sitting down again. Robert followed suit. "You see, Robert, down here, we don't get too much excitement."

"What about that incident out in the hall?" The two men fighting.

"Alas, all too rare. Thing is, heirs might show up for probate and find out Uncle Belvedere loved his dog more than them, and things might overheat, like you saw. But with the Famosas' trust, everyone knew the hearing was coming because of that final accounting. 'Your Honor, I lost all the trust's assets. All of them, Mr. Famosa? Yes, Your Honor. Pretty much all of them.'"

Robert got it now. "And that kind of admission never happens."

"Never *ever*," Bruce said.

"So the other probate lawyers sat in, all except Dragon Lady. She had a conference call, then some kind of lunch after."

"*Dragon Lady?* Who lucked into that handle, Killer?"

"Sharon Sloan, three doors down. Somebody—beats me who— found out her maiden name was *Draganov*. The name stuck for a while because she's the nicest person you'd ever want to meet."

Draganov? Not European, not Asian. Had the ring of a Slavic name. His pulse quickened. Trying to act conversational, he said: "Sure, like you're not really a killer. *Draganov.* That's from where?"

"One of the Dracula countries. Don't know which one. For some reason, she didn't like the handle, came right out and told me so. I just gave her a new one: *Basic Instinct,* and shortened it to *Basic.* Jury's still out on that one."

"That movie with Sharon Stone," Robert said. "Keep 'em coming, Killer."

"Like I said, we don't get much excitement down here."

Robert shook Bruce's hand again, all the while thinking: *Draganov. One of those Dracula countries. Bulgaria?*

Four doors down from Bruce's Madonna tickets, Robert found Sharon Sloan's door, posted with keepsakes, too. First, a picnic photo of her family at a wooden table: Her husband, a nice-looking white guy, and two dark-haired girls, three or four years old. Sharon sat beside her husband, serving some kind of chicken, wearing glasses. Actress Mila Kunis, minus Mila Kunis' looks. Nothing like Sharon Stone, which added, Robert guessed, to the excellence of Sharon's *Basic* handle.

Also posted on her door: a small print of Christ's crucifixion. Definitely not European. Orthodox Christian, Robert believed. The Orthodox cross had three bars intersecting it, not two, like the Protestant cross. It was that third bar, a footrest, that was odd. The short bar for Jesus' feet tilted from Jesus' left to his right.

Very cool of the Romans, he decided. *A footrest in case he was uncomfortable.*

He snapped a few quick shots of her door, headed down the hall, took the escalator to the parking garage, and found an attendant.

"I'm supposed to meet Mr. Keller by his car. Know where his slot is?"

"Killer's on second floor. It's marked."

Backtracking to that level, Robert found Bruce's name on a slot. Several cars down from Bruce's, he saw a sign on the wall: *This Space Reserved for Sharon Sloan.*

Her silver license-plate holder read: *Glendale Lincoln.* He photographed her slot and tag number; once he made it out of the concrete into sunlight, he called Reyes.

"What're you up to right now?"

"Hitting a bucket of balls over in Koreatown."

"You're a golfer?" Robert asked.

"*Estoy el Tigre de East LA.* Working on my short game. S'up?"

Robert asked if they could get together, coming up.

"Sure, homes," Reyes said. "Where's the meet at?"

❧

On the rear patio at Café Pinot, Robert found Erik already seated, waiting in Robert's favorite cityscape. Skyscrapers towered all around them, the heart of downtown, but somehow it felt like an oasis. Besides that, he'd had good luck here before—this being the spot where he'd decided to take on Jack Pierce.

Robert took a seat. "Think I just landed on something that matters."

"Same here," Erik said.

Erik went first. He had wanted to check LAPD's main office downtown and look into those three guys who'd sued the trust.

"Nothing unusual registered," Erik said. "None of 'em career criminals or on anyone's radar. But the old Polack in records started laughing when I gave him the three names. Said, 'Who was it who pissed off all the Slavs?' And I'm clueless, so he tells me, '*Stanley Novak?* C'mon, that one's Slav, front and back.' *Stanley's* from *Stanislav,* he said, and *Novak,* that's Slavic as it sits—means *new man,* if I remember right."

"What about the other two?"

"Not necessarily Slavic but could be, easy. Take *Anton Peterson.* *Anton* could definitely be Bulgarian, and *Peterson* means *son of Petrov.* Third name's the same—*Martin Daniels.* You and me, we'd say *Martin,* but if you say it like *MarTEEN,* you're in downtown Sofia. And *Daniels,* think he said that could be Americanized from *Danielov.*"

Robert said, "So that's one home run and two doubles. Think I stumbled into a grand slam. *Draganov.* That name mean anything to you?"

"Nothing, but it sounds . . . you know . . . Bulgarian."

Robert explained *Sharon Draganov Sloan*'s courthouse role and the Dragon Lady's visibility into the Famosa trust by way of Bruce Keller.

"Not that she'd need Keller," Robert said. "These probate attorneys have access to every file in the system."

"How long's Sharon worked there?" Erik asked.

"Seven years. Definitely working there when the trust's lawsuit troubles started. She's the Draganov link to the trust, and those three assault-and-battery lawsuits—I'm betting they were drummed up. Using Sharon on the inside, the Draganovs coulda been screwing the trust for years. Taking most of the settlement payments away from the lawyers but giving them a cut."

"Sham lawsuits, a piece of the action for Sharon, too. Sounds plausible," Erik said.

"How many Bulgarians you ever meet in LA?" Robert asked.

"On the force twenty years, a handful, and a small one at that."

"A handful more than me," Robert said. "You know, I'm starting to think Carlos' trust could've been some sort of test run. A template for scamming other trusts down the line."

"A trial run," Erik said, nodding. "I think we're getting a handle on this beast."

"Closer," Robert said, grinning. "Much closer."

The waitress came to take their orders. Robert went with the scallops. While Erik quizzed her about fish and chips versus the hamburger,

Robert recalled that Evelyn had settled with Novak, Peterson, and Daniels for thirty cents on the dollar. Knowing what she knew then, hers had been skillful lawyering—bluffing, actually. But this new information meant the lawsuits against Teo had been shams—Teo drugged and framed for bogus drunken beatdowns. From the time Teo had tried to walk away from that boardwalk fight, Robert had never seen him as violent. Underneath, he saw a gentle man, even though he knew it was a sucker's bet, rooting for clients.

So what? As Philip once told him: "The best lawyers always get emotional about certain clients."

"What's dickhead doing here?" Erik asked, glaring at Reyes inside the restaurant through its rear floor-to-ceiling windows.

"I might've mentioned it to him," Robert said. "I want him to follow Sharon Sloan."

Inside, Reyes exchanged elaborate dap with the bartender. After that, he headed their way.

"Maybe he's one of the owners," Robert said, messing with Erik.

"Don't start up with me. Guy owes me three grand on his fairy-tale after-party."

Reyes grabbed a seat at their four-top, still wearing his golf glove. Robert was pretty sure the glove was left on for Erik's benefit.

"Sorry I'm late, homes, had to find a newsstand. Try ya some of the scallops, *Roberto*. They're elite."

"That's what I ordered. How's the fish and chips here?" Erik's dish.

"So-so," Reyes said. "Why come to an upscale joint, go pedestrian?"

"Guess you know this place?" Erik asked, eyeing that golf glove. Robert kept hoping Erik could ignore it.

"Cousin waited tables here five years. I ate here lots. First timer, *Oso?*"

"Where's my money, Ray-Ray? Or as you'd say, Where's my money *at?*"

"Let's let that one go sayonara, a'ight? Your wife, she kill you she find out you lost them two boys' college funds."

"Prove it, Ray-Ray," Erik said. "Prove it happened, that was the bet."

As Erik recapped the exact terms of their bet, Reyes undid the golf glove's Velcro strap, taking his time like a stripper. Then from inside Reyes' leather jacket came a *Hollywood Reporter*.

Reyes folded it flat on the table. The headline: "Santa Monica Pier Gets *Street Cred*." Under that, an article and shots of the party.

"My man, Peter Paul Dickerson," Reyes said.

Billionaire Peter Paul Dickerson. According to the article, Peter Paul had bought all rights to the *Street Cred* franchise. Just to be in the biz, Robert guessed. In a photograph, a Ferris wheel behind them, Peter Paul had his silk-encased arm draped around Raymundo Reyes, both flashing gang signs, acting tough for the camera.

"My homeboy, PPD," Reyes said. "Gonna hit me some *gof baws* wit' him later, bat around some of my movie script ideas over at Bel-Air CC."

Erik looked whiter than usual as the waitress set down the plates. "Careful, plate's hot," she said.

"You, too, *chica*," Reyes said.

She started sucking up to Reyes, asking him about a scoring part in the next *Street Cred.*

Erik stood up and looked at Robert. "Take your time. See you outside when you're done." Then he headed inside.

"Think *Oso*'d mind if I pillaged that fish and chips?"

"I wouldn't," Robert said, signaling their waitress for a doggie bag.

He showed Reyes Sharon's online courthouse photograph and gave him her license plate number.

"She parks inside the courthouse, Level B Two, drives a red Lincoln MKZ hybrid. License plate frame's out of Glendale."

"Home of Bob's Big Boy."

"You say so. I'm thinking she might live there or in Silver Lake."

"Yeah, close in to work. What am I looking for?"

"Who she meets, where she goes. She works at the courthouse nine to four or five. A lawyer, white-boy husband, and two kids, so if she does something that doesn't make sense. Anything . . . you know . . . noteworthy."

"Noteworthy," Reyes said. "Only *mi abogado* gets away with sayin' that. I see anything noteworthy for this upscale *chica abogada*, I let you know."

"How's the event coming along?" Meaning the sale of Carlos' furnishings.

"Want you to go Ethan Hunt on the event."

"Ethan . . . ?"

"Mission: Impossible, baby. You might need to disavow all knowledge."

Reyes was right—he didn't want details.

"So you and me are clear. Erik's a good man, all right?" Robert said.

"How you know that, Roberto?"

"Because I know it." He left it at that.

Twenty minutes later, Robert and Reyes walked out of Pinot. Erik's Prius was parked at the curb. Taking Robert's advice, Reyes didn't burn Erik about his ride, just headed up the street, where an UberBLACK pulled up for him.

Erik squeezed out of his Prius, caught up with Reyes. Robert had a good idea what was coming next: Erik handing a white bank envelope to Reyes, shaking Reyes' hand. Then Erik came back to the Prius.

"What a d-bag. Let's book," he told Robert.

Robert handed Erik his doggie bag.

"Hey, Erik? Reyes, he's a good man."

"You say so," Erik said.

"I do say so," and he looked at his friend till Erik said, "Got it."

They squeezed back inside the Prius and took off toward the Westside.

"You free for a run to the desert tomorrow?" Robert asked.

"Mojave?"

"Joshua Tree National Park."

"Twelve hundred square miles," Erik said. "Can you be a little more specific?"

He'd spent more time with Carlos' gibberish on the way downtown. So he felt pretty good saying, "Don't worry, I'm all over it . . ."

&

Maybe Robert hadn't thought it through when he called Gia from the Prius, telling her he planned to leave town. Delfina was listening and got upset about it. Then Robert thought it through; then it made sense. Her father was *asleep* in the hospital, meaning that part of her life wasn't caving in. Now she heard Robert would be leaving, and in her world, *leaving* could turn into *never coming back*, same as with her mother.

A half hour later, Gia put Delfina on the phone; Robert still heard *upset* in her voice.

"Just for a couple of days," he told her. "Maybe less."

"Mr. Jacobson is going with you?" she asked.

"Both of us are going, and he's going to take care of me."

"Gia already said."

"Want me to bring you something from the desert?" Robert asked.

"Nothing, I'm okay."

"I'm coming back to see you and Gia. You know that, right?"

Erik whispered, *"See her now."*

He caught Erik's clue: "Why don't I come *see you now?*"

"Okay," Delfina said. Funny how her voice brightened, just like that.

Now Gia told him: "We're headed to that camping store on Pico. Delfina wants Evelyn to come, so we're picking her up on the way."

"We on speaker?" Robert asked.

"Not at present, no."

"You're so smart," he told her.

"I keep hearing that," she said. "But only from you, baby."

"Would you two rutting animals cut it out?" Erik said. "Seriously, my wife's out of the country."

Gia said, "Feel you, dude. But not really . . ."

⁂

Erik dropped Robert off at Wilderness Camping. He spotted Evelyn sitting in a camo chair in the first of three large rooms. On the way here, he'd decided to bring her up to speed on the bogus lawsuits, along with the meaning of Carlos' nonsensical work notes and bogus e-mails.

But as he drew closer, she looked drawn, wrung out, and he hesitated. She took pride in the quality of her legal work—would it seem like he wanted to take her down a peg if he revealed that she'd been manipulated by her client?

She managed a weak smile when Robert approached her. Seeing that, his better angels prevailed, and he decided against pointing out her mistakes.

"How you coming along?" he asked.

"This chemo's rocking my world," she said.

"Much longer to go?" he asked.

"A month, they say. You know, Robert, I neglected to tell you something that's been weighing on me. Carlos called me about a week before he died, left a message, and I deleted it without even listening. What kind of person does that?"

"You didn't know he was going to have a heart attack."

"Even so," she said. Pointing over at the second room, she said, "There they are. Better hurry. Delfina's very concerned about your well-being in the desert."

Robert joined them. Delfina had been shopping for helpful desert gear. He checked the contents of her basket: a Suunto A-30 compass—made in Finland, Delfina told him; three pounds of trail mix; a strobing emergency light; a USB-powered light set; Ultrathon insect repellent; a snakebite kit; Aloe Gator sunscreen; four emergency road flares; heavy-duty crampons for mountain climbing; two long coils of climbing rope; a How to Tie Rope Knots kit; two Yeti-brand, eighteen-ounce, stainless-steel beverage tumblers with black plastic handles; and a red Swiss Army knife.

"Basic desert necessities," Gia told him.

Then Gia clued him in—Delfina planned to pay for it from the $300 in Teo's drawer. They couldn't let that happen, so Robert explained to Delfina they had no mountain-climbing plans and no need for crampons; that Robert already owned a Swiss Army knife; and that the compass, expensive, too, wasn't needed because his iPhone compass worked great.

"All this other stuff, let's see. I already wanted to buy rope for Gia's house."

"Rope for what?" Delfina asked.

"Well, in back, there could be a rope swing—"

He stopped. Wished he could take back his words that implied her future with them. Gia picked up on it.

"I asked Robert to make me a rope swing, Delfina. When you come visit us after your daddy wakes up, we can all swing on it."

"Will you take the rope with you tomorrow?" she asked Robert. "You might need it in the desert."

"You're right. I'll probably need it, but I'm paying for it. And I'm buying the road flares, too," he said, putting them in his basket. "Gia and I worry about each other having car trouble at night, so these are perfect."

A half hour later in the checkout line, Evelyn joined them. Robert and Gia had whittled down Delfina's buys to less than forty dollars, including a Joshua Tree National Park guidebook. If Robert paid for any more of it, Delfina would've seen through him.

In the parking lot, Delfina handed Evelyn a small bag. A package of trail mix and cherry-flavored ChapStick.

"To make you feel better from your medicine," she said.

Evelyn seemed moved to tears by Delfina's gesture.

"Thank you, sweetie," Evelyn said, spreading ChapStick on her lips. "You know, I feel better already."

As they neared her car, Evelyn whispered something to Gia. Then Evelyn gave Delfina a long hug and took Robert aside.

"I'll have a first draft of her trust by next week. Would you mind taking a look at it?"

"You know my limitations. Not sure what I can add."

"I learned early on how thorough you are. I always welcome your gimlet eye. Should I start calling you *Joshua Tree Lawyer*?"

"No way, Evelyn, I'm still a big deal down at the beach."

"I've never been to Joshua Tree. Palm Springs, yes. Two Bunch Palms, many times. You and Erik take some shots, all right? I hear it's magnificent, like another planet."

"Will do."

"See to it, then. Delfina's not the only one who'll miss you around here."

On their drive home in Gia's sedan, Delfina said, "Show him what's in your bag, Gia."

"I can't, sweetie. It's a secret."

"What bag?" he asked.

Gia said, "Something I bought before Erik dropped you off."

"More rope?" he asked, taking Gia's hand.

Delfina was laughing. "That's silly. You already bought rope. Guess again."

Gia whispered to Robert, "Not *that* silly . . ."

❧

That night, Robert and Delfina practiced knot tying in Gia's living room. Using a how-to picture and the kit's pieces of rope, Robert showed her a bowline knot. First, he made a loop in the palm of his hand. Then he grabbed the end of the rope closest to his body and brought it back through the loop, then around the free section of rope. Finally, he stuck the end down through his loop.

"The rabbit comes out of the hole, goes around the tree, then dives back down the hole. Nailed it!" he said.

Looking for a high five, he got one from Delfina.

"Your turn," he said.

"Why do they call it a rabbit?" she asked. Meaning the free end of the rope.

He called for Gia, and she came out of the bathroom in a terry-cloth robe.

"What's up, MacGyver?" she asked.

"Why do they call the end of the rope a *rabbit*?"

"*Rabbit's* easy to remember. So you'll remember how to tie the knot."

She took a bow and left the room.

"She's smart," Robert said.

"I know. I acted bad today with Gia. I'm sorry."

"Gia didn't tell me you acted bad."

"I went in the bedroom and slammed the door and started crying like I was still a baby."

Now he got it—Delfina had misbehaved after hearing about his desert plans. The camping store had been Gia's solution, and it worked.

"Did you tell Gia you were sorry?"

She nodded. "Yes."

It was all he could do not to reach over and hug her. Instead, he put a hand on her shoulder, squeezed it, and picked his words carefully.

"Gia is still your friend, Delfina. You did everything right, and we both care a lot about you, okay? A *lot-lot*," he added.

He could see his kind words warming her, and instead of starting to cry, he said, "C'mon, make that rabbit come out of the hole . . ."

Later that night, Robert found a couple of more hours with Carlos' work notes. Each time he did, they made more and more sense to him.

Once he made it to bed, half-asleep, Gia slipped in beside him in a black T-shirt with white letters on the front; he couldn't read them in the dark.

He said, "Erik doesn't want to take my Bronc to the desert. Says it's a *relic*."

"More like vintage," she said.

"A classic, right?"

"Don't push it," she said. "Taking the Prius?"

"Guess so. *His car*, he said."

"Hey, you're the one who told him it was a great family car."

"It's a three- or four-hour drive. I worry about him in that small car."

"About *him*?"

Even in the dark, he knew when she was laughing at him.

Robert asked, "What is up with you and Erik and his Prius?"

"You're just a funny man, baby, that's all."

"At the camping store, what'd Evelyn whisper to you?"

"Nothing much. Something like: *Have children, my dear. It's my only regret in life*. Come here," she said, pulling him toward her prone body. For some reason, she didn't take off her T-shirt. Somehow, he made it work anyway.

The next morning in bed, he peeked at her T-shirt before she woke up; from the camping store, it read: *Leave It Better Than You Found It*.

He nuzzled her till her eyes opened.

"Did I?" he asked.

"What?" she murmured.

"Leave it better than I found it?"

"Much better," she said, slipping the shirt over her head. "Wear it to the desert. You mind?"

He didn't mind at all . . .

CHAPTER 34

"When did you plan on telling me about it?" Robert asked Gia.

"Never," Gia said. "It was too much fun keeping it secret."

Delfina was laughing along with Gia.

"You knew about it, too?" Robert asked.

"A little bit," she said. "Mr. Jacobson took me for a ride."

"C'mon, Beach Lawyer, lighten up," Erik said. "My lads love it, too."

They all stood on the street. In front of them, Erik's rhino-coated Yukon Denali SUV. A ProZ LED light bar rested on top of the cab, a bush grille up front. Inside, an auxiliary battery pack and in-dash TVs, front seat and rear, and all seats heated with headrests.

Damn!

The SUV's name: the Beast. According to Erik, his boys halfway believed the Beast was alive, and they slept inside it whenever their parents allowed it.

"He built a huge gun safe into the floor. Did he show you?" Gia asked.

"No," Robert said. "But he just now told me all about it."

Robert got why Erik's boys had yelled, *"Beach! Beach!"* Wrong. *"Beast! Beast!"* they'd been saying. And, God, did he covet this truck, especially knowing deep down that the Bronc's likelihood of a desert breakdown was roughly 30 percent. Robert swung his sleeping bag and backpack—filled with Delfina's buys—into its cavernous back seat.

"Please take this with you."

It was Delfina's voice. When he turned, she held out her hand. In her palm, she held Teo's rock. He knelt in front of her.

"That belongs to you and your daddy. I can't take that."

"Please?" she asked.

He figured out what she really meant: *Bring it back.* He took the rock. Unable to help himself, he swooped her up and gave her a big hug.

"I'll take it, just for you."

"Keep it in your pocket," she said, "so it'll be safe."

He put her down and snapped it inside his pants pocket.

"That okay?" he asked.

She smiled at him; he knew he'd passed muster.

As they drove the SUV toward Barrington Avenue, Robert looked in the mirror at Delfina and Gia, both waving. He waved back.

Erik said, "My boys can *be* sweet. Delfina *is* sweet."

Robert nodded.

"Gets to you, doesn't it?" Erik asked.

He nodded again.

"Whew." That was all Robert could muster.

CHAPTER 35

Robert's Waze app put the Beast downtown on the I-10, then onto the Pomona Freeway. To their left lay Skid Row, the heart of LA's dark side. Inside Skid Row, Union Rescue Mission, LA's final safety net before darkness descended.

Erik asked, "The trust's apartments, they were out this way, right?"

"Not far. Monterey Park." About five miles east of downtown.

As the sun filled the Yukon's cab with warmth, enhancing its new-car smell and the scent of Gia on his T-shirt, Robert recalled last night's visit with Teo at Saint John's. Delfina had already spoken to her father and had given Robert some time alone in the room. Sliding a chair next to the bed, Robert had taken a shot at bringing Teo's subconscious up to speed:

"Teo, I've been looking into your life and into your brother's life the last several days, and . . ."

He stopped, started over.

"Teo, it's me, Robert. Hey, man. I'm here with Delfina and wanted you to know I've been working for you. Gia and I, we've been taking real good care of Delfina. Think we're doing okay, but we've never done anything like this. We like having her with us, but we're all looking forward to you getting out of here. You, too, right? When you do, no matter what, there's going to be money waiting, enough for you and Delfina to make a new start."

He'd looked out at the nurse's station. Delfina was talking to a shift nurse.

Talking to Teo again: "So anyway, I know a lot more about you and Carlos now. In some ways, more than you knew. Oh, I met Benny, your sponsor, and he told me what you shared in the meeting. It was hard for him to tell me, but that's what he thought best, telling me, and I know he was right. He knows your situation, too, and wants you back on your feet again.

"And what you told Benny about Carlos was right. Your brother did love you. I saw that old rock in his study, the one you saw, too, and I know now how much seeing that meant to you. But Teo, there's no other way to put it—Carlos messed up big-time, and that's what he wanted to tell you. He wanted a chance to meet with you and talk. I know you felt like you'd let Carlos down over the years, but I think he probably wanted a chance to apologize to you. Not what you were thinking, right?

"Anyway, Carlos did something with the trust's money he shouldn't have. He felt terrible about it, wanted to make things right, if that was possible. What I'm going to do is, I'm going to do my best, my very best for you and Delfina, because you two are my first serious clients. That way, you'll give me good word of mouth when you're on your feet again.

"Look, I know you made mistakes along the way. Same here—I made some big ones, believe me. Guess we all do, but you raised a great little girl, and she knows how much you care about her. That's for damn sure, Teo. She knows it top to bottom and inside and out."

He'd waited a minute until he'd stopped crying.

"I think, end of his life, your brother was a brave man. Just like you, Teo. *Lo respeto.*"

Now, as Erik's Yukon passed the exits to Monterey Park, Robert pointed out the one that led to Vincent's fallen empire.

Erik said, "The Famosa family had it made and blew it."

"If Vincent hadn't been such a prick, poisoned his family." Robert shared something Teo once had told him about Vincent: "Vincent never saw Carlos taking over as trustee. He enjoyed the grandeur—in his mind—of being trustee. Lording it over his sons, telling 'em he'd outlive both of them."

"Your own father, rooting against you? Can't imagine it."

A poem by Percy Bysshe Shelley rolled into Robert's mind: "Ozymandias," memorized under threat of a high school *F*. In the poem, an ancient traveler came upon a rubble-strewn desert. All that remained of King Ozymandias' once-great empire: two broken legs from a statue of him, pieces of his arrogant sneer, and a pedestal with this inscription:

> *My name is Ozymandias, King of Kings;*
> *Look on my Works, ye Mighty, and despair!*

"Sure, Vincent, was a big deal," Robert told Erik, "till somebody invaded his rectum with a plastic prick, then beat him to death."

"Or vice versa. How'd a junior hustler like him put together a stake?" Erik asked.

Robert told him about Vincent's bet on the Ramos v. Ramos fight, followed by a decade-long string of winning bets.

"'Then he bought a single-family house—Highland Park, Teo said. Teo has an old photo of Carlos and him on the front steps. Them working, while Vincent brought over a woman, a girlfriend, who knows, to see what a hotshot he was."

"Small-time clown," Erik said. "All Vincent's winning bets. You buy it?"

"Did till you asked. Why?"

"'Cuz shoving a hunk of plastic up a straight man's rectum? That ain't a garden-variety beef."

He was right. Robert had no answer for that one and doubted he ever would.

An hour later, a hundred miles east of Robert's boardwalk slot, the Yukon approached the first of the desert wind farms west of Palm Springs. Robert could see how the gigantic white single-prop whirligigs passed for spaceships to Delfina and robots to Erik's boys.

Erik said, "Okay, there's three entrances to the park. Which one do we want?"

"Let's go to the board first, shall we, contestants?"

On his laptop, Robert had already lined up Carlos' client notes into a columned list:

- Monumental Park
- West Only
- Profit
- Evergreen
- Yuck
- Rx Samuelson
- Truht/Faiht
- granted
- a real chiseler

- O'Meira
- Don't Forget!
- Angle Mann
- Sticky Mickey
- Meet Karen
- a real prick
- Your Decision!
- Dance Wif me 'Inri (not cockney)

"First," Robert said, "*Monumental* and *Park*. Joshua Tree National Park was originally designated a national *monument*, not a national *park*. So in my mind, that makes it a . . . ?"

"A Monumental Park," Erik said.

"Check. Next is *West Only*, so how's this? There are three entrances into the park. Cottonwood entrance is off the I-10, but it leads into the low desert, and as we know from doing our homework . . . ?"

"Joshua trees grow only in the *high* desert. So scratch that Cottonwood entrance."

"Check. That leaves us with the other two entrances: the North Entrance or the West Entrance. What's your raw instinct as a top-tier investigator telling you?"

"Mmm . . . *West* Entrance *Only?*"

They pounded fists. Ten miles later, Erik exited the I-10, the Beast flying along Route 62's miles-long uphill grade.

Erik asked him, "Remember all those wind turbines in *Jerry Maguire?*"

"Turbines were in *Rain Man.*"

"Nope, *Jerry Maguire.* Tom Cruise drove by all those turbines. I can picture him doing it."

"That was in *Rain Man*—Tom Cruise driving by them in *Rain Man.*"

"*Rain Man.* 'Show me the money,' right?"

Either Erik had the movies mixed up or was messing with him; Robert's money was on *messing with.*

Erik kept it up. "*Rain Man.* The autistic brother, Dustin Hoffman, saying, 'Show me the money!' My man, Dusty, autistic but keeping it real."

"Are you vaguely aware of the actor named Cuba Gooding Junior?"

"*Boyz n the Hood,* sure, a classic, like your Bronco. Cuba running up that Crenshaw alley. Gang pulls up behind him—*run, Cuba!*—they gun him down anyway."

Robert knew that Cuba's friend—played by Morris Chestnut—had been gunned down in the movie. So, he was pretty sure, did Erik.

"What ever happened to Cuba Gooding Junior?" Erik asked.

"Other than *Jerry Maguire?*"

"Cuba was in *Jerry Maguire?* You kiddin' me?"

"How long you gonna keep this up?"

"Till you show me the trust money, baby! Show me the money, *Roberto!*"

So Robert started laying out three separate Famosa trips to the desert:

"Back in the '70s, Vincent took Zara and both sons to Joshua Tree. That's where he bought 'em the first two rocks. Then, two years ago,

Teo and Delfina made their desert trip. He bought her a stamped rock, and on this trip, Teo told Delfina he *was looking for Jesus.*

"Desert's a good place for that."

"Now, not long before he died, Carlos went to the desert alone. He hid the cash, bought three new stamped rocks like Delfina's, and framed them back in LA. And while he was up here, I think Carlos went looking for Jesus, too."

"Teo and Jesus, I get. Delfina told you, but how do you figure Carlos and Jesus?"

Robert explained the last of Carlos' work notes: *Dance wif Me 'Inri (not cockney).*

"'Dance with Me Henry' was the name of a raunchy rock-and-roll classic, but instead of writing *H-e-n-r-y*, Carlos used *I-n-r-i.*"

"'Ello, 'Enry," Erik said in terrible cockney.

"*Not cockney,* dude. *I-n-r-i* reminded me of something: the Romans put those letters at the top of Jesus' cross. *I-N-R-I*, an acronym for *Jesus of Nazareth, King of the Jews.*"

"So *each* brother came back to the desert, at different times, *looking for Jesus?*"

"Yep."

"Like it," Erik said. "What about *R-X Samuelson?*"

"What about it? Or him? Or her? Or them?"

"*Granted? Chiseler? O'Meira?*" Erik asked.

"Work in progress, okay, but I think *Meet Karen* is really *Meet Cairn. Cairn,* those stacked rocks we see on the hike. Like, Carlos maybe built a cairn where he hid the dough."

Erik said, "Or he left a woman named Karen standing in the desert with the money."

"Let's go with my *cairn.* And I have ideas about finding Jesus."

Robert told him most rock formations in the park had names like crossword-puzzle clues—the Arch, Elephant Arches, Lost Horizon, Great Chasm, Cyclops, Ghost Rock, Tulip Rock, Wonderland of Rocks,

Iron Door. But two other formation names could relate to Jesus: Stone Temple and Skull Rock.

Taking Stone Temple first, Robert said, "If you Google *Jesus* and *Temple*, you find major hits on Jesus driving the money changers from the temple in Jerusalem."

Erik thought about it. "Money changers? A little bit like Boris, huh?"

"Makes sense, right?"

"Enough. Skull Rock ties in with Jesus, too?"

"Even more, I think. Jesus was crucified on a hill called Calvary, but Calvary's called Golgotha. And *Golgotha*, in Latin, means 'skull.'"

"Skull Rock—*hallelujah!*" Erik said.

At the end of a thirty-mile, winding upgrade, they hit the high desert. The Twentynine Palms Highway flattened out, straightened, and turned east. For the next thirty miles lay the high-desert communities of Yucca Valley, Joshua Tree, and City of Twentynine Palms.

And growing here and there on each side of the road: real clusters of those tarantula-trunk Joshua trees, like the biblical prophet Joshua waving them on.

CHAPTER 36

Indian Cove Campground rested at the end of a windswept road off the high-desert highway. It had one hundred-plus camping slots scattered among hundred-foot-tall rock mounds, sandy washes, and a long wall of tan, odd-shaped boulders. According to the guidebook, that boulder wall was the north face of Wonderland of Rocks.

They'd learned about the campsite at the ranger station near the park's West Entrance. Without mentioning Stone Temple or Skull Rock, Robert had asked if any of the park's rock formations might relate to Jesus. None of the on-duty rangers could think of a single one and wondered why he wanted to know.

Because of the law that applied to any money they might find in the park, Robert stayed mum on his reasons. Even Erik was discreet, once Robert filled him in on Gia's banging legal memorandum on the subject.

California's statute provided that if anyone found property worth more than $100 and the owner was unknown, the finder had to turn it over to local police. If the police could find the owner, they in turn must notify him of the found property and return it to him. If the owner didn't show up within ninety days and the property was worth *more than $250*, police then made a public announcement. If no owner showed seven days after that, the finder became the keeper. But if you found such property and didn't report it to police—you'd be guilty of theft.

Gia concluded, and Robert agreed, that the trust owned the property. That meant the owner was *known*, not *unknown*, meaning the statute didn't apply if he was the finder. Great as far as the law went, but if Robert found the trust's money and law enforcement got wind of it, how would he go about proving ownership? Those two circulars for bogus investments? Bulgarian money launderers? Carlos' so-called work notes?

"Well, Officer," Robert might begin, "it's a funny thing about Bulgarians . . ."

On top of California law, federal law could apply if they disturbed archaeological artifacts or disturbed the desert floor: like digging a hole, Gia suggested.

She ended her memo with: *"Federal law, Roberto? Don't get me started!"*

Erik's reaction had been laced with his usual dollop of common sense.

"If police notified a desert community somebody just found buried millions? The Manson Family reunites for that much money."

When they showed a park ranger named Rachael a photograph of Delfina's rock, she suggested they check out the gift shop up the street.

"They sell desert rocks and minerals, *objets and other stuff* over there," Rachael told them. Smiling because she'd meant *objets and other stuff* to be funny.

Objets and Other Stuff, the gift shop's sign said, too. That and *7 Minute Showers*. Named the Tortoise, the shop's baskets lined its road-facing wall, filled with rocks and minerals: garnet, tigereye, moonstone, gypsum rosettes, hematite, tumbled oco, chrysocolla quartz points, rough fluorite, black onyx, and tourmaline. Iron pyrite, too—fool's gold.

Gold but not really gold, Robert recalled Delfina saying in the hospital chapel.

And in a basket on the top shelf: dark-gray stamped river rocks, just like Delfina's.

While Erik scoured rock baskets for his sons, Robert took a stamped rock to the counter and spoke to the Tortoise's longtime owner, a one-armed red-haired man in his fifties who introduced himself as Baker. First name or last, Robert wasn't sure.

"The store's always sourced 'em from Montana. We're the only high-desert store ever offered 'em for sale. The only manufactured rock in the store, but people go for 'em."

Robert showed him Teo's rock with its etched Joshua tree and clack-mark edges.

"Ever see one of these?"

"Been a while," Baker said, "but when I was a kid, all the time. The artist who made 'em's long gone, turned out a hundred or so a week. Back then, my family bought all he made, sold 'em for a quarter apiece. My dad put one in my Christmas stocking. Don't know what became of it."

Baker didn't recall Carlos or Teo off their photos—four other clerks helped out here, too, and Baker had turnover on top of that—but ID'ing the brothers in this store was secondary to Robert now. Carlos and Teo had been to this store. First, with Vincent and Zara, way back when. And each of them, at different times, in the last two years.

He brought Erik up to speed in the car: "Carlos came to the West Entrance and stopped at the Tortoise. Once he saw that those etched rocks were history, he substituted stamped rocks, the closest thing he could find, and had 'em framed. That's where Teo bought Delfina's rock, too. All because back in the '60s, Vincent stopped there. Somebody—Vincent, Zara, the boys?—paid fifty cents for two etched rocks and took 'em back to LA."

"You're killing it," Erik had said.

After they picked up supplies in Joshua Tree, they made Indian Cove around dark, unloading stacks of avocado firewood, food, and sleeping bags from the Yukon. Their secluded site butted up against an enormous boulder mound with its own fire pit; an iron grill on a swivel lay across the top of it, ready to go.

As part of Wonderland of Rocks, Indian Cove lived up to that name. Once the sun dropped from sight, the pale sky dripped indigo onto the horizon, darkening until thousands of stars punctured the overhead palette. After reconnoitering in the dark—only ten other campers—they built a fire and downed two bottles of wine, four buttered baked potatoes, and two sixteen-ounce rib eyes.

Robert fed the fire pit till it blazed and radiated heat across the dry air. Lying in his bag, watching the sky, Robert understood their long stretches of silence. He felt small, yet very much a part of whatever *it all* was, and tomorrow, he and Erik would be two men—doubters might call them *two deranged men*—scouring this desert for hidden treasure.

From what he'd read, Robert knew they would be in good company. The Mojave brimmed with legends of crackpots and cranks, and the Iron Door cave topped the list. William Keys, a famous local, had built his ranch in the middle of nowhere, decades before the park existed, and set up a mining operation. Iron Door, a cave on his ranch, was to this day sealed by Keys' very real iron door. The cave had been used to store both dynamite and to house Keys' schizophrenic son. Whether both uses occurred at the same time, he had no idea.

As the fire died down, Erik spoke first.

"Seriously, dude, what if Ranger Rachael shows up demanding sexual favors?"

Given the setting, Robert had expected something more profound. "Well, the law's real clear. She's a federal official—comply, or you'll do serious time."

"I will not comply, even with my wife out of the country. Even knowing she'd never learn of my indiscretion—unless someone I trust squealed on me."

"As your attorney, I won't rat you out. But for the record? You need to be out here a few days without water before you start talking crazy shit."

Erik laughed, reached over, held out his fist. "Pound it, boy."

Robert pounded Erik's rump roast of a fist and recalled a sparring session when Erik's gloved meat mallet had caught him with a liver shot. His life force had vacated his body, and he lay down on the pavement for a full five minutes. Time for a little payback.

"Hate to admit it, but I love your truck. Next year, I'm gonna buy the new model. Exactly like yours but a bigger engine, bigger gun safe, and a midnight-blue rhino coat."

"A deluxe gun safe for a man with no guns?"

"Yeah, and bigger than yours."

"I don't care for your tone, sir," Erik said. "Next you'll be telling me you'll have a small secret compartment in your hypothetical truck, same as I have in my real truck."

"I'm calling bullshit." Then: "Where?"

"Can't tell you, Beach, it's a *secret* compartment. Maybe after you show me the money . . ."

CHAPTER 37

At daybreak, Robert and Erik drove back to the park's West Entrance and into the park proper. At the actual gate, Quail Springs Road turned into Park Boulevard, which wound through the park another twenty-five miles before ending at the North Entrance.

It didn't take long for their first setback. Fifteen minutes along Park Boulevard, Robert realized his theory about Stone Temple and Jesus was dubious at best. What was marked in his guidebook as a gravel road to Stone Temple turned out to be an eight-mile hiking trail, no vehicles allowed. Jesus running money changers from the temple was a great metaphor, but Carlos hiking in to Stone Temple did not compute.

Robert told Erik: "No way Carlos made a sixteen-mile round trip hike into Stone Temple weighed down with money. Two or three trips, more likely."

"You or me, solo, it's two days' work. Him? Never."

They decided, too, that Carlos would've worked alone. Neither of them could imagine him asking for help. *Excuse me, sir? I'll pay you a thousand dollars to hide this bag at Stone Temple. Mark it with a cairn, then come back here and tell me where you put it.*

"And no peeking inside the bag," Erik added.

That left them to find Jesus at Skull Rock, farther into the park. As the SUV rolled along, Robert watched the rising sun spill onto the desert floor. The setting was unlike anything either of them had ever seen. Mile after mile of Joshua trees swarmed a vast alluvial plain, an army of hairy-limbed evergreens throwing crazed morning shadows across sand and rock.

Enormous mounds of boulders—the same ochre-colored rocks as back at Indian Cove—seemed to have sprung out of nowhere. Autonomous mounds of White Tank monzogranite surrounded by miles of flat desert floor. Occasionally, a ten-ton circular boulder appeared, resting on top of a flat rock shelf; some rock faces had joints so tight, they looked like a stonemason's master work. A circle balanced on a straight line. Unnatural-looking, but there it was, advanced cosmic design by the celestial landscaper.

They pulled into Skull Rock's parking lot. Robert already knew this place differed from Stone Temple in a good way: the massive rock rested just fifty yards away, across the road.

"Gotta be it," Erik said.

Robert's pulse quickened as they neared the rock's base, first tourists to arrive. The back quarter of this fifty-foot-tall boulder had sheared off, rounding it into a cranium. On its front, facing them: a broad forehead. Below that, two deeply indented erosion-eyes and nasal openings, all of it creating the eerie look of a human skull, minus its jaw or mouth.

"A simple walk for Carlos," Robert said. "Right around dark or at daybreak. Two or three easy trips with the money, even for him."

Erik nodded. "Hides it, buries it, in and out."

Where, though? Robert wondered.

The rock was a popular spot, so Carlos would've hidden the money somewhere out of the way. So they separated and started searching, hoping, too, that Carlos' cairn would mark the money's location.

"Or Karen," Erik added.

After the better part of that day, they met by the Yukon for their fifth water break. They hadn't ignored a single crevice, gulley, rock bed, or diggable sandy spot, but both came up empty-handed.

"Maybe we were too worried about telling the rangers what we were looking for," Erik said.

Robert agreed, despite Gia's legal memo: right now, they didn't have much choice. "We'll have to pick their brains somehow."

Out of the park, on their way down Quail Springs Road, Robert finally picked up a signal and a text from Philip Fanelli about digging into Evelyn's background at her old law firm:

Bradley Holtzmann called back. Evelyn Levine was covered by NDA with his firm. Couldn't get him to violate it. Nerve of that guy!

A nondisclosure agreement. Same thing Robert had with Fanelli at his old firm, meaning that Bradley wasn't at liberty to discuss Evelyn with Philip or anyone else.

Robert texted back, half joking: Maybe Bradley's old flame, Dorothy, will have better luck?

When he finished, he saw that Erik was pulling into the ranger station. A thought struck Robert.

"Forget it. C'mon, let's try Baker first."

The one-armed owner of the Tortoise. Erik liked the idea.

"What's our cover?" Robert asked.

"Our office scavenger hunt."

"Done."

Inside the Tortoise, Baker welcomed the idea of helping two city boys figure out desert clues.

"High school, college reunion, what?" Baker asked.

"For our business," Robert said. "We work for a software start-up."

"What's it called?"

"Priya," Robert said. "It means *beloved* in Sanskrit."

Erik looked at him like a proud father.

"Let's hear what you got," Baker said.

First, Robert tried out the Jesus rock-formation angle; Baker came up empty.

"Try these, then," Robert said. He began riffing on *Rx Samuelson*: *"Rex Samuelson? Doctor Samuelson? Samuelson? Samuelson's pharmacy?"*

"Not ringing a bell," Baker said.

Using *Samuels* instead of *Samuelson*, Robert gave him each variation again.

"Drawing a blank," Baker said, but he was into it. "Gimme some more."

Erik asked, "How about *Truth* and *Faith?*"

"A church maybe?" Baker asked. "Synagogue? A priest? The Bible?"

To be polite, Robert wrote down *church*.

"Church," Erik added. "That's strong."

"How about *Granted?*" Robert asked. *"A real chiseler?"*

"Damn, damn, damn," Baker said. "Keep going."

"O'Meira?"

"Nope."

Then Robert added O'Meira variations: *O'Malley, O'Reilly, O'Neil?*

Three *nopes* in return.

Robert read, *"Don't Forget! Angle Mann, Sticky Mickey, Meet Karen, A real prick, Your Decision!"*

Baker slammed his only hand on the counter.

"Got two of 'em! *Angle Mann* and *a real prick*. That's *Engelmann*. He's the first botanist to write about the prickly pear cactus grows around here, and believe me, when it pricks you, you remember it. Get it?"

"Nailed it!" Erik said. He started to go for a high five with Baker, then thought twice.

Robert wrote: *Engelmann . . . a real prick = Prickly Pear Cactus.*

Baker said, "Got a question, though—did you say *granted?* Or *granite?*"

"Granted," Robert said. "Try *granite* if it helps."

"Back to the beginning!" Baker said. "Go back, go back!"

Robert read it all to him again.

Then Baker asked, "Why do you keep saying *Rex* and *Doctor* and *pharmacy* around Samuelson?"

Robert showed him the *Rx.* "That's our clue."

"I get it, like a prescription. That's what messed me up," Baker said. "I'm going with *rocks* not *Rx*. As in *Rocks Samuelson*—as in *Samuelson's Rocks.*" Then to Erik: "High five, big man!"

Baker raised his only arm and smacked Erik's raised hand.

As Baker explained those rocks and their eccentric Swedish namesake, he filled out the *Truht* and *Faiht* clues, too.

"What's the prize for winning?"

"Trip to Long Beach," Erik said.

"Shit, all this work for Long Beach?"

"Still a start-up," Robert added.

Before he left, Robert bought $500 worth of *objets and other stuff,* and while Erik took a seven-minute shower around back, Robert used his one cell bar to return Gia's earlier call.

Gia told him she and Delfina—in the back seat—were headed down to Venice Beach and mentioned Evelyn had called her earlier in the day.

"She okay?" Robert asked.

Gia said, "Weak but okay. She wondered why there were so many people at Carlos' house, so I dropped Delfina at Evelyn's and went over to check it out."

Robert winced. "What was going on?"

"See if Reyes' photos help," she said. "Had a grill outside, cooking up some *tacos de carnitas, de pollo y enchiladas.* A steam tray with homemade *tamales, chilaquiles.* Oh, and a tasty *salsa de mole.*"

"*Tasty?* You ate over there?" he asked.

"*Sí, Roberto. Delicioso.* Plus, some beers and maybe twenty shots of Patrón. I lost count."

She'd been driving; he knew better.

"How'd the place look?" he asked, closing his eyes.

Gia lowered her voice. "Bangin'. Like an upscale strip club, middle of the day. Stripper pole and four *chicas* from his side of town."

"Dressed in . . . ?"

"Not much but tasteful. Twenty or so elderly gentlemen from, I think, around that neighborhood, or maybe he cleaned out Social Security, bused 'em over. Anyway, it was poppin', *mi amor, y todos los viejos estaban muy excitados.*" Loose translation: All the old dudes were sexed up.

"How'd he do on the sale?"

"Reyes, guessing, said about thirty thousand after hard costs."

"What!" He'd been expecting ten grand, tops. "For that stuff?"

"Not exactly. He had a marketing strategy."

"The girls?"

"*Un poquito.*" She explained how it worked. Two girls would take one guy into Carlos' love-pit bedroom. One girl took pictures while the other two messed around on that zebra four-poster.

Messed around, he wondered.

She ran down Reyes' fee structure: "Picture on the bed with a half-clothed girl, a hundred bucks. Girl's top off, two fifty. Both girls with tops off, five hundred. One girl naked, a thousand. And so on."

And so on? he wondered again. Had he sponsored a whorehouse for Delfina's trust?

"I'd toss out that bed," Gia advised him.

No longer wondering: *Yes, he had.*

Her pictures came through. Old dudes on the bed messing around with those *chicas*. Sitting in those leather chairs, girls in their laps, kings for a day.

So what, he decided. *Nobody died.*

Just to make sure: "Nobody died, right?"

"Not that I heard about." Then he knew she was laughing. "Somebody wants to talk to you," Gia said, and Delfina took over the phone.

Visiting over at Evelyn's, Delfina said, had been fun.

"Evelyn gave me juice and cookies, and we talked about lots of stuff."

"What kind of stuff?"

"Well, she had pictures, and I asked about them. One was of her house where she grew up. With her daddy and her mom when Evelyn was a teenager."

The picture, Robert recalled. *The studio limo driver with his wife and teenage daughter.*

"And then Evelyn and just her daddy when he was real old. He was smiling, and they were standing in front of their house, but it wasn't their house anymore."

He recalled Evelyn's father, his demented smile.

Delfina told him, "Evelyn dated a movie star, and he was so handsome."

"Chet Jordan," he said. "He was a real big star."

"Like Dwayne Johnson?"

The Rock? More like Cary Grant.

"Just like Dwayne Johnson," he said.

"Evelyn said he was real rich but not happy because he was broken inside. He looked sad in the picture with her."

After that, they'd taken out Evelyn's trash, and she'd let Delfina use the garage door opener to raise her garage door.

"Evelyn calls it *a clicker*; it was so fun," she said.

She asked about his camping supplies.

"I ate some of the trail mix, but a bear ate most of it because he was hungry."

"Oso Polar!"

"Yes, and we used your sunscreen and the insect repellent. That was very thoughtful of you, Delfina. We really needed it, especially Mr. Jacobson."

"I know. He's so white. Do you still have my rock?" she asked.

"In my pocket," he said. "Keeping it safe for you and your daddy."

"Okay," she said. "We're at the beach now."

Then Gia came on again.

"Any idea where Reyes is?" he asked her.

"'On the trail to Glendale,' he told me, whatever that means." Following Sharon Sloan.

"Oh, and he said he was taking over as your top investigator." Reyes jerking Erik's chain. "Find the do-re-mi?" she asked.

"No dough yet, but trending, yes," he said.

After Robert finished his own seven-minute shower, he huddled with Erik. They both wanted to hit the park ASAP but had concerns about rangers patrolling campsites for parked cars, checking permits, ending the park's day in good order.

"Trail bikes, right?" Robert asked.

"Bikes it is."

Afterward, they'd drive the Beast as close as possible to the park's West Entrance gate and from there, ride into the park proper.

The girl renting bikes said, "Raining cats and dogs next valley over. Sure you two want bikes?"

Erik told her, "Cats and dogs we can handle. Unless it's raining buckets, we're going."

At the time, Robert smiled at the exchange.

A couple of hours later, there was nothing to smile about.

CHAPTER 38

Nothing about the desert agreed with Kiril or, for that matter, with Penko. Dry air, windblown sand, deceitful cactus with soft spikes that, if touched, caused pain and blistering.

"I ever get chance, I murder the desert," Penko said, drunk again.

Kiril wondered: *Has Penko been sober once since we followed the Yukon SUV from LA? Followed it into this godless high desert?*

Even so, Kiril shared Penko's frustration. Only one Bulgarian desert existed: Pobiti Kamani. The Stone Desert, near the Black Sea. He'd never bothered with it. Sand dunes, rock columns, and lizards, all better left to eurozone tourists with their strap sandals, socks, and short pants.

From the start, following that tricked-out Yukon in this flat terrain, with its five-mile straightaways, had presented difficulties, starting with the SUV's first turn off the main highway. Right after, the SUV had pulled into the ranger station. If he'd had any idea what the SUV was about to do, he'd have never made the turn and exposed himself. As it was, he parked on the shoulder, a hundred yards up the road from the station.

"Why don't I kill them right now?" Penko had asked, looking back at the ranger station.

In the ranger station? Are you insane?

"We must wait," Kiril told him.

"For what?"

"*Gospodar* will tell me when, and we cannot disobey him."

Hearing *Gospodar*, Penko quieted down. Kiril was lying to Penko. *Gospodar* had already ordered the right time to kill them—but what was the use in Penko knowing beforehand?

The same went for the two *kurovi glavi* in the back seat: Niko and Petar. All attitude with their gold chains, mirrored shades, and headphones, heads bobbing to Russian rap, loaded on rakia and talking their constant street shit.

Two turds, Penko called them. The same two *Gospodar* picked to man the Westlake and Playa Vista offices, back when that charade was going on. The pair of men offered so little, Kiril was certain they'd been sent along for only one reason: to make sure that the money, once in hand, came back to San Bernardino.

So far, no one had noticed Ilina's rental car trailing them.

"First," he'd told her, "you follow my car to the desert. Check in to motel." He gave her the name. "Buy food in LA, and do not leave your room. I will come for you."

"How long should I wait?" Ilina had asked.

"Until I come for you," he'd said again.

But absolute clarity on this point mattered to Ilina. She was driving at something else and had pressed him. "How many days before I know you will not come?"

"Three days," he said. "But I will come for you. You believe that, right?"

Enough so that she'd cashed out all her bank accounts—$30,000 total. And he'd believed enough in her to trust her with his own $50,000: his life.

She'd been afraid; he didn't blame her.

For the first time since arriving in America, she'd slipped her higher-ups. As far as they knew, she was with a regular client. But her phone—its location function still switched on—was in an off-lobby restroom towel dispenser, not upstairs in her room.

After eight hours, Ilina would be considered missing. After that, Kiril believed Ilina would rather kill herself than return to LA and face the streets, unprotected like the girl, Radka.

On Kiril's first night in the desert, keeping tabs on the lawyer and cop had proved difficult. Indian Cove campsite lay at the end of a straight road with no turnoffs. Only one reason to drive in—camping. And only one narrow entrance into the campground, making their own entry by car too obvious.

The best option: he and Penko had jogged over to the campsite perimeter. Taking a high position on nearby rocks, they would watch their targets for the night. If at any time the two other men took off on foot into the desert, he and Penko could simply follow them from there and do what needed doing.

Holes in his plan? Many. It was the best he could do on the fly.

That night on the rocks, watching the men camped next to a fire pit, Kiril cursed the wind that found him, even hunkered down in a crevasse. By 10:00 p.m., Kiril had run back to the car, banged on the window, and jumped inside. Niko and Petar were passed out, drunk.

Kiril took the keys from Niko, drove to Ilina's motel, and found her room. The light was on inside. When she let him in, she was crying. No surprise; often, she cried. About a sweetheart back home or about one of her customers, he did not know.

"What is wrong?" she asked.

"Cold. Blankets, I need them."

Top of her closet, she found two and handed them over. He pulled her to him and told her, "Whoever it is makes you sad, you will forget about him with time."

"I know," she said. "Stay warm, be *careful.*"

An hour later, Kiril climbed back up the Indian Cove rocks and tossed Penko one of the blankets.

"Don't need," Penko said, draining his last bottle of rakia.

"Good," Kiril said, taking both.

He passed the rest of the night in peace; when he woke before dawn, Penko had passed out between two rocks. Below him, the targets stirred. Once Kiril saw them packing up the SUV—leaving, not trekking into the desert—he boot-heeled Penko. Hard enough to break a normal man's ribs. Penko stirred.

"We go now," Kiril told him, dropping the blankets between boulders.

In thirty minutes, coffee and Egg McMuffins in hand, they waited on the highway until that SUV exited Indian Cove Road. Twenty seconds later, Kiril pulled out to follow.

Again, everything conspired against him—stoplights, next to no traffic, and long straightaways.

Once into the desert—at a place called Boy Scout Trail—Kiril rolled up on them too fast. The SUV had already stopped. Too late to back up and take a position. Kiril drove past until he came to a parking lot a few miles down Park Boulevard.

He wondered what to do next—go back and risk detection, or wait here—when the SUV passed by. Pulling out and lagging behind them again, Kiril caught his first break. The SUV parked in a lot across from a place named Skull Rock; he pulled onto the shoulder, five hundred yards back.

Rest of that day, through binoculars, Kiril watched the two men searching the area; his mind wandered to his youth in the Pirin Mountains, south of Sofia. Camping in the Rila range to prey on tourists. His favorite targets had been the spiritualists who danced and meditated near the monastery. Dressed only in white robes, they left their passports at their lodgings—for safekeeping with their trusted Draganov guide. That same day, those passports would find their way onto Sofia's black market.

Grown men and women dancing in white robes? Kiril wondered. *They would fit in on Westside of LA.*

By afternoon, back from Skull Rock, the two men had come up empty-handed; they'd driven their SUV past Kiril's stakeout, out of the park.

Two hours later, Kiril knew the situation had changed at last: the two men rented trail bikes, parked the SUV, and rode the bikes back into the park. Three and a half miles in, they steered their bikes off-road, ditched them, and began hiking into the desert.

"This will be it," Kiril told Penko, pulling a U-turn. "Ready to kill them?"

"More than ready," Penko said.

"Kill them and get home," Niko said. "I have tickets to Hollywood Bowl concert."

Kiril could've just as easily asked the three men: "Tell me this, Niko, Petar, Penko: Is each of you ready to die by my hand?"

As he parked at the North View Trail parking lot, his thoughts shifted to Ilina's tears last night. Best girl of the group, she was strong, smart, and beautiful. Even though her body was his, he thought about asking her who it was she cried for. But what good would that do? She would lie or tell the truth, and still he would not know the answer. Better he earn her respect first and worry later about earning love.

Jarring him from his reverie, the sound of Penko vomiting bile and booze into the parking lot storm drain. So Kiril opened the Ford's trunk. Instead of guns, he'd picked Tasers, knives, and telescoping batons.

"In a national park, possession of firearms is legal," *Gospodar* told him. "But noise and ballistics tests, who needs that?"

Kiril agreed. Firearm reports would carry for miles out here. One word of a discharged weapon to rangers could kill his chances of escaping this flat, hostile land.

Kiril and the others ran from the parking lot to the ditched bikes, about a hundred yards off Park Boulevard; they climbed partway up a nearby rock formation, where Kiril glassed the two hikers out in the desert.

For the first time since this trip started, Kiril smiled. *Guns to kill those two? With Penko along, guns would be unfair.*

CHAPTER 39

Walking toward Samuelson's Rocks, Robert and Erik agreed: John Samuelson qualified as a desert legend. According to Baker, Samuelson had worked his own mining operation, won a gunfight, did serious jail time off it, and had an unquenchable thirst for solitude. Even though Samuelson's gunfight and jail time happened back in LA, Robert and Erik awarded him legend status anyway, given what was carved into the rocks spread out ahead of them.

"A Swedish immigrant," Robert said. "One of your crazy homies."

"Respect," Erik said.

After riding into the park, they'd ditched their bikes off-road at a rock-mound formation and began the manageable hike toward these rocks. Each wore a near-empty backpack. They believed the trust's money lay less than a mile across the sandy plain ahead, where a short stretch of granite rocks jutted from the desert floor.

"No path," Baker said, "leads out to the rocks."

The rocks remained an island of private property inside a public park. The hike out to them appeared to be flat and slightly down-sloping, but the terrain was actually more a series of dips and rises, sandy waves invisible to their unpracticed eyes. Along the way, they avoided the occasional prickly pear and let themselves be awestruck by armies of Joshua trees, burnished gold by the last strands of sand-filtered desert daylight.

Halfway there, Robert turned around to check their bearings. Park Boulevard had blended into the desert. He had no way to locate it, other than knowing it lay just beyond that rock formation.

"Hey, look at that," he called out.

Erik had walked forty yards ahead. By now, given the dips, only his head and upper torso were visible. Robert caught up with him; together, they eyed an apocalyptic bank of gray-granite weather rolling over the mountains beyond Park Boulevard, tumbling down onto the distant desert plain.

"How far away, you think?" Erik asked.

"Three, four miles," Robert said, a layman's guess.

"Gonna get wet," Erik said.

"Gonna be worth it," Robert said.

They took off running toward Samuelson's Rocks.

❧

Kiril crouched beside Penko and the other two halfway up in the rocks; he again glassed the two hikers. Without binoculars, the pair was already impossible to pick out of the landscape. Even so, Kiril believed the time to act was at hand—the other men had ridden in on bikes and worn backpacks for the first time. And they hiked into the desert even now, with night coming on.

Through his binoculars, he watched the pair start running toward the large bank of rocks in front of them; nothing in his guidebook clued him to that formation's name.

Kiril stood up. "It is time."

"My God," Niko said, pointing behind them. Petar even removed his mirrored Oakleys.

That storm marched down the face of a mountain. Thunder rumbled against lightning that jabbed a doomsday sky. Kiril's hair tingled with electricity.

They made the desert floor beside the two bikes; the first fat raindrops pelted the sand.

Kiril thoughts turned to the lawyer and the cop:

Find my money now, you two. Find it, so I can take it and get out of this desert.

❦

Even before reaching the rocks, Robert knew they were right on target. Just ahead, he singled out two carved words on Samuelson's closest granite inscription: *Truht and Faiht*. Misspelled, same as Carlos' work notes; both words, and many others, had been chiseled into granite.

Five feet tall, Samuelson's Rock of Faiht and Truht must have broken from a larger section of stone and fallen to earth, where it leaned at a twenty-degree angle against the rocks behind it.

As they stopped in front of it, Robert took in the eccentric Swede's labor-intensive inscription:

THE.ROCK.

OF.FAIHT.

AND. TRUHT.

NATURE. IS. GOD.

THE. KEY. TO. LIFE.

IS. CONTACT.

EVOLUTION. IS. THE MOTHER.

AND FATHER OF MANKINE.
WITHOUT THEM. WE. BE. NOTHING.

JOHN SAMUELSON
1927

Each letter, other than signature and date, ran five inches tall. Robert found it hard to imagine anyone with patience enough to use extra punctuation. Each period must've taken hours to chisel by hand.

"Unbelievable," Erik said.

And it was. Baker had mentioned nine other rocks nearby with Samuelson's inscriptions, touching on everything from the genius of Henry Ford to the greed of banker Andrew Mellon and of all politicians with their hands in your pocket.

"Me and Samuelson might've hit it off," Erik had told Baker.

At the moment, Robert tried to imagine John Samuelson's typical day. Out here in the raw elements, his house somewhere nearby, long ago burned to the ground. This place vibed *shrine* to Robert. Shrine to a half-crazed, hard-assed man doing exactly what he wanted to do, saying to hell with anyone who didn't like it.

"See a cairn anywhere?" Robert asked.

"Nope," Erik said. "You do the honors."

Robert dropped to his knees in front of the rock, reached into the dark space behind it. Nothing at first. Then he reached in farther, shoulder-deep.

"Talk to me," Erik said.

"*Nada* so far."

He began circling his hand. At his circle's nadir, he touched something man-made—cloth or canvas—and grabbing what felt like a strap, he pulled. It weighed forty pounds or so, and as he dragged the canvas backpack into the light, the first raindrops splattered the rocks.

Erik knelt beside him. "Can't believe it."

"Can't, either," Robert said.

He unzipped the backpack's main compartment. Stacks of currency lay inside. Pulling the first stack out, he counted ten $1,000 bills. The other nine stacks were the same: a total of $100,000.

They both gazed at what lay underneath those bills: loose granite stones.

Taking out one of them, Robert looked around; rocks like it littered the area. Carlos hadn't hiked them in. He'd filled his backpack once he was here.

"A hundred grand," Erik said. "That's it?"

"You shitting me, Carlos?" Robert asked.

Searching the side pockets, Robert found Carlos' handwritten note, read it out loud:

Teo, if it's you, you know how to find the rest. You already know I love you.

I'm sorry. Don't Forget!

Your brother, Carlos.

If you're not Teo? Go pound sand! Ha!

"*Ha?*" Robert said. "That's it? *Ha!*"

Erik sat down, rested his back against the Rock of Faiht and Truht.

"Forgive me, Jesus. I hate Carlos Famosa's guts."

Robert couldn't find any words. So he did some simple math instead: $18,000 cash, plus the $5,000 from the hashish, another $30,000 from Reyes' *Risky Business* event, plus this $100,000. That meant about $150,000 in the trust's kitty.

If this is all there is . . .

Erik sprang to his feet.

"Heads up. Behind us, no kidding."

Robert stood. Looked upslope, back the way they'd come, didn't see anything.

"What?"

"Wait," Erik said, slinging Carlos' backpack onto his shoulder, along with his own pack.

Another ten seconds, Robert spotted them. A quarter mile away—four men. One in the lead. All of them now emerging from one of those dips, running headlong at them, like they were pulling that dark storm behind them.

"Boris," Robert said.

"Let's book," Erik said.

In sync, they ran around Samuelson's huge pile of granite rocks, taking themselves farther away from Park Boulevard but putting these rocks between them and their pursuers.

Along the way, Robert pictured that big man, out in front of the others. Not running with the grace of a long-distance runner, his legs pistoned like an NFL running back, punishing anyone in their path. That fierce gait looked familiar—but he couldn't place it.

Still keeping Samuelson's rocks between them and Boris, Robert and Erik made three on-the-fly notes: Boris wanted the money, Boris would kill them no matter what, and stay together.

They stopped at the far end of Samuelson's Rocks and stashed all the bills in Robert's pack. Erik grabbed Carlos' rocks-only pack, and they took off with both packs, their path still directly away from that rock formation, their pursuers, and Samuelson's Rocks.

A few minutes later, Robert stopped. Let Erik run on until his body descended into the next dip. Erik's shallow footprints in the hard-packed sand were invisible to Robert in the growing gloom.

Robert shouted, "Stop!"

Then Robert, his tread light, joined Erik. In the decline together, they started running in the dip, perpendicular to their earlier route. Invisible, he hoped, to their pursuers' upcoming field of vision. An edge, no matter how small, as he and Erik headed for Hidden Valley. That's where Park Boulevard swung deep into the desert. Where they'd hit the blacktop, turn on the afterburners, and leave Boris behind.

He looked behind them. Visibility in the storm had compressed from five miles to five hundred yards, if that. And so far, no Boris.

The storm. Good for me, bad for Boris, he was thinking.

But he was wrong.

In the wetter sand, their steps left easy-to-follow tracks. Nothing to be done; they kept churning through it. Another two hundred yards, according to plan, Erik slung away that rock-filled pack. Boris would stop to check it out or grab that extra weight on the fly. Either way, it would slow them down.

"How you hanging?" Robert asked.

"Okay. You?"

"Easier'n the beach."

They'd been thinking along the same lines: good thing they were in shape. Otherwise, they'd be on their knees in the downpour, playing a losing game of *Let's Make a Deal* with Boris, whose endgame was a given: Robert and Erik, stripped of all money, dead in the desert.

The rain still came hard and strong. The lightning—biblical. He'd never experienced it so close outdoors, where branches of it branched off other branches and struck the desert floor. A cosmic light show to watch from behind double-pane plate glass—not while running for your life.

For the next five minutes, clothing soaked, breathing steady, they kept a good pace, picking their path across the soaked sand. Swiping his iPhone screen clear of raindrops, Robert used its compass to keep them roughly east-northeast—on track for Hidden Valley—jumping rivulets of rainwater that flowed left to right in front of them across the sloping desert floor.

Not tired, not yet, but it was coming. Back of his mind, fatigue was there, and with it would come fear.

Delfina's rock . . . Teo's rock . . . whoever's rock it was . . . bounced in his pocket. He pictured Gia and Delfina waving goodbye in front of Gia's house.

As if he were making his final reckoning, his thoughts turned to the farm. His family. A dominating uncle; his deranged father; his loving, weak-willed mother; the farm's wise foreman, Luis; and his once best friend, Rosalind. All the years he hadn't seen them and maybe never would again.

Still running, he looked over his shoulder. Lightning lit the world behind him. Even though visibility was now a hundred yards or so, at least no one had appeared through the sheets of rain and fog and darkness.

"Don't see 'em," Robert said.

"Pretend they're right on our ass," Erik said.

Robert caught the look on Erik's face. Knew that Erik's wife and kids rolled through his mind in ways Robert didn't fully comprehend. Five years knowing Erik, Robert couldn't recall seeing this expression. He'd only glimpsed it. Most recent, when Erik saw that trio of wasted bullies who'd picked a fight with Teo—a father just protecting his child.

Today's look went even deeper—Erik preparing for war.

Glancing back again—bad news this time. That largest of the four pursuers carried Carlos' rock-filled back. A forty-pound pack, and still this one ran ahead of the others.

And he spotted Robert the moment Robert saw him. Motioned to the others behind him.

"Still with us," Robert said.

"They catch us, they're dead men," Erik said.

Robert dug deep into places better forgotten. Deep hatred. Moments on a Capitola clifftop, fighting for his life with Jack Pierce. On the beach below . . . Jack Pierce drowning . . . Robert's heart hardened enough to kill.

And he realized: he'd twice seen that monster man's gait. Bursting past him on the Santa Monica stairs, and jogging though Gia's neighborhood, his hood pulled up. Plus, Delfina's unexplained, cracked-open bedroom door. The thought of this man coming through the kitchen door off Gia's backyard surged through him; his heart went rest-of-the-way cold.

"Dead men," Robert said.

The next fresh rivulet ahead held more water than others he'd seen. Instead of jumping it, Robert grabbed Erik.

"Follow the water?" Robert shouted over the deluge.

"Yeah!" Erik shouted back.

Tracking it downslope another five hundred yards, they reached the vast plain's low point: a riverbed cut into the desert. A hundred feet across at its widest; sheer five-foot-high sand banks; a channel littered with dead creosote, rocks, and brush; a wet sand bottom pooling from the downpour.

"Like it?" Robert asked.

Erik's answer—he jumped into the channel. Robert landed beside him. They shared a look.

"They catch us . . . ?" Erik asked.

"Dead men," Robert said.

They took off again, using the closest channel bank to shield themselves from Boris. As they ran, Robert saw a place where the far bank had caved in. A Joshua tree had recently toppled into the riverbed, an event hundreds, maybe thousands, of years in the making.

As they neared the next bend, Robert saw their pursuers. Erik saw them, too: four men lit by an electric sky, then cloaked again in rain and darkness. All of them now inside the channel bed together. Inside those five-foot walls.

Given enough time, Robert had a couple of ideas that might help give them the upper hand.

"The tree?" Robert asked.

"The tree," Erik said.

They dashed across the channel, back to that fallen Joshua tree. After clambering up its gangplank-narrow trunk onto the bank, they pushed and kicked its trunk back into the channel. They took the high ground.

Their pursuers ran past as Robert unzipped his pack, removed two coils of rope, two stainless-steel thermoses, and his Swiss Army knife. The emergency flares—those he tossed to Erik.

"For up close," Robert said.

"Pop it, stick it down his goddam throat," Erik growled.

Meaning the big man, Robert knew.

Robert dumped out a thermos, filled it with wet sand. He tied a rope knot around its plastic screw-in-top handle. Swung in a three-to-five-foot circle, it was a weapon. Hit a man's head just right—a deadly weapon.

Out in the channel, Robert saw one pursuer stop. Look right at him up on the bank. He stopped and called out to the other men, who returned and gathered around him.

Their leader, Robert figured, was wearing that camouflage jacket and cap. Robert finished knotting off a second thermos weapon.

Out in the channel, he saw that camoed guy grab Carlos' backpack from that badass lead runner, kneel, and unzip it . . .

❧

Once Kiril opened the backpack and saw the stones, his big-money plans with Ilina went to shit. Before he even stood up, another idea born of fear and desire jumped front and center. Why not slit Penko's throat, kill Niko and Petar? Do it all now instead of later, like he'd planned. Do it now, and for a while trick the pair he'd just chased across this desolation. His only hope for getting the money rested with those two on the bank.

Before he could act, Penko roared in rage and rushed the sand bank. It yielded to his force as he leaped up, clawing for a grip, sliding him back into the channel. The harder he tried, the more that sand yielded.

Tire yourself, Penko. Easier for me to kill you.

Kiril told Niko and Petar: "Go to that tree, climb onto the bank. I will rush them with Penko."

Once they took off, Kiril gave a thumbs-up to that lawyer on the riverbank. The one looking at him.

In his mind, he heard Ilina telling him, *Whatever you do to make it happen is already forgiven.*

Then Kiril watched Petar and Niko clamber onto the tree's unsteady trunk. That put them about three feet from the bank. The lawyer ran toward them as Kiril drew his blade from its scabbard and shielded it inside his sleeve.

🜚

Robert reached the Joshua tree where those two gangster-looking guys were making their move up its trunk. Waiting till the first one got closer—four feet away, he guessed—Robert started swinging his three-pound thermos in a tight circle. As that first man looked up to leap ashore, Robert aimed for the guy's temple. He missed low—the thermos struck his windpipe. The man clutched his throat, gagging as he tumbled into his comrade; the pair wound up tangled in the channel.

At that point, Robert saw the man in camo calling to the fallen pair; the one who could still stand ran back to him. It seemed impossible—the leader gave him a second thumbs-up. Then again.

What the hell . . . ? He's helping us?

Robert jogged back to Erik, who kept booting the animal lunging up the bank. Next try, the monster got his elbows onto the bank, and Erik caught him in the forehead with his heel.

In the channel, face bloodied, the monster tasted the blood dripping into his mouth.

Pointing at Robert, he screamed, "I will take young girl in room where I watch her sleep." Then to Erik: "I will rape your sons in your yard! In that tree house you build when I go back to—"

That's all it took.

"Don't!" Robert screamed. Too late.

Erik had leaped off the bank, feetfirst, striking that big man square in the chest. Both men slammed to the ground, struggling, first one on top, then the other. Erik cracked open his road flare and jammed it into the monster's neck, spewing molten red.

The monster laughed insanely at the pain.

Then on Robert's periphery, the man in camo, the leader, slammed a knife into that second gangster's chest. Another thumbs-up to Robert, another thumbs-up, signaling what? *We're on the same team?*

What the . . . ?

In the channel, the monster caught Erik with a sharp elbow to the jaw and dazed him, sending the flare flying. He rolled Erik off him, regained his feet. Stood over Erik, who tried clearing his head.

No choice now—Robert had to give up the high ground. He made ready to jump down and start swinging the thermos—and that's when they all heard it.

Distant at first, like a surging wind. Then the sound picked up, became a roar, growing.

From his vantage point, Robert saw the flash flood first. A sea of mud and rocks and debris, rolling and churning, the face of it four feet high and growing. The monster saw it, too. No fool, he forgot Erik and ran down the channel, that camouflaged leader not far behind, the water overtaking them.

But Robert's focus was Erik: on the ground, ten feet out from him, five feet below. No way to hoist him up in time.

"Erik!" he screamed. "Grab it!"

Paying out twenty feet of rope, Robert slung Erik the thermos. Erik got to his knees, gave the rope a wrap around his body, tucked the thermos behind his bicep, and clamped down his arm.

"Got you!" Robert screamed.

Erik stood, ran toward him, jumped as high as he could, his feet digging into the riverbank. Not high enough to get out—both of them knew that—even as Robert pulled with all his might. But Erik's momentum and Robert's pull got him just high enough. When that first surge of floodwater reached him, Erik still had a fighting chance, unlike the other men.

They'd be dead as soon as the water hit.

Erik's eyes caught Robert's. Robert nodded.

I got you.

The water swept Erik away.

Robert was instantly on the move, running downstream along the riverbank, dodging several small Joshua trees, knowing that one slip put him in the flood to die with Erik. Looking ahead: a large Joshua tree thirty yards downstream, ten feet back from the riverbank.

But no matter how fast he ran, the torrent rushed faster. He paid out more rope to Erik from his coil as he went.

Erik faced downstream, knees tucked to his chest, Robert's rope wrapped around his body, locked in by that thermos wedged behind his bicep.

Still alive. Still breathing.

That Joshua tree came up fast on Robert. He paid out twenty more feet of slack rope to Erik and ran the other end of the coil around the tree, keeping the rope low on its thick trunk. Once around the tree, then again, hand to hand. Five more feet of rope left when it pulled tight against Erik's body. The tree groaned but held; so did the rope.

Robert watched the flood: the tight rope against the current shot Erik's body underwater. Had he just drowned his friend?

Waiting. Water rising. Tree holding. The rope's angle to the shoreline more and more acute as Erik's submerged body angled closer to shore. Robert tied off the rope and ran to where he guessed the rope ended underwater.

Waiting until Erik—close to the bank now—lunged from the floodwater.

Robert reached out. "Erik!"

Not enough time. Grabbing a breath, Erik went under again. Robert grabbed the rope with both hands. Five tortured seconds passed—Erik lunged free again. Robert dug in both heels and leaned into the rope with all his might. Every force at work—even the floodwater—now helped swing Erik's upper body partway onto the bank.

Erik grabbed Robert around his legs. Robert lay back on the ground, and Erik climbed over him till he was free. Erik collapsed onshore. Robert stood, half dragging, half coaxing Erik another ten yards from the water, where he made it onto all fours, coughed up a mouthful of water-and-sand slurry, then another one, gagging on the horrible mix.

Robert couldn't believe it. Alive, both of them. He leaned back on his elbows, gasping for air.

"You maniac," he said to his dry-heaving friend.

A deep look passed between them—they'd gone into battle together, came out the other side.

Erik raised a weak arm, pointing upstream, behind Robert.

"What?"

"Money . . ." Erik gasped.

Robert stood, whirled. On the bank upstream, his $100,000 backpack floated in a pool of overflow. Not far from the channel and drifting that way.

Running upstream, he summoned reserves he'd never before called on.

Thinking: *Not gonna lose it, not after all this.*

Diving flat at the water, he belly-skimmed across it. Teo's rock dug into his thigh as he grabbed the strap of his errant backpack. He rolled over onto his back in the slush.

Clutching the backpack to his heaving chest, he gazed up into the new night: the storm had passed, and the desert sky was as clear as any sky he could ever remember.

CHAPTER 40

At a Joshua Tree motel that night, Robert lay in the plastic tub, the bathwater running hot on him again. Wrung out beyond anything he could recall, he was still coming to grips with being alive.

Three hours ago, he'd driven Erik to a local ER with a bruised and rope-burned torso. Nothing, they decided beforehand, would be gained by mentioning the four men—one stabbed to death by his partner, the other three surely drowned.

Fortunately, Erik's injuries passed for a rock-climbing snafu. Now, Erik slept in the next room, doped up on narcotics, and Robert found himself reliving the aftermath of what had just happened. Once they'd retrieved their trail bikes, half-buried in rain-slammed sand, they'd ridden out of the park back toward the SUV. Before that, at the North View Trail parking lot, a single car remained.

Belongs to Boris, Robert had been thinking.

"Keep going, I'll catch up," he told Erik, who was grabbing shallow breaths to ease the shooting pain in his ribs.

"Got it," Erik said, and kept going.

Robert rolled into the parking lot, over to a blue Ford sedan. A San Bernardino rental, according to its markings. This blue car, he now recalled, had passed him on Park Boulevard, once or twice at least. The Ford was locked; he peered inside. Nothing of interest to see on the seats or floors; he decided not to press his luck by breaking a window.

And now, lying in his plastic bathtub, he thought about Carlos' backpack note again.

Don't Forget! the note had said.

In each *Argonaut* notice, in Carlos' work notes, Carlos had used the same phrase.

He tried to sort out all the pieces. *San Bernardino*. Sharon *Draganov* Sloan, once nicknamed *Dragon Lady*. Sharon from Glendale, an hour's drive east of San Bernardino.

Reyes' texted reports about Sharon had yielded nothing helpful so far:

Lives in Glendale for sure. Drove home from work. Home near lake. Shopping at Glendale Galleria with two kids. Mediterranean food delivered to her house from Central Cuisine. Had a cousin worked there a few years ago. Yelped it five stars, especially the kabobs. Homegirl Sharon's in for the night.

Good to know if he ever wanted a kabob over that way, but it left Robert with the question: How was a probate lawyer of Bulgarian descent connected to four men who'd just tried to rip off the trust and murder him? The answer seemed impossibly out of reach.

At some point after he'd appeared in probate court, Sharon must've put these killers onto Teo. Then onto him. He remembered what that monster had raged in the channel: that cracked-open door into Delfina's bedroom—that man had been in the room with Delfina. And he knew about Erik's tree house.

How close all of them had come to disaster chilled him. He twisted the tub's hot water handle again.

He'd spoken to Gia a half hour ago: Teo could be brought out of his coma as soon as tomorrow. After that piece of news, Robert had told Delfina how much he appreciated her camping-store buys.

"Especially the rope," he told her.

"Did you go climbing on rocks?"

"No, but we needed rope. We caught an elephant with it, but we let it go."

Delfina liked hearing that, told him: "A man brought over a frame with my Magna Carta Man drawing inside it. Gia and I put it on the wall." Then whispering, "He was fat."

"Mr. Freize," he whispered back. "He's a real nice man."

He lay back in the tub and wondered if this desert trip had put him any closer to answering his client's question: *Why do they want to hurt my daddy?*

He was closer to an answer, he first decided. Then he changed his mind: *No. I'm not closer at all.*

Then there were Carlos' other puzzle pieces: *O'Meira, Sticky Mickey, Your Decision!* Clearly, he didn't have a clue about them; neither had lifelong high-desert resident, Baker.

"Sticky Mickey," Robert mumbled, eyes closing, finally accepting the dead end he'd reached. Knowing he'd done all he could ever do for his client.

Seemed like hours later, Robert bolted from a deep sleep, shivering in cold bathwater. His iPhone on the bathroom floor, his heart jacked, he checked the time. He'd slept twenty-five minutes; he toweled off, got dressed, and grabbed the ice bucket.

From the second floor, he pounded down the concrete exterior balcony. Below him, the empty swimming pool, filled with beer cans and empty tubs of off-brand peanut butter. As he reached for the ice scoop, music drifted to him dimly from across the main drag, out in the world.

At first, he didn't recognize the melody. Maybe it was a recent song, and there wasn't one. He could make out that shit-kicker bar down the highway; he and Erik had driven past it a few times since they'd arrived in the high desert. *Live Music Tonight*, according to black letters on a yellow, backlit sign.

A beer or two. Maybe a few shots to back them up. Exactly what I need.

As he crossed the highway, strains of the Temptations' "I Can't Get Next to You" reached out to him. Closer to the bar, he heard more of that sweet Motown sound.

Passing the sign, he saw the band's name on its flip side. Noticing what it said for the first time, he stopped. Couldn't believe it. His first impulse: to wake Erik, to call Gia. To tell someone who cared how the band billed itself.

Jesus and the Disciples Sing the Temptations.

Inside, the bar brimmed with desert folk. A fifty-and-over crowd, but the first person Robert laid eyes on: Jesus, onstage.

Chica boom, chica boom, Jesus was singing, winding up the number.

A black man in his sixties, backed by two women his age—they had to be the Disciples. One black, one white, wearing Motown-era, sparkling cocktail dresses like the Supremes used to wear.

The lead's given name was Jesus Stone, the bartender said. Jesus played Temptations covers here once a month. Rest of the time, he traveled a small-town cactus circuit.

Robert drained his first beer, ordered another, and listened to Jesus finish his last set with "Get Ready." Guy could sing, that's for sure, and he sang with joy. The same joyful vibe infused the backups, too, even though a third Disciple was out with a bad hip.

Jesus wound up the number, took his bow with the obligatory, "Thank you, thank you very much!" This older crowd started breaking up, filtering out pretty fast.

Robert walked up to Jesus at the bar.

"Jesus, my name is Robert Worth. I came up here from LA, and I need to talk to you. It's very important."

The man turned on his bar stool, smiled. "What's on your mind, son?"

That joy Robert saw earlier wasn't stage presence. There was something about him offstage, too.

"Two men," Robert said. "Teo and Carlos Famosa. Do you know them?"

"No, I don't," Jesus said.

Robert said, "Yes, you do. You must know them. I know that you do."

"Hold on now, Robert. Didn't know them as men, but I did meet two boys, last name Famosa, Teo and Carlos. Didn't know 'em well. Long as I live, though, I'll never forget 'em, and that father of theirs, their mom? Them, too."

Robert tried to keep his thinking steady, his questions simple, but his pulse was racing.

"Carlos and Teo—they never forgot you, either. But I don't know why. Can you tell me why?"

"Not sure about that, but I'll share how I know 'em. Never shared it with anyone else, except my wife, and it's still clear as day inside my head. Want the long or the short of it?"

He'd almost died finding this man.

"Longer the better," Robert said.

"All right, then . . . Back then, back when I met the Famosas, I was a park ranger, but my story started, I guess, well before that. Sure you want the long of it?"

"Going nowhere," Robert said, hitting his beer.

As Jesus Stone's story unfolded, Robert learned the man was from Riverside, a town between the high desert and LA. A senior linebacker, he'd been a high school phenom with college offers when he blew out his ACL.

"And thirty years ago, a blown ACL was all she wrote, but I couldn't accept it. Playing college ball, the NFL, that was my big dream. A kid's dream, but that's how it was."

Robert nodded. His own family came to mind—Robert had some idea what it was like, having the rug pulled out from under your life.

"So I came up here after high school, me and some teammates, and we got drunk for a few days, ran around the desert, caused trouble. Angry, bitter, I was bad company—I mean, the ones I was with, they were going on, and I was stayin' behind—and I got into it with some-body and they took off, left me up here. Had a hundred bucks, no car, and I decided I'd show them. So when they came back, I hid from 'em. Smart, huh?"

Robert smiled. "I understand stubborn."

"Lucky's what it was. I wound up staying. At first, it was I'd show them, but there wasn't no *them*. There's just *me*. But the desert, it works on you, know what I mean?"

"Not really, no."

"Truly, I don't know if the desert finds you or you find the desert, but after a while, you pick up a vibration. I mean, being alone in the park at sunrise or sundown, your place in the world, in the universe, it gets real clear. And if you're paying attention, you take a good, hard look at yourself and count your blessings. Took about six months. After that, I didn't want to leave. Wound up landing a job as a park ranger, met a good woman up here, too—Kay. Got married and lived my life. Only thing missing was kids. Me and Kay were never blessed with 'em."

A blessing. Like Delfina.

"I liked being a ranger, helping folks out. Most are decent, but every once in a great while, you'll run across a jackass."

"Vincent Famosa?" Robert asked.

"One and the same. Got a report, a couple kids running around. Some food went missing from another site, so I went over to where they'd camped. The wife, she was drunk . . ."

"Zara," Robert said.

"*Zara*, right. She was drunk, and the husband, he was an arrogant so-and-so in his city-hustler outfit, saying there might not be any LA to go back to because of . . . can't remember if it was earthquakes or what . . . but somehow this Vincent, *he just knew*. And the woman, she wanted to go hiking, but she was almost too drunk to stand up."

Robert pictured them now in Teo's old desert photo. Zara in hiking shorts. Vincent sitting on that log in his hat, arms crossed, wearing his spit-shined Stacy Adams shoes.

"And then there were the two boys. Nice-looking kids but not getting any direction from the higher-ups, if you dig me?"

"Dig you, Jesus," Robert said, digging how it sounded.

"So I offered to take the boys off their hands for a while, and the parents, they jumped all over it. Got Teo and Carlos in the truck after that, gave 'em each a full canteen, and we drove over to a hike I know. Told 'em it was top secret . . . nobody knew about it except a chosen few."

"Samuelson's Rocks. Faiht and Truht."

Jesus smiled at him. "One of *the chosen few*, sitting right here with me. Now, these two boys didn't get along, and I wanted to let that play out. So middle of the day, I walked them out to the rocks. Must've been a hundred and ten, and I took 'em a long way around . . ."

What Robert heard next came as no surprise: Teo had run ahead and teased Carlos about being slow and weak; pretty soon, Teo had run out of water. That's when Carlos told Teo how stupid he was and told Jesus he wouldn't share his water with Teo.

Famosa family, business as usual, Robert was thinking.

"And all of a sudden, I saw that family's mechanism. Clear to me. Clearer than my own life was to me, know what I'm sayin'?"

"I do," Robert said.

"Found us some boulder shade, sat 'em both down. Told 'em they were brothers and they were supposed to look after each other. 'One of you's fast and strong, and the other one's smart as hell. The two of you ought to lift each other up. Not be selfish with your water, Carlos. And Teo, wait up for your brother; it ain't gonna kill you doing that, is it?'

"Thing is, Robert, and God only knows why—they listened to me. Carlos, he started crying about being selfish, and Teo told Carlos he was sorry for bullying him, teasing him. Things they both musta had in their hearts a long time. And after we left Samuelson's Rocks and went back to the campsite, I let them out the truck, hugged 'em both. And they hugged me, too, I remember. And then, I'll never forget it, both of 'em said: 'Thank you, Jesus.'"

Thank you, Jesus. And there it was. Neither boy ever forgot that moment.

"Right then, though, that shitbird Vincent, he started up. 'C'mon over here, you two. Let's go. Show that man how fast you are, Teo!'" Already setting 'em against each other. That little man, Vincent, trying to set himself above me, too, by bossing the boys. *His* boys, but the thing is, Teo started to run, but he stopped, came back for Carlos, and the two of 'em walked back into the campsite together. Tell ya, if I coulda scooped 'em up right there, taken them home to Kay, we'd'a raised those boys with love, like nature dictates, but . . .'"

Jesus ended that part with a sigh.

Robert felt as if he'd stumbled onto the Famosa tribe's sacred burial site. As if Delfina had chosen him on the Venice Boardwalk to hear every word of it.

Jesus said, "Back then, I knew the owner of the 29 Palms Inn, said she'd put up the Famosas one night, free of charge. So I went back, told Vincent I'd found 'em a place to stay. He made some big-man noise at first, but he wound up taking me up on it. Zara seemed happy about it, too."

A cold breeze hit Robert, gave him a shiver. He looked up—just the air conditioner blowing down on him.

"How are Carlos and Teo doing?" Jesus asked.

Robert had been dreading that question. *What the hell. Just tell him.*

"Carlos died recently. Teo's in a coma; it could go either way."

"Mmm," Jesus said. "I always wondered if they overcame their handicap, how they did in life."

Robert looked Jesus in the eye and gave it to him, straight-up.

"Teo still struggles with drugs and alcohol, but he's fighting for sobriety. He has a beautiful daughter, a real sweetheart, Delfina. Couple of years ago, Teo brought her up here and went by the ranger station—he was looking for you, Jesus, wanted her to meet you. You meant something special to Teo all his life. When he was getting sober, he talked about his trip to the desert. And he never forgot what you told him—about loving his brother. I know that, because he told me he loved Carlos, even if Carlos didn't love him."

"That's something to hear, right there."

"Carlos never forgot you, either. Before he died, I know he was thinking about Samuelson's Rocks, about his hike with you and Teo. He was a CPA, smart, what you picked up on that day. Carlos, he made some big mistakes, but he had tons more courage than people gave him credit for. In his heart . . . in his heart of hearts . . . he wanted to do right by his brother."

Jesus said, "Thanks for that, Robert."

"Your kindness that day rippled through their lives, still does, and I'm so grateful I could share it with you."

They didn't say anything for a minute or so, and he wondered what it was about the Famosas that made him want to cry. He didn't know the answer, but sitting at the empty bar, that's what he did.

Feeling a hand on his shoulder, he heard Jesus say, "Go ahead, Robert. I'll save my tears for later."

⚜

Out in the parking lot, Robert and Jesus walked over to a white Cadillac convertible. A cherry '72 DeVille, Jesus' car, where they exchanged cards.

"We're playing up the road in Twentynine Palms tomorrow night. You stick around, I might drag Kay out of the house to meet you."

Turned out, once Kay had watched a few hundred sets by Jesus and the Disciples and decided she'd done her bit for the band.

"Staying over's not in the cards," Robert said. "One day, I'll make sure Teo brings Delfina up here to meet you and Kay. You're part of her life; she should know who you are."

Jesus lit up hearing that. "My cell's on the card. You ever come up here again, you should stay at the inn, same as the Famosas did. Old adobe bungalows, fireplaces in the rooms. It's tucked up against the desert, a bona fide oasis."

"An oasis? C'mon."

"Palm trees, fresh water: the Oasis of Mara. The real-deal Holyfield, gives you more desert flavor than staying on the highway."

Robert had stopped listening at *Oasis of Mara*—remembering *O'Meira* from Carlos' work notes. Delfina had told him that she and Teo had stopped at a motel on their desert trip. A place with a bright-blue swimming pool they couldn't afford.

"Do they have a swimming pool?" Robert asked.

"Right after you drive in. On the right, a nice one," Jesus said.

⚜

Fifteen minutes later, Robert eased Erik's SUV through the inn compound's open gates. Rolling up its sand drive, past the glimmering pool to his right, he stopped at the inn's office. Lights were off inside, a flipped-over cardboard clock on the door handle: *Closed.*

Open or closed, my client's money is here, and I'm going to find it.

Back at the bar's parking lot, he and Jesus had already studied an online map of the grounds. Each of the adobe bungalows and wood cabins had a name. Jesus pointed out where the Famosas had spent the night in the '60s.

Once he saw that adobe's name, Robert told Jesus: "Everything makes sense now."

Lights dimmed, driving toward the rear of the compound, Robert stopped at a T. To his left: a few parked cars and pink adobes. To his right: more wood cabins joined the mix.

Not a big crowd tonight, he decided.

Backing up, he pulled into designated parking for the very first adobe on the right, its name carved into a simple wooden plaque: *Forget Me Not.* The adobe where, according to Jesus, the Famosa family spent one night.

Forget Me Not.

"Don't forget," Robert whispered. Words from Carlos' *Argonaut* notice, from Carlos' work notes, and from Carlos' note inside the backpack at Samuelson's Rocks.

Forget Me Not, a large, unlit adobe. Slowly, he eased up its iron gate latch and crossed its walled-in, raked-sand yard to the large window. He peered inside at a made-up bed in a moonlit room. Given the flat roof, Robert didn't believe Carlos had stashed the money inside. Going out the way he'd come in, he stopped.

To his left glistened the Oasis of Mara: a quarter-acre pool surrounded by royal palms, dappled by moonlight. So quiet. Gia's peaceful backyard seemed chaotic in comparison as two coyotes padded past him to grab a drink from the oasis.

One slow step at a time, he began to circle Forget Me Not. Stopping and studying the ground ahead. Rounding its first corner, he spotted a small stack of rocks on the ground. A *cairn* below a ten-foot-tall Engelmann's prickly pear.

Angle Mann. Meet Karen.

Racing back to the truck, he grabbed Erik's shovel, came back, and started digging around the cairn. The sand gave way fast. Two minutes later, he hit Carlos' first backpack. Same as the one out at Samuelson's Rocks, except this one was loaded with stacks of thousands. Five minutes after that, two large packs rested on the ground. Shouldering the first one back to the Yukon, he came back for the second. It was only then he noticed the prickly pear's rounded pads, backlit by the moon.

In silhouette, they looked exactly like Mickey Mouse ears.

Sticky Mickey, he said to himself, getting into the Yukon. *Good one, Carlos, but you're a little late.*

Sitting there in the still compound, Robert now knew that the brothers had talked to Jesus Stone in the desert as boys, and spent that same night in this adobe. And he believed, too, that the Famosa family's night in Forget Me Not had been peaceful, a sentiment that had carried into the next day, when the boys bought two rocks at the Tortoise, and clacked them together on their drive back to LA. One shining moment, however brief, that both men had separately treasured all their lives.

And as he drove out the gates of the inn, leaving the oasis behind, the last thing that blazed in his headlights—a square wooden motel sign with words from Carlos' work notes: *It's Your Decision!*

You got that right, Carlos, he was thinking, as he floored the Yukon out of there.

❧

Robert's motel room shades were drawn. Drinking coffee, seated, Erik looked at the money stacks spread out on the second double bed.

"How much?"

"Three million eight and change," Robert said. "Plus the hundred fifty thousand already in hand."

"I'm putting in for a raise," Erik said, wincing as he stood, clearly doped up. Crossing to the money bed, he eased himself down till he was sitting.

"Gonna roll in this dough, Beach Lawyer."

"How many pills you take?"

"This morning or the last five minutes?"

Erik tried to lie down on the money, got a sharp jolt of pain to the ribs, and gave up.

"On our way home, we go to a strip club, make it rain."

"Will do," Robert said. "But listen, man. Rule Number One: Nobody Talks about Fight Club."

Meaning the four dead men.

Erik nodded. "Rule Number Two: Nobody Talks about Fight Club."

Robert stared at the money and had to admit: something about it made him want to roll around in it, too.

CHAPTER 41

"They's trouble in Glendale paradise."

That was Reyes' voice on the Yukon's speaker.

"What variety of trouble?" Robert asked.

"Not exactly sure," Reyes said.

A few hours after not rolling in the money, Robert had driven the long grade out of the high desert. The Yukon was rolling back toward LA when Reyes called.

"Trouble started this morning," Reyes said on speaker. "Ms. Buttoned Up's fighting with her spouse about something. Took it all the way out to the driveway, to her car. So she gets in, takes the kids with her, and drives off. Went to the car wash next, then Taco Bell, and then inside the liquor store and picked her up two bottles of champagne. Veuve Clicquot Brut, if I saw the label right."

"Saw it where?" Robert asked.

"In the store. Man, out in the car, Felicia, she's all over me about, 'Who's this bitch we followin'? You with her or what?' And I can't tell her nothin', having my PI code to deal with, so naturally, I took a stretch inside the store."

"Let me get this straight. Felicia is *with you.* In the car. Right now?"

"Right this second, no. I'm outside it, she's inside, but last I looked, it's her ride, so yeah, she's with me."

Erik mumbled, doped up, his eyes closed: "Hard to argue with that logic, Beach Lawyer."

"Blow me, E-Rick," Reyes said. "So Ms. Buttoned Up, she's coming out the wine store, goes to put the bottles in her car, and one of her kids musta pissed her off. And, man, she went off. First on that one, then on the other one—looked like the second kid got his medicine on general principles."

Erik again, to Robert: "Fights with her husband, loses temper with kids, call in the SWAT team."

"Tell *Oso Estúpido* to shut it on up," Reyes said.

Before Robert could say anything, Erik whispered: "*Oso Estúpido*— that's pretty solid smack talk, right there." Then he closed his eyes.

The pills talking. How many did he take?

Reyes said, "After she dressed down them two kids, looked to me like she changed her mind. Grabbed 'em both up and started hugging 'em, kissing 'em, crying. Unless that's some kinda' Slovak custom, I found her behavior *noteworthy*. Kind of noteworthy item you wanted to hear about, *¿verdad, abogado?*"

Robert mulled it over. "Yeah, it is."

"Then she goes home, and an hour or so later, she comin' out the house, carrying them two bottles, gift wrapped. Dressed up now, and I mean lookin' fine. White dress, matching pumps, that dark hair. Don't get me started, 'cause seeing her? Felicia started in on me again."

"Exactly where are you right now?"

"A convenience store, 210 East. Ms. Fox, she pumped some gas, went inside."

Robert asked, "Where's the 210 go?"

"Redlands, San Bernardino, Moreno Valley, Palm Springs."

Robert recalled Boris' Ford rental—from San Bernardino.

"I'll meet you in San Berdoo. Probably take an hour or so."

"How you know where she's headed?" Reyes asked.

"Just hoping."

After Reyes signed off, Erik sat up in his seat and asked, "Who was that?"

※

In the parking lot of San Manuel Casino, Robert watched Felicia's late-model Camaro pull up beside the Yukon; Reyes got out, headed over. Erik still rode shotgun, but now he was downing a second casino-brewed double espresso, trying to fight through the opiates.

Sliding into the back seat, Reyes slammed the door.

"Yo, Roberto. Yo, Oso."

"Don't slam the door, dickhead!"

Erik's opiates were definitely wearing off.

"Con calma, Oso, and welcome to San Bernardino. City on the move, home of the Inland Empire Sixty-Sixers. I am here, *mi Oso*, to break the case."

Robert said, "Easy with the Chamber of Commerce pitch. *El señor Polar* has had a hard couple of days, so don't wind him up."

"Just sayin' my cousin's in right field for the Sixty-Sixers, plays salsa inside here on Tribute Night Thursdays. *Pero lo respeto, amigo.*"

"Tell me what's up," Robert said.

"San Berdoo, you were right. A subdivision street off Foothill Boulevard," Reyes said. "That's where Ms. Fox parks her car and walks alone into a two-story suburban spread. Looked exactly like the back lot at Warner Brothers, except bigger houses, bigger backyards."

"So not at all like Warner Brothers," Erik offered.

Reyes wasn't going to let it go.

"What I mean, E-Rick, *the street* felt deserted like the back lot when they not shooting. Except for this house, maybe a couple others, they's nobody around. But this crib where the lady went, they's gonna throw down today, f'sure."

A deserted subdivision street. Made sense to Robert. San Bernardino had been hit hard by the housing crisis and a shrinking economy.

"*Throw down.* By that you mean . . . ?" Robert asked.

By now, Felicia was laying on the Camaro's horn.

"I could see the smoke, man, smell the party pig. It's middle of the day, y'know, but everybody's dressed up like they headed off to confession. Same time, two men in suits were standing at the front door, checking out Ms. Fox to make sure she's on the list. You ask me, a fox like her always gets VIP'ed into my gig, but this get-together had a *Sopranos* vibe to it. *¿Comprendes?*"

"*Sí,*" Robert said as Reyes slid out and slammed the door.

Rolling over to that San Bernardino subdivision with Erik, Robert looked around for the first time. To his right lay the arid, barren lands of the San Manuel Indian Reservation—big hills and limited development, from what Robert could see. After that, they passed another undeveloped area, Sand Canyon, drawing closer to Sharon Sloan's party address.

Once inside the subdivision, Robert noticed that no roads ran in a straight line. Cul-de-sacs and looping roads reconnected where they'd started out, limiting ingress and egress. Fresh asphalt, new streetlights, and sculpted curbs.

As Robert wheeled another right, he saw parked cars ahead. Maybe fifty of them lined the street, like Reyes had said. Slowing down, he recognized Sharon's car from the courthouse parking garage. Braked the SUV and saw a Garfield plush toy suctioned onto the rear window.

"That cat's had a long run," Robert said.

"The lads love him and Shamu. And that donkey from *Shrek*. What's he called?"

"*Donkey,*" Robert said. "Sharon Sloan brings champagne to the party, middle of the day. Wedding? Engagement party? Baptism? Christening?"

"Whatever it is, sounded like her husband wasn't too jazzed about her coming."

Robert thought about Sharon arguing with her husband, going off on her kids.

"Maybe Sharon wasn't jazzed about it, either," Robert said.

He drove on, drew even with the house. When he did: motion. Two men—the two Reyes mentioned?—ran out the front door for the street. Robert floored the Yukon, squealed down one of those curved roads with no pedestrians in sight.

Not a cul-de-sac, it turned out, as Robert made the next intersection, blew a stop sign and cranked a right.

Erik checked the side mirror. "Mercedes SUV. They're coming." Unbuckling his harness, Erik leaned toward Robert, reached his left hand across the gearshift.

"What're you doing?"

Robert made a hard left, saw that Mercedes in his rearview, gaining.

"Keep hauling ass, man!" Erik shouted, reaching over for the front of the driver's seat.

Glancing down, Robert saw a compartment slide out of his seat— Erik's secret compartment. Inside it, Erik's Glock. Pulling it out, Erik heaved his body back to his seat, groaning in pain. Grabbing a clip from his glove compartment, Erik jammed it into his Glock.

Ahead of the Yukon, a dead end was coming up fast. Beyond that lay all that Indian reservation land. Whatever was in front of him—no side streets in sight—Robert had no choice. Keep going straight.

"Sorry, dude—buckle up!" Robert shouted.

Erik had just snapped into his harness when the Yukon hit the sloping curb. The front end flew up, left the ground. Seconds later, the rear end landed, jolting them as the Yukon sped over the cracked concrete pad of an unbuilt dream house. Now they went over the edge, diving onto a fifty-yard hillside, Robert wrestling the wheel, keeping the car headed in a straight-enough line. The bush grille smashed aloe and yucca and ocotillo as the Yukon bucked its way to the bottom of the hill.

Robert carved a right in the hard-packed sand and floored it. Glancing through the sunroof, he saw the pursuer's car above them, perpendicular to his own path, flying down the same hillside.

Erik said, "They're airborne, man! Insane people! Kick it!"

They took off across the sand. Putting distance between them and the Mercedes until they hit a deep patch of soft sand and began slowing down. Robert tried to ease through it, pumping the gas, knowing better than to rev the engine.

"Four-wheel drive!" Erik shouted.

"Where!"

"Dashboard on your left!"

Robert turned a left-side dash knob to 4WD. Eased the gas, started moving them out of the sand, but the other car had gained on them. Erik's hand rested on the door handle, Glock poised. Face gray with pain but ready to go.

The Mercedes hit that same sand, going so fast, it was only thirty yards behind them when its wheels churned to a stop.

Two guys in suits jumped out, but the Yukon had already grabbed four-wheeled traction and powered away.

In front of them, an elevated roadbed.

"We're outta here," Robert said, pointing ahead.

But on the rise to their left: two armed men emerged from the brush, running downhill.

"Who's that?" Robert yelled, hitting that roadbed, leaning right into the turn.

"Ugly-ass blue windbreakers," Erik said. "Gotta be the feds."

Blocking the road ahead: flashing lights and unmarked sedans. The FBI.

He screeched the Yukon to a halt.

A young agent in one of those windbreakers approached. Robert rolled down his window. Heard a cocky young agent say: "Robert Worth. Erik Jacobson. Welcome, gentlemen."

And Robert wondered, *How'd he know my name?*

CHAPTER 42

"If we're not being arrested or held for questioning or being interviewed, what are we doing here?" Robert asked the agent in charge.

"I'm just curious," she said.

The agent was Woods Pascoe, and her hawk nose and scowl made her meaner-looking than Robert would have liked. He and Erik had already been told—*ordered?*—to park the Yukon and had then been led inside this subdivision house, across the road, and not far from Sharon's parked car.

At that point, Agent Pascoe told them to sit down on opposing living room couches while a premature raid was carried out down the road. Robert looked around at the used glasses and plates on the kitchen counter. Best guess: these agents had been camped out here conducting surveillance for quite a while.

"Who *isn't* curious?" Robert answered. "But this is an interview, at a minimum, and neither I, nor my client, will answer any questions. Him, on advice of counsel. Me, because I know better."

A federal statute governed talking to federal agents in this situation. Robert remembered that from his corporate practice—it didn't matter what the FBI told them. If any answer or statement could be construed as misleading them, whoever did the misleading was looking at a felony.

Just ask Martha Stewart, he recalled. *She did time for it.*

"Let me be more specific," Pascoe said. "Why are you here? Why were you driving by that particular house today?"

"Are we free to go?" Robert asked. "Or are we being arrested?"

"Do you know the men in the other car?"

"What other car?"

"The one chasing you," Pascoe said.

Everything he wanted to say was wiseassed, so he held his tongue.

Pascoe said, "You aware you were driving on public lands, damaging protected habitat when you were stopped?"

Robert made an educated guess.

"That's Indian land. Let the tribal council tell me if they have a problem with damaged weeds and sand. File *federal* charges, Agent Pascoe, or let us go."

Cut us loose, he wanted to say, but didn't want to sound like a criminal lawyer.

Back of his mind, Robert now knew the FBI had watched the Mercedes pursuing them and failed to stop it, arguably almost costing Erik and him their lives. The feds didn't need that kind of publicity; nobody did. That insight didn't come close to giving him an upper hand, but at this point, it was better than nothing.

Most important, in the hour they'd already been here, Pascoe hadn't asked about their trip to Joshua Tree. *That* was a good thing, as Ms. Stewart liked to say, given that four dead bodies could be found up there at any moment.

"Let's do this," Robert said. "I'm going to take a chance and tell you about you because I don't think I can mislead you about *you*."

Pascoe shrugged. "Give it a shot."

Robert said, "When the two of us got out of the car, one of your agents said, *Robert Worth. Erik Jacobson. Welcome, gentlemen.*"

"So you're not gentlemen. So our agents have good manners. So what?"

"Manners or not, I'm wondering—how'd your agent already know my name?"

Agent Pascoe didn't have an answer for that. Not one she was willing to share.

"My client, it's his SUV," Robert said. "You coulda run plates on it and ID'd *him*. But the Yukon's windows are tinted. I never rolled 'em down, and I don't own my client's vehicle. So maybe you'll tell me: How'd your agent know my name without asking me for it?"

"Which agent called you by name?"

"Doesn't matter which one. Point is, there's only one way you know my name—because you were already following someone who lives on this street or someone at this party. Your agents only know about *me* because you were following *someone* over on the Westside of LA. That's the only way I ever show up on your radar. Would've been decent of you to give me a heads-up, tell me I was caught up with some San Bernardino crew all the way over on the Westside."

Not long after that, Pascoe left the room. Through the window, Robert saw her chewing through that cocky agent who'd screwed up, calling him by name.

Waiting for Pascoe to return, Robert knew one and only one rule—keep your mouth shut. But these weren't city cops like the ones he'd outmaneuvered in Santa Cruz. This was the FBI. If they wanted, they'd find out everything about him. About the trust. About his clients. All of it from the beginning of time.

If they ever looked into it, the FBI could put him in the desert at the same time those guys died. From his credit card buys, cell phone records, Internet history, they could prove he'd been there. Not that he was concerned about murder charges. Three of the dead men drowned, surely; their lungs would be filled with the same gunk Erik had hacked up on the riverbank. The other one was stabbed to death. Good luck finding that knife or Robert's motive. Even so, Robert was concerned about his connection to drug money—because that's what the trust's money could be called. And a desert tie-in between him, his client, and drug money—that ran counter to his client's interests.

Because of that, he decided to go against all his legal training and get the ball rolling. Show Pascoe some belly, too, and help his client in the process. When she walked in, he didn't wait for questions.

"Why don't you look into me, Agent Pascoe, if you haven't already? I'm not a criminal or a complicit criminal-defense attorney. You asked why I'm here today, and so I'll tell you."

"Let's hear it," she said.

"I have a client who couldn't consent to my talking to you even if she wanted me to."

"And why might that be?"

"Because she's a nine-year-old." He let that sink in. "And her father, Matteo Famosa, was a victim of a hit and run over in Santa Monica last week. He's in Saint John's ICU right now, in real bad shape."

Looked to him like Pascoe just wrote down Teo's name.

"Take a look at the Santa Monica police report—the hit and run was intentional, but they have no leads I'm aware of. So my client's father is touch and go, her mother left for parts unknown, and my client asked me to find out who'd want to hurt her daddy. That's why I'm here. I'm here for my client, Delfina Famosa."

"Got a date on that hit and run?" Pascoe asked.

Robert gave her the date, the time of night, and added, "Black Lexus SUV. Female driver, they're saying. I hope that's helpful."

"Might be," Pascoe said.

She went into the other room. Robert could see her huddled with another agent, going to a computer screen and pulling up what might've been surveillance tapes. Robert went to the window.

Outside on the street, only a couple of cars were still parked, and fifty yards away, he caught Sharon walking up the sidewalk toward her car. No doubt, she'd been interviewed by the agents and released. Wearing heels, dressed up and *lookin' fine*, like Reyes had said. In the opposite direction, end of the street, several news vans had gathered, their greedy satellite dishes waiting to fill the empty air.

His eyes drifted again to Sharon, drawing closer to her car. For some reason, his mind began to shift from her and landed square on the two Famosa brothers. Not as men . . . as boys. Sitting on the porch of that rental house with Vincent. And he wondered, why would that be? Was there some connection between Sharon, Teo, and Carlos that he was missing? Or was it simply that his just-discovered link between Jesus Stone and the Famosa boys had edged out the other mental competition?

As he began to shift his focus onto Sharon again:

"Over here, Worth. Listen up."

Behind him, Pascoe had returned to the room, and Robert joined her. Turned out, with the on-scene reporters, she'd decided to give Robert a heads-up on what would soon be public anyway: that these Draganovs had been part of a large-scale pot-growing operation in Northern California with interstate connections.

"Trespass-growing on public land for decades. We were moving in on them up north, but we bit on a decoy dope run they'd set up, and they slipped through. There was evidence they'd swapped out all their product for a significant amount of cash before heading south."

So far, Robert was thinking, he, Gia, and Erik had been on target about Boris.

"Along their way to getting out of the dope-growing business," Pascoe said, "this clan has murdered as many as five people. Small-time growers, primarily, hippies who got in their way, and most recently, a college girl from Los Gatos who got mixed up with them, probably starting off as a trimmer. Her father put considerable heat on us to get to the bottom of what happened to her. Now, these guys in the house right down the street? One of them's the Draganov clan's *Gospodar*."

"And that means . . . ?"

"*Boss* or *master.* Not that bright, from what we can tell. Inherited the job from his father, Ivan Draganov."

Bright enough to screw my clients.

"But he calls the shots now, given how this family was set up, and he's getting some top-notch advice on money laundering. The pot-growing business, sooner or later, will be legal all over the country; profits aren't what they once were, so they're getting out. We had a Draganov body shop in San Bernardino under surveillance—a black Lexus SUV came in with a busted grille, night of your hit and run. There was a lot of talk in the shop . . . vague talk . . . but we never put any of it together with a hit and run way over in Santa Monica. Should've, maybe, but we didn't. That's the *who* of it for your client and her father. But *the why?* That, I can't help you with, because hell if I know why they tried to kill Matteo Famosa."

Robert decided to stay silent about the Draganovs' trust scam, at least for now.

"At this point," Pascoe said, "adding in a couple million they just transported south, the Draganovs have at least twenty million floating around LA. We have no idea where it is. Do you?"

Floating around LA? Some of it, no doubt, had floated up to the high desert. But Los Angeles?

"Twenty million floating around Los Angeles? I do not. That woman driving the Lexus? You ID'd her?" Robert asked.

Pascoe said, "An online escort, Alexandra Pavlov. She's already had a few drug-related run-ins with LAPD. Could be productive to bring her in, see where her loyalties really lie."

Erik woke up on the other couch. Still groggy, he rolled into sitting position. "Hey, Pascoe, you cuttin' us loose or what?"

CHAPTER 43

For the last fifteen minutes, a BMW 7 Series had been parked at a Foothill Boulevard curb. The UberLUX driver and his passenger looked out at the flashing lights ahead, at the FBI agents' activity in the vanilla subdivision.

"Any idea what you'd like to do?" the driver asked, turning around in his seat.

His passenger said, "I'll tell you when I know. Until then, turn around and don't look at me."

Evelyn Levine rose above the growing pain in her abdomen, sitting in this soft leather seat and wondering where the world had gone wrong. Just a christening. A Draganov gathering in San Bernardino, and she'd made a big effort to get here. Gone were both her unnecessary wig and the breast-cancer chemo port she'd threaded into her own arm. With the wasting diuretics now flushed from her system and a few decent meals, her face and skin were—though not normal—full and rosy enough for the San Bernardino crowd. After layering herself with a black Dolce & Gabbana business suit and Jimmy Choo Romy 85s, she would look to them like the picture of success and sophistication.

But doing her song and dance for these people was no longer necessary. Sharon Sloan had driven away about five minutes ago, and Sharon had not returned Evelyn's calls on her own burner phone. That fact, in and of itself, was very bad.

Worse was that she'd also seen Robert Worth being escorted by federal agents. Taken into a house, along with his cop friend. Seeing Robert, she'd gained some visibility into the current situation, but not nearly enough.

Gospodar had never heard from Kiril after he'd checked in from the desert. Last she'd heard, Kiril had her instructions—don't make a move until you see Carlos' money in Robert Worth's hands.

She'd been clear about it with *Gospodar*, and *Gospodar* with Kiril. Get the money, then kill Robert Worth.

Yet seeing Robert here, alive, meant he might've come out on top in the desert. And somehow, he'd learned enough to put himself *right here*.

"Now," she told the Uber driver, "take me back to the Westside. Take the 210."

"App's telling me the I-10's better."

She looked in the rearview until his eyes met hers.

"Do as I say," she told him.

"The 210 it is," the driver said.

Sharon. Best guess, the FBI had already interviewed her. It might help for *Gospodar* to contact Sharon right away, secure a criminal lawyer to ease her anxiety. But in her heart of hearts, Evelyn knew Sharon would cave because Sharon was weak. She had none of the stuff that Ivan, Evelyn's first cousin once removed, had possessed.

Ivan had been a powerhouse. Evelyn recognized that the first time she'd met him at her own father's funeral. The Draganov family had turned out for his open casket service at an Orthodox church in Hollywood, because Emil had been Ivan's first cousin.

One thing had been obvious: Ivan's side of the family differed from Emil's. Violence inhered in them, same as it did in her. That quality made them her kindred spirits. Uncle Ivan——he'd asked that she call him that——told her how beneficial it might be to have a lawyer in the family.

Someone who practiced at a higher level, flesh and blood he could grow to trust in strategic matters.

In her Uber, Evelyn studied the back of her driver's head. Her father and this driver had that much in common: the back of a head to a person of stature. Even though Emil had driven movie stars, he'd speak when spoken to, and when they'd reach their destination, he'd be instructed: "Wait here until I'm ready to leave."

In spite of the studio tales he'd told her when she was younger, the stars were never his friends.

Her father's funeral had been in '95. That same night, she'd serviced Uncle Ivan in his hotel penthouse suite. He was a seventy-year-old man, but still, she wanted him; even at that age, Ivan had been virile, a visionary.

It had been Ivan—not Emil, Ivan told her—who'd murdered that Turk in Chicago. Who'd cut off the Turk's hands and fled that city with Emil for the West Coast.

"But Emil, your father," Ivan had told her, "he cowered in the corner while I did a man's work."

That same night in bed with Ivan, Evelyn had taken the biggest risk of her life, telling him how Emil came to die. Ivan, it turned out, wanted to know everything, so Evelyn had begun to share bitter memories of her molester father.

Starting with how Evelyn's Latina mother begged young Ewa to leave her father, to return with her to Costa Rica. Yet Ewa—before she changed her name to Evelyn in tenth grade—refused to leave. She stayed on in Emil's house, knowing that with patience, over time, she'd find a way to crush him.

In their hotel room, Evelyn had told Ivan, "For fun, I'd tell him I'd spotted my mother down the street, or anywhere else I fancied seeing her. That sent him out of the house in a fury, searching for hours, only to return raging, empty-handed, to his devoted daughter."

With time, she'd told Ivan, came Emil's dementia.

"Soon, he lost his job with the studio. Money was in short supply, a blessing for me. That house," she had told Ivan. "Emil's two-story wooden castle on the hill. That was his pride and joy. A home he owned in a neighborhood of renters, looking down on them all."

"A prick, always," Ivan had said, turning toward her in bed.

"Especially when he drove home in the studio limo," Evelyn had told him. "That's when he would drink his rakia on our front porch, inviting our neighbors up for a drink. None came, of course. They hated him, but liking him had never been Emil's point.

"Once I took charge of his household, a woman's work, important bills went neglected. Taxes on our home, overdue, unpaid. He would beat me for failure, and I welcomed it, remaining to the world a dutiful daughter. Finally losing his home, that broke Emil. Turned him into an apartment dweller on food stamps until I petitioned the court to have him committed."

In the Uber, she checked her Rolex. An old one, a man's timepiece, her favorite ornament. It always made her think of Chet Jordan for one simple reason: it had belonged to him before she'd stolen it from his house.

In the hotel with Ivan, she'd told him, "I would often visit Emil's pitiful apartment, only this time it was me in Chet Jordan's limousine. I would tell Emil, 'He's a real movie star, Emil, like all the movie stars you said you knew so well. Chet looks like Marlon Brando, doesn't he, Emil? Your *good friend* Marlon Brando.' Sometimes, I would tell the chauffeur to take us for a drive. 'How do you like it back here, Emil? You've never seen a driver's neck, have you? It was always your neck important people were looking at.'"

"My Ewa," Ivan had said, using her old-country name, "what a cruel and cunning bitch you are. Tell me. How did you finish it with Emil?"

"In that nursing home, near the end, I waited for one of Emil's rare lucid periods and told him that Turks now owned his home. And every time they walked through the front door, they spit on his Orthodox cross nailed onto the doorjamb.

"In the home," she'd told Ivan, "Emil raved to the nurses with tales of my treachery, but they didn't listen. He was mad, and I was his kind and loving daughter. I allowed him to live another week before paying a final visit. I choked him to death in his bed with my gloved hands. Seeing that happen with my own eyes . . . I witnessed a moment of great beauty."

Once she'd told Ivan how she'd murdered his cousin, she'd said, "Emil was a molester of his own female child. He deserved to die by my hand, but he was your blood, so kill me if you want, *Gospodar*. From you, I welcome it."

Instead, as she'd hoped, he'd become hard again.

Afterward, she'd said: "You are old, your body unappealing. I fuck you out of respect, because I worship you."

Ivan had responded by giving her his confidence. They had spoken of the future. Even back then, the first marijuana legalization laws had been voted on, and Ivan had known it was only a matter of time before his black-market profit margins withered and died of legality.

"Not in a year or two," Ivan had told her. "But eventually. One day we will need to get out. I want you to think strategically. Very, very long term."

After that night with Ivan, word got around to his people that the family had a new resource who was smart, patient, and hard.

Over time, she'd found two deals for him. First, in the late '90s, a concrete parking structure. But even with a legal, hard asset, people had to show up and sit in the booth all day, keep up with maintenance, repairs, cleanup, and reconcile cash reports. Actually work without stealing from themselves. She'd done better with small parcels of semi-improved Nevada desert. She'd caught the initial upsurge of a housing boom, fueled by overheated Las Vegas, and *Gospodar* had doubled his money in three years, all of it now clean and taxed as proceeds from a land sale.

"A fluke," she'd told him.

"Counts the same," Ivan had replied.

As the BMW neared San Dimas, sharp pain seized Evelyn's abdomen. For the next ten minutes, the surge bent her over and brought tears to her eyes. Not from breast cancer; that was her visual prop for Robert Worth. This came from pancreatic cancer, diagnosed by her doctors on the same afternoon Carlos Famosa had been found dead in his study. Facing chemotherapy, no reasonable odds of recovery, only a temporary respite from devastating pain, she'd already chosen to die.

Outside the BMW, LA's downtown skyline hid behind a yellow haze. There were a few last memories she wanted to treasure before the end.

"Excuse me," she said to the driver. "I'd like to go to Highland Park instead."

He checked his rearview, wary of her, and didn't speak.

"I'm terribly sorry how I spoke to you earlier," Evelyn said. "I met with my doctors today—does cancer run in your family, too?"

"No, but I'm so sorry," he said. "Don't worry about it, ma'am, not one bit."

As she chatted him up about his family and his interests—*softball, really?*—she snapped open her Christian Louboutin clutch and took out her chemo port, an item she would need for her last few tasks. Another wave of pain seized her midsection as she started threading the needle back into her arm.

Too many variables were in play now; too much lay beyond her control. The FBI . . . Sharon . . . Robert. No telling how much more time she had on this earth, but she had a few items left on her agenda before the end.

"What takes you over to Highland Park?" her driver asked.

"A house," she said. "Just a house."

CHAPTER 44

Over in Mar Vista, Erik closed the garage door behind the Yukon, and Robert opened the Yukon's rear hatch. They removed Carlos' two money bags from inside the Yukon's gun safe.

In the back of the garage, Erik unlocked his massive, free-standing Liberty safe.

"That's badass," Robert said of the black-enameled behemoth.

"One-inch diameter pry-prevention pins, weighs seven hundred thirty-eight pounds, a thirty-minute fire rating at twelve hundred degrees. Without dynamite, you're outta luck, and even then."

Erik swung open the Liberty's pry-prevention door. Inside: shopping bags from Gucci, Valentino, Balenciaga—Priya's shopping swag.

They loaded Priya's swag into the Yukon's gun safe. Robert gave Erik a ten-second grace period before asking, "Dude, where do you keep your actual weapons?"

"The closet," Erik said, pointing to the nearest corner of the garage. Two combination padlocks secured its door. "Not a word about her shopping bags ever leaves this room," Erik said.

"It won't. I'd never tell Gia who really runs the show over here."

Erik actually liked it when Robert ratted him out to Gia. And Gia loved Erik: the kind of husband who'd let his wife commandeer his cherished Liberty safe for her things.

"Not a word to Priya, either. She'd slaughter me if she found out about this."

"I hear you. She's a frightening woman."

"Tell me about it. The money," Erik asked. "How're you going to pull it off?"

"Not sure yet," Robert said.

He knew what Erik meant. He couldn't show up in probate court or at a bank with a pile of cash. At some point, the authorities, maybe even Agent Pascoe, would take an acute interest in it. Stacking Carlos' desert cash into the Liberty took ten minutes. As he worked, Robert gave the problem more thought.

The concept of *constructive trust* had banged around his brain as a solution ever since leaving San Bernardino. It was one of those ideas law students tossed around that almost never applied to a real situation. The core idea lay in fairness—*in equity*, as judges like to say. Robert needed a judge to look at the money like this: the trust's money had been lost by a corrupt trustee, given in exchange for a worthless investment. At the same time, cash had been paid to the trustee under the table. The question before the court would be: *Who owned the money?* Because it was illegal drug money, the government had a claim to it; so did the trust, because of the trustee's scam. Robert's argument would be: *Because the trust had been most directly wronged, it was more equitable to give the cash to the trust than to the government.*

Surely, there were tons of constructive-trust nuances, but if push came to shove, he liked his clients' chances. His essential fairness argument would always come down to this: "She's nine, Your Honor. She and her father are homeless. Your call. Them or the FBI?"

By the time they made it inside Erik's house, Erik was asleep on his feet, admitting he'd downed two painkillers in the driveway. After he went upstairs and called Priya, he planned to lie down and disappear for twenty-four hours.

"I don't know how to thank you, man. Above and beyond," Robert said.

"You'da done it for me, right?" Erik asked.

"Depends on the circumstances," Robert said.

Erik grinned and pressed the Beast's keys into Robert's hand. As Erik slowly made his way upstairs, Robert walked out the back door, locked it behind him, and climbed in the Yukon.

Before cranking it up, he checked his calls and messages—tons of each. Sonny from the gyro shop; framer Drew Freize; Gia and Delfina; his Ozone landlord; texts from Reyes with attachments; a call and a text from Philip Fanelli; other numbers he didn't recognize—aluminum siding . . . erectile dysfunction?

First, he called Gia and Delfina, asked if they'd already eaten dinner. They had, so he told them he'd bring home a surprise.

"What is it?" Delfina asked.

"Can't say," he told her, because he didn't know yet. "You'll have to wait."

"Evelyn said she was going to drop by," Gia told him. "She has a present for our best houseguest ever."

"Know what it is? Robert asked.

"No, it's a surprise," Gia said. "Bring my T-shirt home, *Roberto*. And bring yourself with it."

Next, the calls from Philip. Several of them with no message and a text: Call Dorothy ASAP. Important. A second text from Philip. Unusual. Philip rarely texted.

A generational thing, he guessed. He called Dorothy, and when she picked up, she got right down to it.

"Robert," she said, "I want you to call Bradley Holtzmann. He's expecting your call. Don't give your name, just say, 'I'm a friend of

Dorothy's.' Hurry, though. He's holding off on his pain medication until he hears from you."

Bradley Holtzmann, he remembered. *Senior partner at the mid-Wilshire firm where Evelyn used to work.*

He made the call; a man answered. "I'm a friend of Dorothy's," Robert said, following her cloak-and-dagger instructions.

Like Dorothy, Bradley Holtzmann got right down to business, too.

"I knew the woman in question," he said, meaning Evelyn. "She left my firm's employ under a cloud. An allegation that she stole a client's personal property. That client was Chet Jordan. You might recall his films from years gone by."

Robert started to answer, but Bradley pressed on.

"The item in question, Mr. Jordan's Rolex. She denied taking it and rightly pointed out Mr. Jordan was often intoxicated and that he was in error. However—"

Bradley drew a deep breath. "If you'll excuse me for a moment, I have a pressing matter to take care of."

"I'll be here," Robert said. Taking his arthritis meds, Robert guessed.

Evelyn's account of why she'd left the firm—tired of *grinding it out*—didn't jibe with Bradley's. Her story didn't much surprise him. Sounded like her departure might've been part of a lover's dispute.

Waiting for Bradley, he pulled up Reyes' texts. The attached photos: Reyes and his girlfriend, Felicia; Reyes with Peter Paul Dickerson on Santa Monica Pier's Ferris wheel; and Reyes' text: Me and PPD. Two ballers!

Several more photos: Felicia with a Slurpee, sticking out her dark-blue tongue. Reyes' text: Brain Freeze!!! Was frozen waaaay b4 the Slurpee!!!

Robert hoped Felicia didn't see that one. He opened the last of Reyes' attachments as Bradley came back on the line, seeming more relaxed.

"The woman in question, her work was excellent, even with her active social life. Usually, we stood behind our junior partners, even if it meant losing a client like Mr. Jordan. However, a prior incident tipped the scales against her."

A sense of dread began pulsing, back of Robert's mind.

"The prior incident involved another client, one of her own. A single-task assignment. The client paid half, fifteen hundred dollars, up front, but something happened. After she did the work, he refused to pay the balance. She had twenty hours on her time sheets, time she had to write off. Because it was her client, not the firm's, she was also told she must eat the unpaid fifteen hundred."

Made sense. Bradley's firm had plenty of its own work to occupy themselves. If a junior partner wrote off work for a firm client, no problem; but for her own client, the loss fell her way.

"Eventually," Bradley said, "she took her medicine, but not before causing a big row. Wasn't a big deal to the senior partners, *but to her?* She did not like being challenged. It was a side of her. . . let's just say her reaction was over the top.

"No matter," he continued. "After the Jordan incident, the firm let her go, paid her off, and signed the very nondisclose I'm violating. She took several clients with her, yet every client came back because she charged too much. *Valued herself too highly*—that's how I'd put it."

Holtzmann's account didn't seem to square with the woman Robert had spent time with. She'd stood up to Judge Blackwell when he'd started running down Carlos, stepped in and reminded him a child was present in his courtroom, and that Carlos had been her friend. Taking the high ground, it seemed. Had there been more to it? Had her reaction stemmed from Judge Blackwell not valuing *her* highly enough?

Bradley kept talking. "And when Chet Jordan died in his drunken accident . . . Dorothy said you'd worked at Fanelli's outfit, so you know how gallows the humor can get."

"Definitely," Robert said, his mouth going dry.

"We used to joke around at the firm that somehow this woman had killed Chet or had him killed. Not normative behavior," he said. "Not that she actually killed him, you understand."

Not normative. Or rational.

"I do understand," Robert said.

"Then there was the cancer," Bradley said.

"What cancer?"

Outside Erik's SUV now, Robert paced the driveway.

"During severance negotiations, the woman let us know she was undergoing cancer treatments." He laughed. "We hired a private detective, and sure enough, she went into a treatment facility. We backed off, paid up, and never regretted being shed of her."

The intimacies Evelyn had shared with Gia and him: her cancer, Delfina's trust, her regrets about not having children, her friendship with Carlos. Robert had assumed the truth of it all.

At this point, Bradley started rambling, the drugs having a private party. Apparently, he'd loved Dorothy and considered losing her a big mistake.

Bradley sighed, then laughed. "Before Evelyn left, we called her one-off client *the little trust with the big name.*"

Saying *Evelyn*, Bradley had forgotten his own rules.

In the driveway, Robert stopped moving and breathing.

Evelyn's client dispute in '95 had been over a trust?

"*Famosa,*" Robert said. "The Vincent Famosa Family Trust."

"You know about it?" Bradley asked.

"About it, yes."

All about it? Definitely not. Evelyn Levine had drafted Vincent's trust. Meaning she'd known Vincent since at least 1995; she'd known all about Vincent's family situation years before she'd met Carlos and had repeatedly lied to Robert about it.

"I have to go," Robert said, then realized Bradley had already signed off. Robert jumped behind the Yukon's wheel and squealed out of Erik's driveway.

He texted Gia: Call me ASAP.

Vincent was murdered in 2005. Evelyn had known him for years. Something had blown up between Evelyn and Vincent over legal work done ten years before Vincent died. Meaning that in 2005, Evelyn didn't *happen to meet* Carlos at a seminar—she *found* him there. Carlos didn't happen to move three blocks from her. His bet: she'd followed Carlos, not the other way around.

Had Evelyn ever been Carlos' friend? The trust's faithful adviser? Robert didn't buy a word of it anymore.

He stopped at a red light on Pico. Glancing down, his eye caught his iPhone screen just before it went dark. A jarring image appeared there, meshing with what he'd seen a few hours ago in San Bernardino. He picked up the phone, hit the "Home" button. His screen shone bright with Reyes' last photo attached to his last text.

Staring at the photo, he'd swear Raymundo Reyes had just sent him a shot of Evelyn Levine from the late '90s: an elegant, slender brunette, that crisp bone structure.

Already dialing Gia's number, he mashed the pedal to the floor.

It wasn't Evelyn in Reyes' photo—it was Sharon Sloan. Her image was up close now, not distant like Sharon had been at the Draganov gathering. She looked nothing like her online photo, or the loving wife and mother serving barbecue to her family in her office-door photo.

A fox, Reyes said, and he'd nailed it. Sharon Sloan and Evelyn Levine looked disturbingly alike. Was it possible Sharon was Evelyn's daughter by Syd Levine?

Doesn't matter if she is or not. Evelyn Levine is a Draganov, too. All these years, she's been the one working against the trust, not Sharon Sloan.

Gia picked up on the other end.

"*¿A dónde, Roberto?*"

"Is Evelyn there?" he asked.

"Do you need to speak to her?"

"You and Delfina—stay away from her. Don't let her in the house."

"Hold on . . . Delfina went down to her car to help her up the front walk. What is it?"

"She's dangerous!" he shouted. "Stay away from her!"

Silence for a moment, then the sound of Gia's footsteps, the front door opening.

Gia screamed. "She's gone!"

She? Robert wondered, hoping. *Meaning . . . ?*

Gia's front door slammed, her breath harsh into her phone.

"Delfina's gone. Evelyn's car's gone. They're both . . . What's going on!"

He heard Gia crying.

"Call 911," he said. "Tell 'em Evelyn Levine kidnapped Delfina, and tell 'em it's not a custodial dispute."

"What?"

"Tell them that."

"Sure, but, Robert, how do you *know?*"

It was impossible to take her from zero to ninety in any logical sequence.

"Because I love you, Gia. *Because I know.*"

"I love you, too," she said, her voice breaking.

Next, he considered a lie he wanted Gia to tell about the abduction. If he was wrong, Gia would be filing a false police report, could possibly face prosecution. But if she told the truth, the police would burn time asking legitimate questions: *How well do you know Ms. Levine? Was she expected at your home? Did the girl know Ms. Levine? Is it possible they drove off and forgot to tell you?*

"Gia, tell the police—"

Her crying stopped, the anger in her voice growing. "I'm telling them I saw Evelyn do it. That Delfina was struggling, scared, going with Evelyn against her will, and I'm a hundred percent sure of what I saw."

"I'll find her, Gia."

Gia screamed, "Find her! And if she hurts that little girl—kill that cunt!"

CHAPTER 45

At the stoplight, Evelyn glanced at the unconscious girl in her passenger's seat. Tonight, Delfina had been watching out Gia's front window. Little girl lost, waiting for Robert, and yes—*waiting for her*. Doing what Delfina always did whenever she expected a loved one's arrival at Gia's.

Delfina embodied all the traits that Evelyn knew she herself lacked. Early in life, Evelyn, and all those like her, knew they were totally alone. Knew they lacked any need to connect with other people—a need both Delfina and her daughter, Sharon, craved.

The little girl had run down Gia's walkway to meet her—making things so much simpler than finishing inside the house, contending with Gia Marquez. What Evelyn had in mind now was so much more pure, an end to her distant beginning with Vincent Famosa.

Vincent had been similar to her father. Not a drunk like Emil, but easy prey. A monstrous ego with nothing to back it up. She'd waited years to punish Vincent after drafting his trust. Looked him up, finally, and told him she'd behaved badly, overreacted.

"All is forgiven," she'd told him.

What Vincent could never understand was how much she had enjoyed deceiving him after that. Letting him manage the properties he'd bought with proceeds from the house he'd sold out from under her. Even letting him take out whatever cash he needed. This was never about cash to her. She had been in no hurry at all. Had even looked forward to their get-togethers, listening to him brag about the trust and about his success.

"You'll outlive us all, Vincent."

She had been in no hurry in that motel room, either, after she paid one of the Draganov girls to lure Vincent there. When he came to from the drugs, Evelyn spent the next few hours toying with him while he was hog-tied, helpless on that cheap bedspread, begging for answers—he was hard to understand, ball-gagged like that. Finally, as she'd taken her time with that dildo, she'd answered him in her own way.

As if you didn't already know, Vincent. We had a deal. You stole from me, then dared me to do something about it—at my own law firm. So really, you left me no choice.

Afterward, she'd beaten him to death with a metal meat mallet and left his broken body for the Draganov men.

"West Hollywood," she'd told them. "Dump the big man's body there."

Carlos was next. Evelyn had arranged to bump into him at an estate-planning seminar and befriended him. In his own way, Carlos' downfall had been more gratifying than Victor's. She'd moved into a house near him on Harvard, knowing that all her money—*everything in the trust*—was now in Carlos' capable hands. Whenever she wanted trust money, she'd dummied up maintenance problems, roof leaks, infestation reports from exterminators, all caused and repaired by her people. Most of the repair money wound up in her pocket.

For big-money drawdowns, she'd staged lawsuits against Teo. Dosing him with Rohypnol that blanked his memory afterward, she'd settled those cases with handpicked lawyers. All the while, her own lawyering and legal maneuvering drew praise from Carlos, and again, just last week, from Robert Worth.

After she'd convinced *Gospodar* to use the Famosa trust as a money-laundering vehicle, she had another challenge: turning Carlos much more vehemently against Teo. That task, she'd relished.

"You're doing all the work, Carlos, and splitting the money with Teo? That setup's so unfair." Often reminding Carlos: "Teo and his wife used trust money to get high while you took care of all the busted plumbing. Addicts never change—don't you know that?"

That left her with introducing Ilina into the mix. Carlos had latched on to her at one of the Draganov mixers. After that meeting, shearing Carlos from his brother had been so simple that Evelyn was almost disappointed.

Post Ilina, Carlos was all in on scamming the trust. To cover her own tracks, Evelyn resigned as trust counsel early on, protesting the investments in writing. In those early e-mails between Carlos and her—she and Carlos had crafted those over glasses of wine—Evelyn voiced her grave concerns about his two risky investments. Protecting herself if Carlos' investments were ever somehow scrutinized by probate court—or by an outsider like Robert Worth.

All along, Carlos had believed he was in on everything with her. Up to a point, that had been true: making the investments, taking dirty money under the table, receiving her formal e-mail resigning as counsel and wishing him the best, sending her copies of e-mails about SoccMom's first interest payment and telling her, *You worry too much!*

She and Carlos had even crafted e-mails to SoccMom's fictional Jake Saxon, who blew off meetings and a showdown lunch. The same went for Carlos' e-mails threatening lawsuits. Those were drafted for Carlos' own camouflage, to show that, if nothing else: *Hey, at least I tried to get the money back. They tricked me!*

But over time, the true Carlos began emerging in his own e-mails, the ones he'd written to Evelyn, unbidden. The ones talking about sunrise for lovers in spiritual Sonora, shopping for his lady at Bulgari up in San Francisco, and moving with her to Santa Barbara in a heartbeat.

None of Carlos' e-mails surprised Evelyn. A wallflower with millions in cash on hand, in love with the perfect woman, who loved him back. Evelyn had relished watching his sick ego bloom like a long-dormant virus. And she had relished him talking down to her—*You should travel more, I insist!*—elevating his own glamorous life over her drab existence. That, she knew, had been the real Carlos. A son channeling his father, mainlining ego behind stacks of cash.

Or so she'd let Carlos believe for a delicious month or two. It made his downfall even more satisfying when she'd jerked the little man's chain—*Ilina has disappeared!*—and brought him to heel. Poor Carlos. A weak little man, after all. Just like Vincent. And just like her father, Emil.

Carlos had crawled to her then, trying to get back in her good graces. What was it he'd said? *Beginning to think I offended you somehow,* and showing up at her house distraught, high, at all hours.

Broken.

To his credit, Carlos eventually discovered her connection with Ilina. Near the very end, he'd even called her from a phone booth to tell her he knew about Ilina. About everything.

Too late, Carlos. Too late finding out about Ilina, weren't you?

Her only true disappointment: Carlos' heart attack while Kiril and Penko held him for her. She'd been delayed by her doctors that day, learning about her own very real, untreatable, pancreatic cancer. Carlos had died before she could tell him how long she'd made him dance for her, about the phony lawsuits, how she'd gone about killing his father and exactly why.

The one compensation for missing Carlos' death was how Carlos had—cleverly, she conceded—lured his derelict brother off the streets and into court. Otherwise, Teo would've been lost to her forever. That meant she could now see to it that Vincent's entire line was rooted up, extirpated. Dead.

As it worked out, having Teo in the hospital, rather than in the ground, turned into a happy accident. Comatose, his daughter distraught, and Evelyn put herself in the middle of it. An angel of mercy, the voice of reason, she'd watched Teo's daughter suffer up close—played the aging, cancer-victim lawyer, now torn with regret over how she'd treated dear friend Carlos—and nobly took credit for a new trust that Delfina would never see.

At the next stoplight, Evelyn recalled waiting outside the hospital till Robert and Gia came out with Delfina, playing a repentant, guilt-ridden lawyer and friend before visiting Teo's hospital room.

She'd recalled, too—savoring the memory—her one-way conversation in Teo's room: "That car running you down tonight was a gift from your own father. I killed him. Stuffed a dildo inside him and dumped his body. Then I ruined your weak-willed brother and killed him as well. And your blessed daughter is now in my very capable hands."

Doctors, she'd learned, believed the subconscious picked up penumbral data beyond consciousness. Now, she hoped so again, as the traffic light changed, and she turned onto her street.

She punched her clicker and eased her car into the garage, the door slowly closing behind her. She and the chloroformed girl beside her were thrown into darkness. In many ways, she hoped Robert Worth would put in an appearance. Such a promising young man. Yet having him bear witness to what he'd done to Delfina? At this point, that would be asking life for a bit too much.

Ah, well. All my pain will soon end. Others can feast on my share of it.

Delfina, she was thinking as she opened her car door. *The last Famosa . . . my true prize.*

CHAPTER 46

Robert wheeled the Yukon onto Wilshire, headed east; he'd already tried calling Erik. No answer on the other end, but better that he not drag Erik into whatever was coming. One thing Robert could do that cops normally didn't: *break the law*. Turning onto Harvard, he parked a hundred yards down the street from Evelyn's house and hit the ground running. Once he made it across her front yard, he slipped onto her porch. Her front door, locked. Her plateglass front window, blocked by thick, drawn curtains.

Whether Delfina was inside—anybody's guess.

Leaping off the front porch, he beat it down Harvard to Evelyn's back alley. He jammed up the alley to her garage; he tried the gate to her narrow walkway. Locked. Grabbing the gate with both hands, he swung over and landed in her small, tidy backyard.

The garage door to his left—locked, too. Looking through the garage window: no car parked inside. He hadn't noticed her Volvo parked out front; that didn't mean she wasn't inside with Delfina.

Heart pumping, he tried and failed to calm down as he moved to her back door. About to boot it open, he noticed the door was ajar.

Easing inside the quiet kitchen, moving through it to the living room, he found that room empty, too; the same went for her bedroom.

In her second bedroom, converted into her office, near-empty garbage bags sagged like tired soldiers on the floor. Stacks of hanging-file boxes lay all around. Looked to him like her leisurely cleanup job had been interrupted.

His eye caught a high school yearbook, middle of her desk. Grabbing it, he read its cover from the '60s: *Franklin High School, Highland Park.*

So Evelyn was from Highland Park.

She'd once mentioned her yearbook to him in passing; he tore it open. On the move again, into the hall, he leafed through the yearbook until he found her senior photograph.

Evelyn Draganov. Age eighteen, he guessed. No mistaking her resemblance to Sharon.

Below her name:

President Photography Club, Math Club.

Senior Quote: Why didn't Marlon B ever show up, Ewa?

Ewa? Must be her Slavic given name, and it didn't match the *Evelyn* above her senior photo. Even back then, Evelyn could've passed for Latina in mostly Latino Highland Park, and knowing her, she probably passed whenever it suited her.

And Brando again? The mocking tone of a third party resonated from her senior quote. Nothing about the words or tone squared with how Evelyn had lightly described it: *I made a joke about Marlon Brando in my high school yearbook.*

Still another lie.

End of the hallway, he stopped. Her house sat on concrete slab, no crawl space lay underfoot. That left the possibility of an attic, so he checked each closet for attic trapdoors and came up empty, doubting all the while that Evelyn, healthy or not, could make that climb with Delfina's body weight.

Delfina was not here.

Back in the living room again, he noticed that two photographs from Evelyn's wall were missing. He knew them: Evelyn and Chet Jordan in the nightclub—her aging, deranged father in front of her white, wooden childhood home.

Chet Jordan had crossed her, accused her of stealing his watch. Even though Bradley had been joking about Chet's death, Robert would bet even money she'd arranged Chet's fatal car crash. Given her father's missing picture—had she murdered him, too?

Scouring his dealings with her for some kind of insight, he recalled all the times Evelyn had toyed with him. Visiting Teo at Saint John's, a man she'd just failed to have killed; buying gifts for Teo's daughter, befriending her; pretending to help her financially. Working him, always testing him, trying to see if he was smart enough to see through the face she showed the world.

He knew he'd been slated to die in the desert and pictured Evelyn at his funeral, comforting Gia, gaming her, too, beside herself with grief. All along, he realized, Evelyn got off on *showing him* what she was doing. Taking him right up to the line. Daring him to see her true self.

Got off on doing that big-time, didn't you, you sick bitch?

Something crossed his mind . . . something Delfina told him on the phone after she'd visited Evelyn's house yesterday: Evelyn let her take out the trash. Same thing Evelyn had done with him. He'd viewed his own moment as helping a woman who seemed to be in pain, but the way he saw it now—she'd looked at him as a servant. Taking out her trash—lesser than her. Looking down on him.

He stepped into her kitchen, asking himself: *What was it she did next?*

She'd asked him: *Get that clicker for me, would you?*

Independent Evelyn. Evelyn who didn't reach out for help. She'd asked him to get the clicker from a kitchen drawer within her own reach. Two garage door openers lay inside: *Clickers*. He'd picked up one of them.

"Not that one," she'd said. "The other one."

The other one had a Harvard Street address label affixed to it: the one she'd needed to raise her garage door in back. But the device he'd first picked up—that one had no label at all.

He slid open that same drawer: *both clickers—gone.* She'd taken both of them.

Showing him those two clickers, she'd taken him right up to the line again: *This is who I am*, she'd been telling him. *Figure it out, Robert.*

He grabbed a hammer from the same drawer and ran out. He should've guessed already. At least, he now knew exactly where he'd find Evelyn and Delfina.

⁑

Running up Evelyn's back alley, Robert drew abreast of that neighborhood eyesore. On their walk to Carlos' house, Evelyn had made a point of stopping here, telling him about her petition to force the owner to clean it up.

Stopping me right here and telling me that. You got off doing it—because this house is yours, too.

In the sand-and-gravel threshold between the alley and this garage: a fresh set of tire tracks. Evelyn's car had to be inside the garage. He forced a gap in the chain-link fence and squeezed through, redlining adrenaline. The garage door, padlocked. No windows. No need to kick it in and make his presence known.

Evelyn's car was in the garage, and she was inside this house. So was Delfina.

The back door to the house lay just ahead. He twisted the handle; it opened. Inside, even in the dead of night, this place seemed to hold a deeper depth of darkness. Half expecting to find bodies hung from the ceiling, he felt his way forward with his iPhone flashlight. Moved into a thirty-foot-long hallway with rooms off each side. Empty, unfurnished rooms with boarded-up windows. Cobwebs spanned each door, not the hallway, so he kept inching down it. At the hallway's end, he faced one final boarded-up window. Nowhere left to go.

Even so, he was dead certain Delfina was inside this house.

To his right—looked like the wall moved. Stepping back, he raised the hammer, pocketed his iPhone. A door began to open; faint light spilled onto him through a growing gap.

"Come in, Robert." Evelyn's voice drifted to him from inside the hidden room.

He eased through the open door into a fifteen-by-fifteen-foot, dimly lit, windowless area. The thick door must've been heavy-duty hinged; it made no sound, automatically closing behind him. Finished walls, an industrial strainer plate over a drain in the center of a slightly sloped concrete floor, a hundred-gallon water tank.

In the center of it, over the drain, Evelyn sat in a slatted, straight-back wooden chair, her chemo port wrapped around her forearm. Leading to it, a fat syringe filled with liquid.

Delfina lay draped across Evelyn's lap. Still drugged, he was sure, from Gia's house. Evelyn gripped a long knife, its tip to Delfina's throat.

A killing room. The drugs for herself and that knife: the trappings of a murder-suicide.

Facing Evelyn, at the base of a six-foot-tall, freestanding partition, were her two missing living room photographs. And a third, the one she'd requested from Carlos' house: Carlos on her front steps. Not a memento after all—*her trophy*.

She eyed the hammer in his right hand. "My people redid this room for me, but I've not yet put it to its intended use." She moved the knifepoint closer to Delfina's skin. "Your hammer," she said.

Robert dropped it at his feet.

"Kick it over here," she said.

He followed her order. She watched the hammer sliding across the floor. He grabbed Teo's rock from his right pocket, palming it in his right hand.

The hammer slid to a stop near the drain. No echo to speak of, same with her voice in this soundproofed room.

She said, "Thought I was at the end of the line with Carlos dead, but he drew out Teo and Delfina. Should I thank Carlos for that—or should I thank *you*? You delivered your clients to me, pennies from heaven, dear boy."

She was transparent now. How she'd craved her decades-long dark game. Even easier to see: from ten feet, he was too far away to rush her without that knife striking home. Taking everything he'd learned about her, he swallowed, his throat raw and dry.

"How is it I show up, what, ten days ago, not knowing the first thing about you or the trust, but I'm standing right here?" he said.

"I wanted you here."

Evelyn. Still on top. Where she needs to be.

"I know you used me, and I know why," he said. "'A real go-getter, this Robert Worth. Why don't I let him find Carlos' money?' But my buddy and me, we lured your people to the desert and drowned them. Oh, yeah—we found Carlos' money, too. Something you couldn't figure out if your life depended on it."

He'd never shown her his hard side, and her reaction was clear. Even in this light, his superior tone grinded on her. Her face drifted down to Delfina's.

"Again, Robert, who came out on top?"

Noticing the man's Rolex on her wrist, Robert searched for any way to disrupt her.

"Chet Jordan's Rolex? I know you stole it. Nothing special about that. Just makes you a common thief. How'd you get away with killing him?"

Murdering Chet Jordan—looked like his guess blindsided her. And engaged her.

She said, "The next-best thing to Brando until Chet's tragic accident. That it? Or is there more you need to get off your chest before this child comes to?"

Brando again.

Taunting her with that senior quote, he said: *"Why didn't Marlon B ever show up, Ewa?"*

A cloud crossed her face, then melted into her facade.

"Daddy's good friend from the studio? His drinking buddy? Daddy was a liar, a pederast, a violent drunk, and the world's full of them."

But somehow her classmates knew Brando had failed to show up. Failed to show *somewhere*.

"You bragged to your classmates about Brando, right? How your father knew him. Why didn't he show up, *Ewa*? You were humiliated, weren't you? Where was it, *Ewa*?"

Delfina moaned. Evelyn stroked her face. He looked for an opening, but the knife didn't move. Evelyn's eyes never left his.

"Why do Famosas have to die? What did Vincent do to you? A bullshit billing dispute at your law firm? Even you aren't that petty."

"Been a busy boy, haven't you? What if I said Vincent was my first lover? Outside my own father, that is. Maybe Vincent broke a young girl's heart?"

Lover? Sure. Broken heart? Unh-uh.

She said, "The answers lie down this very street, Robert, waiting for a resourceful man to unearth them. But you, I'm afraid, will be too filled with remorse to care about finding answers. After all, this little girl would be safe had she not met you. Will you be able to live with yourself after she dies, while you could only watch? I wonder, won't knowing that tear you apart, piece by little piece?"

He stepped down hard on his useless rage. "What'd Carlos say that last time he called you? You talked to him, didn't you?"

"No, there's a recording somewhere. Telling me how he followed Ilina home after she broke up with him, and he saw us together. I believe he said—he was crying, it was hard to tell—he said I was evil. But isn't crying what's supposed to happen when true love follows a whore home?"

"Beats me, but let's face it. You see yourself as a puppet master, but you suck at it."

"Even with all the Famosas dead and dying?"

"Then tell me why, *Ewa*? This girl dies because Brando didn't show up somewhere? Daddy broke a promise? What, Vincent took your virginity?"

"Don't you just love black-and-white boxing photos, the old ones? Sugar Ray Robinson, Rocky Marciano, Ali standing over Liston? High contrast, a lifetime captured in an instant."

Virginity, Vincent, Brando, boxing shots. Is this supposed to make sense to me?

His eyes scoured this small room, looking for any physical leg up and coming up empty.

"Vincent, Carlos, Teo, Chet, your father—it's not hard to kill innocent people."

"Only five people?" she said. "You lack imagination."

He still cupped Teo's rock in his right hand. She glanced down at Delfina—he thought he had a shot at Evelyn, but her eyes found his again.

"Your father was what—eighty? Like drowning a kitten."

Delfina moaned. The sound of it rammed a charge through him. Would he get a decent shot at Evelyn's head, or would he just have to wing it?

Delfina's body twitched. Sweat stung his eyes.

Evelyn said, "Look, she's coming to."

He looked. She didn't.

Robert said, "This is how far you came in the world? Killing a child because . . . because . . . ?"

"Still don't know everything, do you?"

Engaged again . . . good.

"I know this: you hurt her, I'll beat you to death with that hammer."

"The drugs in my syringe won't give you that luxury. You carried the hammer in your left hand. I don't recall you being a lefty?"

"Ambidextrous," he said. "Tried out for pitcher in high school. Didn't make the team."

Two lies. Right-handed, he'd been a decent pitcher, fighting it out for second string.

"What's that in your right hand, love?"

"Hard to see in this light. Want me to come closer?"

"No need. Let's see what you're holding . . ."

His sweat-slicked right hand shook. His lips parted to tell another lie—that Teo had come out of his coma, 100 percent alert and intact— but three things happened. Robert had figured on only one of them.

Delfina's eyes opened. "Evelyn . . . ?" she asked, looking up at her captor. Then a paroxysm of pain overcame Evelyn. Losing control of her body, she bent over. And from ten feet away, Robert stepped forward and slung Teo's rock at her head, harder than he'd thrown anything in his life. By the time it left his fingertips, it was only five feet away from its target.

Teo's rock struck Evelyn's temple. Robert didn't wait for anything more. He scooped Delfina into his arms and ran out the way he'd come, running until they were out in the street, where flashing cruisers just now made the turn from Wilshire onto Harvard.

Delfina opened her eyes and asked him, "What's wrong?"

He couldn't answer.

"Why are you crying?" she asked.

Choking on the words, he said, "Because I'm so happy."

Minutes after that, the police gathered in front of Evelyn's house. Gia was with them, and he handed her Delfina. Gia was overwhelmed with emotions as fierce as any he'd ever witnessed. Later, they were told children's services was on the way, and both Robert and Gia understood: their role in Delfina's life had just changed forever.

∾

Evelyn was dead, the police told him, before walking him back through the killing room. Booties, latex gloves, the works, so he could help them reconstruct what had happened. Her dead body was still seated in the slatted chair, black blood dried around her temple.

With the lights up, he learned more about the room. That six-foot-tall, six-inch-thick partition ended three feet shy of the ceiling; it was topped by a varnished two-by-six. That wall partially blocked off a bathroom he hadn't seen. No door, just an opening into a space with another portable water tank, a claw-foot tub with an industrial-size drain, and a toilet.

Robert explained Evelyn's hammer and Teo's rock lying on the drain, Evelyn's knife at Delfina's throat, Evelyn's surge of pain, and Chet Jordan's watch.

Her three photos still rested against that wall, and he explained his belief that she'd murdered Carlos, her father, and Chet Jordan.

Kneeling down, they all checked the photographs.

"Who's the old guy?" one of the cops asked.

Robert kept staring at the blurred, out-of-focus left doorjamb behind Evelyn and Emil.

"Her father, Emil Draganov."

By now, he knew that Gia's juiced-up kidnap report had helped him out with the police. Almost anything Robert did to get Delfina back was justified once it was on the record that Evelyn had forcibly taken her. Drug testing of Delfina's blood would back up Gia's story, too, and because of it all, he faced no criminal jeopardy.

Every so often, the cops would step out of the killing room into the hallway and confer with each other. When they did, Robert checked a curious aspect of the room. Curious because of something Evelyn said, minutes before she died. Something like: *Everything I wanted is here in this room.*

He slipped into the bathroom, stood on that claw-foot tub, and tried to reach the plank on top of the partition wall . . .

CHAPTER 47

That night at Gia's house, Robert came in the bedroom and checked on her, wishing more than anything he could join her and decompress. Finally, she cried herself out and drifted off before dawn. On his end, he had no choice—he would spend his time in the living room drafting a narrative that followed the bouncing ball of his clients' money.

Even so, bone-deep exhausted from the desert, from San Bernardino, and from witnessing Evelyn's obscene agenda, he dozed in and out that morning.

Scenes of coulda-been-a-contender Brando in *On the Waterfront* melted into Evelyn; her father, Emil; and her daughter, Sharon. Those images collided with those of Vincent and his two sons. Maybe that's how part of the answer came to him. He was never sure, half-dreaming, half-awake, how he'd grasped the image that had eluded him when he'd first laid eyes on Sharon Sloan in San Bernardino.

A simple image: that Orthodox-cross postcard on Sharon's court-house-office door. A cross with its slanted footrest.

Awake and agitated, he'd riffled through the trust's files for Teo's photographs and had come up with that shot of hypocrite Vincent, posing with Carlos and Teo on the steps of Vincent's first rental house.

Before today, Robert had focused on the human story on the steps—not the blurred image on the left doorjamb.

He'd seen that same image in the killing room: Evelyn's father on the front stairs of her family home. On that left doorjamb, too: the identical object from the photograph of Vincent's rental house.

Identical Orthodox crucifixes appeared in both pictures—slanted footrests pointing up to heaven and down to hell. Vincent's Highland Park rental house and Evelyn's Highland Park childhood home—they were one and the same.

Evelyn and Vincent had a definite connection years before their law-firm beef. Was it possible Evelyn had told the truth, at least part of it? That Evelyn and Vincent had a sexual relationship?

Before he could dig deeper, Agent Pascoe called him. She already knew Robert's client had been kidnapped and about Robert's part in saving her. Because of that, he'd turned a corner with her, becoming *one of us* rather than *one of them*. *Them* being lawyers. She was on the Westside, and, sure, she could meet him in an hour over at Evelyn's.

For now, he slammed the doors of that Highland Park house and concentrated on the task at hand: securing his clients' money.

❧

Later that morning, Robert met Pascoe in the alley behind Evelyn's residence. What Robert had told her about Teo's hit and run had borne fruit. Alexandra, the woman driving the Lexus that struck Teo, had been pulled in, questioned, and asked for a lawyer.

"We're confident she'll cop a plea," Pascoe said. "Apparently, these escorts were part of a larger extortion ring, working private mixers all around LA and Orange County."

Hearing that, Robert had no doubt Carlos had attended just such a mixer. That's where he'd started dating and where he'd eventually met *the girl*. The one Evelyn called *Ilina*.

Pascoe said, "Sharon Sloan lawyered up, too, late last night, rolled over on the Draganovs and her mother. Pregnant, two kids, fears for her life, Ms. Sloan wants immunity in the worst way. Turns out, her mother reached out to her while Sharon was still in college, before law school, and blamed their lifelong estrangement on some horrible lies told to Evelyn by Syd Levine."

Robert was thinking: *A mother's long-lost love, finally found. Sharon was easy prey for Evelyn.*

"Think the Famosa trust was a template for more money-laundering down the line?" Robert asked.

"Looks that way. Now, what's this you said on the phone about locating my money?"

"Believe I know where it is," Robert said. "First, though, let's talk about my clients' money."

"Let's hear it," Pascoe said.

"My client might be in possession of some cash, arguably traceable to an illegal source. Originally, that money was stolen from my client, and if it ever saw the light of day, the government might assert a claim against it. A wrongful claim, by the way."

"Claims happen. Even more so now that you opened up about your cash."

"Possible cash," Robert said. "What if I could find your money? That twenty million or so in Draganov drug money floating somewhere around LA? Would you think that—I'll pick a number at random—three-point-eight million might be a fair swap for finding it, and you guys calling it a day?"

"You have a good idea about my money's whereabouts, don't you, Worth?"

"What can I say? I have a good idea now and then."

Robert e-mailed her his bouncing-ball money narrative in the form of an affidavit. It laid out his clients' claim to the money as sole benefi-ciary of the Vincent Famosa Family Trust: Carlos' bogus investments and Evelyn Levine's involvement; Carlos getting cash back under the table, hiding it in his floor safe.

Parts of the story he asserted on *information and belief*, but the gist of it was clear and true—the money was stolen from the trust by its trustee, his client had first dibs on it, and wherever that money might be, it was held in constructive trust for his clients' benefit.

"*Constructive trust*. What's that mean?" Pascoe asked.

"Lawyer stuff. Means it's my clients' money, not the FBI's."

"Let me call Westwood HQ, see what they think about your constructive line of crap."

"Better hurry. Bet the Draganov bees come buzzing around their money before long."

Robert waited until she'd explained the situation to her Westwood higher-ups, forwarded them his e-mail, and hung up.

"They like it," she said.

"Only one condition."

"You wait till I go out on a limb before you . . . ?"

"Promise you, it's an easy one. I just want inside Evelyn's study. It's not a crime scene, and besides, my clients'll wind up owning every atom Evelyn ever owned for what she did to them."

Pascoe thought it over.

"Want to know why Evelyn had such a hard-on for the Famosas?" Robert asked.

"Did you actually just say that?"

"Long night. Evelyn told me all the answers I needed were right down the street. Pretty sure she meant inside her study. C'mon, we can wear those cool latex gloves."

"Starting to like you, Worth, and take my word for it—it's pissing me off."

Several hours later, Robert's search of Evelyn's study yielded two instructive items: a title report for Evelyn's childhood home in Highland Park, plus a thick envelope filled with black-and-white photographs, all taken by Evelyn.

While Pascoe leafed through photographs, Robert delved into the title report and gleaned some quick answers.

"Serious city and county tax liens had been filed on Emil Draganov's home, and he's forced to sell it to Vincent Famosa, one step ahead of tax foreclosure."

Then he showed Pascoe the signatures on the deed—Emil Draganov selling the house to Vincent Famosa. And Evelyn's signature as notary public.

"Before law school, Evelyn worked in real estate, and here she is, notarizing her father's signature. The deed taking away her father's home—him a proud homeowner in a neighborhood of renters. It was more than paper to her. It was a trophy. She was in the closing room at the transfer and witnessed her arrogant father's humiliation."

"But that left Vincent on the title, not her."

"Just a front man, a straw man, someone she believed she could control and hide behind."

"Hide from her father?"

"Yeah, a violent drunk, she said. If he ever saw her name on that deed . . ."

He explained that Vincent and Evelyn must've had some sort of deal about the house—20 percent of profits to Vincent when they resold it, 50 percent, who knew? But by the time Vincent came to her firm—according to the title report and what Robert already knew—he'd sold her house and bought four apartments. And all of them in Vincent's name. That's what caused the big blowup at her law firm.

Robert said, "Vincent nullified her vengeance against her father, then challenged her at her own firm—*do something about it, Evelyn.*"

"I get it, but why go to her to draw up the trust? Go anywhere else but to her, right?"

"For a normal thief, sure, but Vincent was a narcissistic egomaniac, and he had leverage on her. Evelyn was half-Bulgarian, half-Latina, and back then, from way, way over on the wrong side of town. She'd been a party to taking away her own father's home, maybe a party to fraud, and Vincent held it over her head, dared her to defy him, and she backed down."

"For the time being anyway," Pascoe said. "Balls on that Vincent."

"Vincent had no idea he was dealing with a psychopath. She liked lying in wait, preferred it, I think. Waiting for Vincent, waiting for his son, Carlos, waiting for her own father and for Chet Jordan, reeling them in slow before she gaffed each one."

"Wrong gal to tangle with, huh?"

"I'll say."

Her envelope of photographs told a story, too. Landscapes, downtown LA, Chet Jordan posing for her in Mexico—*Zihuatanejo*, she'd written on the back, alongside the date.

Farther back in time: a match to Teo's photograph of Vincent and his two boys on the steps of Vincent's rental house. On its flip side: *Highland Park, Vincent, Carlos, and Matteo, 1979.*

Evelyn had shot the original of Teo's print. That made Evelyn the mystery woman Teo had mentioned to Robert—Vincent's girlfriend or the investor with a car—who had shown up with big-dog Vincent at the rental house.

From even earlier in Evelyn's life: shots of five high school girls in a row of stadium seats. Her Franklin High classmates, he guessed. On the back of each shot, Evelyn had written each girl's name, the date and location: *Downtown LA, Olympiad 1970.*

Pulse quickening, he recognized the date and place: *Night of the Ramos.*

343

The next shot took his breath away: Vincent Famosa, jacket buttoned, fedora snug, standing in the ring with Sugar Ramos. On the back, she'd written the same date and location she'd used for her classmates: *Downtown LA, Olympiad, 1970, Vincent Famosa.*

Robert said, "My client Matteo Famosa has a print of the same picture. Teo kept it after Vincent died. Vincent got his print from Evelyn's original shot."

All of Vincent's bluster to his sons—his decade-long string of brilliant boxing bets—had been fiction. Evelyn had made the down payment on the rental house, not Vincent. All Vincent had was his lie about knowing the Cuban-Mexican fighter, backed up by a photograph of him inside the ropes, taken by teenage Evelyn, a girl he'd met at the fight.

Looking at Evelyn's classmates again, Robert understood the taunt behind her senior quote: *Why didn't Marlon B ever show up, Ewa?*

Robert said, "Emil bragged to Evelyn he was driving Brando to the fight—still the most charismatic star in the world—so Evelyn did her own bragging and invited her classmates to meet him there."

"And Daddy never shows," Pascoe said.

He recalled Vincent's boast to Teo about that night: that he'd *bedded a sweet young thing.* Evelyn's own chilling words: *What if I said Vincent was my first lover? Outside my own family.*

"She was humiliated in front of her peers, and I believe, she left the fight with Vincent Famosa."

Robert finally knew the answer to Delfina's question: *Why do they want to hurt my daddy?* Same as the answer to the question he'd put to Evelyn: *What's your beef with the Famosas?*

The answer was as simple and as complex as the human condition: In 1970, Delfina's grandfather Vincent met and seduced a teenage psychopath at a downtown LA prize fight. Years later, Vincent double-crossed her over a piece of real estate. Simply killing Vincent hadn't been enough for Evelyn—she'd wanted to wipe out his entire family.

One question remained unanswered—whether he would ever find the right opportunity to explain the full scenario to Delfina. Only time would tell.

⁂

Later that day, Robert and Agent Pascoe's supervisor signed off on a memorandum of understanding about the drug money. The meat of it was this—the *found money* had to be at least $20 million; the *kept money* could be no more than $3.8 million. For every million below twenty in found money, the kept money went down by 5 percent.

By the time Pascoe lifted the varnished two-by-six on top of that killing-room partition, the negotiation didn't matter. The found money inside the wall totaled $27,400,000.

Robert was relieved hearing the final tally—even though he'd already looked inside and seen stack after stack of Draganov drug money.

Two nights after the FBI seized the Draganovs' stash and staked out the house, *Gospodar*, Pinky, and two of *Gospodar's* top guys snuck into the killing room. Middle of the night, they'd already stacked close to $1 million for transport when Pascoe and two other agents busted in on them.

Later, after transporting Pinky to processing in her sedan, Pascoe told Robert: "That perfume Miss Pinky soaks in? It was so nasty, I had to steam-clean my back seat."

CHAPTER 48

Robert and Gia were driving over to Saint John's Hospital to visit Teo, who had been brought out of his coma a few hours ago. She carried a vase of yellow roses she'd cut from her front yard.

"Yellow's the happiest color rose to me," she said. "And in China, it's the emperor's color, the color of royalty."

"Teo's royalty, all right."

They were halfway to the hospital, wondering if Delfina would be there, when Dr. Wan called Robert. He tried to keep his heart from sinking as he answered.

Dr. Wan said, "I'm sorry, Robert, Teo passed away two hours ago from a massive stroke. It was over very, very quickly."

Robert thanked her and pulled to the side of the road. Looked over at Gia and shook his head, but she already knew the essentials from the tight expression on his face.

They held each other for a minute, then drove over to Ozone and crossed to the beach at the spot where Teo had knocked out Whitey. A languorous low tide let them walk out a hundred yards with Teo's yellow roses, hopping over hissing, rippling wavelets. Scuffing their feet across the sandy bottom, they spooked a school of stingrays and stopped, knee-deep in a tidal pool. One by one, Gia slipped the flowers in the sea. They held hands and watched the roses undulate in the water, this way and that.

Robert said, "When I met Teo, I wondered if trouble followed him around. It didn't. Evelyn did."

"Tough guy, but a real sweetheart."

"Sure was. A restaurant owner named Sonny, he told me Teo had a big smile on his face before he was hit. And I know for a fact that Teo was sober."

"Good. Think we'd ever do as good a job as Teo did, raising a child?"

He nodded. "If we tried half as hard as he did, cared half as much. That what you want?"

"I don't know. It hurt so much, thinking something terrible would happen to Delfina. And that was after one week, not even my own child." She turned into him. "You were so sweet with her. I've never seen that side of you."

He pulled her closer. Gia, the coolest girl he'd ever met as she glided through life. But when it really mattered—he had seen it after Delfina was abducted—Gia was on fire.

"You're ferocious, Gia, and I'm not going anywhere." The last of Teo's roses floated past, caught in an unknown current. "Let's see what happens."

"Let's," she said.

⁂

At Teo's graveside service, a caseworker from children's services showed up with Delfina and her new foster parents. Delfina was thinner than Robert remembered. Sadder, too. She ran over to Gia first; Gia hugged her for a long time. Watching them cry tore Robert up inside. Then it was his turn to kneel and hug the little girl. That tore him up even more.

"Are you sad about Daddy, too?" she asked him.

"Very, very sad, Delfina. I think I liked your daddy as much as you love him."

She thought about what he said, then whispered, "My foster parents are nice, but you and Gia are more fun."

"They look nice to me, Delfina. You're so lucky to be with them. A man down at the courthouse gave me a nickname because my middle name is Logan."

"What is it?

"*Wolverine*. Like it?"

That drew a smile from her. "Yes, a lot. I like Magna Carta Man better."

"Me, too. Much better."

Erik and Reyes were there. Benny Smartt from AA showed up off a call from Robert. Drew Freize, the framer, showed, too, because he was a decent man. Gia told Robert she had expected Reverend Andy from the Mission to make an appearance, but she guessed the Mission had enough on its hands with the living, so Reverend Andy got a well-deserved pass.

Carlos' grave and his blank headstone rested right down the row; a preacher he'd never seen asked Robert to say his prepared words about Teo, and he was glad to do it.

"Teo Famosa was a courageous man," he said. Delfina waved at him. He waved back. "I saw him do things he didn't want to do and face things he didn't want to face—difficult parts of his life he'd tried to forget. Family issues, mostly. Families, they're a funny thing. They come and go, some work better than others, but I'm beginning to think they're judged, not by what they do, but more by the love the members show one another. And these two Famosa brothers, they did love each other, and did care about each other, and they felt that way despite what had lined up against them as boys. Their timing was bad, that's for sure, but their feelings for each other, deep down, I know they were loving. And I know, too, Delfina, how much Teo loved you. You, and the way you are, you are the Famosa family's greatest accomplishment. One time—it was the last time I talked to your daddy—he told me you were his rock. You were his higher power, and you still are. You made him feel stronger and made him believe in himself. You and your daddy made me feel stronger, too."

He thought it a little odd that Delfina had stopped looking at him. Then again, she was only nine. But when she took off running across the cemetery, toward the cars, his eyes followed her. Reverend Andy stood next to a woman, as fair as she was thin. Gia was looking at her, too. From Teo's description, he knew she had to be Bee, Delfina's mother.

Robert wrapped up his eulogy, then joined Gia, and together, they watched Delfina and her mother hugging each other, talking and crying. After a few minutes, they walked over to join Reverend Andy, who filled them in on Bee's treatment up in Bakersfield.

"Meth changes the brain," he told them. "It needs time to repair. But she's had over a year of sobriety, thought she was ready to step up for Delfina."

Delfina pulled Bee over and introduced her to Robert and Gia.

Bee said, "What you two did for my daughter, I can never thank you enough."

"Our pleasure," Gia said. "She was a delightful houseguest, and welcome back anytime."

Robert gave Bee a big smile and mustered kind words, too, knowing full well that no matter how long Bee stayed sober, she would always feel the pull of the streets. And what was it Teo had told him? *Once Bee gets high, she's open to suggestion.*

He and Gia clutched hands, watching Delfina and Bee. Every so often, he felt Gia shudder and knew she was choking back her emotions because he was fighting the same fight.

He asked himself, *You can be as strong as a nine-year-old girl, can't you?*

Something to shoot for. Still, he would miss this little person in front of him. Miss making her pancakes, teasing her and getting teased back, tying silly knots, but he looked forward to toiling on her behalf as trustee. And he would protect her because that was his job. After all, he was Magna Carta Man.

At the first court hearing downtown, he planned to make a motion to change the trust's name. A name that *looked forward, not back*, as Teo once said. Something more fun, as Delfina might add. He would mention it to Delfina another time, knowing that if they put their heads together, the two of them would come up with the perfect name.

EPILOGUE

Sitting on a shaded California oak limb two weeks later, Robert looked far below his perch through a gap in the foliage. He could just make out his family farm's empty army Jeep, parked in front of the farmhouse outside Gilroy. The house where he had been raised.

The night before, he and Gia lay in bed on Ozone. Even before Teo's funeral, they'd begun to stay at the beach. There was no discussion about it; her place felt a little too quiet right now as they picked up again with their lives. Robert didn't bother quite yet with setting up his conference table in his boardwalk slot, but Gia returned to law school full-time.

Three nights ago, the first time since the kidnapping, Gia had sat up in bed and slipped off her T-shirt. Looking over at him, she'd stroked his face.

"Missed you, baby," she'd said.

She'd come to him without waiting for his move, and after they'd made love—that's what it was—she'd lain in the dark on her back, the salted ocean breeze playing over them, her arms outstretched, his head on her belly, gently rising and falling.

"Drive up to the farm," she'd said. "Go home."

He'd thought it over, then looked up at her.

"I'm so smart," he'd said.

She'd stroked his hair, knew what he meant: *smart for being with her.*

"Want to come with me?" he'd asked.

"A lot, but you should go alone. You have unfinished business."

From his oak limb, Robert glimpsed a man and a woman coming out of the farmhouse's wide porch, piling into the Jeep. It would take a few minutes for them to make it up the hill.

He pulled a postcard from his jacket. It was addressed: *Beach Lawyer, Venice Beach, California.* Mail carrier Sharon had slapped the card in his hand yesterday on the boardwalk and once again gave him her sitcom pitch for *Mailman's Dog!*

On the postcard's picture side: a guitar-shaped swimming pool in Nashville, Tennessee. On the stamp side, a short, potent message:

I fell in love with Carlos. I did not know what would hap-
pen to him. I am very sorry. Ilina S.

Ilina. *The girl.* She must've read *Beach Lawyer* references in newspapers and online, and wanted Carlos' death off her conscience for the price of a postcard. In spite of taking part in scamming Carlos, before it was all over, Ilina S. had fallen in love with bespectacled Carlos.

You never know . . .

Driving up to Gilroy earlier today, he'd decided that love—all kinds—was often a matter of timing: Ilina and Carlos, Robert finally finding Gia, Philip waiting years for Dorothy, Erik running into Priya in Thailand. And surely, the brotherly love of Carlos and Matteo Famosa.

What if Teo had come to his brother and introduced Delfina? *I'm in AA now. I need to get clean, Carlos. Can you help me?*

Or if Carlos somehow managed to find Teo and Delfina on his own and helped them off the streets?

Robert didn't believe any of the bromides—*Love is the answer* or *Love will set you free*. But if a loved one has gone MIA, better that you try to do something about it while you still can.

Through the foliage, he gazed down the sere hillside. The army Jeep bounced its way uphill toward him. A Latino was driving, an Anglo woman beside him: Luis, the farm manager, and Rosalind, his estranged first cousin. He'd loved her like a sister until their family had split over money and land and loyalty, and Rosalind had been forced to choose sides.

Now, on the uphill side of this spreading oak, Luis stopped the Jeep. Robert heard Rosalind's voice over the rattling engine.

"What hawk, Luis? Where the hell is it?"

"Inside the tree, *mi jefa*," Luis said. "A broken wing, it needs help."

She stepped onto the hillside. When she did, Luis ground the Jeep into gear and bucked away.

"Damn it, Luis!" she yelled after him. "What's wrong with you today?"

Then it was quiet.

"Rosalind," Robert said.

A raw-boned woman now, she peered into the shaded tree, looking at him on that limb.

She sighed. "Not this, not now," she said.

"Please?"

"Shoulda cut down this tree years ago."

"Why didn't you?" he asked.

This tree. Sitting on this limb. This had been where they'd hidden from the world, where they'd talked and laughed, and where they'd been *just kids* together.

"I couldn't," she said.

She stepped onto the wide limb where it angled into the hillside. She walked twenty feet toward him. Once she sat down, he opened the

Igloo cooler beside him and showed her the iced-down bottles of Yoo-hoo and Abba-Zaba bars, their childhood junk foods of choice.

"Yoo-hoo?" he asked.

She cracked one open and took a swig. He did the same.

"I'm a lesbian," she said.

Finally, she looked him in the eye. He put his hand on her shoulder. "Me, too."

For a while, they didn't say anything more. Then they did . . .

ACKNOWLEDGMENTS

For their early reads, support of *Beach Lawyer*, and essential research: Lawrie and Ben Smylie, Sensei Rooney, Ana Shorr and Doctor Bobby, Ryan Gustafson, Jacqueline and the Lads of Steel, Blackwell Smith, Happy Baker, Libby Duff, Elizabeth Woods, Avery Woods, T. J. Hall, Andrea Mattoon, Hacker Caldwell, Kay Kendall, Surfer Dave, the guys at Nick's and Urth Cafe, Alan Wertheimer, and Bret Carter.

My deepest thanks to Reverend Andy Bales of Skid Row's Union Rescue Mission, the largest mission of its kind in the United States. Andy is truly an unvarnished man of God. There are no words that come close to describing his devotion to the so-called *least among us*.

My manager, Chris George; his wife, Rebecca; and their lovely daughters, Charlotte and Maya.

My intrepid and enthusiastic agent, Beth Davey.

Publicist Ashley Vanicek of Amazon, copyeditor Valerie Kalfrin, and proofreader Jill Kramer.

Caitlin Alexander, my preternaturally patient and wildly talented development editor.

And then there's Liz Pearsons at Amazon. She gave all of those listed above a reason to help me out in the first place.

ABOUT THE AUTHOR

Avery Duff was born in Chattanooga, Tennessee, where he attended Baylor School and graduated summa cum laude. After graduating Phi Beta Kappa from the University of North Carolina at Chapel Hill, he earned a JD from Georgetown University Law Center and joined a prestigious Tennessee law firm, where he became a partner in five years. Duff's screenwriting credits include the 2010 heist drama *Takers*, starring Matt Dillon, Idris Elba, Paul Walker, Tip "T. I." Harris, Chris Brown, Michael Ealy, Jay Hernandez, Zoe Saldana, and Hayden Christensen. Duff lives at the beach in Los Angeles and spends his time writing fiction. His first published novel, *Beach Lawyer*, was an Amazon Charts Most Read and Most Sold book.